# THE REAPER'S SON

A.L. BRODY

The following is a work of fiction. Names, characters, places, events and incidents are either the product of the author's imagination or used in an entirely fictitious manner. Any resemblance to actual persons, living or dead, is entirely coincidental.


Paperback Cover and jacket design by Mimi Bark
Hardcover jacket design and interior chapter headings by Maldo Book Designs
Page edge design by Painted Wings Publishing Services

Hardcover ISBN: 979-8988386-95-7
Trade Paperback ISBN: 979-8988386-94-0
eISBN: 979-8988386-93-3

First edition August 2024 by Sageline Books

## ALSO BY A.L. BRODY

The Mating & Monsters Series

DATING & DISMEMBERMENT

WEDDINGS & WITCHCRAFT

**as Jason Pinter**

The Henry Parker series

THE MARK

THE GUILTY

THE STOLEN

THE FURY

THE DARKNESS

The Rachel Marin series

HIDE AWAY

A STRANGER AT THE DOOR

Standalones

THE CASTLE

PAST CRIMES

# CONTENT WARNING

This book contains depictions of violence, illnesses both physical and mental, underage drinking, ideations of suicide, bigotry, grief, and death.

If you or someone you know is hurting, call or text 988 or visit 988lifeline.org

*For everyone*
*who has ignored their head*
*to follow their heart*

# PROLOGUE

## The Fire

In less than ten minutes, Samael Zagan's entire family would be dead. Of course he could not have known this. But if he had, he would have spent his last precious few moments with them aboard their private plane doing something, anything, other than complaining about his boredom and tormenting his little sister. But given that Samael figured they all had many years, and many more flights together, he made no effort to tell his parents he loved them, made no effort to tell his sister he truly did care for her beyond his jabs, and could not have possibly known that what he saw that day would change the trajectory of his life, not unlike a plane in an unstoppable nosedive

Samael was a thin, pale young man with legs too long for his body and dark hair that fell over his deep-set brown eyes. He was smart and curious, but not particularly charming or outgoing, and the wealthy Zagan family's transient lifestyle emboldened Samael's preference to keep to himself. Samael had always preferred being thousands of feet above ground than on it, gazing down at the vast oceans and grand mountain ranges, bemusedly watching people the size of ants scurrying about, leading their boring, ordinary lives. When people asked Samael where he lived, he would peer out from behind his shock of hair, offer a thin smile and respond, "First class."

The Plata Air jet dipped suddenly, and Samael's thirteen-year-old sister, Arianne, gripped her armrest hard enough to turn her knuckles white.

"This is your captain speaking," Samael said with a mocking baritone. "Please remain in your seats until the fasten seatbelt sign is turned off. In the event that you're a giant wuss, we have placed a paper bag in the seat pocket in front of you for your barfing pleasure."

"Stop it, Sam," Arianne said. "I really don't feel well."

"Quit being such a drama queen," he said. "Don't tell me you're getting air sickness from a little turbulence."

"I'm going to get air sickness all over you if you don't shut up."

Their father heard the sniping and turned around. Mortimer Zagan had kind eyes and his warm smile always put Arianne at ease.

"Just think of it as air hiccups," Mortimer said. "I've flown through every kind of weather imaginable. I promise there's nothing to worry about. Just remember: air hiccups."

"Air hiccups," Arianne repeated, breathing deeply. "Air hiccups."

Mortimer signaled the flight attendant and asked for a cup of water. Within moments, Arianne was gulping it down greedily.

"I have an idea," their mother, Alice, said. She was a former model who dressed for every flight like she was attending a star-studded gala. Her blonde hair cascaded down her shoulders in ringlets, and her gold hoop earrings jangled as the plane rumbled. "When we land, I'll call ahead and make sure the hotel has a special dinner waiting for us."

"Sushi?" Arianne said.

"Pizza?" Samael said.

"Why not both? You can even put sushi on your pizza if you're so inclined."

"That's gross," Arianne said.

"And you," Alice said, glaring at Samael with a stern but loving smile. "Find something besides torturing your sister to occupy your time."

Samael huffed and picked up one of the on-flight magazines. He flipped through it but found nothing but recipes and junk. Did anyone actually buy antique jukeboxes at thirty-five thousand feet? Maybe he would demand his father buy it. Mortimer was frugal, despite his wealth, but Samael knew if he pushed hard enough, he would get what he wanted.

He always got what he wanted.

Then a crackle came over the plane's speakers.

"Folks, this is Captain Davis. Just to let you know, we'll be entering some rough airspace ahead. I'm going to ask that you keep your seatbelts on until further notice, and to stow your tray tables and secure any loose items."

Samael looked at his father. Mortimer didn't appear concerned. And if his father was calm, Samael had nothing to wor—

Suddenly, Samael's stomach felt like it had been sucked into his throat. The plane dropped like a roller coaster plummeting from its apex. Samael's father gripped his armrest, knuckles pale. His mother's eyes were closed, her teeth clenched together. Her hair and hoop earrings were upright, as though gravity had inverted itself.

"*Arianne!*" Samael shouted.

His sister's mouth was wide open. If she was screaming, he couldn't hear her over the madness.

Time seemed to slow as they fell. Then Samael heard a deafening *boom*. His first thought was that it was thunder. But thunder didn't come from *inside* an airplane.

A moment later, Samael felt something that made his heart leap into his throat: wind. Why was he feeling *wind*?

Samael turned around in his seat. What he saw wasn't real. *Couldn't* be real.

*No*, he thought. *Oh my god.*

When Samael boarded the plane, there were twenty-two rows of passengers behind him.

Now, there were none.

Where the rest of the plane had once been was now nothing but an open, yawning mouth. The entire tail section of the plane had been sheared off, leaving a jagged hole of sharp, twisted fuselage. Samael could see dark, angry clouds through the gaping maw, lightning snapping inside them like glowing whips. Samael felt the wind pulling at him. His seat rattled against its moorings and he could feel himself being torn away from the jet.

He needed to get free. If he remained in his seat, he would be sucked out into the sky. Samael looked at his mother and father, their eyes wide with terror. His father reached back, arm outstretched.

"*Give me your hand!*" Mortimer shouted, his voice barely audible over the roaring wind. "*Samael!*"

Samael used to roll his eyes when flight attendants showed morons how to buckle their seatbelt. Who didn't know how to buckle a seatbelt? But now, as he tried to unlatch his own seatbelt to reach his father, Samael found his hands fumbling against the metal clasp.

"*Dad!*" Samael yelled. He locked eyes with his father. Then his sister. His mother. The last thing Samael Zagan said before he was sucked into the sky was, "*Help me!*"

---

Samael coughed. Seawater spilled out over his chin as his lungs emptied themselves. He could feel coarse sand against his skin and slimy seaweed on his face.

*I'm not dead*, he thought. *Dead people don't cough.*

He lay unmoving for what felt like hours, but in reality was no more than a few minutes. He squeezed the saltwater from his eyes, then opened them.

He was on a beach somewhere, half submerged in the water.

Samael got to his feet and felt a sharp pain in his right leg that made him cry out. His body ached. His ears rang. His face felt raw and sunburned. A few hundred yards away he could see a small wooden fishing dock with a rowboat tied up. Wherever he was, it was near civilization.

But then Samael looked out over the tree tops and his breath caught in his throat.

Rising into the sky above the canopy of foliage was a thick plume of black smoke.

*The plane. My family.*

Samael stumbled toward the forest, dragging his wounded leg. His shoes were waterlogged, the soles flopping about like leather tongues. He pulled them off and tossed them into the sand, ignoring the rocks that bit into his feet. Every step brought agony.

When he got to the tree line, Samael smelled gasoline. It made him nauseous. He limped faster. His feet were bleeding. Branches ripped at his face, taking skin with them.

Finally, he broke through the woods and came to a large clearing. And there he saw the wreckage of the Plata Air jet the Zagan family had boarded that morning.

Or at least most of it.

The fuselage and cockpit were a smoldering mass of twisted metal. The tail section was gone. The wings lay a hundred yards away from the main cabin. One engine was still attached. The other was gone. It was something straight out of a nightmare.

Samael closed his eyes, hoping that when he opened them, he would wake up in his seat, an unread book in his hand, and Arianne across the aisle holding a barf bag to her mouth.

He opened his eyes. The wreckage was still there.

Samael limped into the clearing, hoping, praying his family had somehow survived. Seats were scattered about, along with broken meal carts, sheared-off tray tables, and even singed pages from in-flight magazines. But he did not see his family.

Then, Samael saw something glittering on the ground. He ran towards it, and in his hurry he didn't see the tree root front of him.

His foot caught on root and he fell, a shard of glass tearing through his leg and slicing his knee to the bone. His brain seemed to explode in a white light. The pain was bright and brilliant, like a wildfire under his skin, and Samael screamed. But then through the tears he saw the object again, and the pain subsided into a dull ache, like an echo in the back of his mind. He limped forward.

When Samael reached the object, he picked it up. His heartrate quickened. In his hand was one of his mother's dangly earrings. A pinprick of blood dotted the gold clasp. He closed his fist around it. Tears fell onto his fingers.

"Mom? Dad? Arianne?" He screamed their names until he was hoarse. "*Mom? Dad? Arianne?*"

Then he saw something in the distance that made him freeze. The echo of pain disappeared. He wiped his eyes. It couldn't be.

He wasn't looking at something. He was looking at some*one.*

Samael rubbed his eyes. He had to be dreaming. Or dead. There was no way he could be seeing what he was seeing.

Through the haze of burning fuel, Samael saw a man. He stood at the edge of the clearing, just beyond the wreckage. Samael limped closer. He was not dressed like a pilot or flight attendant and did not appear to be injured. He wore a black suit with a white shirt and a black tie. His shoes were black. His hair was shoulder-length, slicked back and neatly combed. His clothing was unsoiled, his skin unblemished. Samael could not see a speck of blood or dirt or ash on him.

The man stood there, looking up at the sky as though something was descending from the heavens. Who was he? And how the hell had he gotten there?

"Hey!" Samael shouted. "Hey, you! Please! Help us!"

The man did not move. He simply said, "The Quieting is done. The Exortus is complete."

"What are you talking about? Who are you?"

Samael shivered, like someone had traced a frozen finger down his spine. He no longer wondered *who* the man was—he wondered *what* the man was.

The man looked at Samael with sympathy in his eyes, as though he knew the tragedy that had just befallen his family. Looking back up at the sky, he uttered a strange word and vanished, leaving Samael standing alone, screaming in a field of fire.

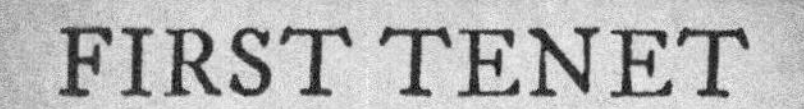


*Dominus is the Lord*
*of the Underworld,*
*the true face of Death,*
*keeper of the Ankou, and*
*responsible for the Exortus*
*of all mortal souls.*

*The Dominus is tasked*
*with raising an heir,*
*or Aegis, who will*
*assume the mantle upon*
*their eighteenth birthday.*

# 1

TWENTY YEARS LATER

Alex Sonnum was asleep in the passenger seat of a rusty moving van, a thin string of drool hanging from his lower lip. His father, Byron, was driving eastbound on the interstate when, distracted by Brahms's Quintet in F Minor, he hit a large, completely avoidable pothole that splashed his cup of peppermint tea all over the windshield and bounced his sleeping son's head off the car window.

"Ow, come on, Dad," Alex said. He rubbed his temple and glared at his father. "How is it possible you're *still* such a terrible driver? You've had more time to practice than literally anyone alive."

"I'm actually quite a good driver," Byron said. "But I was in Rotterdam after the bombing in 1940, and let me tell you, I-80 has far more potholes."

"Sure, blame the road and not the fact that you can't drive straight. What's that saying? A crappy carpenter blames his tools?"

Byron Sonnum laughed. "Not a fair comparison. I didn't pave the interstate. Besides, it's time for you to wake up. We're almost there."

His father's deep soothing voice always put Alex at ease, even during the dark times. And they'd had plenty of those. And even more were to soon come.

Byron Sonnum had dark brown eyes with speckles of obsidian near the iris. His shoulder-length black hair was graying slightly at the temples and tied back in a ponytail. At a glance, he appeared to be in his late forties, which was exactly what he wanted people to see.

"Where are we going again?" Alex asked, yawning.

"Whisper Valley," Byron replied. "Population eleven thousand seven hundred and six, at the moment."

"Whisper Valley," Alex said sarcastically. "Sounds like a a ton of fun I can picture the brochures. 'Looking for excitement? Come to Whisper Valley.'"

"If taking over the family business doesn't suit you, you'll have a robust career writing advertising copy."

Alex stretched his legs. Another move, another city. New school, new neighborhood, blah-blah-blah. Alex had grown used to their transient lifestyle a long time ago. When you left nothing behind, you didn't spend much time thinking about what lay ahead.

Byron took the Whisper Valley exit. They drove past rows and rows of townhouses, mid-level moderns, ranches and Victorians, both run down with overgrown grass and newer construction with fresh, bright paint and neatly trimmed lawns. The sidewalks were lined with maples and oaks and firs, hedges trimmed to identical heights like someone had taken a scythe to the neighborhood. The town seemed pleasant and quiet, if cookie-cutter. The kind of town where people left their doors unlocked at night, where kids played hockey in the street, where you knew the names of your neighbors, and their pets.

Alex didn't trust quiet towns. They had a veneer of amity, of neighborliness, but there was always something lurking beneath the surface people didn't want to acknowledge.

"Here we are," Byron said. He pulled the van into the driveway of the townhouse at 72 Marigold Lane. All of their earthly possessions had spent the last nine hours rattling around in the back of the small moving truck. Byron had one rule when it came to material possessions: only keep what you can pack in a single day.

Byron had adopted Alex after his biological parents abandoned him as an infant. Byron raised him. Loved him. He was his father if not in blood, then certainly in word and deed. And he was the only family Alex had ever known.

His dad's *unusual* vocation necessitated moving at the spur of the moment. Just last week, they'd been living in Fairview, New Mexico. But then the Quieting happened, and that meant it was time to go.

They were on the road to Whisper Valley the next afternoon. Neither Alex nor his father said goodbye to anyone.

Alex wouldn't miss Fairview, just like he didn't miss Worcester, Massachusetts, where he'd spent the first semester of his freshman year, or El Paso and Sioux Falls, where he'd split the second. He would go to school, come home, and keep to himself. One day, the Quieting would come to Whisper Valley, and then it was on to the next city.

In his seventeen years alive, Alex had been enrolled at no fewer than twenty schools on six different continents. Upon being told by his father the day of first grade graduation that they were moving from Bennington, Vermont to Strasbourg, France, Alex asked if he could send letters to his classmates so they wouldn't forget him. Byron said no.

"I know it's hard to understand now," he'd said, "but we *want* them to forget you."

"Why am I being punished?" Alex wailed as tears poured down his cheeks. "Why don't you want me to have friends?"

"You're not being punished," his father had said, wiping away Alex's tears with his thumbs. "I didn't have friends either. All we have is each other. All we *can* have is each other. I promise, one day you'll understand."

"What did I do wrong? Why don't you love me?"

Byron had taken his son into his arms and clutched him tight. "I love you more than life itself. You did nothing wrong. You are *perfect*. I know this is hard. Many years ago, my father told me what I'm going to tell you: your future is more important than you can possibly know. All of these sacrifices are in service of your destiny."

There was that word. *Destiny*. A promise wrapped in chains. But Alex loved his father, and knew he was loved back. Byron would never hurt him. So, Alex listened. And he obeyed.

There would be no playdates. No sleepovers. He would not play any sports or join the debate team or go to parties. He would exist in peoples' lives like smoke—there one moment, gone the next. Alex would never be like other kids, and his dad would *definitely* not be like other dads. That was the way it was. The way it would always be.

Alex and Byron got out of the van and took in their new home.

"Well, what do you think?" Byron said, gesturing to the town-home before them. "Not bad on such short notice."

"It's a house," Alex said.

"I know it's a house, smart guy. But what do you think of it?"

"Does it have central air?"

"It does," Byron said.

"Heat? Running water? Indoor plumbing?"

"Yes, yes, and yes."

"And I have my own room, right?"

"Yes, you have your own room."

"Good. Because after putting up with your chainsaw snoring in Toowoomba, I'm never sharing a room with you again."

"Thankfully, you won't have to. This could be our last move before you take over the family business."

"You make it sounds like we're in the mob or something."

"The mob would be much easier that what we do," Byron said. "Fewer dead to deal with."

"I can't believe this might be our last move before I…you know."

"I know you're ready," Byron said. "You've been ready for some time now."

"Glad one of us thinks so."

"I know so," Byron replied. "Now come on. Let's unpack. We'll order in dinner."

"Hey, Dad," Alex said. "Can I ask you something?"

"Always."

"When you were my age, about to, you know, take over…did you ever feel tired?"

"Of course I did," Byron said. "You're still a teenager. Hormones all out of whack. When I was your age, there were days when I felt like I could run two marathons back-to-back, and then some days I felt like I could sleep for a year. Times change but kids stay the same. People who climb Mount Everest complain about exhaustion less frequently than the average teenager."

"First off, don't ever mention my hormones again if you want me to be able to keep dinner down. Second, that's not the kind of tired I was talking about."

"Ah, *that* kind of tired. It was a long, long time ago, but I remember the months leading up to taking over for my father were very difficult. Anxiety and pressure are very normal, given the enormity of what you're about to undertake. But you have nothing to worry about, Alex. You are going to be *exceptional.* This is your destiny, and I—"

"Stop right there," Alex said. "I've listened to speeches about destiny for eighteen years. If I have to listen to one more, I take over right now. Sorry, but that's the new rule."

"Is that what you'd really want?" Byron said. "To take over sooner?"

Alex thought for a moment. "No. I'll be ready. But I'm not yet."

"Fair enough. Now let's get going. I want to be finished in time for *Shark Tank.*"

"If you want to watch people walk into a room bursting with optimism only to get ripped apart emotionally before having their dreams crushed by undeserving authority figures, you should come to school with me."

"You're too young to be so cynical," Byron said.

"And you're too old to be, well, pretty much anything."

Byron smiled. "Touché, son."

Alex wiped the crumbs from a long-ago eaten granola bar off his pants. A cool breeze shook the leaves. It was a pretty street. Clean sidewalks, lush trees, well-manicured lawns. Toddlers pedaled around on bikes with training wheels. Friendly-looking dogs sniffed the ground. Whisper Valley was one of the nicer neighborhoods they had lived in. He thought about the dilapidated one-room shack they shared in Newton, a suburb of Toowoomba in Australia. They were lucky to get running water four days a week, and thanks to the near-nightly brawls at the grungy pub down the block, police and ambulance sirens wailed constantly. Alex had even devised celebrity nicknames for the rodents that skittered across their floor daily. He had fond memories of HarRatson Ford and Kim KarRatshian.

But two months after they moved to Toowoomba, faulty wiring at the bar led to an electrical fire that killed thirty-seven and, well, then it was time to move on.

The longest he and Byron had ever stayed put was the eight months they'd lived in Tokyo, near the National Arts Center in Roppongi. Alex had actually begun to enjoy the lively district, with its buzzing nightlife and close proximity to foreign embassies. Not to mention the former TSK.CCC terminal building which was torn down after purportedly acting as a Yakuza headquarters for decades. The Ankou must have been busy as hell back in the day, shepherding the souls of mob victims. But just as Alex was getting accustomed to life in Japan, it was time to pack up and move to Louisville. Eventually they would move on from Whisper Valley and the cycle would repeat itself. The difference was that, in just a few months, Alex would be the one in charge.

Byron lifted the truck's gate and they began to unload their meager belongings.

"I was wondering who would move into the Thibodeaux place."

Alex turned to see a guy about his age standing in the driveway next door. He was about five seven, thin but not skinny, with dirty blond hair long on top and cropped close on the sides. He wore a lime green tank top and a pair of mesh gym shorts, and there were white smears on his forehead and neck where he'd failed to blend the suntan lotion into his skin.

The boy walked over and extended his hand. "Ignacio Molina. Call me Iggy."

"Byron Sonnum. This is my son, Alex. Pleasure to meet you."

Alex and Byron took turns shaking Iggy's hand. "I would have brought a fruitcake or something," Iggy said, "but the last time anyone in my family tried to bake we almost burned the house down."

"I don't think I've ever cooked anything more complicated than pasta," Alex said. He pointed at Iggy's neck. "You missed a spot."

Iggy sighed and rubbed the errant lotion in. "Track starts in the spring, but we have to log at least fifteen miles a week until the season starts. I'm heading out for a four-miler. Last year I was an alternate on the four by eight-hundred-meter relay and the eight-hundred-meter dash. This year I plan to be an ex-alternate. Do you run?"

"No, but if you consider the couch to kitchen shuffle an athletic competition, then my dad is an Olympian," Alex said.

"The weather should hold up for a couple of months. If you ever want to tag along—"

"Hard pass," Alex said. "No offense."

"Sorry," Byron said. "My son's manners are lacking."

"Yours would be too if you had my role model," Alex said.

Iggy laughed.

Then they heard a woman's voice shout, "Hi, neighbors!"

Iggy's cheeks reddened. An attractive middle-aged woman sat in an Adirondack chair on the Molinas' porch, wearing a large yellow hat and holding a glass of white wine. A bottle sat in a bucket of ice next to her.

"My mom," Iggy said. "Dorothy if she's drinking white wine, Doro if she's drinking red, and 'please get off the floor' if she breaks out the vodka."

"Hi, Dorothy," Alex said. He and Byron waved.

Doro waved back enthusiastically. "YOLO!" she yelled, raising her glass.

Iggy sighed and squeezed the bridge of his nose. "She doesn't know what that means."

Dorothy's gaze shifted to Byron. Her lips spread into a wide smile. She took the bottle from the bucket and frowned when she realized it was empty.

"I'll grab another from the fridge," she shouted. "It's rude to welcome new neighbors without a proper toast!"

"Rain check," Byron said, "but thank you."

Dorothy shrugged, downed the rest of her glass, and went inside.

Alex was accustomed to neighborhood women acting...peculiar...around his father. Single dad moves into a small town. Gives off a vibe of mystery, which was a polite way of saying he didn't talk much. That allowed people to create their own backstories. Maybe he was a widower. Maybe he was a gambler. Maybe he was just a decent guy who might be up for some witty, harmless banter at PTA meetings and a drink at the end of a long day. For whatever reason, married women flocked to Byron Sonnum. It never went anywhere, but the awkward and unrequited flirting never ceased to entertain Alex.

"So, are you going to school at Dubya V?" Iggy said to Alex.

"Dubya V?"

"Whisper Valley High. WV High. Hence, Dubya V."

"That's the plan," Alex said. "Starting my junior year there tomorrow."

"Same. I'm in Mr. Ryerson's homeroom. You're starting school tomorrow and you moved here the day before?"

Alex shrugged. "We do it a lot."

Iggy paused, confused. "How many schools *have* you enrolled at before?"

Alex thought for a moment. "I honestly don't know. Twenty?"

"Damn, son. You get around," Iggy said.

"My job requires a lot of travel, often on very short notice," Byron said. "Alex is a good sport about it. Mostly."

"Twenty schools," Iggy said, shaking his head. "I've had the same view from my bathroom window for seventeen years. Must be cool to get to see the world a bit."

Alex shrugged. "Eh. You get used to it."

"*Get used to it*, he says. I'd kill to 'get used to it' too."

"Don't say that," Alex said.

"Say what?"

"That you'd kill for it."

"Figure of speech, man. Guess those twenty schools made you a bit uptight."

"Maybe a bit," Alex said.

"So where are you from?" Iggy asked as they unloaded boxes.

"Right now we're from 72 Marigold Lane," Alex said.

"Okay, but what about before that? Where are you *from* from?"

Alex shrugged. "Nowhere, really."

"Nowhere. So you're drifters. Like in those old westerns, traveling from town to town with nothing but a horse and a gun."

"Exactly like that, only with U-Hauls instead of horses."

"Don't get me wrong. I like Whisper Valley, but you can feel suffocated sometimes," Iggy said. "Everyone is up in everyone else's business."

"Yeah, well we won't be," Alex said.

"They're not all bad. I can introduce you to—"

"Nope," Alex said. "No introductions necessary. I'm not looking to meet anyone. Everyone else's business is none of my business."

"That is totally a thing some dude in a western would say. You might act all brooding loner right now, but since the most exciting things to happen in Whisper Valley usually revolve around parking violations, you're gonna get bored real quick if you don't have a guide."

"And I'm guessing you're volunteering for the job," Alex said.

"Hey, nobody knows this town better than I do." Iggy paused, as though waiting for a question that didn't come. "Go ahead. Try me."

"Alright," Alex said, "best pizza in Whisper Valley."

"Leo's. Hands down. Not too doughy and there's a little kick to the sauce. And before you ask, the best burger is Mac's Shack on Pavilion. But just call it the Shack, or people will assume you're a tourist."

Alex looked up and down the block. "Anyone in the neighborhood we should avoid?"

Iggy offered a knowing smile. "Mrs. Higgenbottom at 188 Marigold. She'll pretend to be this nice, sweet old lady and butter you up, get you all comfortable, but the second you say the wrong thing or talk smack about someone the whole town will know before you get home. I've seen her staring out her dining room window with a pair of binoculars the size of my head like she's on safari."

"I'll do all my drug deals when she's asleep, then," Alex said.

Iggy's eyes widened.

"That was a joke, Iggy."

"I figured. But dude, we literally just met. It's going to take some time for me to get when you're being sarcastic."

"Sarcasm is Alex's first language," Byron said. "Sometimes I think it's his only language."

"Ignore my dad. His sense of humor dried up about a hundred years ago." Alex's father shot him a look.

"There are also a bunch of WV students in the neighborhood," Iggy said. "Good people, if you change your mind about the western movie loner thing."

"Like who?" Alex said, mainly so he'd know who to avoid.

"Nia Solomon lives right across the street, Francine Cha lives at 13 Honeysuckle Drive, Arvind Seth is down at 277 Woodthrush Court, and Ayesha Nazar lives at…wait…694 Van Buren Lane." Iggy lowered his voice. "Just be warned, you're totally Ayesha's type."

"In what way?" Alex said.

"You're a mammal," Iggy said dryly. "I'm not saying she'll stalk you, but…actually, there's a pretty good chance she'll stalk you."

"I'll just ignore her, then."

"Good luck with that. The last guy Ayesha crushed on moved to the Netherlands," Iggy said. "And speak of the devil. Hey, Nia!" He waved to young woman walking to the mailbox in front of the Dutch Colonial house across the street. Alex felt a strange sensation in his finger tips, almost like the electrical current when a limb falls asleep. He wrung out his hand. His father noticed.

"Hey, Ig," Nia said back.

"Come here hon, say hi to our new neighbor."

Nia pulled a package from the mailbox and walked across the street. She had a pretty, almond-shaped face and wavy reddish-brown hair that reminded Alex of a sand dune at sunset. Her eyes were light blue and sparkled in the light. Alex felt the tingling return. He clenched his fist and hid it behind his back.

"Nia Solomon, this is Alex. He has the honor of being a new Dubya V student."

"Not sure how honored he should be, but nice to meet you, Alex." She waved shyly. Alex merely nodded.

"Ready for tomorrow?" Nia said to Iggy.

"Not in the slightest," Iggy replied. "It's going to be a dumpster fire of epic proportions." He mimicked an explosion with his hands.

Nia laughed. She was holding the package across her chest as though she was cradling a child. She noticed Alex looking.

"Pencils," she said.

"I've never seen anyone that excited about pencils," Alex replied.

"These aren't regular pencils," she said.

"I'd hope not," Alex said. "They'd better be gold tipped or edible or something."

"Even better. These are Polychromos pencils."

"Polywhatnow?"

Nia laughed. "Polychromos pencils. They're oil-based instead of wax-based like most colored pencils. I'm an illustrator."

"Professionally?"

"No. Maybe one day."

"She's being modest," Iggy said. "Nia is amazing. One day she's going to be launching her latest book as some swanky art gallery and I'm going to sell a tissue she used to blow her nose at Sotheby's."

Nia blushed and smiled. Alex felt heat like a finger trace down his spine.

*What was happening?*

"Meet for the bus tomorrow morning?" Iggy said.

"I'll be there."

"Good. 'Cause every time I see James Mungro and Billy Wootens pull up to drive you, I want to barf."

"Don't start with James," she said. "Just stay away from each other this year."

"I might forgive," Iggy said. "But I don't forget. Actually, I don't usually forgive either. How are your folks?"

Nia looked down and toed the asphalt. "Mom is okay. Dad is…"

Iggy nodded. "You ever need to talk, you know where I live."

"Thanks, Ig."

Alex was about to ask Iggy another question, but stopped. He felt a faint humming sensation, like a tuning fork in his bones. He knew what that meant. Ever since that day in the woods, his body had been attuned to them.

Alex looked up and saw the familiar glow descending from the heavens. The glow was shapeless, formless, and circled in the air like a vulture waiting for prey. Then another descended. And another. Until dozens of them were circling the sky, a tornado of faint white light. Alex looked at Byron. He was watching them too. They exchanged a look of recognition.

*The Convergence*, Alex thought. The Ankou were here. This was why they had come to Whisper Valley.

"Uh, everything okay?" Iggy said. "You both just got, like, super quiet."

"Just, you know, looking at the trees," Alex said. "Whisper Valley has some really nice trees."

"Trees," Iggy said, unconvinced. "You were looking at…trees."

"What can I say. I really dig trees trees."

"Okay, then, tree guy," Iggy said. "Anyway, you should meet up with us to take the bus tomorrow. It stops two blocks away at the corner of Marigold and Third in front of Macklin's Hardware. I meet Arvind, Francine, and Ayesha most mornings. And Nia, when she's not getting a ride from the Prince of Darkness."

Nia gave him side eye. Then she looked at Alex. "Come with us," she said.

"I'll think about it," Alex said.

Nia said, "Well, if your thinking ends in a yes, we meet at eight twenty. The bus usually gets there around eight twenty-five."

"He'll come," Iggy said. "Even loners needs friends."

"No they don't," Alex said. "That's the whole definition of a loner."

Iggy looked back towards his house. Doro appeared to have fallen asleep on the porch, wine glass resting precariously in her fingertips.

"Hey, cool to meet you both," he said. "Hope you like Whisper Valley, also known as the quietest town on Earth. You do anything remotely interesting, people will be talking about it for years."

"Then we'll do our best to be totally uninteresting," Alex said.

"Anyway, gotta log those miles," Iggy said, setting his watch. "I'll see you in about twenty-eight minutes." He jogged off.

"Nice to meet you, Alex," Nia said.

"Nice to meet you too."

"See you tomorrow."

"See you."

Nia walked away. Alex turned towards his father, but watched her from the corner of his eye.

"Nice kids," Byron said. "You know, I ran a bit when I was your age. I saw Jesse Owens win four gold medals in Berlin. I think every kid alive wanted to be him."

"You saw Jesse Owens?" Alex said. "You never told me that."

"It wasn't in person, sadly," Byron said. "My father and I were in Taipei for a Quieting during the 1936 Olympics. But even there, Owens was all over the news. I've forgotten a lot of things I've been around for. But that's one that stuck with me."

"That would stick with anyone," Alex said. He tried to think of things that had stuck with him in his seventeen years, but the only memories he had were ones he'd tried to forget.

"Come on," Byron said. "Let's finish up. I'll return the van and we can Netflix and chill."

"People stopped saying that about three years ago," Alex said. "You need to stop trying to be cool."

"I used to be cool."

"Maybe. But that train left the station, like, fifteen U.S. presidents ago." Alex paused. "Hey, Dad?"

"Yes?"

"They might not make it," he said. "Iggy and Nia."

"We both know that's possible," Byron said solemnly. "The Quieting will happen in this town, and we need to be ready. Everyone here could be a part of it. Including those two. Now come on. Let's get settled."

Alex looked back at the Molina home. Iggy seemed like a good guy. Across the street, he saw a light go on in Nia's house. For some reason, he was still thinking about her eyes, that brief flutter in his chest when she smiled, the feeling of electricity in his fingertips.

Alex hoped that when the Quieting came for Whisper Valley, Iggy and Nia and their families would be spared. But he knew hope was pointless. He had no say over their destinies, just like he had no say in his own.

Then Alex Sonnum, heir to the mantle of Death, went to finish unpacking.

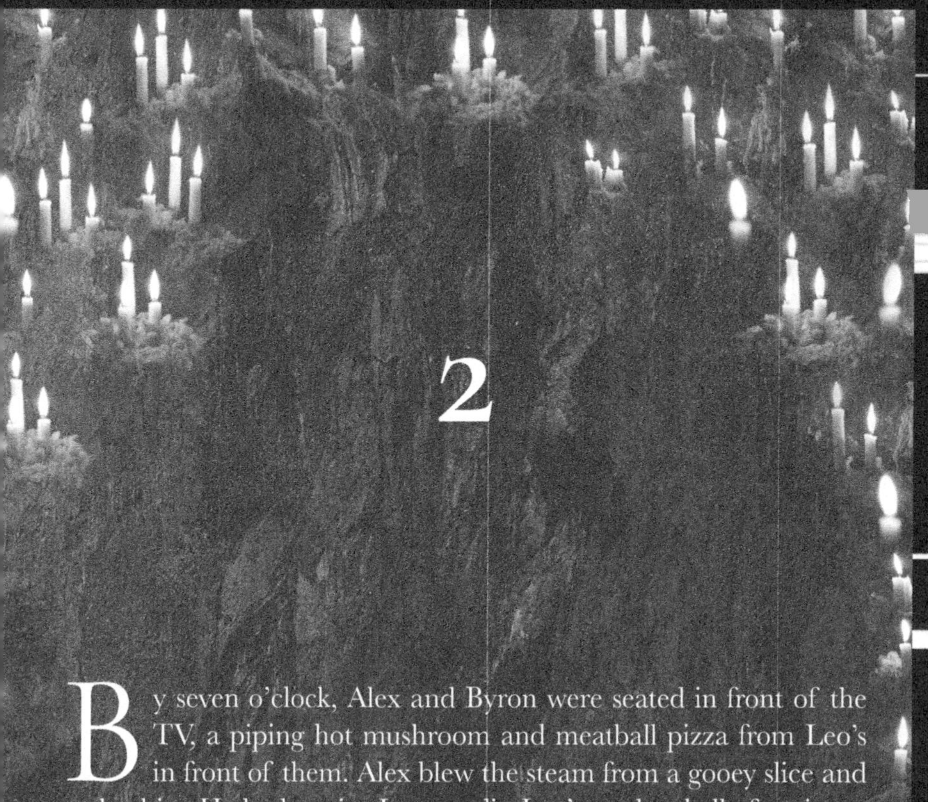

# 2

By seven o'clock, Alex and Byron were seated in front of the TV, a piping hot mushroom and meatball pizza from Leo's in front of them. Alex blew the steam from a gooey slice and took a bite. He had to give Iggy credit: Leo's made a hell of a pizza.

As usual, they dined on paper plates. Byron refused to lug glassware all over the globe, and the one time Alex saw him load a dishwasher it looked like someone had lost a game of Tetris. When Alex took over his dad's job, that would be his first change. No more dishes that collapsed under the weight of pizza grease.

Byron plucked a strand of cheese from his slice, dropped it into his mouth, and took a swig from a large glass of raspberry iced tea. He looked at Alex and offered a tomato sauce-coated smile.

"Iggy was right about Leo's," Byron said.

"Isn't one of the Tenets 'An Aegis shall always befriend those who know where to get the best slice'?"

"I don't think so, but I can ask the Conclave to create an amendment," Byron said. "I've had a lot—and I mean a *lot*—of pizza in my life, and this is up there. Did you know I actually ate at the original Ray's Pizza in Little Italy back when it opened in 1959?"

"I did. You're starting to repeat your stories, Dad."

"Hey, after almost a hundred years as Dominus, anyone's

memory would start to go. I'd easily rank Leo's in my pizza all-time top ten. What about you?"

Alex shrugged. "Top twenty. *Maybe.*"

"Top *twenty*?" Byron said with disbelief. "You can think of nineteen slices you've had that are better than Leo's? I don't believe you."

Alex nodded and took another bite. "Off the top of my head, I can think of two places in Venice and two in Chicago alone. Plus Naples, Copenhagen, Phoenix, Toronto, Singapore, Los Angeles, and New York City."

"Thankfully, my job performance is not reliant on memories of food," Byron said.

"I try to remember things I like," Alex said. "Unlike some people."

The words hung in the air. After a few moments, Byron said, "I remember what I need to remember. I don't get the comfort of forming attachments to the inconsequential."

"Don't worry, Dad. I promise I won't get attached to Leo's pizza."

"It's not a joke. When you choose this life, you forsake attachments."

Alex took another slice from the box. He held it without taking a bite, then put it down.

"Everything okay?" Byron asked through a mouthful of cheese. "You seem…distracted."

"Did I?" Alex said.

"Did you what?"

"Choose this life. I don't remember you ever asking if I wanted all of this. To take your place. Sometimes it feels like I'm just a moving box you throw in the back of a truck."

Byron put his slice down and wiped his hands.

"You are my son and my heir," Byron said. "And I love you more than anything in this world. You know that."

"I do. It's just…sometimes I look at a guy like Iggy, who's stayed put his whole life. And I can't help but wonder what life would be like if we were, you know…"

"If we were what?"

"Normal."

"What exactly is normal?" Byron said. "If you think normalcy equates to happiness, just wait until you've held the mantle for a while. Normal people can suffer just like anyone. Oftentimes more. By living this life, we agree to sacrifice many things you might call normal."

"I don't remember agreeing to anything."

"Neither did I," Byron said. "But I followed in my father's footsteps just like you are mine. The tradeoff is hard, but it is worth it. And when your time comes to take my place, I have no doubt you will match my legacy, if not exceed it."

Alex nodded.

"You are an extraordinary young man, Alex, and your potential is limitless. But emotions can't interfere with our duties."

"They never have," Alex said. "You know, this whole thing started because I was talking about pizza."

Byron leaned closer to his son. "We both know you weren't *just* talking about pizza."

That was the downside of his father having lived through nearly a century of human existence: he had a *really* good B.S. detector.

They ate the rest of their meal in silence, wrapped up the remaining slices, threw out their grease-soaked plates, and wiped down the table.

"Time to go to work," Byron said.

"Need me to come?"

"Nah. Just need to supervise an Exortus a few towns over. Sit this one out. Get some rest. You have a big day tomorrow."

Alex nodded and went upstairs. It was a decent-sized bedroom, bigger than the one in Fairview, which had barely fit a twin bed and small desk. He had room for actual furniture, but it felt silly to decorate. Alex had lived in many houses, but he'd never lived in a home.

Over the last few years, Alex's baby fat had begun to melt away, uncovering sharp cheekbones and a strong chin. His hair had darkened slightly, his voice deepening. He had lengthened out to a sturdy five foot ten. Free weights had given him strong shoulders and a broad back. He was discouraged from participating in extracurricular activities, so working out relieved some of the boredom. Still, his cardio could use improvement. Maybe he'd been hasty, and should have accepted Iggy's offer to tag along on a run. It would be embarrassing for an Aegis to die from exhaustion.

Alex went to the two unopened cardboard boxes stacked in the corner. He used his new house key to slit open the top one. Inside were dozens of travel guidebooks and city maps Alex had collected from newsstands and kiosks around the world.

At first, his father discouraged it. *An Aegis keeps memories in their mind. Not in boxes.* But Alex wore him down. As long as he adhered to the Tenets, Byron said, Alex could keep his books. Packing them up, though, was all on him.

Alex placed the travel books on the small, espresso-colored bookshelf next to his bed. Whoever furnished this house had done a pretty good job. Then he opened the next box. It was filled to bursting with novels. Poetry. Books of art. Books of photography. Biographies. Books about movies. Music. Books about other books. They were well-worn, with frayed bindings and yellowing pages. Alex caressed the creased covers, ran his fingers down the cracked spines. This collection represented a fraction of the books Alex had read over the years, but these were the ones that meant the most to him. The ones he refused to leave behind.

Wherever they went, Alex would find the nearest bookstore or set up camp in the school library, and disappear among the stacks. If he couldn't have real friends, he would befriend those within the pages. Reading eased the solitude. If he liked a book, Alex would finish it in a day. If he *loved* a book, he would take his time, savoring the words and scenes, allowing them to unfold like flower petals in his mind, the voices reverberating around his head like echoes in the dark.

He unpacked the second box, leaving one book on his pillow. It was yellowed with age and love. The diamond of his collection. The book that had come to be a part of him.

He could vividly remember the day he bought it from the small, musty bookstore in Gothenburg, how the illustration on the cover had transfixed him. The image was of a young boy entering an ominous, snow-covered forest, the bare, gnarled tree branches reaching for him like the claws of some wicked beast. He'd bought the book for sixteen Krona, then sat on a bench along the misty banks of the Göta älv and read. From the first page, Alex was captivated. With each chapter, the world around him disappeared as he lost himself in the world of the lost young boy. And when he finished it, he felt an emotion he'd never experienced: remorse. Because he could never again read the book for the first time. The book was called *A Cold Winter's Night*, and he would never, *ever* leave it behind. That book was Alex's home more than any of the houses, apartments, shacks, or shanties he had ever lived in.

He picked up the book and looked out the window. In just a few months, he would be eighteen, and he would have to give up everything. His books, his life, everything he hadn't already abandoned.

*Most people carry the weight of the world on their shoulders*, Byron had told him. *You will carry the weight of the underworld on yours.*

He could see people moving in the Molina house. He wondered if Iggy was nervous for the first day of school. If he would get a good night sleep or if nerves would keep him awake. He looked across the street to where Nia Solomon lived. He could picture her eyes in his mind, the way she held the package like it was her world. Pencils. Weirdly enough, Alex understood.

As he watched, a car with a logo that read Ashburn Pharmacy on the side pulled up in front of the Solomon home. A man exited and walked up the driveway carrying a paper bag. He rang the doorbell. Nia opened the door, took the bag, and shut it behind her.

Alex closed the blinds. It was a bad habit, watching other people. He needed to get out for a bit. Get his mind off of things. Off of Nia and those eyes.

Alex went to the garage and took out his bike. He put on his helmet, made sure the reflective lights were attached, dropped a pin on his phone's GPS app to make sure he knew how to get back to 72 Marigold Lane, and pedaled off.

He rode down Marigold and turned onto Cedarmont Street. He took it slow, enjoying the late summer evening breeze. He had no destination in mind, and that was the point. Alex's path had been laid out for him years ago. On his eighteenth birthday, his world would change. So sometimes it just felt good to be aimless.

Whisper Valley felt peaceful, sleepy. The kind of town where you married someone you met in grade school and raised your family around the corner from your childhood home. The kind of town where kids constantly complained about having nothing to do, but then, when the time came, they never left.

Alex could see families bustling inside their homes. Mothers. Fathers. Sons and daughters. He wondered which ones would survive the Quieting. The Conclave only knew where they needed to go, never how many would die. Sometimes it was hundreds, like in Fairview. Sometimes, thankfully, just a few. That was one benefit to being alone: it was easier to mourn people you didn't know.

The first Quieting Alex had ever witnessed was the collapse of a mine shaft in West Virginia that killed seventeen. He was six years old. He watched in horror as his father went into the tunnels and the Ankou descended from the heavens to Exort the souls of those who died. Alex had cried for days.

"Every life is a candle," Byron had told Alex. "And one day that flame goes out. For all of us."

"Even you?" Alex asked.

"A Dominus is immortal until they relinquish the mantle," Byron said. "When you take my place, my candle will begin to burn. Then, one day, my soul will be Exorted, and the time will come for you to raise an Aegis of your own."

In just a few months, Alex would become Dominus. That day also marked the beginning of the end of his father's life. Alex tried not to think about it as he pedaled. He sped away from the residential neighborhoods lined with maples and elms. At the junction of Willow Road and Route 49, which bracketed the northern perimeter of Whisper Valley and led out to I-80, Alex turned onto the highway, panting as he pedaled, cars whirring past so close that the drag nearly blew him off his bike. He had no idea how far he was from Marigold Lane, or even how long he'd been gone. And he didn't care. He needed to clear his head.

He continued east on Route 49, but at the turnoff to Mossflower Boulevard, Alex saw a beat-up wooden sign that read Scenic View – Larrimore Hill. The rock-strewn road led uphill through gnarled trees into the darkness. The road reminded Alex of the cover of *A Cold Winter's Night.* He turned onto the bumpy path and began the ascent.

The climb was rough and arduous, but Alex kept going, his lungs burning, a sheen of sweat beginning to coat his body. The trail was dark. Alex turned his cell phone light on and held it out to illuminate the winding path. He could no longer hear the highway, only the rustling of leaves, the crickets and animals hidden in the night. He was alone.

At the top of Larrimore Hill, Alex found a small parking lot and stone steps leading up to a row of wood and iron benches arranged in front of a chain link fence.

The vision atop Larrimore Hill was breathtaking. Spread out before Alex was a full, panoramic view of Whisper Valley. Alex took a seat on a bench, wiped his forehead, and took it all in. He could see hundreds of houses, pinpricks of light as cars sped through the town's arteries, stars in the sky flickering white against the blue-black curtain of night.

Attached to the fence were dozens of locks, likely placed by couples who sat right where Alex was. Holding hands. Kissing. Taking in the view's grandeur and intimacy. Alex wondered what it would feel like to hold the hand of someone he loved, to be so sure of your future together that you would clasp a lock in place to signify its permanence, knowing his own lonely future had been locked in place long ago.

Despite this being his first night in Whisper Valley, the sense of isolation felt achingly familiar. He walked to the edge and looked down. Beyond the rusty four-foot fence was a dizzying drop into darkness. Alex sat back down and zoned out peacefully for a few minutes. Then he checked his phone. It was getting late. Tomorrow was the first day of school. It was time to head back to his not-home.

Alex made his way back down Larrimore Hill and turned west

onto Route 49. As he pedaled along, he saw a heap on the side of the road that made him stop short. He put down the kickstand, climbed off the bike, and stood there, frozen, a terrible wheezing sound coming from the broken creature just beyond the shoulder. The deer swiveled its head to look at him.

*It was still alive.*

Alex approached slowly. The animal lay on a patch of low grass. Light from a lamppost reflected off a pool of blood that had begun to seep onto the asphalt. It was dying, all alone for its final breaths.

The animal's eyes had begun to glaze over. Its head craned slightly as Alex came near.

He knelt down beside the deer. It pawed at him weakly, its life fading away with every weak breath. Alex reached out. The animal bared its teeth and its eyes went wide with pain and terror. It made a pitiful noise that lanced at Alex's heart.

"*Shh*," he whispered. "It's okay. Just stay still. It'll be over soon."

Alex held his hand above the animal's chest. Blood soaked its fur. It had mere seconds of life left. It was now or never.

Alex closed his eyes.

He felt his body grow warm, like coils heating inside an oven.

*You've done this before. You can do it again.*

The Blaze pooled and spilled out into his limbs and extremities. His palm began to glow a deep red. Low flames ignited at the ends of his fingertips. He placed his hand on the animal's chest. It struggled weakly. He could feel the wetness of its blood. The deer's eyes went wide.

*It'll be over soon.*

Then he released the heat from his hand and there was a flash of bright white light, like a firework had been set off on the road. The molten surge flowed through him and into the animal. Alex's skin began to burn, every molecule of his body a glowing ember, the heat radiating through him as he gritted his teeth through the searing pain. Then, just as quickly as it came, the white light faded away, the night returning to darkness.

Slowly, the deer stood up.

It was still coated in its own blood, but its limbs were mended, its breaths steady and strong. Alex could see the outline of his handprint in the blood on the animal's fur.

The deer looked at Alex for a moment, as if trying to understand what had just happened. Then it bounded off into the forest, leaving Alex alone by the side of the road.

Alex stood up. His legs felt like wet noodles. He knew this feeling. It always took a little time to regain his strength. He waited until he was strong enough to pedal, then got back on his bike and sped home, a smear of red on the handlebar.

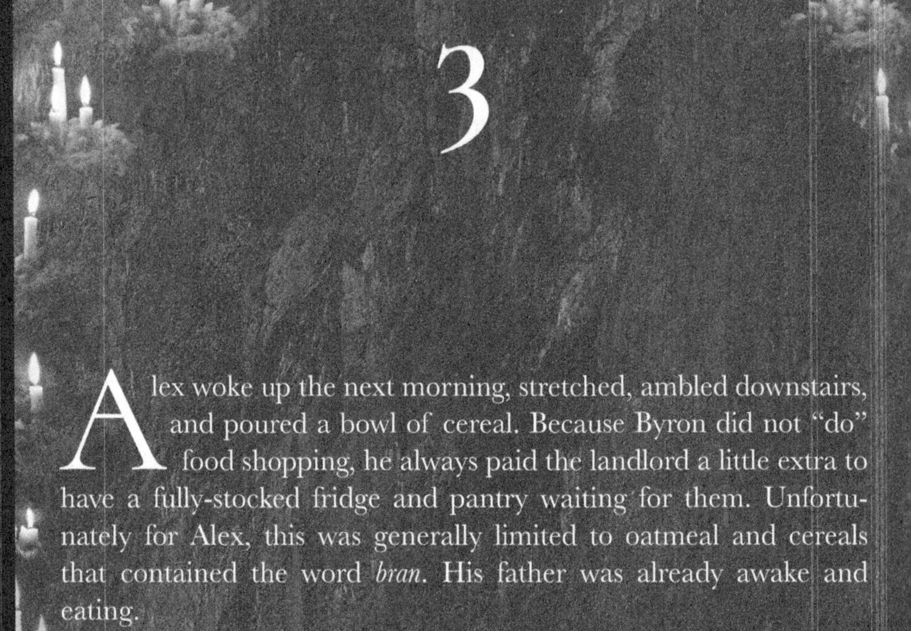

# 3

Alex woke up the next morning, stretched, ambled downstairs, and poured a bowl of cereal. Because Byron did not "do" food shopping, he always paid the landlord a little extra to have a fully-stocked fridge and pantry waiting for them. Unfortunately for Alex, this was generally limited to oatmeal and cereals that contained the word *bran*. His father was already awake and eating.

"Next time we move, can we at least get some eggs? Maybe even bacon?" Alex said.

"Too much bacon is bad for your heart," Byron said through a mouthful of toast. "Gotta watch your cholesterol." He sipped from a mug of peppermint tea and eyed Alex over the steam.

"When I take your job, it won't matter. I'm going to eat bacon at every meal."

"Fine. Gross, but fine," Byron said. "So, what did you do last night?"

"Went for a bike ride," Alex said. "Just wanted to check out Whisper Valley a little. I only have a few more months before I'm wrangling Ankou twenty-four seven."

"Where'd you go?"

Alex paused. "Biked up to the summit of a cool lookout point called Larrimore Hill. One of those scenic view places."

"So was it scenic?"

"Super scenic. Then I came home."

Alex left out the blood he had to wipe off the handlebar.

"So?"

"So what?"

"So, what do you think of Whisper Valley?"

"It's nice," Alex said.

"Nice? I'm not sure you have a future in poetry."

"Come on. Does it matter how I feel about this place?" Alex said. "I mean, it's not like we go on Zillow and check the crime rates or how good the school system is. Once the Convergence begins, we go wherever the Conclave sends us."

"You are permitted a large amount of freedom. "

"Sure, compared to the average death row inmate."

"I don't spy on you, and neither does the Conclave."

"You're saying I should be thankful that Death isn't a helicopter parent?"

Byron checked his watched. "While you're busy being snarky, you're going to miss the school bus. Why don't you meet up with Iggy and Nia?"

"After all this time, are you trying to get me to make friends?"

Byron laughed. "Of course not. But I want you to fit in. Or more importantly, not stick out."

"Because it makes us seem normal."

Byron raised his mug as if to say, *Exactly right.*

Byron finishing his tea, stood up, and clapped Alex on the shoulder like he'd just finished giving him a pep talk.

"Have a good first day of school. You still have a lot to learn. I have a feeling this is going to be a memorable semester."

---

It was a clear, crisp late summer day. Alex put on dark blue jeans and a long-sleeve green button-down, untucked. He walked toward the bus stop and saw Iggy chatting with three other kids. Nia was not among them, and Alex found himself a mixture or disappointment and relief. Iggy smiled when he saw Alex.

"I wasn't sure you'd come," Iggy said as Alex neared. "You and your dad give off pretty strange vibes."

"I've heard that before."

"I figured I'd either see you at the bus stop this morning, or I'd get home from school and your house would be empty because you'd already moved to, like, Manitoba. Now come on. Meet fellow Dubya V-ers Francine Cha, Arvind Seth, and Ayesha Nazir. Francine, Arvind, Ayesha, this is Alex…sorry, what's your last name again?"

"Sonnum."

They all waved awkwardly.

Francine Cha was almost as tall as Alex. She had straightened, bleached blonde hair, a diamond nose stud, and wore a thin black sweater and jeans that looked like they'd been caught in a lawnmower. Arvind Seth had a wispy mustache and his clothes were so baggy that they had to be hand-me-downs. Ayesha Nazir's hijab, sweater, and lipstick were all the same shade of cherry red. A not dissimilar shade of red crept into Ayesha's cheeks when she was introduced to Alex, and he remembered what Iggy said about her warp speed tendency to develop crushes.

Alex offered a pleasant hello and a wide smile, just like he'd done with a thousand other kids he'd met on previous first days of school.

"Where'd you move here from?" Francine said.

"Fairview, New Mexico," Alex said. "It's about half an hour north of Santa Fe."

"Fairview. Why does that ring a bell?" Ayesha said. Then she snapped her fingers and said, "Holy crap, wasn't there some sort of accident there where a lot of people died? Like, really recent?"

"The Phenon energy plant," Arvind said. "It was all over the news. They said it was one of the worst power plant disasters since Chernobyl."

Alex nodded. "We left right after it happened."

"A lot of people died," Ayesha said.

Alex nodded. "Twenty-nine."

"That's so awful," Ayesha said. "Did you know anyone?"

"No," Alex said. "Not personally."

"So you moved here for junior year. You must be in witness protection or on the run or something," Ayesha said. "Let me guess. Your dad had an affair with a mob boss's wife."

"*Shhhh*," Alex said. "You have to swear you won't tell anyone you know we're here. Please. Our life is in your hands."

Ayesha leaned in close to Alex, a mischievous grin on her face, and said, "Your secret is safe with me." She nudged him playfully, her hand grazing his wrist. Apparently, Ayesha had set the land-speed record for developing a crush.

"So how did you end up here?" Arvind said. "There are deserts more exciting than Whisper Valley. And I wouldn't exactly call Dubya V an Ivy League feeder school."

"We came for my dad's job," Alex said. "Nothing sinister or exciting, unfortunately."

"What does your dad do?" Francine asked.

"It's complicated," Alex replied. "Let's just say he's in acquisitions."

Ayesha said, "And your mom? Does she acquire stuff too?"

"No mom in the picture," Alex said. "I'm adopted. Byron took me in solo. I've actually never met my birth parents."

"Oh, I didn't know," Ayesha said. "I didn't mean to pry."

"No worries. It's not a secret. It's just part of who I am."

Arvind said, "I have a friend who was adopted. But it turned out his foster dad belonged to QAnon and got arrested for organizing a raid on this bagel shop because they thought it housed a syndicate trafficking in—" Iggy elbowed Arvind in the ribs. "Long story short, my friend goes to therapy three times a week and his family has been banned from every bagel shop within a hundred-mile radius. But I'm sure your dad is, you know, not insane."

"So no wife or girlfriend?" Ayesha asked.

"Nope, I've never been married," Alex replied.

"I meant your dad."

"Let's just say he's married to his work."

"Sounds like my dad," Arvind replied. "And my mom. And my older brother. Now that I think about it, I've pretty much been raised by my Nintendo Switch."

"There are days I'd absolutely trade my parents for a Switch," Francine said. "Even a refurbished one."

When the bus arrived, Iggy, Francine, Ayesha, and Arvind got on and gave hugs and hellos to a bunch of other students. Alex took an aisle seat next to Arvind. Just as the driver began to close the door, Alex heard a girl shout, "Wait up!"

The driver opened the door and Nia Solomon got on. She thanked the driver and headed toward the back. She stopped when she reached Alex and Iggy's row.

"Hey again," she said, looking at Alex.

"Hey," he said, looking up. Nia's smile made his heart pound. He forced himself to turn away.

"Missing the bus on the first day would be a really bad omen," Iggy said to Nia. "Like breaking a mirror while trying to kill a ladybug."

"Well, good thing I didn't miss it, then. Dad wasn't feeling so great this morning, so I got a late start."

"I'm really sorry," Iggy said. "How is he?"

She shrugged. "Hanging in there. That's all we can ask for."

"How's your mom?"

Nia shrugged.

Iggy nodded, as if something unspoken passed between them. Alex knew he shouldn't want to know what that unspoken thing was, but he did.

Then without warning, the bus stopped short. Nia stumbled. She reached out and grabbed Alex's hand to keep from falling. The moment her hand touched his skin he felt a searing heat, like he'd touched a hot stove. He instinctively jerked away from Nia's touch and looked at his hand. *What the hell was that?*

"I…I'm so sorry," Nia said, clearly embarrassed.

"It's okay," Alex said, trying to seem nonchalant. Even though her hand was no longer touching his, Alex still felt the lingering sensation of warmth on his skin. It unnerved him. "I was just zoning out and it surprised me."

"Are you causing problems, Nia?" Iggy said.

"Just giving Alex a proper welcome to the neighborhood by falling on top of him."

"There are worse ways to get welcomed," Alex said.

"Thanks for not being a jerk. I promise my balance is usually better. Usually."

"You can fall on me whenever you need to," Alex said. Nia's cheeks reddened. "Wait, no, that came off wrong. Don't fall on me. Ever. Unless you lose your balance. Then it's okay. Know what? I'm just going to shut up."

Nia laughed. "I give you credit. Most people don't know when to stop digging."

Alex stood up and motioned to his seat. "Please sit," he said.

"That's silly. There are plenty of seats in the back," she said.

"Yeah, but these are your friends. It's ok. Really."

Nia seemed impressed. As she slid in next to Arvind, Nia's wrist brushed Alex's arm, his skin warming at the spot they touched.

"Maybe chivalry isn't dead," Nia said to Iggy as she sat down. "I think Alex could teach you some manners."

"Giving up my seat for you reinforces the notion that women are physically inferior to men, which promotes the patriarchy," Iggy said. "In fact, my *not* giving up my seat for you is far more chivalrous than giving it to you because it says you are just as capable of standing on a moving bus as I am. Besides, you're in better shape than me."

"If that's the case, maybe I should run track instead of you," Nia said.

"Ooh. You're getting personal. Maybe that fall was a ploy to get Alex's seat."

"And maybe you're just lazy," Nia said.

"Now *that* is a distinct possibility," Iggy said.

"Thanks again," Nia said.

Alex nodded and smiled, but he felt thrown. He took a seat

several rows back next to a girl who gave him one look and went back to her phone. He watched Nia, trying not to be too obvious.

She rummaged around in her backpack, took out a sketchbook, and opened it on her lap. Alex could make out an illustration of a young woman with unruly reddish-blonde hair, not unlike Nia's. She had a pair of golden-tipped white wings, and her arms were outstretched like she was welcoming the sun. The background was brown and yellow and looked to be in motion, like a sandstorm. Nia took out a dark red pencil and began shading in the horizon, a blood orange sun above the storm that encircled the winged girl. Nia worked carefully, oblivious to the bumps and stops. Her hand moved fluidly, like a violinist skimming her bow effortlessly across the strings. Alex tried not to stare, but he must have failed, because Nia looked up.

"Are those the pencils you got yesterday?" he said.

She nodded. "Just a little hobby."

"Looks like much more than a hobby."

She smiled and said, "Maybe it is. Maybe I'll show you more."

"Maybe I'd like that. Maybe I…"

He trailed off. Alex felt the familiar humming sensation in his bones. He looked out the window and saw a familiar glow descending from the sky.

*Another Ankou. Another soul about to be Exorted.* Alex watched the Ankou disappear below the tree line. He should have been desensitized to them long ago, but he'd never been able to accept death the way his father did. He would have to, soon enough. His time was coming.

"What are you staring at?" Iggy said, interrupting Alex's thoughts.

"Oh, just…the trees."

"Maybe you're not in witness protection, but you definitely have some freaky tree fetish. I mean, I get it. All the green leaves and thick branches," Iggy said sarcastically. "You have the same weird look on your face you did in your driveway yesterday. Like the sky is falling and you're the only one who can see it."

"I just…zone out sometimes. That's all."

"So if I see you staring off into nothing, I'll assume you're just lost in some sort of erotic tree daydream."

"You're making this way weirder than it really is.

"You say that, but if I see you making googly eyes at any of our shrubs, you will *definitely* not be invited over for dinner."

The bus pulled up outside of Whisper Valley High and the students filed out. Nia put her sketchbook back in her backpack. A blonde girl with spiky hair ran up to Nia and squeaked like a chipmunk as she threw her hands around her.

"Alice D'Agosta," Iggy said. "She and Nia have been friends forever, which mean Alice has good taste in girl firends. But she's been on and off with this cretin named Billy Wootens, which means she has terrible taste in boyfriends."

Then Alex saw a tall, broad-shouldered guy approach Nia and Alice. They separated and turned to him. The guy gave Alice an emotionless peck on the cheek. But when he turned to Nia, he enveloped her in his arms like he was a soldier returning from war. Nia hugged him back but seemed tentative, almost hesitant to fully embrace him.

"Who's that?" Alex asked.

"That would be James Mungro," Iggy replied. He said the guy's name like it was a dirty word. "Trust me. Stay away, tree guy."

"He doesn't look so bad," Alex said.

"Neither does a can of Spam. It's when you see what's inside that you want to hurl."

"Isn't that a little harsh?"

"Not in the slightest," Iggy said with a conviction that made Alex wonder just what James Mungro had done to him.

James must have heard Iggy, because he let go of Nia and turned toward them. Nia went off with Alice. James locked eyes with Iggy. There was something behind the stare that let Alex know that whatever animosity existed between Iggy and James, it was deep and it was bad. Then James gave Iggy the finger, spat on the ground without breaking his glare, and headed toward the entrance.

"He seems delightful," Alex said.

"James is a festering boil on the asshole of a yak that's been infected by the bubonic plague."

"Congrats, you just won today's Mad Libs. Is there a reason James looked at you like he wanted to bury you in the desert somewhere?"

"I plead the fifth."

"I'm taking it there's history between you two."

"That's the understatement of the century," Iggy said. "If you listen to a single word of my advice, just try to be where James Mungro isn't. You'll thank me later."

"I don't think that'll be a problem." Given Alex's intention to steer clear of most everybody in Whisper Valley until the Quieting was over, he didn't think avoiding one douchebag would be all that difficult.

They merged with the throng of kids funneling into Dubya V. Most were wearing brand new clothes, sporting shiny shoes and clean sneakers, faces adorned with sun-kissed summer smiles.

"This is Dubya V," Iggy said, extending his arms melodramatically. But to Alex, it was just a school. Five stories high with a red brick façade and wrought iron fencing. Most of the schools Alex had attended were interchangeable. Some were red brick, some were limestone, some were metal and glass, some had bars on the windows and metal detectors and security guards who searched every backpack, and some you could have smuggled a tank inside with no questions asked. "So, before you're sucked into the ravenous maw of small-town academia, do you have any questions?"

"How's the food?" Alex asked.

Iggy made a *so-so* gesture. "Avoid most red meats. And white meats. Actually, just don't eat any meat. The lasagna isn't half bad, and the veggie pot pie is surprisingly tasty. But if it looks like it got a sponge bath in a vat of grease, that's because it probably did."

"I'll stick to bread and water."

"The prisoner's diet. Smart. The blander the meal, the greater chance your bowels live to see another day. Come on. Time to register."

They entered the school through a wide set of dark blue metal double-doors. Alex got on the on S-Z registration line. Alex looked at the students in front and behind him. They exchanged wide smiles, tight hugs, and enthusiastic claps on the back. There were even a few chaste pecks on the lips. Some of the girls wore shorts scandalously close to their upper thigh, showing off golden summer tans. Some of the boys wore shirts a size too small, strained sleeves showing off summer gains. Some seemed content to stay in the corners and watch life unfold around them.

Two boys and a girl came up to Iggy and took turns hugging him. He beamed, talked for a moment, then nodded at Alex. They eyed him skeptically, then offered tentative nods. Alex offered a listless smile in return. He heard Iggy whisper, "New kid. Alex. Moved in next door yesterday. Just him and his dad. Seems cool. Has a weird thing for trees."

When Alex got to the front of the line, a plump woman wearing a white sunflower dress and ear-to-ear smile said, "Name?"

"Sonnum. Alex."

"Sonnum, let's see..." She riffled through a box of manila folders until she found Alex's name. "Here you go."

There was an N in the upper right corner. When she noticed it, the woman said, "Oh, you're new to the Dubya V. That's what we call Whisper Valley High." She winked, as though she'd let Alex in on a state secret.

"So I've heard."

"Inside you'll find your homeroom assignment and your schedule for this semester. It also has your email and login, your assigned guidance counselor, and school contact list. It should answer any questions you might have."

"Thanks," Alex said. "I think I'll be okay."

"I'm sure you will. Nice to meet you, Mr. Sonnum. Welcome to the Dubya."

Alex skimmed the packet. It was pretty much the same as the dozens of other welcome packets he'd received over the years. His schedule included European History, biology, English, Algebra II, phys ed, comp sci, lunch, and a healthy amount of free periods. He had twenty minutes to get his bearings before homeroom.

Bright, cheery *Welcome Back WVH Students!* banners draped across the hallways. Yellow and red streamers hung from lockers and doors. As he headed toward the stairs, he saw Nia Solomon talking to James Mungro. She saw Alex and waved him over. Alex remembered Iggy's warning, but he'd already been rude to Nia once. He went over. She put her hand on his arm. His skin grew hot, the same feeling as when they'd touched on the bus. He took a step back. Whatever was happening was freaking him out.

"Alex, this is James," she said. "James, this is Alex. He's new."

"Good for him," James said with the enthusiasm of someone getting a tetanus shot.

"Just wanted to say have a good first day. Oh, and don't eat the sloppy joes unless you have a death wish."

"Iggy already warned me," Alex said. He noticed James flinch when he said Iggy's name. "Anyway, gotta run. Nice to meet you."

James didn't respond. "See you around," Nia said.

"I hope so," Alex replied. He saw red creep into Nia's cheeks.

He went to the third floor for homeroom, where Mr. Ryerson, a slightly frazzled, sixty-something history teacher, welcomed the class.

"I'd also like to introduce a new student to the Dubya V, Mr. Alex Sonnum. Alex is a junior and coming here from…where are you coming from again?"

"Fairview."

"New Jersey?"

"New Mexico."

"Close enough. Welcome, Alex!"

He was greeted by a few unenthusiastic "Hey's" but mostly silence. That was fine with him. All he had to do was make it through the first few days and everyone would forget he was there. It was a solid plan.

At least until lunch, when it all went to hell.

# 4

After third period biology ended, Alex followed the crowd to the cafeteria on the second floor. He could smell fried chicken and something cooked in enough garlic to kill Dracula. Alex got in line behind a big dude with a shaved head wearing a WVH football jacket. His arms were around the waist of a slim brunette in front of him. Every few steps she turned back for a kiss. Alex rolled his eyes. He thought about letting the people behind him cut the line before his brain liquified from the PDA.

He took a plate of pasta with a side of broccoli and a piece of bread soaked through in oil and garlic, then found a chair by the windows, sat down, and ate a forkful of pasta. He was surprised at how edible it was.

"Alex!"

He turned to see Nia seated at the far end of the table. Her sketchbook was open in front of her, multicolored pencils tucked into the spine.

He waved timidly and said, "Hey."

"Are you following me?" she asked.

"No, I swear, I just saw this chair and—"

"I'm kidding. Didn't mean to interrupt your…whatever that liquid oozing from your bread is. Anyway, just wanted to say hi."

"Hi back."

Nia smiled and returned to the sketchbook. He watched her for a minute. She had completely tuned the world out, her hand moving effortlessly, fluidly like water over stone. He wanted to ask her who the winged woman was. Where she'd come from.

But then Alex felt a tap on his shoulder and he looked up to see James Mungro standing over him.

James Mungro was solidly built, maybe a hundred and eighty pounds, with neck-length brown hair parted down the middle, green eyes, and a chin sharp enough to open a soda can without using the tab. He wore a long-sleeve gray thermal with the top two buttons undone. He had a toothy smile that made Alex think he was about to threaten him, politely.

"I'm James," he said.

"I remember. We met earlier. Can I help you?"

"I saw you talking to Ignacio Molina before school. Are you two friends?"

"Iggy and I are neighbors. Why?"

"What were you two talking about?" There was an air of both menace and vulnerability in James's voice.

"Nothing," Alex said. "I'm new, and Iggy was being polite and pointing out some of the kids in our class."

"And what else?"

"And nothing," Alex said. "If you have an issue with Iggy, you can take it up with him."

"Just tell me what he said to you and I'll walk away."

"No," Alex said. "I don't think I will."

"Just so you know," James said, "Ignacio Molina is a goddamn liar and you shouldn't trust a single word that comes out of his mouth. If he's spreading rumors about me, I need to know. So just tell me what he said and we'll forget any of this happened."

"What exactly *did* happen?" Alex said.

"Look, asshole, I tried to be nice, but…"

"No, you didn't."

"Excuse me?"

"You didn't try to be nice. You tried to be a raging shithead by bullying me and insulting Iggy, and congratulations, because you succeeded. I've seen a hundred guys like you in schools all over the world. You're all the same. Some amoeba-brained doofus who takes it out on everyone else because Daddy doesn't hug him enough."

James took a step back. His lip quivered. His face darkened. Alex got a bad feeling, like he'd accidentally jabbed an exposed nerve.

"Look," James said. His voice was full of quiet rage but there was something wounded underneath. "You don't know me. This doesn't have to be a thing. I just want to know what Iggy said to you."

"I agree, this doesn't have to be a thing, but you—"

"Are you bothering my boy, asshole?" came another voice. Alex looked up. A fleshy, pink-cheeked guy stood next to James holding a tray so full of food Alex wondered if there was anything left for the other students. He was shorter and stockier than Mungro, with narrow, cruel eyes and forearms the size of Alex's thigh.

"Easy, Billy," James said.

*Billy Wootens*, Alex though. The two guys Iggy had warned him about. Perfect start to the semester. Billy set his tray down, picked up Alex's fork, and stabbed a piece of greasy pasta. He then tapped the utensil so the noodle fell into Alex's lap, spattering sauce on his pants.

"Okay, congrats, you win," Alex said with a sigh. If he didn't defuse the situation, it could get way worse. "I'm gonna go eat somewhere else."

"Smart guy," Wootens said.

Suddenly, Nia marched over and stood chest-to-chest with James. She glared at him and said, "It's literally the first day of school. You couldn't get through one day without acting like a couple of dipshits?"

"It's not like that," James said. "Everything is cool. I was just welcoming Alex to Dubya V."

"Yeah, like the Germans welcomed the allies at Normandy," Alex said.

"James, let this go," Nia said. "For me."

Alex looked at her. What did she mean *for me*?

James's face softened. He took a step back, looked at Billy and said, "Come on."

"No way," Wootens said. "This shitstain doesn't get to win. Tell my boy what he wanted to know. I'm only going to ask one more time."

"I'm honestly impressed you can count to one," Alex said.

"You're not funny," Billy said.

"Your mom disagrees."

Billy slapped Alex's tray off the table. Food splattered all over the linoleum. The garlic bread went skittering across the floor where it came to rest under the chair of Mr. Ryerson. Ryerson looked at the errant piece of bread, then traced its trajectory. When he saw it led to James and Billy, Ryerson walked over with the exasperated look of a sheriff in a western movie preparing to admonish a pair of drunken bar patrons.

"Is there a problem, Mr. Mungro? Mr. Wootens?" Ryerson said. Alex got the sense they'd been asked this question many times before.

"No problem at all," James said. "We were just welcoming Alex to Dubya V."

Ryerson looked at Alex. He'd obviously had enough confrontations with James and Billy to know they were lying.

"Everything alright here, Mr. Sonnum?" Mr. Ryerson said.

"The bread is a little too garlicky, but otherwise everything is fine. Just enjoying my first day. And you can't beat the welcoming committee."

Ryerson lowered his voice and tapped James on the chest. "Mr. Mungro, don't start this semester like you ended the last one. I know your father's cell phone number by heart by now."

"Please don't call him," James said. There was something pitiful and desperate in his voice.

"I'll think about it," Ryerson said. "I think you owe Mr. Sonnum an apology. Mr. Wootens? Mr. Mungro?"

"Sorry," Billy said, head bowed.

"Ditto," James added.

"Ditto is not an apology," Ryerson said.

"I'm sorry," James said, staring daggers at Alex. Alex got the feeling this chastisement was likely going to have the opposite effect Mr. Ryerson intended.

"Thank you, gentlemen. There's not a lot of patience left in this school for you," Ryerson said. "With any luck you'll both be in college next year and you'll be someone else's problem. But for now, you're mine. So get your acts together."

They both nodded.

As they walked away, James looked back over his shoulder, his icy glare giving Alex chills. James wasn't a run-of-the-mill bully. Alex had a feeling he might be something worse.

"Sorry about those two," Nia said. "Billy is an asshole. James is…complicated."

"Thanks for standing up for me," he said.

"You literally stood up for me on the bus, so we'll call it even."

"So are you two…together or something?"

"It's not *that* kind of complicated."

"I didn't mean to pry, you just seem…cool. And he doesn't."

"I'll take that as a compliment."

"It was meant as one."

Red crept into Nia's cheeks and she smiled. "See you later, Alex."

"See you, Nia."

As Alex left the cafeteria, his finger brushed against hers and he felt the now-familiar heat. When he got outside, he stared at his hand as though expecting an explanation. Alex had lived in a dozen countries. Attended dozens of schools. Met hundreds of people, shook a thousand hands. And he had *never* felt this before.

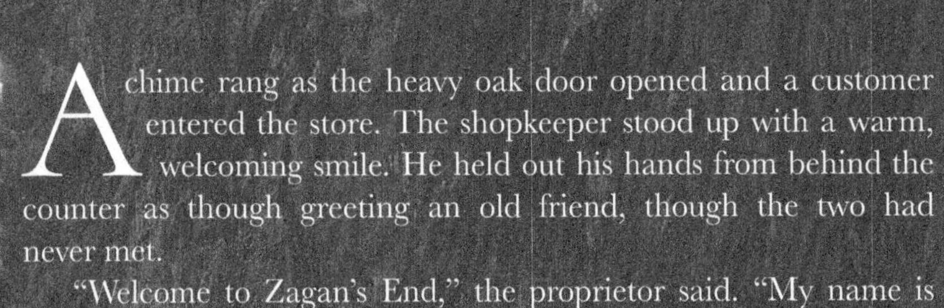

# 5

A chime rang as the heavy oak door opened and a customer entered the store. The shopkeeper stood up with a warm, welcoming smile. He held out his hands from behind the counter as though greeting an old friend, though the two had never met.

"Welcome to Zagan's End," the proprietor said. "My name is Samael Zagan. What can I do for you?"

The man did not answer. Instead, he began to inspect the shelves as Samael Zagan watched. The customer wore a cream-colored suit and alligator loafers. He was clean shaven, wore thin, rimless glasses, and his thick brown hair had the tangy scent of heavy gel. He paced the store slowly, deliberately.

The showroom of Zagan's End was about a thousand square feet, with another thousand in the basement for storage and other activities. The walls were a dark cherry wood and lined with thick maple shelves. The shelves were not cluttered, each one occupied by a single item, most encased in protective glass. The items were not labeled.

Black steel light fixtures with gold leaf trim hung from the ceiling. The floor was polished ebony. The dark walls and black floor gave off the appearance of stepping inside a coffin—and that aesthetic was not an accident.

Samael Zagan himself was tall and slender, with an aquiline nose and high forehead. His jet-black hair was neatly parted down one side, and there was just the slightest hint of mischief behind his hazel eyes. He wore a black button-down shirt under a pinstriped black suit, accented by a purple tie and a white pocket square. The tie was held with a clip in the shape of a grinning skull. *It adds humor*, Samael said, though the humor tended to be lost on most. At thirty-six years old, the ensemble made Samael resemble either a hip mortician or the doorman at an occult-themed nightclub. Either way, Samael Zagan blended in seamlessly with his shop's décor.

The customer picked up one of the items from a shelf and looked it over.

"You have good taste," Samael said. "That is a very special piece."

"It's a silver belt buckle," the man said skeptically.

"It is most certainly *not* just a silver belt buckle," Zagan said. "That is the belt buckle worn by the great Jesse James on the very day he was murdered in cold blood by Robert Ford."

"No kidding," the man said, adding an impressed whistle.

"I do not kid when discussing such priceless artifacts," Zagan replied.

"So, what is this, some kind of witchcraft store? You do pagan rituals here? Eye of newt and things like that?" the man asked derisively.

"If you're looking for ghosts and goblins," Zagan said, irritation in his voice, "there is a quaint little costume shop over on Norfolk Avenue. I'm sure you can find cheap wigs and plastic wands there."

"No need to get so defensive," the man replied. "So how much for the buckle? There's no price tag."

"This is not a souvenir shop," Zagan said. "If a customer is interested in one of our items, I prefer them to make an offer so we can negotiate like gentlemen."

The man nodded and rubbed his chin. He moved along the wall and pointed to another item.

"I'm guessing that's not just a butterfly brooch."

"You'd be correct. That brooch was a gift from George P. Putnam to his wife, Amelia Earhart. Mrs. Earhart wore that brooch to dinner in Miami on the night of May 31, 1937. The next day, Mrs. Earhart departed Miami in a Lockheed Electra in her second attempt to fly around the world. It is the last piece of jewelry she ever received."

"How can I be sure these items are authentic?"

"I opened Zagan's End the day before my twenty-first birthday. Since then, I have sold thousands of priceless end of life artifacts to hundreds of customers. Not one piece has ever been returned, nor have I ever been accused of selling counterfeit merchandise."

"So that's why the place is called Zagan's End," the man said, "because it's literally filled with things from the end."

"My shop is the closest you will ever get to death without seeing a white light."

The man chuckled. He examined an off-white item contained inside a long, clear, circular tube, three inches in diameter, with rubber stoppers at either end.

"You sell bones, too? Isn't that illegal?"

"That law only applies to grave robbers or for items obtained through illegal means. This bone was obtained quite legally. And this bone in particular killed millions of people."

The man cocked his head. "Come again?"

"Does the name Gavrilo Princip sound familiar?"

"No. Should it?"

"Yes, it should. Gavrilo Princip was a member of the Black Hand, a secret society of Serbian dissenters," Zagan said. "On June 28, 1914, Princip was buying a sandwich at the Moritz Schiller delicatessen on Franz Joseph Street in Sarajevo. As luck would have it, the motorcade carrying Archduke Franz Ferdinand of Austria stalled right outside the deli. The Black Hand had already failed in an assassination attempt on the Archduke that very day. Princip saw his opportunity and marched up to the motorcade, drew a FN Model 1910 pistol, and shot the Archduke in the neck and his wife Sophie, Duchess of Hohenberg, in the abdomen."

The man held up the tube. "What the hell is this?"

"After the assassination, Princip was arrested and chained up in solitary confinement at the Terezin military fortress in the Czech Republic. It was there that he came down with tuberculosis, which necessitated the amputation of his right arm."

"You're not telling me…"

"I am," Zagan said proudly. "That is the ulna bone from the arm of Gavrilo Princip, the man who killed Archduke Ferdinand and lit the powder keg that ignited World War I. So when I say that bone killed millions of people, I speak the truth."

The man stepped back. "I don't know whether to be impressed or to throw up."

"One of those reactions would require far less cleaning for my staff."

The man approached the counter. "I was told on good authority that you also buy items of interest to, well, death."

"Those authorities you speak of are correct. I'm a resourceful man, but I also rely on a network of trusted dealers and investigators. But I almost never buy goods from someone I have not worked with before."

The man nodded, as if thinking.

"You said 'almost never.'"

Zagan smiled, but did not respond.

"I have an item that might be one of those almosts."

"I'm listening," Zagan said.

The man opened his briefcase and took out a small cardboard box, wound with blue string. He laid it on the countertop. Zagan's eyes narrowed. The man untied the string and opened the box. When Samael saw what was inside, his lower lip began to tremble.

"Is that…?"

"It is. Washed up on a beach in Kiribati ten years ago," the man said. "And it sat in an evidence locker collecting dust for a decade. Nobody put two and two together. Until…"

"The documentary about the plane crash that killed my family," Zagan said.

The man smiled. "I heard it was streamed over half a billion hours it in its first week alone."

"Eight hundred sixteen million hours," Zagan said, proudly. "But who's counting?"

"Well, then, you know when the documentary premiered there was huge renewed interest in the Plata Air crash. Environmental and aviation experts around the world tried to trace where the plane went down. They charted weather and sea patterns, where the debris might have floated to, etcetera. And directly in that path was..."

"Kiribati," Zagan whispered.

"Kiribati. A local cop got smart and smuggled it out of the evidence locker. It was then purchased on the black market by a dealer of rare antiquities named Desmond Brinks. I believe you know Mr. Brinks."

Samael nodded. "I know Desmond. Or did. I haven't heard a peep from Mr. Brinks in a long time. I was never very fond of him or the unethical means through which he obtained his wares, so I can't say I hope he's well. How do you know Desmond?"

The man took out his wallet and handed Zagan a business card. It read Marvin Watterson, Attorney-at-Law, Watterson & Associates.

Watterson said, "I represent the estate of Desmond Brinks."

"Ah, so how is my old friend Desmond?"

"I wish I could say I knew. I haven't heard from him in a year. He didn't speak very kindly of you either, Mr. Zagan He wasn't of a fan of this...*cult*...you associate with."

"I do not belong to any *cults*, Mr. Watterson. Like I said, I merely have a network of trusted associates."

Watterson smirked. "Network of associates. Right. Don't you all have a funny name you call yourselves? The Children of the Corn or something like that?"

"The Children of Azrael," Samael said.

"Wasn't Azrael the name of the bad guy's cat in *The Smurfs*?"

"There are many people, like me," Samael said, ignoring the jab, "who are fascinated by death both as an abstract and as a cultural presence. The Children of Azrael are merely a group of like-minded individuals who, shall we say, *investigate* death."

"Mr. Brinks seemed to think you did a little more than *investigate* death. He seemed to think you might have even caused it for people who got in your way."

"That is slanderous. I have never participated in any illegal activities. Do people who play Dungeons and Dragons actually smite their opponents with spells and battle axes? The Children of Azrael have an interest in death. There is nothing wrong with that. In a perfect world, Desmond and I could have done a lot of business together. But when Desmond walked into a room, between him and his ego there was no room for anyone else."

"Desmond did think highly of himself," Watterson said. "But somewhere along the way, he must have decided to put your mutual animosity aside."

"What do you mean?" Samael asked.

"Three weeks ago, I received a signed letter from Mr. Brinks which stated that, to paraphrase, he felt he had wasted his life in pursuit of material possessions. It had cost him two wives and his relationship with his children. He made the decision to go off the grid, to find himself and discover his true path, to use his own words. He left his liquid assets to his children, and instructed that most of his possessions be auctioned for charity. Some items, however, Mr. Brinks said could be used to pay off his many outstanding debts."

Samael shook his head. "I would not have expected Mr. Brinks to possess that kind of self-awareness."

"That makes two of us. So, per his wishes, we sold off most of his assets with the proceeds either going to charity or into a trust for his children and grandchildren. But I kept one piece for myself. According to Mr. Brinks, it was the most valuable piece he owned. As it would happen, the only other instructions in his letter were that under no circumstances did he want this one item to fall into your hands."

"So why are you here, if this is explicitly against Desmond's wishes?"

"When Desmond went on his spirit walk, or whatever you want to call it, he left me with a mountain of unpaid bills. Let's just say after this, he and I are even."

"May I?" Samael said.

"You may."

Samael removed the item from the box. It was a rusted metal container, about a foot and a half long, six inches high, and six inches wide, and coated in chipped orange paint. Samael caressed the surface lovingly, like one might a baby's cheek.

"I always wondered why they called it that," Watterson said.

"Called it what?" Zagan said.

"A black box. Since it's, you know, orange."

"This is it," Zagan said. "Desmond Brinks told you this is *really* it?"

Watterson nodded. "This is the flight recorder from Plata Air Flight 172. The plane your family was on when they died."

A single tear fell from Samael's eye.

"So, Mr. Zagan," Watterson said, "I would like you to make me an offer for this item so we can negotiate like gentlemen."

---

Marvin Watterson exited Zagan's End with a smile and a certified check for $750,000. Once Watterson was gone, Samael bolted the front door and turned off the lights. He went behind the counter, rolled back the black carpeting, and pulled up a heavy, lead-lined trapdoor to reveal a narrow metal staircase. Samael flicked a light switch and descended, cradling the flight recorder in his hands like it was a Fabergé egg.

When he reached the bottom, he flicked another switch. A row of iron wall sconces illuminated a large wooden table twelve feet long and eight feet wide. Scattered across the table were dozens of warped, twisted, and charred pieces of metal, plastic, and cloth. Zagan approached the table and set the flight recorder next to a four-foot-long piece of aluminum with a faded blue insignia that read Plata Air. Next to it lay a wheel about two-and-a-half feet in diameter. The rubber was shredded, the metal scorched. On its final flight, the landing gear for Plata Air Flight 172 had never even been deployed.

Since his family had perished, Samael had spent nearly twenty years acquiring every piece of debris he could from the crash that had killed them. Some required money. Others required favors. He supplied both, gladly. The largest pieces had been claimed by Plata Air. But various scraps—seats, luggage, wiring, etc.—had found their way into Samael's hands. His efforts had been bolstered by his family's considerable fortune—of which he was the sole heir—as well as an eight-figure settlement from Plata Air itself.

Samael turned off the light, shrouding the airplane wreckage in darkness. He then walked deeper into the basement and approached a thick metal door. He slid open a small grate and peered inside.

Samael smiled.

The emaciated man rocked back and forth in the corner, his clothes and skin covered in filth. The floor and walls of the cell were assembled from dark red brick and ash-colored mortar. There were no windows and no ventilation. The man's hair was stringy and unkempt and his clothes hung loosely from his bones, like a child playing dress up. On the floor was a paper plate with chicken bones that had been sucked clean, and a plastic cup that had been licked dry. The cage smelled of body odor, dried fluids, and antiseptic.

The man blinked as though waking from a nightmare and looked up. His eyes widened, filled with hope and fear.

"Hello, Desmond," Samael said.

Hope left the man's eyes.

Desmond Brinks skittered back against the wall. Samael watched, entertained.

"I bet you'd like to know who just visited my store," Zagan said. Brinks blinked. "Marvin Watterson."

The man's eyes widened.

"Why…?" Brinks's voice sounded like he'd spent a month rubbing sandpaper against his vocal cords.

"He received our letter. Well, the letter I forged. And he did exactly what I knew he would do. You would have never sold me the flight recorder willingly, and stealing it from you would have attracted the authorities. This way, I am now its *legal* owner, as I should have been the moment it washed up in Kiribati." Zagan paused. "Would you like to know how much I paid?"

Brinks shook his head.

"Seven fifty."

Brinks gritted his teeth as if in pain and said, "You're a psychopath and a thief."

"*You're* the one who refused to part with the most important relic from my family's demise, Desmond, and you call me names? If you'd sold it to me like I'd asked, you'd be eating amuse bouche at Guy Savoy in Paris as opposed to chicken bones on my basement floor."

Brinks gave Zagan a wobbly middle finger.

Samael snickered. "Now, Desmond. There is certainly no love lost between us. But *you* are to blame for your current situation. I extended my hand many times over the years."

"You didn't *extend* anything," Brinks spat. "You just wanted me to join your sick cult. To what—help you murder more people?"

Samael's eyes narrowed.

"Oh yes, Samael," Brinks said. "I know *exactly* what you've done in the name of finding Death. Do your 'friends' know what you really are? Or do they still think you're just some harmless true believer or rich treasure hunter, doing your bidding while financing your psychotic search? You're a murderer."

"You're wrong, Desmond. Not about the murderer part, for that I plead the fifth. But I *am* a true believer. The only difference between me and the other Children of Azrael is that my ambitions are grander than hunting down a few expensive trinkets."

"You'll never find him," Brinks said quietly. "Death doesn't exist."

"We can add that to the long list of things you and I disagree on."

"You got what you wanted, Samael. Now *let me go*."

Samael tapped his lower lip. "I have a confession to make. I told you that once I got the flight recorder, I would set you free, that I took no enjoyment from your incarceration."

"You did."

Zagan waited a moment, then said, "I lied. In fact, looking at you right now in such a pathetic state brings me more joy than I ever thought possible."

Brinks tried to scream, but the only sound that came from his throat was a pitiful rasp. He ran to the metal door and pounded it with his bony fists. Zagan simply waited until Brinks ran out of energy.

"Please…" he moaned, slumping to the floor. "Just let me go. Anything you've done will stay between us, I swear."

Zagan clucked his tongue.

"I have been searching for Death for twenty years, Desmond," Zagan said. "In ancient Greece, Thanatos was the embodiment of Death, the son of Night and Darkness. In the fourteenth century, as the Black Plague decimated Europe, folklore depicted Death as an old hag named Pesta, who would travel from town to town. If Pesta arrived carrying a rake, the town would survive the pestilence. If she brought a broom, everyone who lived there would perish."

Brinks listened, trembling.

"Death is not merely the moment your heart stops beating, when your final breath has exited your lungs. I believe Death is real. Because I have *seen* him. Death came for my family. Death is a man. And before I take my own final breath, I will make Death feel the same pain I felt when my family fell from the sky. I will rip out Death's heart, like he ripped out mine."

Brinks rocked back and forth, muttering to himself.

"Have you ever read Edgar Allen Poe, Desmond?"

Brinks shook his head.

"Only an intellectual fraud like you would have skipped the world's foremost chronicler of the darkness of the human heart. *The Raven* is Poe's best-known story, but my personal favorite is *The Cask of Amontillado.* In the tale, the vengeful Montresor takes retribution on a man who has wronged him by plying him with drink and leading him deep down into a catacomb, where he proceeds to slowly seal him up inside a tomb. I enjoy that story because, like Montressor, I believe revenge should be savored."

Desmond held out his hands, desperate, pleading. He opened his mouth. Nothing but a thin string of saliva came out.

"Some think it odd that I have dedicated my life to such... morbid pursuits. But I think it's the most natural thing in the world. Do you know why, Desmond?"

Brinks's head wobbled, his neck barely strong enough to hold it up.

"Because the one thing every living creature has in common is that Death comes for us all," Samael said. "He's just coming for you sooner than most." Then he slid the grate closed.

# 6

One benefit to it being the first day of school: nobody had a real reason to use the library yet. It was bigger than some school libraries Alex had seen, smaller than others, but most importantly it was quiet.

After comp sci, Alex found a spot among the stacks, took the copy of *A Cold Winter's Night* from his backpack, and was quickly sucked back into the story.

He was on page twelve when a now-familiar voice said, "You're sitting in my favorite spot."

Alex looked up to see Nia standing over him. "Now I'm starting to think *you* might be following *me*," he said.

"Don't flatter yourself," she said. "I come up here during most of my free periods."

"I think I'm going to start. I have free period after lunch three days a week. Good place to read and digest." He paused. "Wait, is this really your favorite spot?"

"No, I was messing with you. But this is my favorite aisle and I do need to reach the shelf behind you."

"See, you could have led with that and it would have come across as way less aggressive."

"But less fun."

"I question your definition of *fun*."

"Iggy said you had a dry sense of humor," Nia said. "But I refuse to call you Tree guy."

"How about Alex?"

"Alex works," she said. "Unless you prefer Alexander."

"Nope. Just plain Alex. What about Nia? Is that short for anything?"

"My full name is actually Yevgenia, but I've always just been called Nia. I was named after my grandmother. And she was named after Yevgenia Ginzburg, the Russian author and dissident who spent eighteen years imprisoned in Stalin's gulags. What about you? Are you named after some famous Alexander? Hamilton? Graham Bell? Trebek?"

"Nope, nope, and nope. Pretty sure my dad picked the name Alex out of a hat."

"Well, I like Alex."

"I'm glad. And I like Nia."

She blushed, then gestured at the shelf behind him. "Excuse me, plain Alex, mind if I get to that shelf behind you?"

Alex scooted to his right and looked at the colorful spines lining the bookshelf she was pointing to.

"Graphic novels?" he said.

"Yup."

Nia knelt down, rifled through the books, and pulled one out. She showed it to Alex. The cover was an image of Earth being orbited by another planet that appeared to be a smaller, black-and-white mirror of Earth.

"*Terrarium*," Alex said. "What's it about?"

She seemed pleased that he asked. "In 2299, Earth receives a distress signal from a planet whose inhabitants call it Terrarium. They claim their natural resources are running out, and ask Earth for assistance. Earth sends a crew to visit Terrarium, and when they get there, it seems like Earth in many ways. But their technology is far superior to ours, so naturally we begin to suspect that they had a nefarious motive for contacting us. So, do we decide to help Terrarium? Or do we start an intergalactic war and try to destroy them as a preventative measure?"

"That's uplifting," Alex said.

"The next one on my TBR list is about rainbows and bunny rabbits. I like to balance it out. What are you reading?"

He shielded the cover from Nia and said, "It's nothing."

"Seriously? You're not going to show me? It's porn, isn't it?"

"You got me. I'm looking at porn in the middle of the library."

"Seriously, what is it?"

Alex had never shown the book to anyone before. His father had seen it on his shelf, but to Byron it was nothing more than pages held together by cheap glue. Byron didn't know how much the book meant to Alex. He'd never asked.

"I'd like to see," Nia said. "Please."

Alex turned the book to face Nia.

"*A Cold Winter's Night*," she said. "That's a gorgeous cover. Kind of spooky. What's it about?"

"A guy."

"A guy? That's all you got for me?"

"It's about a guy…who gets lost."

"And what happens to him after he gets lost?"

"Stuff." Alex shoved the book into his bag.

"Okay, now I'm starting to think it really *is* porn."

"It's not. I swear. I'm just…I don't really like talking about it."

"Okay. I'm not going to pry."

"You must have some things that are little too personal to share with someone you just met."

"Of course I do," she said. "Maybe one day we won't be strangers and then you can tell me what the book is *really* about."

"Maybe," he said.

"Maybe you'll even tell me why you really moved here," Nia said.

"Maybe."

"Maybe you'll let me borrow that book so I can read it for myself."

"Now you're pushing it," Alex said.

"Okay. I'll quit while I'm ahead. Mind if I hang out here and read?"

"Here?"

"No, on the roof. Yes, here."

"Like, with me."

"Not *with* you, just here." She pointed at a spot across from him. Alex felt his heart begin to beat faster. "Is that okay? If you need alone time for your book of not-porn…"

"No. It's fine."

"Okay, then." Nia sat down across from Alex. She dropped her bag on the ground, put a pair of ear buds in, and opened up *Terrarium*. He could hear the faint sound of music and tried to figure out what she was listening to.

"*La Bohème*," Nia said, as if reading his mind. "What I'm listening to."

Alex mouthed, "You're talking super loud."

Nia laughed and took the buds out.

"That's opera, right?" he said.

She nodded. "My dad introduced me to it when I was a kid. It calms me. What about you?"

"I definitely don't listen to opera." He tried to think of anything Byron had ever introduced him to and came up blank.

She smiled. "No, I mean what calms you?"

He thought for a moment, then said, "Reading. Just being surrounded by stories."

"I know what you mean," Nia said. "Sometimes it's nice to get lost in other worlds."

"To not think about everything going on around you," Alex replied.

"Let other peoples' problems help you forget about your own for a little while."

"Especially if those problems are an intergalactic war," Alex said.

"*Especially* if their problems are intergalactic war." Nia held out an imaginary glass. "To other worlds."

"To other worlds."

They both leaned forward and "clinked" their glasses.

Alex reopened *A Cold Winter's Night*, but he couldn't focus with Nia sitting there. He pretended to read, but instead watched her as she scanned the pages. He noticed the gentle curve of her neck, the small freckle just under her jawline, how she bobbed her head with each turn of the page, making her curls bounce ever so slightly. He studied the small dimple in her chin, the way her blue eyes sparkled as she read.

"What?" Nia said.

"Huh?"

"You were looking at me weird. Do I have something in my teeth?"

He didn't know how long he'd been watching her, and he hadn't realized she'd noticed. He felt silly, embarrassed.

"Your sock," Alex said, pointing to her right sock. "The thread is unraveling."

Nia rolled her eyes, reached down, and yanked out the errant thread. "My mom has knit me a pair of socks for the first day of school every year since kindergarten," she said. "It's sort of our little ritual. Unfortunately, her sock-making skills have declined over the years."

"The things we do to make our parents happy," Alex said.

"You have no idea," Nia said.

"I might."

Nia put her book down. The gesture unnerved him. It felt intimate, like she wanted to give Alex her full attention.

"Do you have any first day of school rituals?" Nia replied.

Alex held up his book. "I always reread this when we move," he said. "I don't get the chance to have a lot of consistency. This book is pretty much it."

"Well, now I *have* to read it. Maybe you'll let me borrow it sometime."

"Maybe," Alex said.

"So other than the lunch drama, how's your first day going?"

Alex thought for a moment. "I guess I feel a little lost," he said.

"You mean today," Nia said, "or in general?"

"I don't know. I'm not sure. Maybe both?"

He didn't know why he said it, but something about the way Nia was looking at him cracked a barrier he barely knew was there.

"Lost how?" Nia said.

Her book was flat on the floor like she'd forgotten about it. She was focused on him. Alex wanted to talk to her. To tell her why he felt lost. How his life felt like a train speeding down tracks toward a destination he didn't know if he wanted to reach.

Nia moved her leg slightly to the left to get more comfortable. It was just inches from his and Alex felt his heart begin to beat faster. Warmth flooded his body, and he couldn't tell if it was real or in his mind.

"You okay?" Nia said. "You look kind of—"

Before she could finish her question, Alex said, "Sorry, I have class." Then he got up and ran out of the library.

"Alex?" he heard her call after him. He ignored it and bolted through the stairwell door, taking three steps at a time until he was far away from the library.

For some inexplicable reason, Alex felt like when he was around Nia, he was no longer in control of himself. Every word, every look into her eyes broke the walls down more. And if an Aegis couldn't control their emotions, they would find themselves out of a job.

Or worse.

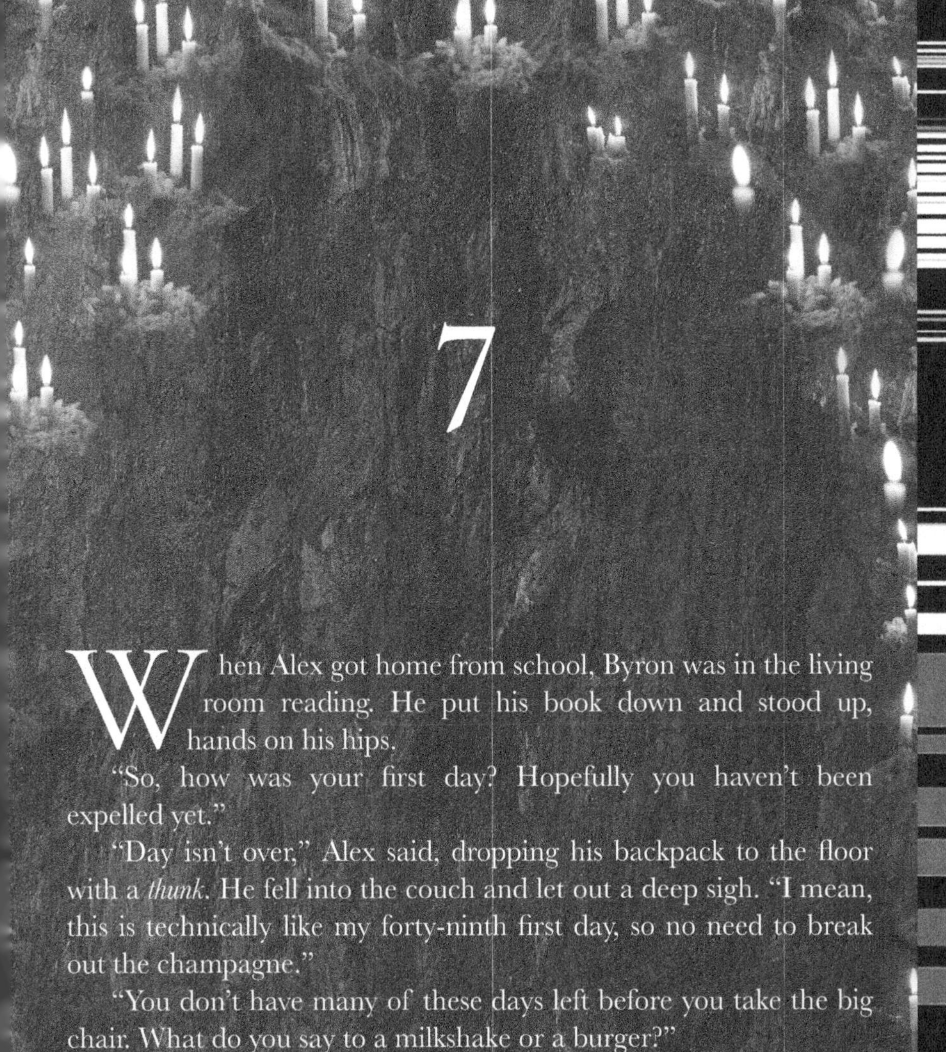

# 7

When Alex got home from school, Byron was in the living room reading. He put his book down and stood up, hands on his hips.

"So, how was your first day? Hopefully you haven't been expelled yet."

"Day isn't over," Alex said, dropping his backpack to the floor with a *thunk*. He fell into the couch and let out a deep sigh. "I mean, this is technically like my forty-ninth first day, so no need to break out the champagne."

"You don't have many of these days left before you take the big chair. What do you say to a milkshake or a burger?"

"A milkshake?" Alex said. "When was the last time either of us had a milkshake? Is this the 1950s? I mean, I know you're older than dust, but you don't have to make it so obvious."

"I'm not old. I'm retro."

"That's what old people say."

"So, did you meet anyone nice?" Byron said.

"Nice?"

"You know. Other students."

"No. I'm actually the only junior so it was just me and a bunch of teachers."

"Your sarcasm is getting old."

"So are…never mind. Yes. I did meet other people. I'm sure it'll be a huge shock to hear that they weren't all nice, though."

"What do you mean?

"Just stupid stuff. A couple of guys gave me a hard time at lunch."

"About what?" Byron said.

"One of them has some personal issue with Iggy and somehow I ended up in the middle of it. He tried to bully me. So I pushed back."

"You have to be careful," Byron said. "I don't expect you to be a pushover, but you can't incite conflict. We need to avoid drawing unnecessary attention to ourselves."

"I didn't incite anything," Alex said. "They started it."

"Anyone who says 'they started it' is fifty percent of the problem."

"I don't think there's science to back that up. And I won't be a doormat."

"You need to find a middle ground between antagonist and doormat. Deference is always the preferred course of action."

"So why am I in school to begin with?" Alex said. "It's not like comp sci will prepare me to control the Ankou."

"You may be shocked to hear this, but an education is necessary for your growth as an Aegis. I went to school until I took over from my father. You can't quell a turbulent soul if the world the souls inhabit is foreign to you. Next time, don't take the bait. Just walk away. Real strength is calming the storm. If you can avoid conflict with the living, it'll better prepare you to prevent it among the dead. You get me?"

"I get you," Alex said.

"Glad to hear it. So, what's your night like?"

"I have thirty pages of European history to read and an algebra problem set."

"First day of school and they give you homework," Byron said, shaking his head. "Are you planning to take your bike out again?"

"I might. Do you have a problem with that?"

"You know you have freedom. As long as you're responsible."

"When am I ever not?" Alex said.

They ate grilled cheese sandwiches and canned tomato soup for dinner. Alex began his homework, and after the sun had set, Byron came into Alex's room and said, "I'll be home late. The Conclave has alerted me to a possible rogue Ankou."

Alex put his pen down.

"Are you going to have to…?" Alex pointed downward.

"If it doesn't perform its next Exortus with flying colors, then yes."

"You'll banish it to become a Mors."

"That's right."

"You never told me what they look like," Alex said. "The Mors."

"You'll see them for yourself soon enough," Byron said. "They are the undying. All I'll say is that they look like it."

"I can't wait," Alex said dryly.

"Night, son," Byron said. "If you go out, be careful."

"Always am."

Byron went upstairs. When Alex heard his father's door close, he took his bike from the garage and rode out into the dark. As he passed by the Molina house, Alex could see Iggy seated at a dinner table with his mother, father, and a tween girl who was presumably his younger sister. They were all smiling and laughing. They looked so normal. Happy. Alex pedaled faster.

He turned right onto Lakeville Drive, a winding road that encircled Hammermill Lake. The sharp breeze coming off the water felt cool and invigorating. Lakeville was a one-lane road, with a narrow bicycle and pedestrian lane bracketed by a guardrail that overlooked the ravine down to the water. Alex felt calm. At peace. Today was rough, but it was over. He let his mind empty out as he stared at the dark road ahead.

Which is why he didn't notice the Mercedes until it was next to him.

No sooner did Alex realize that the car had slowed to keep pace with him than a soda bottle hit him square in the chest. The bottle was empty, but it made Alex swerve and nearly crash into the guardrail. He skidded, kicking up gravel, but managed to stay upright.

*What kind of psychopath…?*

And when Alex saw who was driving the car, he knew the answer to that question.

James Mungro. When his dad told him deference was the best option, he probably didn't consider what to do if an asshole steering three thousand pounds of steel tried to squish you against a guardrail.

"Hey there, new kid," Billy Wootens shouted. Billy was in the passenger seat, his window down. James Mungro was behind the wheel. Two girls were in the backseat. One was Alice D'Agosta. The other was Nia Solomon.

*What the hell…why is Nia with them?*

Billy called Alex a name he presumably learned in biology. Alex could hear Nia screaming at James.

"James, stop it! Watch the road, you're going to kill somebody! I'm calling 9-1-1. James, *stop the car!*"

"Put the phone down, Nia!" James shouted as he swerved the Mercedes directly into the bike lane, narrowly missing Alex's front tire.

"Are you *insane*?" Alex yelled.

James swerved again. This time Alex had to squeeze the handbrake so as not to slam headfirst into the car. He kept pedaling, faster now, his heart thrumming in his chest. He had nowhere to go.

"James, *stop*!" Nia yelled. "Yes, 9-1-1, I'm calling to report a—LOOK OUT!"

James was too focused on Alex to notice the deer that had stepped into the middle of the road.

"HOLY SH—" James yanked the wheel hard to the left. The headlights illuminated the animal. Alex could see dried blood coating the deer's fur…and a handprint in the center of its chest.

The Mercedes began to spin out of control. The deer bounded back into the woods. Alex kept pedaling, watching the scene unfold as if in slow motion.

James tried to turn into the skid, but he'd lost control. The car hit the guardrail head on. Alex heard a sickening *crunch* as the hood crumpled. There was a horrific sound of squealing metal and shattering glass. The guardrail buckled, and the car began to teeter over the ravine. Smoke poured from the mangled hood.

*Oh my god…*

Alex did not have time to think. He pedaled to the wreck as fast as he could, hopped off the bike, and ran over. When he looked inside, he felt lightheaded. The blood drained from his face.

The windows were shattered. Glass covered the interior. Alex went to the backseat, reached in through the broken rear passenger window, and put his hand on Nia's shoulder. When he touched her skin, Alex felt heat radiate up his arm.

"Nia, are you okay?" Alex said.

"I…I think so," she replied.

Alex took out his cell phone and dialed 911.

"Hi, there's been an accident on Lakeville Drive. I'm not totally sure where, but…"

"We're a mile south of the Cosmos Diner," Nia said.

Alex nodded and repeated it to the dispatcher. Then he yanked open the door and unbuckled Nia's seatbelt. He wrapped her arm behind his neck, every inch of skin she touched feeling like it was aflame, and led her away from the smoking wreck.

"Jesus, Alex, your arm."

Alex looked down. There was a ragged hole in his shirt sleeve and through it he could see a deep two-inch-long gash on his forearm. Blood had begun to soak through the cloth.

"I must have cut it on the glass," he said. "I didn't even notice."

"Let me see it," she said. She grabbed his arm before Alex could protest. A searing pain the likes of which he'd never felt before shot through his body. He pulled his arm away.

"There's no time," Alex said. "I called 9-1-1. We need to get everyone else clear before this car ends up in the ravine or a giant fireball. You get Alice. I'll get Billy."

"On it," Nia said.

Alex ran to the passenger's side and Nia went to get Alice. Billy Wootens was leaning back against the head rest, holding his head and moaning. A trickle of blood seeped through his fingers, but the cut over his eye looked superficial.

Alex couldn't open the passenger side door; the lock had been damaged.

"EMTs are on the way," Alex said. "Are you hurt?"

"Get the hell away from me," Billy said, swiping at Alex with a bloody palm. "This is *your* fault."

Billy was fine. He was an asshole, but he was fine. Alice screamed and cried as Nia led her away from the car, but other than the hysterics she seemed unhurt.

"James, let's…"

Then Alex saw the driver's seat. Bile rose in his throat.

"Nia…" Alex said. "Where is James?"

Nia walked to the driver's side. When she saw what Alex was looking at, she covered her mouth and dry heaved.

The driver's seat, where James Mungro had sat just seconds earlier, was empty. There was a gaping, ragged, body-sized hole in the windshield. Blood dripped down the punctured glass like outstretched, macabre fingers. The driver's side seatbelt hung loosely, unused.

When Billy noticed the horror-movie scene next to him, he began to scream.

"JAMES! Oh my god! Oh my god! Somebody *do something!*"

Alex ran to the dented guardrail and peered down into the ravine. There was a steep incline, dotted with shrubs, rocks, and small trees, leading all the way down to Hammermill Lake which lay beyond the gloom. Somewhere in that darkness was James Mungro. And he was badly hurt. Or worse.

Alex opened the flashlight app on his phone and climbed over the guardrail.

"What the hell are you doing?" Nia shouted.

"I need to find James," Alex replied. He grabbed a branch for balance and began to descend.

"Alex, wait for the police and EMTs. That doesn't look remotely safe."

Alex hopped back over the guardrail and returned to Nia. She was shivering. He put his hands on her arms and held her, tight. Warmth flooded through him, but this time it didn't hurt. He kept his hands there until her shivering stopped.

"You're warm," she said softly, looking up into his face. "How are you so warm?"

"I'll be okay," he said, ignoring the question. "I promise."

She nodded. "I'm holding you to that."

Then Alex released her, stepped over the guardrail, and climbed into the darkness.

He held the cell phone out in front of him, sweeping the light back and forth. His stomach roiled at what he might find. A chill traced his spine like an icy finger.

"James?" Alex yelled. "James, say something!"

Alex heard crickets and the sound of rocks becoming dislodged, but nothing human. He ducked beneath the branches but slid on some stones and skinned his knee. The pain barely registered.

He could feel blood thumping in his temples. The sky was pitch black and full of nightmares. He continued down. He'd lost all track of time. Then, to his surprise, Alex heard Nia's voice.

"Alex? Alex, are you okay?"

She was coming after him.

"Stay there!" Alex yelled back. "It's not safe!"

"I can take care of myself!" she shouted.

"I'm getting that sense," he whispered to himself.

Alex ventured further down the ravine. He was afraid of dislodging a mass of stones and getting caught in a rockslide. He swept the cell phone light back and forth, using the trees and branches to brace himself. He saw nothing but rocks and shrubs and dirt until…a shoe. A single white sneaker half buried in the dirt. Alex picked it up. There was a splash of blood near the heel.

"*James!*" he yelled. "James, where are you!"

Then Alex heard something from below. He stopped. Listened. It sounded like a moan. The sound was soft, but given the silence it may as well have been a thundercrack.

Alex hurried down the ravine, carelessly, half running, half sliding among the rocks. He heard it again. Another moan. This time closer.

He swept the cell light again. And this time he saw James Mungro.

Alex put his hand to his mouth and bit his thumb to stop himself from screaming.

James lay at the bottom of the ravine. He was on his back. He was not moving. The lower half of his left leg was bent perpendicular to his knee. The fingers on his left hand were all pointing in different directions like a discarded glove. His right arm was tucked somewhere underneath his body, twisted in such a way that defied human anatomy. He looked like a rag doll that had been tossed haphazardly across a room by a petulant child.

Then he saw James's head.

His face was a mask of red. Blood seeped from what looked like a hundred cuts. Shards of glass protruded like small icicles from James's scalp, his head, his neck.

But from somewhere within the mangled mess came breath. He was still alive.

Barely.

Alex did not hear any police or ambulance sirens. Wherever help was, they were too far away. James would be dead in minutes, if not seconds.

Alex looked up. He saw a glowing form descending from the sky.

It was an Ankou. And it was coming to take James Mungro's soul.

"You…"

The word hissed from James's lips like air from a tire. Alex couldn't tell if it was an accusation or a cry for help. Alex knelt down next to the boy's mangled body.

"It's okay," Alex whispered. "It's okay."

James was pretty much the farthest thing in the world from okay, but words escaped Alex. Then he heard a noise. From somewhere above. The sound of rocks spilling down an embankment.

"Alex? James?"

It was Nia.

There was no time. The Ankou was close. James's soul would be Exorted in seconds. Alex had to do it *now.*

Alex placed his hands on James's chest. He could feel the boy's heart beating faintly.

"No..." James mumbled.

"It's okay," Alex said. "It'll be over soon."

Then he closed his eyes and felt the Blaze rising. The fire roiled and simmered inside of him, pouring from his chest into his arms, then down into his wrists and spilling into his fingers, which began to glow like embers. Small flames leapt from his fingertips as the flame from Alex flowed into James's body. The heat rose within him. It was nothing like what he'd felt with the deer, or any of the other animals over the years. Using the Blaze on a dying animal felt like placing his hand on an oven. Using it on a dying person felt like he'd stepped inside one.

Alex cried out as the dying boy's eyes widened. His mouth opened. A stream of blood trickled from his lips down his cheek. Then James unleashed a terrifying scream, and a brilliant white light blotted out the world.

---

"James! Alex!"

Nia held her cell phone light in front of her. So far, she had seen nothing other than some footprints and broken branches where Alex must have come through. Then Nia heard a scream from somewhere below her and the night sky vanished behind a flash of white.

Then, just as quickly as it appeared, the light vanished.

Nia stood there, her heart pounding. *What the hell was that?*

"*Hello?* James? Alex? Anyone?"

"Nia! Down here!"

It was James.

She scrambled down the ravine.

"James? Where are you?" She scanned the hillside with her cell.

"Over here!"

She followed his voice.

"Here!"

Then she saw him.

*How in the hell…?*

James was sitting on a tree stump, hands on his knees, head bent. He was shaking.

But he was alive.

"James…" Nia said. "James, are you okay?"

James nodded. "I…I think so."

Nia shined her cell light on him. His shirt and pants were shredded and covered in blood, like he'd been chewed up by a shark and then spit back out.

But other than his clothes, James looked—fine? How was that possible? Underneath the grime, his skin was intact. She couldn't see a single cut or laceration on him.

"You went through the windshield," she said. "You fell all the way down here. How…?"

"I don't know," he said. His voice trembled, but his breathing was steady. She walked over to him and pressed two fingers against the side of his neck. His pulse was fast, but strong.

"What happened?" she said. "Where's Alex?"

"I don't know," James said again.

"You don't know what happened or where he went?"

James shook his head, and then he began to sob. Nia took James in her arms and looked around the ravine. There was no sign of Alex. He was gone.

*Who the hell—or* what *the hell—was he?*

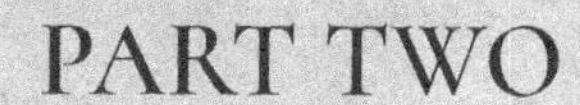

PART TWO

# SECOND TENET

*Both Dominus and Aegis are forbidden from interfering in the balance of life and death, either by preventing a soul from being Exorted or by Siphoning a soul before its flame burns out. Defiance will be met with punishment by the Conclave.*

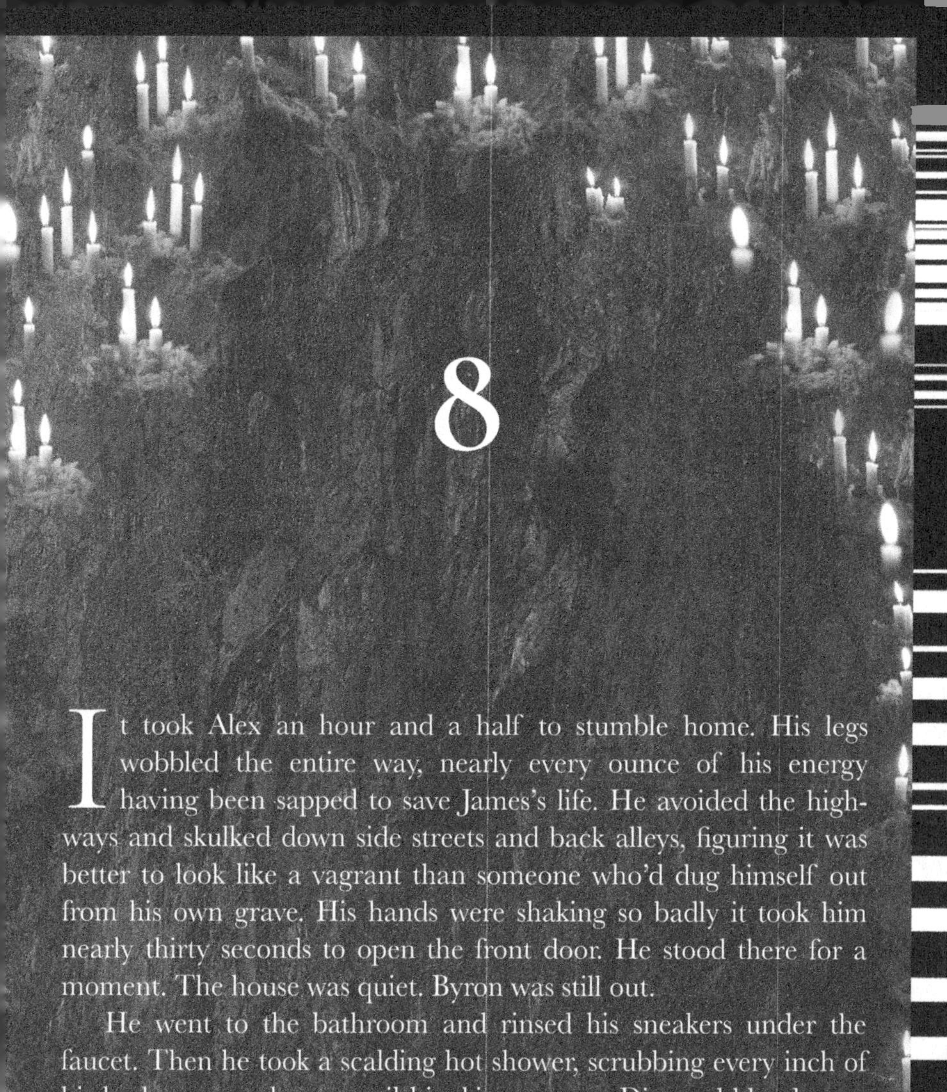

# 8

It took Alex an hour and a half to stumble home. His legs wobbled the entire way, nearly every ounce of his energy having been sapped to save James's life. He avoided the highways and skulked down side streets and back alleys, figuring it was better to look like a vagrant than someone who'd dug himself out from his own grave. His hands were shaking so badly it took him nearly thirty seconds to open the front door. He stood there for a moment. The house was quiet. Byron was still out.

He went to the bathroom and rinsed his sneakers under the faucet. Then he took a scalding hot shower, scrubbing every inch of his body over and over until his skin was raw. Dirt and blood went down the drain in a pinkish-brown swirl.

He gingerly cleaned the angry red gash then taped a gauze pad over the wound. He put on clean clothes and threw the soiled ones into a garbage bag. He took the bag outside, walked swiftly down the street, and tossed it into a garbage can by the side of 34 Marigold Lane.

Then he slid into bed and tried to let his racing pulse subside. A new layer of sweat had already begun to seep from his pores. Alex shut his eyes and took slow, even breaths. He tried to forget the image of James's broken body lying in the dirt, tried to forget the burning, searing pain he felt when he placed his hands on the boy's failing heart.

Alex had only felt that kind of agony once before. He had used the Blaze ten, maybe twenty times in his life. But other than one notable exception—the very first day he'd received it from his father—Alex had used it only on animals. Deer, rabbits, birds. Wounded creatures he'd found and pitied. But the moment he touched James, the memory of that day, that very first pain, came rushing back. He could still feel the heat burning his veins and scorching his bones. Alex closed his eyes tightly and prayed for sleep.

But sleep did not come. The image of James looking up at him, his face covered in blood, would not go away. He lay there, staring at the ceiling, trying to convince his mind to think about something else. *Anything* else.

He lay there for hours. He could not shake it. The crash. The blood. James's body. He would give anything to make the thoughts go away.

Then, he felt it. The sensation started low in his body, near his abdomen, a rancid feeling like he'd eaten something bad. At first Alex thought it was psychosomatic, the way you might get nervous before a test and feel nauseous. But then the sensation rose. It climbed into his chest, enveloping his heart and lungs until he was coughing and fighting for breath. It spread outward into his arms. To his horror, Alex saw that his body had taken on a dark, purplish color. His skin itself had begun to feel moldy, spoiled.

*What was happening?*

A faint, purplish-brown vapor seemed to be rising from his body, almost like smoke from a poisonous candle. His breath grew short. Alex clutched at his throat, trying to claw it away, to allow him room to breathe. He rocked back and forth, trying to cry out but was unable to. It felt like his body was putrefying from the inside out.

Then his father appeared in the room, eyes wide with both fear and anger.

"Stop this, now!" Byron called out. And just as quickly as it had come, the terrible feeling vanished. The vapor disappeared.

He gulped down sweet air. Sat up. Checked his body. Everything was the way it was just moments before, right down to the cut on his arm.

"Alex," Byron said, "what did you *do*?"

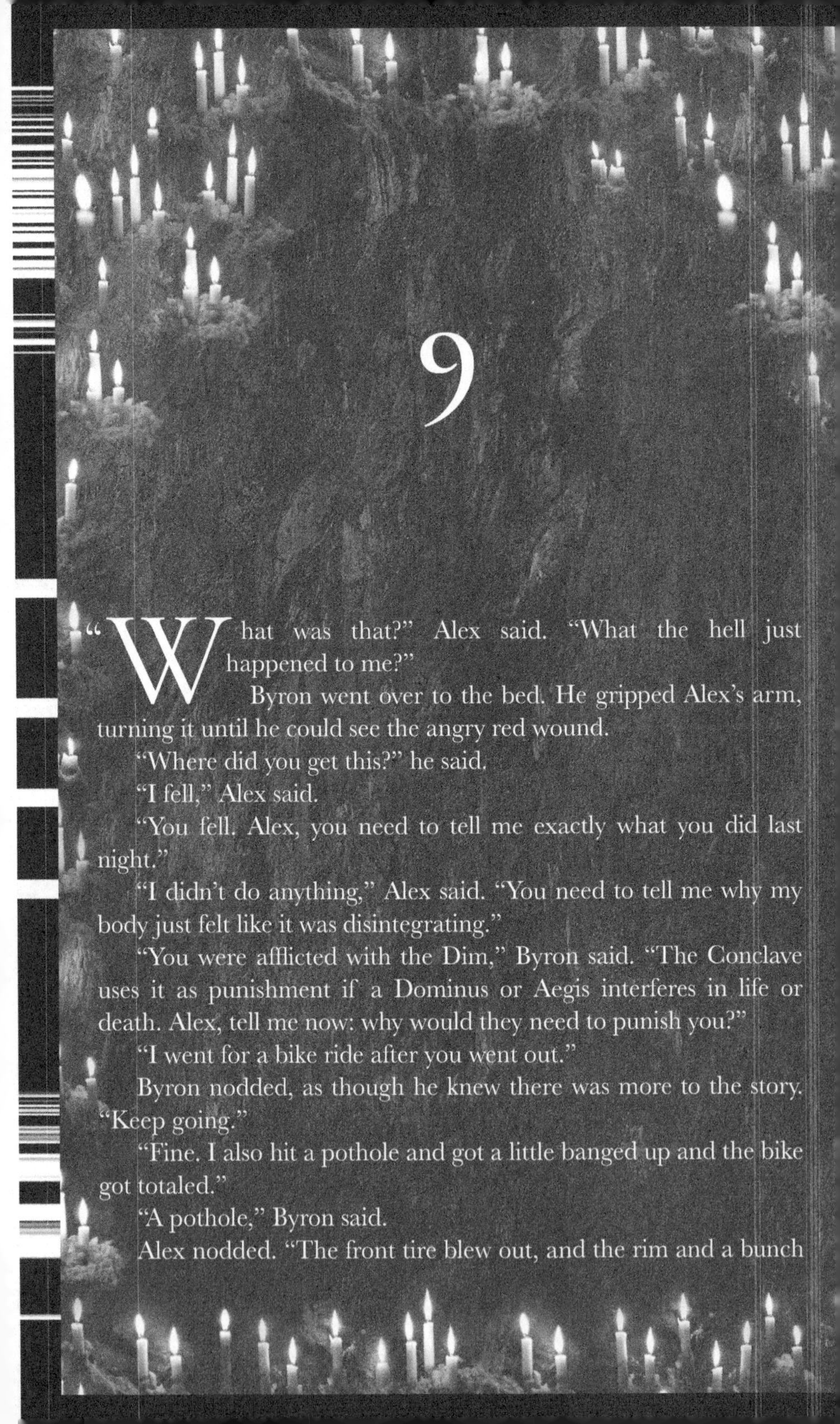

# 9

"What was that?" Alex said. "What the hell just happened to me?"

Byron went over to the bed. He gripped Alex's arm, turning it until he could see the angry red wound.

"Where did you get this?" he said.

"I fell," Alex said.

"You fell. Alex, you need to tell me exactly what you did last night."

"I didn't do anything," Alex said. "You need to tell me why my body just felt like it was disintegrating."

"You were afflicted with the Dim," Byron said. "The Conclave uses it as punishment if a Dominus or Aegis interferes in life or death. Alex, tell me now: why would they need to punish you?"

"I went for a bike ride after you went out."

Byron nodded, as though he knew there was more to the story. "Keep going."

"Fine. I also hit a pothole and got a little banged up and the bike got totaled."

"A pothole," Byron said.

Alex nodded. "The front tire blew out, and the rim and a bunch of the spokes got bent to hell. It was an old bike anyway, it would have probably cost more to fix than to get a new one."

"So…you just left it, where? On the side of the road?"

"No. There was a garbage dump nearby and I tossed it in."

"So you took your bike to a garbage dump and…just tossed it in?"

"Yup."

"If you didn't have your bike, how did you get home?"

"I walked."

"You walked home…in the middle of the night…from a garbage dump. Do I have this right so far?"

"I'm not going to subject myself to the third degree. I answered your questions."

"Not truthfully, Alex."

"Welcome to my world. You never want to answer any questions honestly. I'm sick of my life being a guessing game. It's bullshit."

"Watch your mouth," Byron said. "I'm your father and I've earned more respect than to be talked to like that."

"No, you're not my father," Alex replied. He felt a sour taste in his mouth and instantly regretted the words. He saw Byron deflate slightly, shoulders hunching over like he'd been punched in the gut.

"I'm sorry. I didn't mean that."

"You're right. I'm not your biological father," Byron said. "But I raised you, alone. I cared for you, fed you, clothed you, and loved you from the time you were small enough to fit in the crook of my arm. I love you like my son because you are my son. Your life is more important to me than my own. Do you *ever* doubt that?"

"No," Alex said.

"I need to trust you, Alex. You just saw what the Conclave is capable of if we disobey."

"You told me they weren't omniscient," Alex said. "That they couldn't see everything."

"They are not omniscient, but the Conclave can feel when a life is disrupted." Byron sat down on the bed next to Alex. "Tell me. What happened last night?"

Alex took a deep breath.

He told his father about the crash. How James had been thrown through the windshield. How Alex had found his broken body at the bottom of the ravine. How he'd used the Blaze to save James before the boy's soul could be Exorted.

Byron nodded as he listened. The more Alex spoke, the more concerned he looked.

"So your bike," Byron said. "The one that was 'totaled.' Where is it now?"

"I left it there," Alex said.

Byron rubbed the bridge of his nose. "You left your bike at the scene of a car crash," he said, sighing. "Alex, you will be Dominus in mere months. You will be responsible for maintaining the balance between this world and the underworld. You can't be so…*irresponsible*."

"I know. I'm sorry."

"Did anyone else see you use the Blaze on the Mungro boy?"

"I don't know. Maybe. A girl in our class. Nia Solomon. She was in the car too. She came down the ravine to look for us. She might have seen it."

"Alex," Byron said. "Do you hear what you're saying? That you left your bike at the scene of a car crash? That not only did you use the Blaze to interrupt an Exortus, but somebody else may have *witnessed* it?"

"Does this mean we have to leave Whisper Valley?"

Byron shook his head. "We can't leave here until the Quieting is over. You know that."

"I know," Alex said. "Now you answer my question. What is the Dim? Why did it feel like my body was putrefying?"

"Because it was," Byron said. "Just as the Blaze represents the fire of life, the Dim is the manifestation of life ebbing away. As our candles burn, the smoke they emit is concentrated death. The Conclave used that on you."

"Why were they trying to kill me?" Alex said.

"They weren't. They were making a point. You are next in line to be Dominus. If you interfere with life and death, they're letting you know that they will hurt you. Badly. This was only a reprimand. Learn from it."

"I never want to feel that way again," Alex said.

"That is entirely in your hands. When the day comes for you to take my place, I will show you the flames of life. Then you'll understand where our power comes from."

"You're talking about the Cavern of Orcus."

"That is where life and death are balanced," Byron said. "Now if anyone asks you about last night, deny everything. You simply got scared and ran off."

"You want me to tell people that I'm a coward? That I left people to die?"

"Our job is more important than your dignity."

Alex said nothing.

"The Conclave will only forgive a certain number of mistakes. They need to know that once you become Dominus, you will not abuse your powers."

"I couldn't just let James die, Dad."

"Our job is to shepherd the souls of the dead. Not to decide who lives and who dies."

"But we can," Alex said.

"We can. But we don't."

The words hung in the air.

"When you gave me the Blaze that day in the woods, you interfered with death. Why didn't they use the Dim on you then?"

"That was different. You are the first Aegis who has not come via the ritual of Corpus Sanguis, where the blood of a Dominus is infused into the soul of a newly-Exorted child. Because you are not from my blood, I had to transfer the Blaze to you physically. To do that, I needed a vessel."

"A vessel. You mean the guy we saved."

"That's right," Byron said.

"Would the Conclave ever go further?" Alex said. "Would they ever kill an Aegis?"

"They can," Byron said solemnly. "And they have. Please learn from this, Alex. I can protect you from a lot of things. But I can't protect you from them."

# 10

Iggy talked the entire bus ride to school, convinced that a senior named Trevor Michaelson was likely head over heels in love with him based solely on the fact that Trevor had liked a six-month-old Instagram photo of Iggy running track. Alex tried to listen, but he had two things on his mind: how the Conclave had let him think he was dying that very morning, and that Nia Solomon had not gotten on the bus. That worried him. Was she avoiding him? Had she seen him use the Blaze on James? He needed to know what she saw. What she might have told people. But underneath all of those concerns was something else: he just wanted to see her.

"My arms looked *good* in that pic," Iggy said. "I mean, Trevor's the captain of the swim team, so he could probably get with anyone. But do you know how many pics he had to scroll through to get to that one? It has to mean something, right?"

"Oh, definitely," Alex said. "Hang on, Iggy, my dad just texted me."

"Oh, of course. Sorry if my love life or lack thereof is boring you." Iggy leaned across the aisle to talk to Ayesha.

Byron hadn't texted, and he felt bad lying to Iggy, but he needed to know something. He opened the browser on his phone and searched for the *Whisper Valley Press* website. To his surprise, he couldn't find a single story on the crash. He checked the websites of all the local TV stations. Nothing. He googled "James Mungro" and narrowed the search to the past twenty-four hours. Nothing came up except for James's social media feeds, and they made no mention of it.

Strange. *Very* strange. How could a crash that nearly killed five people go totally unreported?

"Hey, Iggy, can I ask you something?" Alex said.

"Oh, so you don't want to hear about my romantic laments, but when *you* have a question, I should drop everything."

"Sorry, Iggy. I promise I want to hear nothing but stories about Trevor Michaelson's trap muscles. Just a little distracted this morning."

"Don't sweat it, Tree guy. I don't blame you, I'm pretty sure I'm overthinking this. Or maybe not. Anyway, what's up?"

"You said the other day that you know everything about Whisper Valley."

"If you're talking about gossip, I consider myself the Bravo TV of the Dubya V," Iggy said proudly.

"That's catchy."

"I know. I've tried to pitch a *Real Housewives of Whisper Valley* but they won't return my calls."

"So you hear things."

"Occasionally," Iggy said with a mischievous smile. "Let me guess. You like someone and want to know if they're hooking up with anyone before you make a move and her name definitely doesn't rhyme with Maya."

"What? No, nothing like that."

"Sure. Someone told me you two were talking about books in the library yesterday and that you seemed cool if a little weird."

"Nia told you that?"

"Maaaaaybe. Then she stopped returning my texts. Okay, I might have been a little pushy and I probably would have stopped returning my texts too."

"We just talked, that's all," Alex said. "But that's not what this is about. Did you hear about anything that might have happened last night? After school? It might have been bad."

Iggy's eyes narrowed. He looked around, as if scanning for eavesdroppers. Then he whispered, "I did hear something."

"Like what?"

"It's crazy. I'm not even sure I fully believe it."

"What is it?"

"Okay. Well, first thing you need to know for some context is that James Mungro's family is connected. I'm talking like if AT&T and Sprint and T-Mobile merged with Facebook and TikTok connected. When I told you to steer clear of James, it wasn't just because he's an asshole—which he is—but it's because you do not want to get on his dad's radar."

"What do you mean?"

"Don't you know who James's father is?"

"I just moved here, Iggy, I don't even know where to buy milk."

Iggy pulled up the internet browser on his phone, tapped it a few times, then showed the screen to Alex.

"Well, I guess that explains it," Alex said.

The website read Whisper Valley Police Department. Iggy zoomed in on a photo of a bald man in his late forties or early fifties, with a thick brow and severe gray eyes. The name read Dean S. Mungro. The title underneath read Chief of Police.

"Holy crap," Alex said.

"Dean has been grooming James to join the department basically since birth," Iggy said. "Not only that, but the Mungro family has money. Not just Whisper Valley money, but *money* money. If you look outside the Oberst Auditorium in school, you'll see a plaque thanking Dean and Lillian Mungro for the recent renovations. If you're going to be a screwup like James Mungro, it helps to have a rich cop for a dad."

Alex thought about the crack he'd made in the cafeteria about James's father probably not hugging him enough. He hadn't just touched a nerve. He'd jabbed it with a pitchfork.

"What exactly did you hear?" Alex said.

"There are rumors that James did a battering ram job with his dad's Mercedes last night. Thankfully, nobody was seriously hurt. A few bumps and bruises. James got lucky."

"Where'd you hear that?"

"I'm friends with Billy Wooten's ex-girlfriend, Rebecca Hayes. Apparently, Billy texted Rebecca a pic of his stitched-up Frankenstein forehead last night. Rebecca asked what happened and who he was with, and since Billy makes your average pet rock look like Mark Zuckerberg, he told her about the crash and said he was with James, Nia, and Alice D'Agosta. Apparently, Billy and Rebecca hooked up a few weeks ago because he said he was ending it with Alice, so Rebecca flipped the eff out when she heard they were hanging out again. And since I somehow became Rebecca's designated shoulder to cry on when Billy does something dumb, which is pretty much every day, she texted me about the crash."

"I didn't hear anything about a crash on the news this morning," Alex replied. "You said this is a slow town. Wouldn't it get covered somewhere?"

"You'd think so, but this wouldn't be the first time Dean Mungro pulled some major strings for Prince Dickhead. James already has like two-point-nine-nine-nine-nine-nine strikes, and that's even *with* his dad cleaning up his messes. With something like that on his record, he'd have a hard time getting past college admissions boards. Let alone into the police academy," Iggy said. "James would be in juvie or worse right now if it wasn't for his dad. Last year, on July Fourth, James got arrested for selling oxy *and* setting off illegal fireworks on Somerset Beach. *In the same night.* But James was in school on Monday like nothing happened—with a splint on his wrist. He told people he fell down the stairs, but that wasn't the first time James came into school with a mysterious injury and an excuse flimsier than printer paper."

"You think Dean hurts James."

"I know he does. To protect and serve, my ass," Iggy said. "Which is why I'm scared what Dean might have done to James if he *did* get into an accident last night."

"Jesus," Alex said.

"Nope. Jesus healed the wounded. Dean Mungro just gives him more work."

They got off the bus and walked toward school. Alex looked around for James, Billy Wootens, and Nia. He didn't see any of them.

"So why does Nia hang out with James?" Alex asked. "He's a giant asshole and she seems pretty cool."

"I think there's a history between them, but the details are above my paygrade because she's never told me. And she's got enough on her plate with her folks that I don't pry. Let me ask you this: if you and Nia were just talking, that's all, why are you so interested in her?"

"I'm not."

"Riiiiight," Iggy said with a smirk. "And I don't stalk Trevor Michaelson's Facebook page. I love Nia. And most of the time she's fine. But then she'll go three days without saying a word to anyone. She'll just sit in a corner alone reading or drawing. Some days she's all smiles, then the next she's the human embodiment of an Elliott Smith song. The James thing—I don't know. It doesn't make sense to me. I think she wants to cut him off, but there's something between them that keeps her from doing it."

"And you're *sure* they're not dating."

"Trust me, tree guy," Iggy said, "they're definitely not dating."

---

When Alex hadn't seen James, Billy, or Nia by lunch, the worry in his gut began to fester. He wasn't hungry, but he took a grilled cheese with mashed potatoes and broccoli in the hopes the food would change his mind. He scanned the cafeteria looking for Iggy. But he didn't see Iggy. Instead, he saw Nia. More importantly she saw him.

She was sitting at a table, notebook open in front of her, but when their eyes met, she stood up, threw everything into her backpack, and made a beeline toward Alex. The look on her face said *I saw something messed up last night and you need to explain what the hell happened RIGHT NOW.*

*Play it cool*, Alex thought. *Remember what Dad said. Deny everything.*

But when he saw the look in her eyes and felt the knot in his stomach, Alex knew he couldn't lie to her. So he did the next best thing. He put his food down in front of a random kid, apologized, and ran away.

*I'll just avoid her the rest of the semester. That should be easy. Yup. No problem.*

Alex threw open the cafeteria doors and saw Mr. Ryerson.

"Men's room?" Alex asked impatiently.

"Fourth floor, first door on your right. Something the matter, Mr. Sonnum?"

"Nope, just *really* gotta go," Alex said.

Alex sprinted to the stairwell, nearly taking out a trio of sophomores. He took the stairs two at a time, then banged open the door to the men's room and closed the door. He was alone. Alex went inside one of the stalls, locked it, and sat down. The bathroom smelled like piss and disinfectant. He wished he'd taken a moment to open a window or find a better hiding place.

*Well, now what, genius?*

Unfortunately, Alex didn't have time to answer the question. The door swung open and he heard Nia say, "Unless you're actually taking a dump, get out here, Alex. We need to talk. *Now.*"

Alex remained silent. For some reason, his current predicament reminded him of *The Odyssey*. His AP English class read it last year at Fairview. Alex had particularly enjoyed the chapters where Odysseus was forced to navigate his ship between the monsters Scylla and Charybdis. On one side of the narrow strait was Scylla, an enormous multi-headed sea monster that could devour several sailors at once. On the other was Charybdis, a ferocious whirlpool that could engulf entire ships within its swirling maw. The choice between Scylla and Charybdis was essentially deciding between the lesser of two evils: lose a few men, or lose them all.

Alex had a similar choice at that moment: the toilet where both his body and his dignity were balanced very, very precariously, or

Nia Solomon, the girl who had witnessed him do something that no human being should be able to.

So the toilet, or Nia.

Which was the lesser of two evils?

*Well*, he thought, *Nia smells better than this stall.*

Alex slid the bolt back and opened the door. Nia stood there, arms folded across her chest. The look on her face was somewhere between anger, bewilderment, consternation, and awe—all of which mixed together to come across as: *Start talking*.

"Um, hi," Alex said. "Come here often?"

Nia did not react.

"Last night," she said. "What happened in that ravine?"

"What happened is that *your* friends nearly got five people killed," Alex said.

"First of all, Billy is *not* my friend," she said defiantly.

"But James is."

"Sometimes. It's complicated."

"No shit. You hugged him on the first day. You were in the car with him last night. You spend an awful lot of time with James for *sometimes*. It makes me wonder what kind of person would be friends with someone like that."

"You have no *idea* what kind of person I am," Nia said with quiet anger. "You don't know anything about me."

"And you know even less about me," Alex said.

"I know what I saw last night," she said. "I know it's not possible for James to be alive, let alone walking around today like nothing happened."

Alex said nothing. He could still feel the echoes of the poisonous Dim scraping against his bones. He could hear his father's voice in his head: *Deny. Deny. Deny*.

"Nothing happened," Alex said. "I don't know what you think you saw."

"Don't lie to me. I know what I saw," Nia said. "I saw the windshield. I saw the blood. Nobody just walks away from that. James should be dead."

Nia took a step forward. Alex took a step back. He had one foot in the stall.

"I don't know what you want from me," he said.

"I want to know the truth," she whispered. "When I followed you to the bottom of the ravine, I saw a bright light and then I found James without a scratch. How do you explain that?"

"I don't have to," Alex said.

"I *saw* you go down there. James *told* me you were there."

"Then ask *him* what happened," Alex said.

"James has no idea. He doesn't remember anything before that light. He just knows, like I do, that nobody could have survived that crash without looking like Swiss cheese."

"I have nothing else to say. I need to get to class."

"Don't give me that 'I have to get to class' crap again," she said. "Tell me—"

Just then, they heard a pair of voices outside the bathroom door. Nia pushed Alex backward into the stall. She followed him in and locked the door behind them. They stood there, face to face, unmoving. He could feel her breath on his neck, could smell a faint whiff of sweat and deodorant. Her finger brushed up against his and it felt like he'd grazed a hot pan. But this time he didn't pull away. Nia didn't move her hand. One of her curls flicked his cheek. Alex's pulse raced. Their fingers were touching by mere molecules, but neither of them moved. He could hear her breathing quickening. *It's not just me.*

"Nia, I—"

Then the bathroom door opened.

"I swear those sloppy joes go right through me," one guy said.

"You're better off licking a toilet seat than eating anything they claim came from a cow," the other one replied. "One day last semester I ate a beef taco, veggie lasagna, and bread pudding and my body basically shut down."

"I mean, you have nobody to blame but yourself for that."

One of them entered the adjacent stall. The other one went to a urinal. Alex looked down. Nia's eyes were closed. She was shaking her head as if to say, *How the hell did I end up here.*

They remained silent as the guys went about their business. Alex tried to stay calm, steadying his breathing. He wondered if her heart was beating as fast as his.

After what felt like an eternity, they flushed, washed, and left the bathroom. When the door closed, Nia unlocked the stall and pulled Alex out by his shirt. She was about to continue the interrogation, but then glanced at his sleeve.

"Your arm," she said, concerned. Alex looked down. A thin line of red had begun to seep through the fabric. She rolled up his sleeve, each touch of her fingers like the pelting of hot water—and not entirely unpleasant.

"It's not a big deal," he said.

"Look at this," Nia said, "are you *trying* to get an infection?"

He'd taped gauze to the cut before school, but the bandage was nearly soaked through with red. She took the gauze off and touched the skin around the laceration.

"Does it hurt?" she asked.

"Can I say yes and still be considered manly?"

She said, "This really needs stitches."

"I can't go to a doctor."

"Don't tell me you're one of those new age weirdos who uses sound therapy to cure brain tumors."

"No, it's not like that."

"Whatever it is, if you don't take care of this, you're going to get an infection." She grabbed a wad of paper towels from the dispenser, ran them under the sink, and dabbed at the wound. Alex winced. She placed a dry towel over the cut and said, "Hold it there. Tight."

Nia took a first aid kit from the wall and removed an alcohol wipe, gauze, and medical tape. She cleaned the cut, dried it, placed the gauze over it, and secured it with the tape.

"Change it two or three times a day," she said.

"Thank you, doctor."

"Hold up," Nia said, rolling his sleeve up a little further. "Is that—?"

"It's nothing," Alex said, quickly rolling his sleeve back down and buttoning it.

"It's a tattoo," she said. "Let me see it."

"No."

"Okay, fine. Be all secretive. Now, back to last night. Talk to me."

"I can't."

Alex tried to walk past Nia, but she grabbed him by the shirt collar and yanked him back.

"Tell me the truth. What did you do to James? Who are you?"

Alex turned to face her. For some reason, for the first time in his life, Alex felt like saying things he'd sworn never to say. She had a power over him, something elemental, something he could not explain. The heat when she touched him. He'd never felt it before. It meant something, even if he didn't know exactly what that was.

He thought about the pain. What the Conclave had done to him. But. He also remembered what his father said. *They are not omniscient.*

"I shouldn't have done what I did to James," Alex said softly.

"What does that mean?" she said. "Did you…*heal* him?"

"Please," Alex said. "Just let it go. For both our sakes. It's safer that way."

"*No,*" she said. "Tell me, Alex. What *are* you?"

"I'm just like you," Alex said. "Only not at all like you."

"How…" Nia said, "…how are you not like me?"

The anger in her voice was gone. It was gentle. Probing. It made him want to tell her.

Everything.

"I…"

"Alex," she said, moving toward him. Their bodies were close enough for him to feel the electricity between them. "Please. Talk to me. I want to know who you are."

The words took Alex's breath away. Nobody had ever said that to him. Nobody had ever cared who he was.

Seventeen years keeping it inside. Seventeen years without anyone to talk to except the one person who couldn't—wouldn't—

understand him. Seventeen years and nobody had tried to know Alex the way Nia was in that moment.

"I'm..."

Just then, the door banged open. Mr. Ryerson stopped when he saw Nia. His lips formed a scowl of disapproval.

"Ms. Solomon," he said. "I'll assume you're in the men's room because you forgot to put in your contact lenses this morning and couldn't read the sign. Am I right?"

"Yes," Nia said. "That's it. I'm crazy farsighted. I actually thought this was the biology lab."

"That's what I figured," Mr. Ryerson said with a wry grin. He held the door open for her. Nia looked back at Alex as she walked out, her eyes pleading with him. Then, as the door began to close, Alex said four words.

"Larrimore Hill. Nine. Tonight."

Nia smiled as the door closed.

# 11

Samael woke up coated in sweat. He checked his watch. He'd been asleep for three hours and twenty minutes. His felt a cramp in his leg and ran his fingers over the thick, four-inch-long scar on his calf, a souvenir from the many surgeries required to fix the badly broken leg he'd woken up with on that beach. Three hours was plenty. It was time to get to work.

Samael slept at most four hours a night. When he relayed that to pleasant company, it was met with an eye roll, an assumption that he was bragging about his work ethic rather than making a simple statement of fact. Samael rarely slept because he chose not to. It had taken years of training to gradually reduce the amount of rest he needed to function at a high level. He had excised all alcohol, nicotine, and caffeine, worked out regularly, and slept in a soundproof room on a soft mattress with high thread count sheets so as to maximize the rest he got from those sparse hours.

The hours between dusk and dawn were the most productive of the day, when Samael could work in solitude with no impositions on his time. A side effect of his sleep habits was that Samael's skin had developed a dull, pale pallor, with circular, wine-colored shadows below his eyes. More than one person had remarked that Samael resembled a wax sculpture more than a man of flesh and blood.

The silver lining, Samael supposed, was that this morbid trait actually benefitted his business. It didn't hurt for a man who trafficked in death to resemble Death itself.

"If I *were* Death," Samael had responded recently to one overly-lubricated portly banker at a charity auction, "I wouldn't have to work quite so hard."

But that wasn't *quite* true. Samael held a great deal of respect for Death's work ethic. Which is why he needed to rival it. How else could one expect to hunt down Death—let alone destroy it—if you didn't understand it?

Since the plane crash that had killed his family, Samael had spent the majority of his life looking for the man—if you could call him that—who had watched his family burn. Samael kept a veneer of respectability in ordinary society, hence Zagan's End, but the shop was a means to an end. Every night when he closed the store, Samael spent the dark hours searching for the man in black, at the edge of the clearing partially obscured by the heat and haze, as if overseeing a wake.

Death.

Samael scoured news reports, websites, blogs, anything and everything all over the world looking for hints, rumors, crumbs, morsels. Unfortunately, most so-called legitimate news sources did not believe in Death the way he did, and refused to acknowledge that there may exist phenomena beyond rational comprehension.

When his family was killed, Samael Zagan was a fixture in the news for weeks. *The Boy Who Fell From the Sky and Lived*, the country's largest newspaper called him. Camera crews waited on the tarmac to capture video of the sunburned, malnourished Samael returning home. He was offered vast sums of money for interviews. Film, television, and publishing companies beat down his door hoping to capitalize on his incredible story of survival. Dozens of families offered to take in the now-orphaned teenager. Overnight, Samael had gone from being a member of a family, someone who was loved, to an item. A trinket to be kept on a shelf. Something to be both pitied and exploited.

At his family's wake, Samael wailed and cried. But the moment the caskets were lowered into the ground, his tears dried up. Grief would not bring his family back. The emotion that monopolized his thoughts was not sadness or despair.

It was anger.

Anger at the man he had seen that day. The man who watched his family burn.

Death.

Samael had no doubt that Death was a man. Even human, perhaps, in some way. But finding a man who did not want to be found, who had the ability to vanish like smoke, could be no mere hobby. So Samael had spent thousands of hours scouring the world for rumors of any activity that could not be rationally explained. He did not believe in the supernatural or paranormal, per se. But he believed someone, or some*thing* walked among the living, reaping the souls of those who perished.

But Death was cautious. Death was not a rubbernecker, gawking at catastrophes for dinner table conversation. Samael had a theory. Death, Samael believed, was a nomad.

Death went where Death was needed.

Pandemics. Violence. Strife. Chaos.

A plane crash.

There were simply too many deaths on any given day for Death to be present at all of them. Just like kings had soldiers, Death surely had minions to help him reap souls. Death himself only made appearances when it was special. At the intersection of unexplained phenomena and mass tragedy, that was where Samael would find Death.

The problem was, Death was always one step ahead of Samael. By the time Samael found a clue, Death had already vanished.

Seven years ago, Samael learned of a train that had left Plovdiv, Bulgaria heading to Istanbul that had gone off the rails outside of Esenyurt, killing two hundred and forty-nine people. Miraculously, the conductor had survived the crash despite the lead car being crushed like a tin can under a tank tread.

Unexplained phenomena and mass tragedy. Death had been there. Samael knew it.

Samael had flown out to Istanbul the very next day. The city was in mourning. Samael paid the right people and managed to gain access, along with an interpreter, to the conductor who was being monitored at Acibadem Hospital in Taksim Square.

The conductor, a sharp, middle-aged woman named Fatma Kocak, was not only unhurt, but even irritated that she was being forced to remain in the hospital for observation. Samael introduced himself as an insurance investigator from the United States. Ms. Kocak was skeptical. Instead of trying to convince her, Samael showed her his phone. His bank was prepared to transfer three hundred thousand lira, or approximately forty-four thousand dollars, into an account of her choosing. All Ms. Kocak had to do was answer a few questions. She agreed.

Ms. Kocak told Samael that inspectors had performed a routine safety evaluation on the train just that week, and not a single thing was out of place. There were no issues with the tracks, and the weather that day was twenty-one degrees Celsius; beautiful and sunny. It was as if God himself, Fatma said, had lifted the train's wheels off the tracks and moved them just *slightly* to the right.

At that point, Ms. Kocak did not know she was the only survivor. Samael asked her if she had seen anything peculiar, anything extraordinary. She said she could not be sure, but she believed she had seen a strange man as she lay in the rubble. The man did not move and made no effort to help. He was just *watching.* Ms. Kocak said she assumed he was a passenger. He wore a black suit with a white shirt and a black tie. His shoulder-length hair was slicked back and neatly combed. She could not see a speck of blood or dirt or ash on him. Fatma said the man's presence seemed odd, but she was hardly in the right frame of mind. Samael felt a shiver of hope.

Samael did not say it to Ms. Kocak, but he was positive that the man she spoke of was Death. Death was at the crash, just as he was at the Zagan family's demise. Then Fatma said something strange: the man, she said, had a boy with him. *How old was this boy?* Samael asked. Fatma couldn't be sure, but she guessed somewhere between ten and twelve. That part puzzled Samael. *Are you sure?* Samael asked. *About this boy?* Fatma scoffed, as though insulted Samael would doubt her memory.

Unfortunately, the rest of Ms. Kocak's answers were unhelpful. And when Samael was sure he'd learned everything she knew, he left her room. But he remained in the hospital.

Because the crash had been deemed an accident, the Turkish police did not see a need to guard Ms. Kocak's room. Which was why, after she'd fallen asleep, there was nobody to object when Samael reentered and injected a bubble of air into the IV attached to her arm.

Samael then stepped into the hallway and waited.

Within minutes, doctors and nurses were hurrying to Ms. Kocak's bedside. But it was too late. The bubble would have already traveled through her intravenous system and into her heart, causing a pulmonary embolism. Fatma Kocak was dead within minutes.

*Amazing*, Samael thought. *One tiny bubble of air did what ten thousand tons of steel could not.*

He'd killed Ms. Kocak for two reasons: first, he did not want her telling people about the man who'd visited her room. Second, and far more important, he wanted to see if Death would reap Ms. Kocak's soul the same way he'd reaped those who died in the crash.

But other than the medical workers frantically trying to revive Ms. Kocak, nobody came. Samael felt no remorse for the woman's death, but was devastated by the fact that Death had already moved on.

That was why Samael had spent millions of dollars funding the Children of Azrael. Samael could not chase Death the entire world over. The Children of Azrael could be his eyes and ears. Even if they errantly believed that Samael's interest in Death was curiosity rather than obsession. Many were willing to turn the world upside down to aid Samael's quest. But they could never know that Samael's curiosity went beyond obsession and into murder.

Once a week, Samael would receive a briefing from Morton Yen, secretary and treasurer of the Children of Azrael. The briefing contained links to dozens of articles, blogs, photos, and websites with potential leads culled from hundreds of COA members around the world. There were Children of Azrael in nearly every developed country in the world, stretching from Greenland to Argentina, from Svalbard to New Zealand. Because Death took on so many guises in so many different cultures, it was important to have as many perspectives as possible. Certainly, some COA members were more *reliable* than others. Which was why Samael needed to filter these leads through a trusted lieutenant. Namely, Morton Yen.

It was three thirty in the morning when Samael's cell phone rang. The caller ID read M. Yen. Samael picked it up before the first ring ended. Morton did not call often, and when he did, it was for good reason.

"Good morning, Samael," Morton said. That was one of Morton Yen's many idiosyncrasies. He never waited for Samael to say hello.

"Morning isn't for a few more hours, yujin," Samael said.

"I didn't wake you, did I?"

"Have you ever?"

Morton laughed. "No, I suppose not. That's good, because I have information that may interest you."

Samael sat up. Morton did not make such remarks lightly.

"Tell me," Samael demanded.

"It involves a disappearing police report," Morton said.

"I'm hoping you're not calling in the middle of the night due to a magical, vanishing police report about some stolen wallet or bar fight."

"Would I call you if it was that trivial? No, this missing police report involves a dead man."

"A dead man? You have my attention."

"More precisely, a man who *should* be dead."

"I'm afraid you lost me, Morton. What do you mean a man who *should* be dead?"

"A member of the Children of Azrael works with the NAAB, the National Automobile Accident Database. He informed me of a police report that was filed the other night in a small town called

Whisper Valley. The report in question disappeared from both the Whisper Valley PD and the NAAB servers without any explanation."

"How does our contact know this report disappeared?" Samael said. So far, Morton's leads had led only to footprints that vanished in the sand. Samael knew not to get his hopes up.

"Our friend receives notifications when there are changes to accident reports, since they'll be needed for insurance purposes, especially if there may be criminal charges filed. For example, if a hit-and-run graduates to manslaughter because the victim died in the hospital, or if a motorcycle accident involves the child of a foreign diplomat and necessitates federal intervention. But this was different. Nothing was *added* to this report. It just…vanished."

"What does that mean?" Samael said.

"It means somebody with a great deal of influence or money, or more likely both, made it disappear because they did not want the report to become public knowledge."

"You said there was a body—or lack thereof. I'm still not understanding how this missing report is relevant to our pursuits."

"If what our friend in the NAAB told me is true—and I would trust this man to take my son up in a hot air balloon—this *should* have been a fatal accident."

"Should have been fatal?" Samael said.

"I'm sending you some pictures. Check your email."

Samael refreshed his inbox and moments later found a message from Morton Yen containing half a dozen photo attachments. Samael opened them. He examined the photos while Morton waited. He furrowed his brow. It didn't make sense…

"You're telling me there were *no* fatalities?" Samael said in disbelief.

"Not only were there no fatalities," Morton said. "There were no *hospitalizations*."

"That's impossible," Samael said.

"I confirmed it myself before calling you," Morton said. "There were no hospitalizations to any medical center within a fifty-mile radius of Whisper Valley with injuries that would have been consistent with an accident of this kind. There were no media reports on the crash, and no mention of it in any police blotters."

"How…?"

"I know," Morton said. "Like I said, this is most unusual."

"Agreed," Samael said. He enlarged the first photo. It was of a silver Mercedes S-Class. The front of the car was crumpled like a can hit with a hammer. It was nestled against a dented guardrail along a dimly-lit one-lane road. The timestamp read 9:48 p.m. But what drew Samael's attention was not the mangled heap of metal. It was the windshield.

Or more precisely, what remained of it.

There was a large, jagged hole in the driver's side windshield. Broken glass littered the hood, and the windshield itself looked like it had been used as a prop in a horror movie. Blood dripped from the glass. Red-stained shards glittered atop the car's silver hood like rubies. The car had obviously hit the guardrail at high speed and the driver, who was not wearing a seatbelt, had been thrown through the windshield.

Beyond the guardrail was a steep ravine, and whoever was driving had been launched down the incline. There was almost no chance the person who suffered this fate could have survived, at least not without immediate and significant medical attention. And even then, it would have taken an act of God for the driver to pull through, given that they seemed to have left the majority of their blood on the Mercedes.

"The license plate is visible," Samael said. "Whose car is this?"

"The car is registered to a Dean Mungro of Whisper Valley," Morton said. "We ran a thorough background check and as if this isn't crazy enough, it turns out Dean Mungro is the town's chief of police. And the Mungro family's connections run deep. Official charitable financial filings reveal Dean Mungro has donated hundreds of thousands of dollars to various political campaigns, and the Mungro family has a wing named after them at the Dearborn Medical Center. Bottom line, if Dean Mungro wanted to make an accident disappear from the public record, he could without too much effort."

Samael examined the rest of the photos. He zoomed in.

"There was more than one person in the car when it crashed," Samael said. "Does Dean Mungro have family?"

"A wife, Lillian, and a son James. Lillian is Dean's third wife."

"I can appreciate a collector," Samael said. "But why would the police chief and his family be out driving a Mercedes on a Tuesday at ten at night?"

"I don't think the Mungro family was in the car. At least not most of them," Morton said. "I think it was Dean's son, James, who was driving at the time of the crash. James has an impressive rap sheet for a high school junior. Drugs, assault, disturbing the peace, and on and on. A motor vehicle accident could land him significant juvenile detention time. Unless, of course, his father intervened."

"Who were the other passengers?" Samael said.

"I don't know yet, but our people are on it. Assuming they're friends of James Mungro, they may be loyal to him and the family and refuse to speak."

"And the car itself?"

"Most likely a cube of scrap metal in a junkyard by now."

Samael nodded. The picture was coming into focus. James Mungro went for a nighttime drive, which culminated in a horrific accident that should have killed him. Only it didn't. And then his father wiped the crash from the face of the earth. But it didn't answer the question: how could James have survived such a gruesome maiming without medical attention?

Samael tapped his finger against his lower lip. There was a piece of this puzzle missing. Samael scanned the photos. Zoomed in. Then he saw it.

"There," Samael said. "The fourth photo in the set. What do you see in the lower right-hand corner by the crash site?"

There was a pause on the other end as Morton Yen pulled up the photo.

"I see a bicycle," Morton said. "Do you think the car hit the biker?"

"No. The bike is upright and the kickstand is down. I think

whoever was on the bike either witnessed the crash, or came upon it. But look lower. Zoom in."

Another pause. Then Morton said, "Are those…footprints beyond the guardrail?"

"Exactly. The person on the bike stopped aside the wrecked car, climbed over the divider, and went down into the ravine. Do you have any pictures from the ravine itself?"

"No," Morton said. "These were all the images we could get. It appears the investigation got shut down before forensics were called in."

"The elder Mungro didn't want his son facing criminal charges," Samael said, "and used his pull to get the accident wiped away and the car disposed of. But it doesn't explain why there are no records of the injury sustained by the driver. And if Dean went to such great lengths to keep this off of his son's record, it's doubtful he would have let him die from his injuries. Unless, by the time the evening was over, James *had* no serious injuries."

"I don't follow, Samael."

"Have you ever heard of San Pascualito Muerte, Morton?"

"I have not."

"In Guatemalan folklore, San Pascualito was a saint known as King of the Graveyard. San Pascualito is said to have appeared in a vision to a man dying from the cucumatz epidemic, whereupon he told the man that if he was adopted as the patron saint of San Antonio Aguacaliente, he would end the plague. They did, and he did. What I'm saying, my friend, is that in some cultures, Death not only has the power to take a life, but to *prevent* the end of life."

"This could all be a dead end, Samael. It's possible there's a rational explanation for all of this."

"If this accident is real, it seems impossible. And I've spent years searching for the impossible. I want to know everything about Dean and James Mungro. Police records, finances, personnel files, marriage licenses, property deeds, school transcripts, even their preferred brand of toothpaste. I will need sufficient leverage to persuade Mr. Mungro to come clean about an incident he desperately wants to keep quiet."

"You'll have all the leverage you need by the time you have your morning coffee."

"I can always count on you, my friend. I'll be on the next flight to Whisper Valley. Death's trail may still be warm. I want to know how James Mungro survived that accident. And, perhaps more importantly, who was riding that bicycle."

Alex spent the rest of the day wondering what the hell he'd gotten himself into. His offer to meet Nia at Larrimore Hill was an insane, spur-of-the-moment decision. He could take it back. Walk into school the next day and avoid her until the Quieting was done. He could leave Whisper Valley without ever speaking to her again. Sure, he'd have to deal with more bathroom intrusions, avoid the library, and never be able to ride the school bus again. But soon Alex would be a Dominus and his concerns would be far greater than smelly bathrooms. What happened to James would be long forgotten. *He* would be long forgotten.

It would be simple.

It would be clean.

It's what he should have done.

But it's not what he did.

Because deep down, Alex wanted to see her. He wanted to keep his promise to Nia.

So, at eight thirty, with his father out Exorting souls, Alex took an Uber to Larrimore Hill. He'd hoped to have a few minutes alone to figure out what the hell he was going to say, but when he arrived, a beat-up brown sedan was already parked there. Nia was sitting on one of the benches overlooking Whisper Valley. A lump rose in Alex's throat as he got out of the car.

Nia's back was to him as she stared out at the gorgeous expanse, a strong breeze making her curly hair look like it was dancing in the wind. Both the view and the girl took his breath away. She looked like a painting come to life. A perfect memory he wanted to lock inside his mind and call up whenever he needed to feel calm.

"How long are you going to stand there, creeper?" Nia said without turning around.

"A few more hours," he said. "Hope you don't mind."

"Nope. Just stand there staring at my neck. That's not at all weird."

Alex took a deep breath and walked toward the bench. His pulse quickened. Nia moved over and Alex sat next to her, careful not to touch her.

"So…how's your night going?" Alex asked.

Nia laughed. "You're not really going to try small talk after what happened," she said. "You know, I was surprised you suggested we meet at Larrimore Hill. I figured you'd pick a coffee shop or a diner or something. How'd you even know about this place?"

"Total accident," Alex said. "I went out on my bike the night we got into town and just happened to see the turn-off."

"That's a fortunate accident," she said. "Lucky for us you made that turn."

Alex nodded. "I figured if you didn't show tonight, at least I'd be stood up with a nice view."

"You were worried *I* wouldn't show," she said.

"A little. Wait, were you worried *I* wouldn't show?"

"Worried? Now. I was pretty positive you wouldn't. You surprised me." Nia turned to face him. Alex felt his stomach do a flip.

She was wearing black pants and a light blue denim jacket with a patch over the pocket on the left side. He noticed a small birthmark in the shape of a crescent moon just below her right jawline. She was wearing perfume, which threw him a bit. He probably smelled like a combination of biology lab chemicals and hot school bus leather.

"My parents used to bring me up here for picnics on weekends when I was a kid," Nia said. "We'd pack drinks and sandwiches and just sit here and eat and look out at the city."

"I've never been on a picnic," Alex said. "My dad and I…we've been all over the world. But we've never really stopped to look at anything."

"Well that's a waste of the world," Nia replied. "I want to see what you've seen. As much as I love this view, I bet even people in Athens get tired of looking at the Parthenon sometimes."

"I didn't."

Nia's eyes widened. "You've been to Athens?"

Alex shrugged nonchalantly.

She shifted closer to him. "Tell me what it was like. Make me feel like I'm there."

"I still remember how it glows at night atop the Acropolis," Alex said. "I don't know how to describe it other than it looks like there's a fire burning inside the walls. It turns the sky gold. Beautiful isn't even the right word. I think you'd love it."

Nia seemed to shudder just thinking about it. "When were you there?"

"We spent a few months in Greece, living in the village of Skala, in southeastern Cephalonia," Alex said. "It was, I don't remember exactly, about five years ago?"

"You don't remember when you lived in Greece?" Nia said. "I feel like that's the kind of thing you wouldn't forget."

"It's not that it wasn't memorable," Alex said. "It's just that when you travel as much as we do, cities and towns start to blend together. When I was younger, I think I appreciated what I saw. The different cultures and sights. But at some point it just started to feel like 'Okay, here we go again, new town, new people, yup, been there, done that.' It gets old, never sitting down." He paused. "That makes me sound like a spoiled dick, doesn't it?"

"Just a little," Nia said with a faint smile. "Where else have you lived?"

"Off the top of my head: Italy, Australia, New Mexico, Istanbul, San Francisco, Honduras, Tokyo, Marseilles…"

Nia's jaw dropped further and further as Alex spoke.

"Kuala Lumpur, Taipei, oh, and Cape Town. And that's just the last seven or eight years. I still drool when I think about the bunny chow in Cape Town."

"*Please* tell me bunny chow isn't what it sounds like.".

Alex laughed. "No, Bugs is safe. Bunny chow is basically curry inside a hollowed-out loaf of bread. No actual rabbits are harmed. But it. Is. *Delicious*."

"You moving around so much. Does it have to do with what happened in the ravine?"

"Sort of," Alex said. "We move because of my dad's work."

"What does he do? Flight attendant?"

Alex laughed. "Not exactly."

"What, then? Politics? Military?"

"No and no."

"Cruise ship director?"

"*Definitely* not. That requires a personality."

"And you always go where he goes?"

Alex nodded. "We've been a package deal as long as I've known him."

"What do you mean as long as you've known him?"

"Byron adopted me when I was a baby. I never met my birth parents. I don't even know their names."

"Did you ever try to find them?"

"When I was eight or nine, I asked my dad where he adopted me from. He gave me the name of the orphanage, but I found out they'd closed down a few years earlier and I couldn't find anyone who had access to the records. I took that as an omen."

"I'm sorry," Nia said softly. "That must be really hard."

"Not really. Byron is all I know. I have nothing to compare it to."

"So he's not a mafia kingpin or a Senator. What *does* he do?"

"It's complicated."

"Sounds illegal."

"It's not, I swear. But it's also not exactly the kind of job where he gets healthcare or a 401k."

"Does his job have anything to do with what you did to James last night?"

Alex nodded.

"I'm going to ask a question," she said, "and I need you to be honest."

"Okay…"

"Are you a vampire?"

"What? No! Where did that come from?"

"Then you have to be some kind of wizard."

"Don't even go there."

"Then tell me," Nia said. She put her hand on his. "Who are you?"

He moved his hand away.

"Every time I touch you, you act like I'm about to stab you," Nia said. "Why?"

Alex looked down at Nia's hand. "I don't…I'm not good at talking about myself."."

"You don't have to be good at it," she said. "I just want you to be honest. And I promise you, Alex, you can always trust me."

For some reason, hearing those words, hearing her say his name cut deeper than any blade ever could. He looked into her eyes and felt his heart open.

"When I was young," Alex said, "maybe five or six, we were living in upstate New York, near Rochester. One day, my dad told me to get in the car. He didn't say where we were going. After a few hours, he pulled onto a dirt path and led me into the woods. I remember being so afraid he was going to leave me in the middle of nowhere."

"Why would you think that?"

"I got abandoned once. I thought it could happen again."

He paused. She seemed to sense his hesitation. "Go on."

"I don't remember how long we walked. It might have been fifteen minutes, it might have been two hours. And then I heard this noise, like a wheezing. At first, I thought it was a bird. Then I saw a man lying down in the middle of the path. He was wearing shorts and a t-shirt and there was a water bottle next to him leaking out into a little puddle. He'd gone out for a run and had a heart attack and just dropped right there."

"Oh my god," Nia said.

"He was so scared. I'll never forget how his eyes looked. Like he knew he was dying. He was pale as paper and kept whispering *help me*."

"What did you do?"

"I begged my dad to call 9-1-1. But he didn't. I screamed at him. *Why aren't you doing anything? He's going to die because of you*. Then my dad turned to me and said, 'No, he won't. He's going to live because of *you*.' He told me to place my hand on the man's heart. I thought my dad had lost it. He said if I waited too long, the Ankou would take him."

"An-who?" Nia said. "What was he talking about?"

"Just let me finish. So I did what my dad said and put my hands on his heart. The guy tried to push me away, but he could barely breathe. Then my dad placed his hands on top of mine."

Alex paused.

Nia said, "It's okay."

He didn't know if he should go on. If he could go on. Or what the Conclave might do to him if he did.

*They are not omniscient. They're only concerned with matters of life and death.*

The Conclave didn't own him. He only had a few months left before he was chained to the dead forever. A few months left to call his own. He wanted to make the most of them.

"When my dad put his hands on mine, it felt like he was pressing hot coals onto my skin. The pain was unbearable. I screamed and tried to pull away, but he held my hands there. '*Stay strong*,' he said. So I did. And then I began to feel the heat transfer from his hands into mine. My hands began to burn from the inside and then I saw fire go *through* me and into the dying man."

Nia sat silent, unmoving.

"And then there was this, I don't know how else to describe it, this surge of energy, like a lightning bolt through me. And this huge burst of white light lit up the entire world."

"Like what I saw in the ravine," Nia said.

Alex nodded. "When the light went away, the man was still on the ground but his cheeks were pink. He was breathing. Then he got up and ran away so fast he left his water bottle in the mud. I asked my father what we'd just done. He said, 'Now you possess the Blaze. Now you are an Aegis.'"

"The Blaze—is that what you used on James?"

"Yes."

"So what is an Aegis? Who is your father? Alex, who are *you*?"

Alex looked into Nia's eyes. He held out his hand, palm-up, took a deep breath, and concentrated. Small flames began to dance on his fingertips. He could see them reflected in Nia's eyes, flickering in her irises.

"My father is Death," Alex said. "And I'm his heir."

# 

*Death.*

*Death's heir.*

If Alex had been Nia, he would have laughed all the way down to the bottom of Larrimore Hill, continued laughing until he got home, gone to sleep laughing, and kept laughing until the men in white coats came to take him away.

But Nia did not laugh. She did not smile. Alex wondered if she'd heard him. He felt silly repeating himself, so he sat there.

She took Alex's hand. She ran her hand above the flames, then looked at him.

"It's warm," she said. "I was kind of hoping it would be, I don't know, an illusion. That you were just some wannabe magician."

"I'm not," he said.

"So…Death," Nia said, as if mulling over the words in her brain. "Your dad is…Death."

"His technical title is *Dominus,* lord of the Underworld."

"Your dad is the lord of the Underworld."

"Yup."

Nia laughed. She put her hand to her mouth. "I'm sorry. How am I supposed to react to that?"

"Don't look at me. I've never had to."

"I mean, I guess *Dominus*, lord of the Underworld must look pretty cool on a business card."

Alex laughed. "I keep telling him he needs business cards."

"No you don't."

"No. I don't."

"Don't mess with my head. Half of me thinks either you're crazy or I'm crazy.

"I'm not crazy. Not a hundred percent certain about you yet."

Nia smiled. "And so you're a—what's it called again—Aegis?"

"That's right. Essentially an apprentice."

"So how long has your dad been…Death?"

"A hundred years, give or take," Alex said. "But when I turn eighteen, it's my turn. So in four months and nineteen days…"

"You become…Death," she said, incredulously. Alex nodded. "And I thought going to college at eighteen was a lot of pressure."

"Oh, it still is," Alex said, "just a different kind, I guess."

"Four months. Wow that's soon. How do you feel about it?"

Alex thought for a moment, then said, "Honestly? I have no idea. Nobody's ever asked me that."

"Not even your dad?"

"Nope. It was always just a foregone conclusion. Like it's happening whether I like it or not. Nobody asks how you feel about the sun rising. It just happens."

"So your dad is a hundred years old," Nia said.

"Give or take."

"He looks good for his age. Being Death is better than Botox."

"Cheaper too. A Dominus can alter their appearance. He needs to pass for the parent of a seventeen-year-old. It wouldn't work if he looked like something found in a sarcophagus."

Nia let loose a quick burst of laughter. "I'm sorry. I've heard of being groomed to take over the family business, but this is like a whole other level. So does your dad turn into a skeleton who wears a flowy robe and carries around a giant knife?"

"You mean a scythe," Alex said. "And no. That skeleton and robe stuff is all just folklore. Most people have been brainwashed to think of Death as this horrifying monster, when that's not true at all.

The idea of Death as the Grim Reaper began around the fourteenth century during the Black Plague. The plague killed nearly twenty percent of the population of Europe, and doctors who treated the sick wore these big billowy robes to protect themselves from 'infected air.' So artists began portraying Death as a skeleton, wearing those robes, carrying a scythe because it was said he reaped souls from the Earth. Not to mention that I helped pack up our moving van when we moved to Whisper Valley and I didn't see any scythe, unless it's like a fold-up Swiss army scythe."

"So when you take over, does your dad retire, head down to Boca, sip mai tais?"

"A Dominus is granted immortality while they hold the mantle," Alex said. "Once their successor takes over, they live a mortal life until it's their time to go. Just like everyone else. My dad isn't really a lounge chair Mai Tai kind of guy. He'll stay by my side as an advisor. It's hard enough to have the world figured out at eighteen, let alone the underworld."

"So other than giving you the ability to heal nearly-dead joggers and bad teenage drivers, what actually is the Blaze?"

"The Blaze is our connection to the underworld," Alex said. "Every living person has a flame that corresponds to their lifespan. There are billions of flames, and the Blaze draws its power from them. Think about the Blaze like a flamethrower, and life itself as the fuel. The Blaze is also our connection to the Ankou."

"Your dad said a...*thing*...would come for the guy in the woods. An Ankou."

"The Ankou are servants of Death, souls sentenced due to misdeeds committed while living. But if an Ankou Exorts enough untethered souls, they are permitted to move on."

"You used those words before. Exortus. Untethered. What do they mean?" Nia asked.

"When someone dies, their soul is untethered from their body. But an untethered soul is turbulent. Disturbed. A body is all the soul has ever known, and when the soul is untethered, it's like a child being ripped from its parent. An untethered soul needs to be given peace or it will become lost. For a soul to be given peace, an Ankou must appear to the untethered, turbulent soul in the guise of someone whose appearance will calm it. A loved one."

"Like a lullaby for the departed," Nia said.

"In a way."

"What do the Ankou look like?"

"Formless. Kind of like spiritual jellyfish. I can feel them before I see them. Sort of like those old men whose bum knees let them know when it's going to rain."

"What if the Ankou can't calm the untethered soul?"

"If a soul isn't properly Exorted, it stays on earth as what we call a Perdita—a lost soul. And too many Perditas roaming the earth are very bad."

"Why?"

"Every soul has an energy. Like a battery. One battery can't power much. But a million batteries could power a nuclear reactor. If there are too many Perditas here, it upsets the balance of spiritual energy. It's my dad's job to make sure that spiritual energy remains stable. If the balance tips too far, if there are too many lost souls, it would be like using a car battery to power a flashlight."

"What happens when an Ankou screws up?"

"They're banished to the underworld to spend the rest of eternity as a Mors."

"A Mors?"

"Mors are failed Ankou. Their punishment is a fate worse than death. My dad calls them the Living Undead."

Nia shuddered. "I don't know how you live with knowing."

"Knowing what?" Alex said.

"How it ends," Nia replied. "For everyone."

"I've known since I was a kid," Alex said, lowering his head. "I've never had a choice whether or not I could live with it. I just did."

"It must be hard."

Alex merely nodded.

Nia said, "You know, I can be kind of cynical, but the last few days have completely obliterated my bs meter. I'm going to believe pretty much anything anyone tells me from now on. So thanks for that."

"Hey, you were the one who wanted answers."

"Couldn't your answers have been more, I don't know, *grounded*? Like, 'Yeah, I rubbed some Neosporin on James and gave him a pep talk and *voila*.'"

"That would have to be some extra strength Neosporin."

"So all these…*things*…report to your dad. Does he report to anyone?

"My dad is kind of chairman of the undead board. He reports to the Conclave, which consists of the previous seven Dominii. And when he is Exorted, he'll join them."

"And one day, you will too."

"That's right."

"So that means your grandma or grandpa is a member of the Conclave?"

"My dad's dad is on there, and his dad, and his mom, etcetera, etcetera."

"Figures that there's nepotism in the underworld too."

"What's good enough for the living is good enough for the dead."

"You said you've never told anyone any of this before," Nia said. "Why me?"

"I've lived all over the world," Alex said. "Every continent except Antarctica, and that's probably only a matter of time. I've met thousands of people. I've traveled a million miles. I've been caught in soccer riots and flash mobs. And when you brushed by me on the bus, I felt something I've never felt before. And I don't mean that figuratively. I tried to ignore it. And it would be a whole lot easier if it wasn't there. When I use the Blaze, it feels like I'm burning from the outside in. When I see you, it feels like I'm burning from the inside out. I don't want to ignore it. I can't ignore it. Because in a few months I'm going to regret everything I didn't do while I still had the chance. I don't want to regret not telling you the truth."

"You mean about you and your father."

"No," Alex said. "I mean how I feel when I'm around you."

They sat in silence. Alex felt calm. It surprised him. He would have thought he'd be nervous, hesitant, even terrified. But he felt none of that. If anything, he felt relief.

"This is…a lot to take in," Nia said. She walked to the fence and placed her hands gently atop the rusty railing.

"Just imagine being told all of this when you're six," Alex said. "I just wanted to have a cool lunchbox."

He walked to the fence and stood shoulder to shoulder with Nia, gazing out over the white and yellow lights, the endless horizon. He listened to her breathing. Her smell, like lilacs dipped in sugar, made him dizzy. He looked down. Their hands were millimeters apart. He moved his pinky slightly, until it was just a hair from hers. He wanted to touch her desperately.

"Okay, my turn," Alex said. "You got to ask me a hundred questions. I should get at least ten."

"Ten?" she said. "No way. One."

"Not a chance. Eight."

"Three."

"Seven."

"I can live with four."

"Deal. First question. Why didn't you tell anyone what happened last night?"

"Because I didn't *know* what happened last night," Nia said. "What, am I going to go to the cops and tell them I saw fireworks after a car crash and a guy I barely know bring someone back from the brink of death? You know who James's dad is, right? Dean would have me locked up or committed. I needed to know the truth. And to save you a question—no. I won't tell anyone. I said you can trust me and I meant it."

"Thank you," Alex said. "Second question. You believe Dean Mungro covered up the crash for James?"

"Of course he did," Nia said. "Dean has been grooming James to follow in his footsteps since he could walk. But James won't get near the academy if he does time. And Dean would commit seppuku before letting James fail. As messed up as James is, his father is a thousand times worse."

"Third question. Why do you even bother with James? You seem like a decent person. He doesn't."

"You just don't know me well enough," Nia said.

"Question stands."

"It's complicated," Nia said. "People want black and white. It's easy to understand, but it's not real. James and I, we have a *lot* of grays. You of all people should know that what you see is never the full story. James and I have a history. Don't you ever do things you don't want to, or might even regret, because you feel you owe someone?"

"Of course I do. I told you who my father is."

"So just understand there's a history. And that's all you need to know."

"Okay. Last question. What are you drawing in those notebooks?"

"Now *that's* personal," Nia said with a smile.

"After everything I've told you, *that's* personal?"

Nia debated for a moment, then said, "Her name is Arumaya. She's a demigoddess, born on the planet Iyanrin to Queen Harana, goddess of sand, and Avrahim, a great descendant of Ishmael, son of Abraham and his servant and mistress Hagar. Harana was killed by her brother, Marte. Avrahim was framed and executed for the crime, and Arumaya was banished to Earth by Marte before she could claim the throne. On Earth, Arumaya fights evil while trying to find a way back home to overthrow Marte and avenge her parents' deaths."

"You just up and invented a superhero?"

"Not just a superhero," Nia said. "I invented a whole world in Iyanrin. Arumaya is one part of it. Iyanrin is a desert planet. I modeled it on the ancient land of Canaan. On Earth, Arumaya has the power to conjure sandstorms."

"So you really don't want to piss her off at the beach."

"I wrote an epic battle scene where Marte's forces attack her while she's sunbathing. Let's just say never anger a demigoddess while she's trying to get some vitamin D."

"Well, now I *have* to read it," Alex said.

"Arumaya is incredibly powerful and decent and people on Earth consider her a beacon of hope. She tries to be a bridge between nations. But her powers mean people are afraid to get close to her. She feels like an outcast. So Arumaya has to deal with the paradox of having the power of a goddess, but also feeling like she must go through life alone."

"How long have you been drawing?"

"I started getting really serious about the draft four or five years ago, but I've been doodling since I was a kid. I have dozens of old notebooks filled with little cartoon princesses and unicorns. I want to be an illustrator. Comics, animation. I already have enough Arumaya stories for a whole graphic novel. Besides, the world needs more Jewish superheroes. I mean Magneto is awesome, but one more wouldn't hurt anyone."

"I thought Magneto was a bad guy."

Nia laughed. "You of all people should know that the best bad guys are the heroes of their own stores. The greatest villains believe deep down that their actions are justified. That what they're doing is right."

"Just let me know when it comes out and I'll order a billion copies."

"I don't need you to buy a billion. Just one would make me happy."

"As long as you sign it for me."

A strange smile spread across Nia's face.

"Why are you looking at me like that?" Alex said.

"You didn't laugh. At Arumaya. Or judge me."

"My dad is lord of the underworld and likes peppermint tea," Alex said. "I don't have the right to judge anything."

"Fair point," Nia said. "I don't like to tell anyone about her because they usually think I'm kidding. Then when they figure out I'm not, they're embarrassed and I feel like crap. Then they assume it's some silly hobby. But it's not a hobby to me. This is what I love. I think about it when I go to sleep. I want to create new worlds for the rest of my life."

"Have you shown them to anyone besides strange boys?"

"You might be strange but you're not a stranger."

"To everyone else it feels like I am," Alex said. "But it doesn't feel that way with you."

"No, it doesn't."

"So have you done anything with your illustrations?"

"I applied for an mentorship program in Austin," Nia said. "It's over winter break. If I get in, there will be a ton of workshops and panels with some of my idols, and pitch sessions where I can show my portfolio to industry professionals. It could open a lot of doors. If I get in and decide to go."

"What do you mean *if* you decide to go?"

"I have responsibilities," she said.

"Don't we all?"

"Yours are to the dead. Mine are to the living."

Alex said nothing.

Just then, the fence buckled, and before he even knew what was happening, Alex teetered forward. He instinctively thrust out his arm to try to grab something to keep him from falling into the abyss. He felt Nia's hand grasp his wrist. A fire raged through him where their skin met.

"I got you," she said. He grabbed her around the waist and she pulled him back onto solid ground. "You okay?"

"I think so. They really should post a warning sign up here," Alex said. He looked down. She was still holding his arm. He still had his hand around her waist. Their bodies were millimeters apart. Her fingers were searing into him. Neither of them made any effort to move.

"You said when we touched that day on the bus, that you felt something. That you needed to get away," Nia said softly. He could hear his own heartbeat like a drum in his chest. "But you're not trying to get away right now."

"Maybe I don't want to get away." He could feel her breath on his neck. "Do you...?"

"Do I what?"

"Do you feel something."

Without hesitation, Nia said, "Yes."

Alex didn't move. It was as though his body and mind had frozen together. Their eyes were locked onto each other, the vast dark sky looming above them as hundreds of lights from the city twinkled below. The night was silent except for the sound of their breathing, their heartbeats.

Nia seemed to be waiting for Alex to say something. Do something.

Alex whispered, "I kind of want to kiss you."

Nia held his gaze and said, "What's stopping you?"

He put his other hand on her waist. Nia took a sharp breath, seeming to tremble at his touch. They moved closer, slowly, as if each of them was gauging their desire, to make sure they both wanted this, *knowing* they both wanted this, but savoring these few, breathtaking moments before their lips met.

One hand slid down Alex's wrist. The other slipped around his neck and pulled him to her. Then their lips met and warmth flowed through his body, traveling down his arms, his legs, pooling into every inch of him. Nia's lips were smooth and soft and inviting. The sensation was like nothing he'd ever felt. He never wanted it to end.

And then it did.

Nia slowly pulled away, letting her lips linger on his for one more moment.

"Well, I did not come here tonight expecting *that*," she said.

"I did."

"No, you didn't."

"No, I didn't." Alex paused. "But I'm glad it happened."

"Me too," Nia said. She checked her watch. "We should probably go."

"We probably should. Can I hitch a ride?"

"I *could* leave you here," she said, "but I'm starting to like your company."

They got into Nia's car. When she turned the key, a voice came over the stereo.

"Welcome to *The Creative Brain*. I'm your host, Jacqueline Camereti. Today I'm pleased to be joined by—"

"Sorry," Nia said, turning the stereo off. "I was listening to a podcast on the way here."

"Keep it on," Alex said.

"You sure?" she said.

"Of course. I want to know the kind of stuff you do when no one's around."

She smiled and turned it back on. They drove in silence, listening to the host and guest discuss the intricacies of character design. As they approached Marigold Lane, Alex said, "I'll walk from your place. Thanks. For listening."

"Thanks for trusting me."

"I've never told anyone what I told you tonight," he said.

"That's why it means more."

Nia pulled up to the curb in front of her house.

"Hey—maybe I should get your number," he said. "You know. Just in case."

"Sure," she said with a sly smile. "Just in case."

She typed it into Alex's phone. He called it. Nia held up her phone up so he could see.

"That's you?"

"That's me," she said. "By the way, how's that cut on your arm?"

"Doing better, thanks to your medical expertise."

"May I?" He hesitated, but nodded. Nia rolled up his shirt sleeve. Then she stopped. "Your tattoo."

"It's the only thing that's come with me everywhere I've been."

She traced her finger along the lines of black ink. Alex felt fire in her every touch.

"Can I see it?" she said.

He rolled his sleeve up further, exposing his forearm. Nia placed her hand underneath his elbow and brought it closer. The tattoo was a silhouette of a boy encircled by gnarled tree branches, wandering into a dark wood. It was all black, with thin lines. Simple yet elegant.

"I recognize this. It's the cover of the book you were reading the other day in the library. *A Cold Winter's Night.*"

"You have a good memory."

"The book means that much that you wanted it on your skin?"

"It does."

"Why?"

"I'm pretty sure you used up your question allotment," Alex said. "Besides, I need to leave a little mystery for our second date."

"Oh, so this was a date?" Nia said.

"You didn't say it wasn't."

She smiled. "Good night, Alex."

"Good night, Nia."

As he opened the door, Alex felt Nia's pinky finger brush his.

"Do you still feel it?" she said.

"Yes. Do you?"

"Yes."

His heart soared as he got out of the car and walked home. He could still feel Nia's lips on his, her skin on his hand, the electricity that surged through his body every time they touched. He didn't know how he'd be able to sleep. How he'd be able to function. What he would say to her the next time he saw her.

As it turned out, he didn't have to think about it.

When Alex opened the front door, he found his father standing in the foyer, fully clothed.

"Good timing," Byron said. "We have work to do."

Then his father placed his hand on Alex's head and said the word *Evanescet*, and an instant later they were gone.

# 14

Nia opened the front door and the familiar antiseptic smell of medicine and tangy scent of lemon polish hit her immediately. The wood flooring was shiny and spotless. The countertops and staircase bannisters gleamed. She took off her shoes, banged them against the steps outside, and placed them, gently, onto the straw mat inside the front door.

The house was silent. A light was on in the kitchen, and she could smell the faint chocolatey aroma of fresh-brewed coffee. Her mother, Rivka, always made a small pot before she began her nightly housework. The pleasant sound of opera music came from upstairs. Puccini's *La Bohème*. Her dad's favorite.

When Nia was younger, she would sit on the floor with a chocolate éclair as Stephen Solomon played opera records on his turntable and translated the lyrics for her. She was enchanted by the story of the Parisian bohemians and the doomed romance between the poet Rudolfo and the seamstress Mimi. She dreamed of one day visiting the Latin Quarter, of sitting in sunny outdoor cafés and flirting with lean boys with dark eyes and sharp cheekbones. She asked her parents, with increasingly annoying frequency, if they could ever visit Paris.

*Of course*, they told her. *We'll go as a family*.

They never went.

Nia crept upstairs, careful to stay quiet in case her father had fallen asleep, the euphoric memory of Alex's kiss making her feel lighter than air. The hallway was dark except for a sliver of light peeking through the crack at the bottom of the bedroom door. She knocked softly.

"Who is it?" her mother asked.

"It's me, Mom."

"Oh, come in, hon," Rivka said cheerfully. Nia opened the door.

Rivka Solomon sat in a faded green loveseat, knitting. She did not take her eyes off her project, the needles making a *click clack* noise as her hands moved fluidly. The curly hair she had passed on to her daughter was pulled back in a ponytail, silver streaks amidst the auburn.

"What are you making?" Nia said.

"A winter hat," she said. "Isn't it adorable?"

"You know it's September," Nia said. "It looks kind of small. Who's it for?"

"A baby."

"A baby? Is somebody we know pregnant?"

"No," her mother said with a detached smile, "but it never hurts to be prepared. You know I would love to be a grandmother more than anything."

Nia felt a twinge in her stomach, like someone was poking her with a needle. "Don't get your hopes up. I want to graduate college before I take Lamaze."

"It's just…your father would love the chance to hold his grandchild before he leaves us."

The needle in her stomach became a knife in her heart. Nia felt a sob rising, but she tamped it down. She had gotten good at delaying pain.

"Mom, did you take your Donepezil tonight?" Nia asked.

"Yes, dear."

"Galantamine?"

"Of course."

"Rivastigmine?"

She nodded. Every night, Nia rattled off her mother's medications like she was assembling a grocery list.

"Mom, are you *sure* you took all your medications?"

She nodded absently. Nia went to the bathroom and found the pill bottles in the medicine cabinet supposed to combat the effects of her mother's Alzheimer's disease. She opened each one and counted, then opened the Notes app on her phone. She kept a daily log, and made sure the number of pills left matched. There was one extra Rivastigmine pill. Nia took it out, filled a glass of water, and handed it to her mother.

"Take this," she said. Rivka swallowed the pill and washed it down.

"Shhh," Rivka said. "Don't disturb him."

Nia turned to the bed where her father lay. Stephen Solomon was covered up to his chest by a brown duvet. His bald head rested propped up on two thick pillows. His sallow skin was so thin and pale she could see thin blue veins beneath the surface. His face was deep-creased and worn, his breathing ragged and wet, the sickness in his lungs loud enough for her to hear from across the room. Nia's father was fifty-five but looked twenty years older.

"Nia?" he said. His voice was weak and raspy.

"Hey, Dad, I thought you were asleep."

"Come on, you know I like to wait up for you."

"But you need your rest."

"I'll have plenty of time to rest," he said. "So I want to be with you and your mother every moment I have left."

Nia felt her face grow flushed. She pulled an ottoman to the side of his bed. He lay his withered hand on top of the sheet and opened his fingers. Nia placed her palm on his. He closed his fingers around hers and squeezed just hard enough that she could feel his pulse.

"Did you go out tonight?" he asked.

"For a bit."

"Staying out of trouble I hope."

"You know me, I'm just a regular menace to society. I just met a friend for a bit at Larrimore Hill."

"Larrimore Hill," Stephen said. "I used to love going up there with you and your mother. I miss our picnics."

"We'll do it again soon, Dad. I promise. I bet you'll even be strong enough to give me a piggyback ride up the hill, like you used to."

Stephen managed a sickly laugh. "Flattery, my dear daughter, will get you everywhere."

"How do you feel?"

"Been better. Been worse."

"Did you take your Cisplatin?"

"I did," he said, and she knew he was telling the truth.

"How's Mom today?" Nia said. Rivka did not seem to be aware of the conversation and had not taken her eyes off the half-formed pink hat in her lap.

"The same," Stephen said.

"The same is good," Nia said. "I love you, Dad."

Her father smiled weakly. "I love you too, baby girl."

Pressure built up behind her eyes with those words. *Baby girl.*

"Nia?" Rivka said, as though she suddenly just realized her daughter was in the room. "Did you pick up the roast chicken like I asked?"

"You didn't ask, Mom," she said, "but I'll pick one up tomorrow."

"Oh, and James called for you earlier."

"James?" Nia said, suddenly alarmed. "Did he say why?"

"No, I just told him to try your cell phone."

Nia took out her phone. She'd put it on silent when she left to meet Alex. Sure enough, she had three missed calls from James. She cursed under her breath.

"I heard that," her father said.

"Sorry."

"So did you meet Justin Perlmutter tonight?" Rivka said.

Nia sighed and said, "Mom, Justin and I broke up freshman year."

"He brought me flowers when he came to pick you up for the prom."

"I remember. Tulips. Your favorite."

"Tulips. My favorite."

The sadness came from out of nowhere, as it often did, compressing her chest and making her lungs feel like they were trapped in a vice. How could she feel so elated from a first kiss, then moments later so weary and helpless? Nia felt tears welling up but refused to let her parents see them. She had to be strong. Even if it was only on the outside.

"If things don't work out between you and Justin, you really should give James a chance," Rivka said. "You should be so lucky as to end up with a boy like that. And he comes from such a good family."

"Mom, please stop," Nia pleaded.

"Oh, and did you pick up that roast chicken like I asked?"

Nia felt her cheeks growing hot. Her eyes were wet. She wiped them on her sleeve. "I did, Mom. Yesterday. You made it for dinner tonight."

"Thank you, hon. Maybe I'll make it for dinner tomorrow. What would I ever do without you?"

"I don't know," Nia said, tears now sliding freely down her cheeks. "I really don't know."

"Good. Because you know how much I need you. *We* need you."

Rivka went back to her knitting. Slowly and surely, the disease was chipping away at her mother's once-formidable mind. Nia sat there, hand in her dying father's weak grasp, watching the world slip from her mother. The two people she had always counted on to help pull her through were now fully reliant on her and her alone. Every day it felt like the weight of responsibility was crushing her. She could barely hold it up for them—let alone herself.

When Nia looked back at her father, he was asleep. Nia kissed his dry hand, his skin discolored from the needles and treatments that had, so far, only prolonged his pain. She placed her father's hand in his lap, kissed her mother's cheek, and went to her room, gently closing the door behind her.

Nia saw an unopened envelope on her desk and her heart began to race. The mentorship program said it could take eight to twelve weeks for a response, but what if they moved faster? She grabbed the envelope, but her heart sank when she saw the return address was from a college in California she had no interest in attending. She tossed it in the garbage without opening it.

But what if it *had* been an acceptance to the mentorship program? *We need you*, her mother had said, and she wasn't wrong. Getting into that program could change her life. But what about her parents? The doctors had given him mere months—would he even be alive come winter? What if her mother got worse while she was gone? What if—god, she couldn't even imagine it—her father died while she was away? She would never be able to forgive herself.

It was all too much. Her heart rate began to speed up. She tried to take deep breaths, like her therapist had told her to do. Every morning she took the latest SSRI he'd prescribed, then fought through the nausea and dry mouth that came with it. During the day they helped. But by the time night fell, the effects had begun to ebb, the darkness breaking through.

*Find things to help quiet your mind*, the therapist had told her. Nia opened her laptop and played *Questo Mar Rosso*, the soaring, playful opening from *La Bohème*. As the music began, it felt like a balloon was slowly inflating in her chest, filling her, forcing the sadness out through her pores, suffocating her from the inside until she could barely breathe. Finally, the flood overcame her. Tears streamed down her cheeks as she sank to the floor, back against the wall.

The darkness always snuck up on her at the worst times, robbing her of moments of joy, like the electricity of a first kiss. She was jealous of her friends like Alice who could spend their nights obsessing over unrequited crushes, stalking social media feeds, analyzing text messages like they were encrypted files. She would give anything to be preoccupied by such simple, uncomplicated dilemmas.

So, Nia sat on the floor, trying to focus on the feeling of Alex's lips on hers, the small beauty of their fingers intertwined, and prayed for the music to take her somewhere far away.

# 15

They were standing in the foyer of a small house Alex did not recognize. He could smell the acrid scent of blood, but there was something else in the air. Something bitter and metallic. Gunpowder. He had smelled that scent before. Then he felt the familiar humming in his bones and knew why his father had brought him to this place.

Moments ago he had been kissing Nia Solomon, every nerve in his body on fire. He had felt alive, truly alive. But that moment was over. Now it was time for death.

"Let's go to work," his father said.

"I already feel the Ankou," Alex said. "What happened here?"

Byron merely said, "Follow me."

Byron led Alex into the living room. It was there that they saw the bodies.

Alex turned away. Byron gripped his shoulders and said, "Look at them. You must be able to face the dead like you face the living."

Alex turned back. He took a long breath.

"Who are they?" he said.

"Suzanne and Cory Westin," Byron said. "Earlier tonight, Cory accused Suzanne of being unfaithful. She told him she was not. He told her if she didn't admit to her infidelity, he would kill them both. She refused and told him she had been faithful."

"But he killed her anyway."

Byron nodded. "One of the Ankou assigned to this Exortus is unreliable. There is already one Perdita in Whisper Valley. We are here to make sure the Ankou performs this Exortus properly. And if not..."

"There's always room for another Mors," Alex said.

Two Ankou descended through the ceiling, shimmering orbs pulsating with light. But as they neared the bodies, the Ankou began to stretch out, elongate. Limbs unfolded, necks and heads extended from the glow, until the Ankou began to take on human form.

The first Ankou hovered above the body of Suzanne Westin. Its face was that of a kindly looking older man with a crown of gray hair and a neatly-trimmed beard. The old man reached down with a glowing hand. Then, slowly, tentatively, a luminous hand reached up to grasp it.

Alex heard a woman's voice say, "Dad?"

The Ankou nodded and said, "I'm here, sweet pea. I'm here."

The Ankou began to rise, still in the guise of the old man, smiling lovingly, still holding the hand of the dead woman's soul. The rest of Suzanne Westin's soul rose with the Ankou, fully Untethering from its mortal body, which lay still on the carpet. Then the Ankou disappeared through the ceiling, still gripping the soul of Suzanne Westin.

"Well, that was thankfully uneventful," Alex said. He pointed to the man on the ground. "What about him?"

As if hearing Alex's question, the other Ankou hovered over the body of Cory Westin. The glowing hand of the dead man's soul reached out from his body, grasping for something.

The Ankou hesitated. Its shimmering shape did not change. Cory Westin's soul began to writhe, pulling loose from its body like a phosphorescent snake shedding its skin.

"Dad," Alex said nervously. "Dad it's untethering."

"I know," Byron said. "This Ankou has failed. You need to step in. Prove you're ready. *Now*, before it's too late."

Alex stepped forward. He raised his hand toward the Ankou and concentrated. The Blaze burst forth from his fingertips. He placed his hand directly into the Ankou, connecting with it. He unscrambled the spiritual confusion and saw who the Ankou needed to be to complete this Exortus. And when he did, he knew that Cory Westin's soul would not be joining his wife's.

Alex forced the Ankou to change its shape. It grew limbs and a head. Its visage became that of a man of about thirty-five, with an oily black goatee and unkempt hair, its thin eyebrows wickedly arched, a sneer on its thin lips.

The Ankou's hand reached down and grasped Cory Westin's soul. Then, once it had a firm grip, the shimmering white light surrounding the Ankou turned a fiery red as it began to pull the soul from its body.

When Cory's soul saw the visage above him, it began to scream. The soul made an inhuman, guttural sound, like that of a dying animal caught in a trap. The Ankou held fast to Cory Westin's soul and began to pull. But unlike the Ankou that appeared above Suzanne Westin, this Ankou began to pull Cory Westin's soul *down.*

Alex disconnected from the Ankou as it continued to descend. Cory Westin's soul screamed and shrieked and twisted, but the Ankou held fast. Both the Ankou and the soul began to disappear through the floor. Cory Westin's soul clawed at the floor but could not grasp the material world. The soul's legs disappeared through the floor, then its waist, torso, neck, and face. Finally, Cory Westin's soul was gone. Pulled down below. Far, far down below.

And like that, the Ankou and souls were gone, leaving only their bodies behind.

"The Exortus is complete," Byron says, "but our job is not done."

Byron held his hand out and said, "*Penancium.*"

A white light rose from the ground. It was the Ankou that had Exorted Cory Westin's soul. Its face was still of the goateed man. Then Byron closed his fist and the Ankou was sucked into his grasp.

"One more Mors for the Cavern," Byron said. "Now we can go."

"Quicker than a trial," Alex said.

"You did well," Byron said. "You prevented another Perdita. You're ready."

"The first Ankou," Alex said. "It took on the guise of Suzanne Westin's father."

Byron nodded. "He passed away from emphysema two years ago. Seeing her father gave Suzanne's soul peace, and allowed it to be Exorted."

"Who appeared to Cory Westin?" Alex said.

"His name was Jeremy Vine," Byron said. "Ten years ago, Cory believed Jeremy Vine made a pass at Suzanne in a bar. He followed Jeremy outside and stabbed him in the heart. It was only right that the last person Cory saw before being Exorted was the man whose life he ended."

Alex heard sirens in the distance as Byron again placed his hand on Alex's forehead. He said *Evanescet* and, after a flash of light, they were back at 72 Marigold Lane.

"Get some rest," Byron said to Alex as he headed toward the stairs. "We've both had a long night. You more than me."

"What's that supposed to mean?"

"You will become Dominus in a matter of months, Alex," Byron said. "Your focus needs to be on that and nothing else right now. I saw you get out of that girl Nia's car tonight. You have the potential to be an exceptional Dominus, but now isn't the time to lose your focus."

"I didn't lose focus," Alex said angrily. "I did my job, just like I've done for years. I've Exorted thousands of souls. I've traveled around the world with you. Given up my *life* for you."

"Not for me," Byron said. "The responsibilities of a Dominus are great, Alex. Things will only get harder once you take my place. Remember, I've been where you are. I know what you're going through."

"You don't understand anything about me or Nia," Alex said.

"I understand more than you could possibly know," Byron said.

"What does that mean?"

"Nothing," Byron said.

"My being with Nia doesn't interfere in life or death. The Conclave shouldn't care and neither should you."

"You need to distance yourself from people or you might not be able to do your job when the time comes. You should be preparing to take my place, not playing games with this girl."

"That girl was more interested in me today than you've been my entire life," Alex said. "I'm ready. You said so yourself. What I do between now and the day I take your place shouldn't matter. You can't stop me from seeing her."

"You're right," Byron said. "But we are not meant to have companions. Love only brings pain. I hope you don't have to learn that the hard way."

Then Byron went upstairs and closed his bedroom door, leaving Alex alone in the dark.

# 16

Alex was not prepared when his alarm clock went off. His dreams had alternated between heaven and hell: Nia Solomon's lips softly pressing against his, and Cory Westin's shrieking soul being dragged into the underworld. Dreams of the living and nightmares of the dead battling for dominance as he slept.

They ate breakfast in silence. There was no mention of the previous night. Alex left for school without saying goodbye. It had been a long night and he was exhausted. He had a free period after lunch and couldn't wait to hide in the library and think about Nia sitting across from him. When Nia got on the school bus, their eyes locked. She smiled at him and mouthed, "Hey."

"Hey back."

As Nia walked toward the back of the bus, she let her hand graze his shoulder, smiling as she did, knowing it would send a finger of flame up his neck.

Iggy wanted to DM Trevor Michaelson, but needed Alex's opinion on how exactly to phrase the message. Alex questioned the intelligence of Iggy asking him, of all people, for romantic advice, but he listened and did his best, and the fact that Iggy nodded as he spoke meant his advice couldn't have been total garbage. Or that Iggy was just being kind. Alex preferred to presume the former.

When they got off the bus, Alex and Nia held a lingering gaze before heading in opposite directions.

"Put your tongue back in your mouth," Iggy said.

Alex spun around. "What are you talking about?"

"Come on, Tree guy, you think I didn't notice you staring at Nia like you were on death row and she was your last meal?"

"Please don't say anything to anyone," Alex said.

"Don't worry. I don't kiss and tell, and who anyone else kisses is none of my business. I assume you two *have* kissed, otherwise staring at her like that is kind of creepy." Iggy paused. "So, have you kissed?"

"I thought you said that was none of your business."

"Under ordinary circumstances, yes. But I love Nia like a sister. Consider it protective."

Alex said, "I don't kiss and tell."

Iggy smiled. "I approve. Nia is awesome, and she deserves someone just as awesome. So be good to her. Otherwise, I will beat you to death with my bio textbook."

"That's a fair punishment."

"Long as we're clear. But seriously, if she's happy, I'm happy. Maybe it'll even convince you to stick around. For once."

Iggy headed off to homeroom.

*Be good to her. Stick around.*

Alex knew he could commit to one of the two.

---

"Mr. Sonnum," Mr. Ryerson said during homeroom, snapping Alex out of his daydream. "Are you present today?"

"I am," Alex lied.

"Good. Because your body appears to be here but your brain is somewhere else."

Mr. Ryerson wasn't wrong.

Last night was like nothing he'd ever experienced. It both

thrilled and terrified him. What would he say to her now? He wanted to tell Nia that she was all he could think about. He wanted to know more about her illustrations, about Arumaya, about the worlds she'd pulled from her imagination, and what inspired her. He wanted to know everything about Nia.

But he had to be careful. His father. The Conclave. He was walking a thin line. Spending time with Nia was pissing his dad off for some reason, but he wasn't *technically* doing anything wrong. Nothing Alex had ever done made him feel the way she did. How could he ignore that?

When his free period came, Alex went upstairs to the library. He threaded his way through the stacks until he came to a familiar spot. He found Nia sitting against the bookshelf with a graphic novel open on her lap. When she saw him, she smiled.

"I'm guessing your being here is not an accident," he said.

"You mentioned you have free periods after lunch three days a week," she said. "I figured there was a sixty percent chance you'd be here."

"Okay, but you are sitting in front of the shelf I need to get to."

"Is that right?" she said.

"Yeah. Mind if I just grab a book from behind you?"

"Free country," Nia replied.

Alex leaned forward, as if to take a book off the shelf, but as he did, he kissed Nia. Gently. Sweetly. She pressed her hand against his chest and he felt a warmth spread through him. When Alex stepped back, he pulled a book from the shelf.

"Did you find what you were looking for?" she said.

Alex nodded. "I did." He looked at the book in his hand, laughed, then turned the cover to show Nia.

"*Sadie Scout and the Perilous Piranhas of Doom,*" she said. "I haven't heard of that one, but, you know, you do you."

Alex put the book back and sat next to Nia.

"Am I the only one who had trouble sleeping last night?" she said.

"Nope. I don't think I got to bed until three."

"Anything in particular on your mind?"

"Two things."

"Was I one of them?"

"You were."

"What was the other?" Nia said.

"I'd rather not talk about it," Alex said. "Had to help my dad with some work stuff after I left you."

"Work stuff," Nia said. "You mean…?"

"Yeah."

"If you want to talk about it, I'm here."

"I'd rather just sit here with you and take my mind off of it for a bit. Is that okay?"

"Of course it is. You're a nice distraction too."

"That's exactly what I'm going for. I'm playing it cool so that at first I'm a nice distraction, but then when you least expect it you realize you're completely falling for me."

"Don't play it cool," Nia said. "Playing it cool is overrated."

"That works in my favor, because I really don't know how."

"Maybe that's why I like you," she said.

"So you're admitting you like me?"

"I might. What about you?"

"Definitely, definitely, definitely, maybe," he said. They both smiled.

"Since we *might* both like each other, I have an idea," Nia said. "You said last night was our first date, but I don't consider it an official date if you have to confront the guy in the men's room first. So, I have an idea for our first official date. It's a little more, how should I put it, normal."

"I'm fully on board with normal."

"There's an author reading at the bookstore in town in a few weeks. It could be fun, unless—"

"Sold," Alex said. "I'm in."

"Well, that was easy."

"I'm pretty easy."

"You might not want to say that too loud."

Alex looked around. There was one other kid sitting a few aisles down, but he appeared to be engrossed in a textbook. "So, any plans tonight?"

"Easy, tiger. I have work. Two nights a week at Scoop N' Sprinkles."

"Guess I'll have to find another way to occupy my time."

"Maybe avoid taking your bike out," Nia said. "Bad things happen when you do."

"Tell me about it."

Then, as if responding to that comment, Alex heard a voice that made his stomach clench.

"What the hell are you?"

It was James Mungro. James was standing in the aisle, staring at him.

"James, listen, I—"

James stormed over to where Alex and Nia were sitting and loomed over them.

His eyes were filled with anger and confusion. Alex noticed a large, dark bruise by James's right cheekbone. When Alex used the Blaze, he'd fully healed James—which meant he'd sustained that bruise *after* the crash.

Dean. James's father. Dean had covered up his son's crash, but not before he let his boy know just what he thought of his recklessness.

"What did you do to me?" James said in a whispered rage.

"James, let it go," Nia said. "Please."

James looked at Nia, and something in his face softened. But then he looked back at Alex and said, "My clothes were covered in blood. But I was *fine*. Why? What did you do?"

James was clearly not rational, which was understandable given the circumstances. Alex thought about what his father said. He had to stay calm. Deferential.

"Listen, James," Alex said evenly. "Forget anything happened. Let's both move on. It's better that way."

"Not a chance, you goddamn freak," James said. "Answer me. What did you *do*?"

The boy a few aisles down had put his book down and was watching them. Alex had to diffuse the situation *immediately*.

"I saved your life," Alex whispered. "Isn't that enough?"

"No, you almost *killed* me!" James shouted.

"Keep it down," Alex said. He could feel his blood pressure rising. *Don't let him get to you. Defer.* "Just pretend you never met me. In a year, you'll forget all of this, I promise."

James grabbed Alex by the shirt and lifted him off the floor. Nia leapt up and shouted, "Stop, James! Let him go!"

Alex wrenched himself free and said, "Get your hands off me. I'm the only reason you're still alive."

"I wouldn't have been at the bottom of that ravine if not for you," James said.

"You were driving, not me," Alex said. "Come on. Just let it go."

James took a step back, seemingly recalibrating the situation. Wondering how much truth there was to what Alex was saying.

Then it went from bad to worse. Billy Wootens appeared beside James. Billy had half a dozen stitches above his right eye, and his forehead looked like it had been rocked a few times with a meat mallet.

"I almost lost my eye because of you," Billy said, pointing at Alex. He turned to James. "He wrecked your car. Look what your dad did to your face because of this asshole."

When Billy mentioned Dean, James's face darkened. He grabbed Alex's shirt and brought his fist back.

"James, stop it!" Nia grabbed James's arm, but he wrenched free, flinging her ribs-first into the shelf, spilling books onto the green carpet. Nia cried out.

Alex did not think. He did not weigh consequences. Anger had been simmering within him, but now it had boiled over into pure rage.

So much for deference.

Alex placed his right foot behind James's heel then drove him backward. James tripped and hit the floor with a loud *whump*. Then, before Alex knew what he was doing, he had one hand on James's throat and the other raised above his face in a clenched fist.

"I swear to God," Alex said, "if you ever so much as *look* at her again, I will..."

What Alex saw next scared him more than anything in his entire life.

James's face began to darken. Not red with blood, or blue from lack of oxygen. A dark, poisonous purplish-brown color began to crawl upward from below James's collar, like something rotten was spreading underneath his skin. It rose past his chin, his lips, until his entire head began to turn the color of rancid meat. It looked like James was putrefying from the inside out. He began to choke. A faint vapor began to rise from the boy's skin.

*The Dim*, Alex thought. *I'm using the Dim on him.*

Alex took his hand off of James's neck and staggered back. Almost immediately, the unnatural color began to drain from James's face, leaving him gasping for air. Alex held up his hands and stared at them as if they belonged to somebody else. Some*thing* else.

A librarian appeared in the aisle and shouted, "What in god's name is going on?"

"I..." Alex said, but he couldn't finish the thought.

"What...?" James said, still on the ground. "What did you do to me?"

Then Alex sprinted from the library, the doors banging closed behind him. He sprinted down the stairs, flung the school doors open, and ran.

Why did he have the power of the Dim? Why did he have the power to kill?

He needed answers. And as Alex ran home, lungs burning, scared beyond belief, the most important question raced through his mind: *What am I?*

# 17

Alex threw open the front door to find his father sitting in the den sipping from a mug of peppermint tea. Alex slammed the door shut and marched up to his father. Byron went to take another sip, but Alex slapped the mug out of his hand. The cup went spinning across the room, spilling tea in an arc before shattering against the wall.

"What the hell am I?"

"Sit down," Byron said, wiping the liquid from his hands.

"I think I'll stand."

"We need to talk," Byron said.

"Yeah, no shit."

"Langua—"

"Enough of the *language* crap." Alex marched right up to his father, close enough to smell the peppermint on his breath. "What am I?"

"You're my son."

"Am I? Because fathers aren't supposed to lie to their sons."

"I never lied to you."

"Then why the hell didn't you tell me about…this?" Alex held up his hands. They were shaking. "Whatever the Conclave did to me the other day, with the Dim, I was able to do to someone else. I almost *killed* someone."

"But you didn't."

"I *could* have."

"But you didn't."

"Stop saying that!"

"It may seem like splitting hairs," Byron said, "but there is a difference between lying and withholding necessary truths."

"So you just kept it from me? You didn't trust me? Why? Did you think I'd go around killing people? Is that what you think I am?"

"It was for your own good, Alex."

"Tell me. Right now. Why am I able to use the Dim?"

"The Dim is the counterpart to the Blaze. You can't have life without death, and you can't have the Blaze without the Dim. Every life has a candle. And that candle begins to burn out the moment you are born. And like fires emit smoke, the fire of life emits the Dim."

"So when you gave me the power of the Blaze, I also got the power of the Dim."

"Yes," Byron said.

"You should have told me," Alex said.

"Being a Dominus means being able to balance both life *and* death. You controlled your powers before they got the better of you. Not everyone can. Not everyone has. The Dim has been used for evil in the past."

There was a look in Byron's face Alex had not seen before. Remorse. Sadness. Like a memory he'd suppressed had come flooding back to him.

"It's time you see where our powers come from," Byron said. "I had to know you were ready. That you were strong enough. It's time for you to see the truth. It's time for you to see the Cavern."

Before Alex could reply, Byron placed his hand on Alex's forehead, whispered *Evanescet*, and the world disappeared in a flash of light.

# 18

A woman in her late fifties with silver hair and an apron tied around her waist answered the door. Samael Zagan smiled at her and said, “Afternoon, ma’am.”

She smelled of dust and lemon polish and wore fake pearl earrings with a cubic zirconia necklace. Samael already knew the woman’s name was Carolyn Wool, that she had worked as a housekeeper for Dean Mungro for twelve years, and that she was paid off the books.

“Can I help you?” she asked, a skeptical look on her face. This was not the kind of neighborhood where strangers showed up at your door unannounced.

Samael offered a wide, friendly smile that seemed to put her at ease. His clothing was more understated than usual. Olive pants with a light blue shirt under a tan sportscoat. His brown loafers were well-polished, and his hair was combed and neatly parted. He looked like a friendly accountant.

“Miss Wool?” Samael said. The woman’s smile shrank ever so slightly. “Ms. Carolyn Wool?”

“That…that’s me. May I ask who you are?” Her voice was defensive. She was used to opening the door for guests. She was not used to the guests asking for her.

On a mahogany table behind Carolyn was a photo of Dean and Lillian Mungro. Lillian was thirty-one, twenty years Dean's junior, with blonde hair, dark roots, and a figure that could raise the pulse of the dead. Dean's spouses had gotten progressively younger over the years, as though he were trading in cars.

Next to that photo was a large portrait of Dean Mungro wearing his police uniform. He looked stern and professional. There was something behind Dean's eyes that Samael recognized. It was the look of a man who dared you to cross him.

Samael peered around Ms. Wool and nodded approvingly. "You keep a clean home, Ms. Wool. Cleanliness *is* next to godliness. My name is Samael Zagan. I would like to speak with Mr. Mungro."

Ms. Wool looked over her shoulder, then turned back to Samael.

"I'm sorry. Mr. Mungro isn't home right now. If you'd like, I can tell him you stopped by Mr…what was your name again?"

"Zagan. And that won't be necessary. I know Mr. Mungro is upstairs. I have no interest in upsetting this happy family, but tell Mr. Mungro that if he doesn't come downstairs to meet me, I will entertain myself by conference calling his wife Lillian and Ms. Jeanette Trevino."

The lack of surprise on Carolyn Wool's face told Samael the housekeeper already knew about Jeanette Trevino. Ms. Trevino was a twenty-three-year-old graduate student who currently lived in a rental apartment in an upscale building she could not afford on her salary alone.

"I'll see if I can find Mr. Mungro," Ms. Wool said, her voice shaking.

"Thank you, dear."

Ms. Wool allowed the door to close. Samael listened. He could hear Ms. Wool's footsteps going upstairs. Then he heard two voices: Ms. Wool's was soft. Dean Mungro's was not. A minute later, Samael heard the *clump clump* of heavy feet. Then the front door was ripped open, revealing a man about six feet tall, with wide shoulders, burly arms, and a bald head. He had a dark brown goatee with such even coloring that it most likely came from a bottle. His voice was deep. He spoke like a man who did not repeat himself.

"The last person who threatened me is doing eight years in San Quentin," Dean Mungro spat. "Now get off my property."

"After I speak with your son, I would be happy to leave. But not before that."

"My son?" A look of surprise crossed Dean's face. "You have two seconds to tell me why you're standing in my doorway or you'd better hope we don't make a detour to a dark alley before I book you."

"I would advise against threatening me," Samael said. "For your sake."

"For my sake?" Dean said with a disbelieving laugh. His eyes narrowed. "Are you one of James's…friends?" Dean said the word *friends* like he'd tasted rancid meat.

"I have never met your son before," Samael said. "But I would like to speak with him about the Mercedes he crashed the other night."

Dean's voice lowered. "My son didn't crash any cars. Leave my property right now."

Samael sighed. "Clearly my knowledge of you and Ms. Trevino is not motivation enough. But I'm reasonably sure the constituents of Whisper Valley, not to mention the IRS, would be interested in why a man who claims to uphold law and order received one point two million dollars from Charles Harrison of Gemstone Development. Especially since Mr. Harrison has been granted numerous construction contracts in Whisper Valley. I bet I can guess who went to bat for Mr. Harrison with the city council to award him those contracts."

The color drained from Dean Mungro's face. "Who *are* you?"

"Someone you never have to see again," Samael said. "But that depends on you."

Dean grew quiet. He seemed to be weighing his options.

"In case you're thinking about doing me any harm," Samael said, "you should know that I'm hardly a computer whiz or financial genius. But I have friends who are. And they know where I am. So if anything were to happen to me, rest assured that a ream of text messages, photos, and emails exchanged between you and Ms.

Trevino will arrive in your wife's Gmail account. And your bank records will go directly to the IRS and every financial crimes reporter within a hundred-mile radius."

Dean stood there, unmoving. Samael got the sense he could have knocked the man over with a feather.

"James is upstairs," Dean said weakly. "Follow me."

"Thank you, Mr. Mungro."

Dean led Samael upstairs. His right hand was clenched into a fist. He was clearly used to being on the other side of the threat.

Dean led Samael down a long hallway and stopped in front of a white door. Dean tried the doorknob, but it was locked. He then rapped on the wood twice, hard.

"James," he said. "Need you to open up."

"I'm working," came a voice from inside.

"I don't care. Don't make me ask again."

There was something in the way Dean said *Don't make me ask again* that let Samael know it was not an idle threat.

The door opened. Samael was expecting the young man inside to be tall and confident and smug, as he appeared in the photos Morton's team had found online. And while the boy who appeared in the doorway may have been tall and broad like his father, his shoulders slumped inward, arms held in front of him like he might need to cover up at a moment's notice. Samael noticed a dark bruise above the boy's eye. Samael looked at Dean, then back at James. He felt disgust, and debated making good on his threats despite Dean acquiescing to his demand.

"I said I'm working," James said, irritated. Then he saw Samael. "Who's this?"

"His name is Samuel," Dean said.

"Sam*ael*."

"Whatever. He has some questions for you," Dean said. His voice was polite but there was a layer of menace beneath it. "About the other night."

James's eyes widened. He stuttered, "I thought we…you said…"

"I know what I said," Dean said. "You're going to talk to this man. *Now*."

"Dad, I—"

Dean pushed past Samael into the bedroom. James shrank backward. Dean reached out, quick as a rattlesnake. With one hand he grabbed the back of his son's neck, and with the other pinched his cheek so tight his thumb and pointer finger were practically touching. He dragged James over to the bed.

"Ow, Dad, please…" James pleaded.

"You're going to talk to this man," Dean said. Tears sprang up in James's eyes. "Or so help me god…"

"Mr. Mungro," Samael said sternly. "Your son did not threaten you. I did. There is no need for this aggression. Let he and I talk like men."

"My son and I are men," Dean said. "I don't know *what* you are. You talk to your kids the way you want, and I'll talk to mine the way I want."

Samael's eyes narrowed into slits. He was shorter than Dean and outweighed by at least fifty pounds. But there was a glint of madness in Samael's eyes that had stopped men far larger, and far more dangerous, in their tracks.

"Let go of him," Samael said, "or I will do things to you that will give your son nightmares for the rest of his life."

Dean's mouth opened, exposing a slug-like pink tongue.

"Whoa," James said.

Dean was clearly not used to being spoken to in such a manner. He stared right back at Samael, as if judging his sincerity. Then he released his grip on his son. Samael could see pale white marks where Dean's meaty fingers had sunk into his son's flesh.

"Talk to him," Dean said to James. He took a menacing step toward his son. James rubbed the back of his neck and nodded. Dean turned to Samael. "Everything said within the walls of this house, stays within the walls of this house. You got it?"

"You have my word," Samael lied.

Dean said, "Okay. Now, talk."

"I said I want to talk to your son," Samael said. "Not you."

Dean shook his head. "I'm not leaving this room. I need to

know what you two talk about. I need to know what's going on between you and my son."

"There is nothing 'going on' between us. Like I said, this is the first time we've met, and that's the truth."

"Fine," Dean said. "But if I find out there's something else happening here, and that James is still doing *things* behind my back, I don't care who you are but I will not have my son ruin his future or disgrace our family name."

"I can assure you, Mr. Mungo, you are the only one disgracing anything. Your son and I will be having a conversation. Nothing more."

Dean didn't look like he believed Samael, but he left and slammed the door hard enough to rattle the pictures on the walls. Samael waited until he heard Dean's footsteps descending, each one accompanied by a colorful four-letter word. Then Samael turned to James.

"Please. Have a seat," Samael said, pointing at James's bed. James sat down. Samael took James's desk chair. James eyed Samael warily.

"Thank you for agreeing to speak with me," Samael said.

"I didn't *agree* to anything," James replied icily. "You threatened my dad. Nobody does that. You'd better watch your back."

"My back is watched at all times, James, but I appreciate your concern. Now, I'll get right to it. I want to know more about the crash the other night."

"I don't know what you're talking ab—"

Samael held his finger up and James stopped speaking. "I'm just here for answers. Not to cause you any trouble."

"You're causing me trouble right now," James said.

Samael smiled. "You have your father's temper," he said. "You should try to rein that in, lest you end up a small, vituperative man like he is."

"I will *not* be my father," James said.

"That," Samael said, "is entirely up to you."

Samael took a cell phone from his pocket. He opened the Photos app and held the device up so James could see it. Then he swiped through the photos.

"These are pictures taken of the crash before your Mercedes was *disposed* of," Samael said. "You were driving the car, correct?"

"Where did you get those?" James asked, his voice panicky.

"That doesn't matter. It only matters that they're in my possession."

"Those look photoshopped," James said quickly.

"Your father may be law enforcement, but you wouldn't last sixty seconds in an interrogation room. I know you were driving, so there's no point arguing otherwise. But I'm more interested in what happened *after* the crash. You went through the windshield. Didn't you?"

"I'm here, aren't I?" James said. "I mean, you saw the photos. If I went through that windshield, I'd be cut to pieces."

"You're absolutely right. Nobody could have survived those injuries. So explain it to me. How is it that you're here and not, as you said, cut to pieces?"

The young man's hands began to tremble.

"I only want the truth," Samael said. "I have no intention of getting you in trouble. Believe it or not, I think you and I may have a common interest."

"Who *are* you?" James asked, his voice quivering.

"All I want is to understand how you're still alive. Same as you. Now tell me what happened."

James shook his head, as though trying to rid himself of a bad memory. "I don't remember going through the windshield," he said, "but I remember how there was so much pain it was just this big echo. Like if you're at a concert and the music is so loud you almost can't hear it. There was so much pain it was like my body tried to turn it off."

"You were likely in neurogenic or cardiogenic shock, perhaps both," Samael said. "Your body was shutting down, and your organs were in catastrophic failure."

James looked up. His eyes were red-rimmed. A bubble of snot

popped in one nostril. It was a pitiful sight, and Samael felt a modicum of pity for the boy.

"And then what happened?" Samael said.

"I saw *him*," James said.

Samael leaned closer. His heart began to thump against his chest.

"You saw who? *Tell me*. What did this man look like?"

"It wasn't a man," James said. "It was a kid. A student."

Samael sat back. That did not make sense. The person he saw at the wreckage twenty years ago was certainly not a kid. And though he didn't believe Death aged like most, he also couldn't understand why Death would appear as a *student*. He began to wonder if the trip to Whisper Valley was a mistake. If he'd been so hungry for a meal that he'd eagerly devoured the meager morsel Morton had provided.

"Who was this…kid?" Samael asked.

"His name is Alex Sonnum," James said. "He's a junior."

Death most certainly was not a high schooler. Samael felt sick.

"Alright," Samael said with a sigh. "Tell me about this Alex Sonnum."

"He's new. I think he just moved to Whisper Valley. Like he and his dad literally got here the day before school started."

"His dad?"

"Yeah. They supposedly moved because of his dad's work. I heard that they move *a lot*, and nobody can figure out what his dad does."

*A transient.* Samael's head perked up slightly.

"What else?"

"Alex was there that night on the road. Riding his bike. I was just out driving with some friends. We weren't doing anything wrong. And out of nowhere, he tried to cut us off."

"He tried to cut you off," Samael said drolly. "On a bike. While you were in a Mercedes."

"That's right," James said.

"Alright, then," Samael said. "What did this psychopath on a Schwinn do exactly?"

"I tried to swerve around him, but I lost control. I remember trying to turn into the skid like they taught us in driver's ed. I remember hitting the guardrail. After that, I really don't remember much except the pain. Until I saw him."

"Him? You mean the Sonnum boy?"

"Yeah."

"What did he do?"

"I'm not really sure. He must have gone down the ravine to find me. I just remember seeing him standing there."

"This boy who tried to cut you off then climbed down a mountainside to help you? And why were you not wearing your seatbelt?"

"I don't know. It must have been defective or something."

"Right."

"Hey, asshole, that's what happened. If you don't want to hear what I have to say, then you can get the hell out of my house."

"I'm sorry. Go on. You saw Alex Sonnum at the bottom of the ravine. And then what?"

"He…I don't know. Like I said, my brain wasn't really working. But I remember he walked up to me and knelt down. I thought he was going to either finish me off or start praying. Then he put his hands on me. On my heart."

Samael felt his pulse quicken. "And then?" he said.

"There was this huge white light, like something exploded. Only there wasn't any sound. Then when it was gone, I was just…fine."

"Fine?"

"Except I was covered in blood—I think it was my blood—but I didn't feel any pain. I got up and checked myself out. No broken bones or even any cuts. Not even a headache."

"What happened to Mr. Sonnum?"

"I have no idea. By the time my head stopped spinning, he was gone. He probably didn't want to stick around since he'd nearly killed all of us."

"And then what?"

"My friend Nia found me."

"Did she see what Mr. Sonnum did to you?"

"I don't think so."

"And that's when you called your father. To help."

James hesitated, then said, "Yeah. I'd already gotten in trouble a few times—for things that were totally not my fault—and I knew people would get the wrong impression and assume I had something to do with the crash. My dad wants me to join the police academy after college."

"And having this crash on your resumé wouldn't aid either effort." Samael nodded, thinking. "What else do you know about this Sonnum boy?"

"That he's a goddamn freak who should be sent to some X-Men facility to be studied. Especially after what he did to me in the library."

Samael's eyes narrowed. "The library?"

James took out his cell phone and scrolled through his photos and videos. "The kid who took this video texted it to me. He didn't start recording until it was almost over. You don't see much. But you see enough."

James held the phone so Samael could see the screen, then pressed play. Samael recognized James on the ground, terror in his eyes. Another boy had one hand on James's neck and the other raised in a fist. The other boy was smaller than James, but there was rage in his eyes, and Samael knew firsthand that focused rage could subdue a far larger opponent.

"That's Alex Sonnum?" Samael said.

"He's a freaking psycho, right?"

Samael did not respond. The video was taken from about ten feet away, and it was unfocused and rocky. But Samael still saw something that made him shiver.

James's skin was turning a color Samael had never seen before. Alex Sonnum was killing James, but not by cutting off his air supply or crushing his windpipe. Alex Sonnum was doing something *unnatural* to him, as though he was rotting James's body from the outside in. Then Sonnum let go of James and ran off. The video ended.

"May I?" Samael said, gesturing to the phone. James handed it to him. Samael watched the video again, this time focusing on

Alex's hands and the discoloration on James's face. He paused it and zoomed in.

*There*, he thought. There was a faint light emanating from Alex Sonnum's hand as he gripped James's neck. It had a similar coloring to the discoloration in James's face.

*The color of death.*

He thought about how Fatma Kocak had seen a man and a young boy amongst the train wreckage. Could it be possible that the boy Fatma saw back then was the teenager Samael saw now on this video?

"Do you know where Alex Sonnum and his father live?"

"They rented a house on Marigold Lane near my friend Nia."

*Death is a renter*, Samael thought. For some reason that amused him.

It had been twenty years since he watched the flames lick at the charred debris of the plane that carried his family. Twenty years since Samael saw Death through the fire. Twenty years he had searched and waited, as patiently as a person could, for a clue that could bring him closer to Death, the creator of all of Samael's pain.

But if Samael's eyes and ears did not deceive him, and James was telling the truth, then an even greater prospect had presented itself.

"I take it you're not a fan of Alex Sonnum," Samael said.

"You're perceptive," James replied.

"Then I have a proposal for you. If you're telling the truth—"

"I am," James said.

"Then I think a brief partnership will be mutually beneficial. At the end of it, you will never see me again, but we will have dealt justice to those who have inflicted pain on us. You on this Sonnum boy. And me on someone very close to him."

James looked up. His lips spread into a wide smile. "I'm listening."

# 19

The white light faded, like a linen sheet being gently pulled away from Alex's face. He blinked, allowing his eyes to adjust. Then he blinked again, because what he saw in front of him, *all around him*, couldn't possibly be real.

"Dad…where the hell are we?"

"It's not hell," Byron said, "but you're not far off. Welcome to the Cavern of Orcus."

They were standing in a cave. The word *cave* came to mind because Alex didn't know how else to describe it. But calling this place a cave was like calling the Grand Canyon a divot. The cave, as it was, stretched as far as Alex could see. Rooms upon rooms upon rooms, for what must have been literal miles. Looking up, he could not see a ceiling, only a darkness where a ceiling *should* have been. The rock bed they stood upon was a deep, rich red, like hardened mud mixed with blood. Its coloring was consistent, and strangely it did not reflect any light. There was no dirt. No dust. No water or moss or mold. The rock floor was impeccably clean, as though it had never once been trod upon.

The distance between the walls was about a city block. But it wasn't the width of the cave that made Alex's jaw drop. It was what was on the walls themselves.

Lining the walls were hundreds—no, *thousands*—of shelves. Each shelf was an off-white, almost ivory color with just the slightest tinge of yellow.

*Bone*, Alex thought. *The shelves are made of bone.*

The shelves stretched the length of the cavern and did not appear to be held up by any sort of columns or brackets. They simply existed.

Adorning each of the shelves was an endless sea of candles. The wax was a bright red, the color of blood the moment it touched oxygen. Each and every candle was lit. Alex could not feel any wind but the flames still flickered, the ever-moving shadows making the walls feel alive.

He moved closer. No two candles seemed to be at precisely the same height. Some were tall and strong, their flames reaching nearly a foot into the air. Other flames rested in pools of melted wax, gasping their last breaths before they were snuffed out. The cavern was silent. Alex could hear each breath he and his father took.

"These are the fires of life," Alex said, awed.

"That they are," Byron said. "This cavern holds a candle for every person currently drawing breath. This is where the Blaze draws its power from. The fires of life are the connection between our world and the underworld."

"There must be—"

"Billions," Byron said. "Now hold out your hand. Use it. The Blaze."

Alex held out his hand, palm up, and began to breathe deeply, harnessing the energy. He began to feel a heat spread through his body and into his hands. Small flames leapt from his fingertips. As they did, the light in the room seemed to glow even stronger, brightening the cavern. Byron nodded in approval.

"This is where it all comes from," Byron said.

Alex closed his fist, and the glow receded. "Why are the candles different lengths?"

"Each candle represents a life. Its length mirrors how much life that person has left. Some are long because there is much life left to live." Byron pointed at a candle whose flame fluttered in a pool of wax. "For some, their Exortus is right around the corner."

Just as Byron finished speaking, the flame Alex was looking at flickered briefly, as though gasping for air, then went out, releasing a small trail of smoke. But the smoke was not black, or even white. It had a purple, brown color that James recognized immediately.

"That's the color of the Dim," Alex said. "The smoke is life draining away."

"Precisely."

Suddenly, as if conjured out of thin air, a figure appeared in front of the extinguished flame. The figure was shrouded in a black robe that hung to its feet, with a hood that covered its features. Alex could not see a face, only a shadow where a face should be. A hand slipped out from beneath the robe to collect the candle. When Alex saw it, he shivered.

The hand had no flesh. It was simply jagged bone, connected by no tendons or muscles Alex could see. The bones were not white and ivory, however. They were cracked, nearly blackened, as though they had been decaying for decades.

The figure took the hardened wax from the extinguished candle into its pale, skinless hand. Then both the hand and wax slipped back into the robe. And as quickly and suddenly as it appeared, the figure vanished.

Another flame flickered out several feet away. Then another. Then another. They were going out all around him. And each time a candle went out, a hooded figure appeared, took the wax into its skeletal hand, then disappeared. As he watched, Alex noticed that each skeletal hand looked different. Some were cracked and blackened with age. Some were milk-white with a hint of yellow, as though the bones had been freshly buried. None of the figures cast a shadow.

No sooner had the expired candles been cleared away than new ones appeared in their place with a strong orange flame. Some were several feet tall. Others were mere inches. Immediately, faint trails of purple and brown smoke began to waft from each candle.

"Life replaces life," Byron said. "This is the cycle. Souls depart. Others take their place."

"This is…I don't even know what to say."

"Magnificent, isn't it?" Byron replied.

"It's about time I finally get to see your office," Alex said.

Byron laughed. "Sadly, we're still waiting for a decent coffee machine."

"Those are the Mors, right?" He pointed at the robed figures.

"They are. Damned to spend eternity in this cavern," Byron said. "They serve only to create room for new life. They are the living undead."

Byron pointed to one robed figure, hunched over, approaching a pool of wax. As the hand extended, Alex could see literal dust falling from its cracked, bony fingers.

"Many years ago, that man was a king," Byron said. "One of the most powerful and feared men alive. But he used his power to divide his people for his own selfish means, stoking violence and hatred rather than unity. Remember what I said. Having power but not wielding it is the truest test of strength. Some die with remorse for their misdeeds and are given a chance to redeem themselves as Ankou. Some, like this man, never deserved a chance at redemption."

The figure turned to face Alex. For an instant, the flames illuminated the Mors and Alex saw what lay beneath the hood. He said a silent prayer.

Inside the shadowy hood was a skull. It was clean of flesh, as though it had been boiled off. It had no lips. No nose. But above the hollow where its nose once sat, Alex could see two perfectly clear, unaffected eyes in the lidless sockets. For a moment, the creature locked eyes with Alex. It stared at him. Then the figure turned away.

"It looked at me," Alex said. "That thing *looked* at me. Is someone…in there?"

"They can't speak, but the Mors are as sentient as you and me," Byron said. "That is their prison, to be trapped inside these hollowed-out, crumbling bodies, with nothing but eternity to consider their deeds."

"Oh my god."

"No," Byron said. "God gave up on the Mors a long time ago."

Alex watched as a puff of smoke drifted up from a burnt-out candle. A new one formed in its place, less than an inch long. Its flame would burn out before long.

"Sadly, some souls enter the world without much life to live," Byron said. "Their flames won't last long. When it's time for you to raise an Aegis of your own, the Conclave will perform the ritual of Corpus Sanguis and imbue your blood into one such soul."

Alex watched as the short candle began to burn, smoke of the Dim drifting into the air.

"Can't you do something? Use the Blaze to save it?" Alex said despondently. "I can't bear to think of a child being Exorted."

Byron's voice grew stern. "We can't use the Blaze whenever we see fit. If we heal everyone who is sick or injured, the balance between life and death would tip. Souls must be Exorted as planned. If a Dominus or an Aegis can't wield their powers responsibly, their soul will be Siphoned."

"The Conclave wouldn't dare Siphon a Dominus and Aegis," Alex said.

"Not both of us together," Byron replied. "There must always be one who wields the Blaze. But if I defied the Tenets…or you did…they would Siphon us. Let's not even talk about that. Siphoning is reserved for only the most desperate measures."

"Have you ever Siphoned someone?"

"Once," Byron said. "And I never will again."

"Have you ever brought someone back?"

"Have I ever used the Transference?" Byron said. "No. Transference is the trading of a flame for a flame, or a soul for a soul. Using it would kill me."

"So who did you Siphon?"

"That isn't important. It happened before you were born and has no bearing on your future. I brought you to the Cavern because in just a few months, you will become its caretaker."

"This is…a lot to process."

"I know it is. It was for me too. But I grew and I learned. You will too."

Alex watched as another flame went out. They were going out all around him. Mors were everywhere. Coming and going. The bones. The flames. The smoke. The Dim. The Death.

He felt woozy.

"I want to go back. Get me out of here," Alex said.

Byron whispered *Evanescet* and just like that, they were back in their living room on Marigold Lane.

Alex sat down. Byron brought him a glass of water. Alex downed it.

Byron said, "Your time as an Aegis is nearing its end. Soon you'll have my job. It's a lot of responsibility. But I know you can handle it."

"What if I can't?" Alex said.

"I know you can. And I know you will. You are needed, Alex. Being a Dominus has almost taken more from me that I can bear, but I know that when my flame is ready to go out, I'll look back on my life and be proud of what I've done."

"What would have happened, Dad," Alex said, "if I had killed James?"

Byron stood there. Silent.

"What if I'd gone too far? If I wasn't strong enough to stop the Dim before it was too late? What if I couldn't handle it?"

"We don't have the fortune of hindsight, Alex. You did stop yourself. I trust your judgment and your abilities. Now good night, son."

Then Byron went upstairs.

Alex watched his father walk away. It felt like all the energy had been sapped from his body. He couldn't shake what he'd seen. The cavern. The Mors. Those terrifying eyes buried in the fleshless skulls. Every time he closed his eyes, every time he *blinked*, he saw them. That was his future. Overseeing the living undead. Lord of the Underworld. Now that he'd seen his destiny with his own eyes, now that he knew he possessed the power to both give life and take it away, it changed everything.

*Think of something happy. Think of something happy. For the love of god, think of something happy.*

Alex took his cell phone from his pocket. His hands shook as he tapped out a text. It needed to be eloquent. It needed to be witty and thoughtful and wise.

**Hey, Nia. What's up?**

Less than a minute later, he got a response.

**What's up? I've been calling and texting you for hours. Are you okay? What happened in the library?**

**There are other sides to what I am that I'm just learning about. I swear I didn't know I could do that. It'll never happen again.**

**I think it's best if you and James stay far, far away from each other.**

**That's the understatement of the century. Are you still working?**

**Yup. At Scoop N' Sprinkles until 9. I currently smell like vanilla ice cream and chocolate fudge.**

**That sounds kind of delicious. Need any company to watch you scoop n' sprinkle?**

**Much as I'd like to say yes, I'm always beat when I get off here and then I still have some stuff to do at home. But ask me spur of the moment on a non-work night and I'll say yes.**

**Wait...are you asking me out?**

**Depends. Would you say yes?**

**Maybe. I know we have our first "official" date coming up. But how would you feel about a few hundred mini-dates before then?**

**What exactly is a "mini-date?"**

**I don't know. As long as you're there, I'll be happy.**

**That sounds lovely. Anywhere you want. Just not the men's room.**

**I'd send an emoji back but I'm not very good at them**

**and I'd send something that either made no sense or was totally inappropriate.**

**Why sell yourself short? Go for both. I like that you're an emoji plebeian. It's old fashioned.**

**Old fashioned in a cool, retro way, or in a "reminds you of someone's grumpy uncle" way.**

**It's a fine line. Tread carefully.**

**I will. Hey, is it weird to say I'm still thinking about the other night?**

**It'd be weirder if you weren't still thinking about it. I am.**

**Just FYI, I have fifth period free.**

**Well, I might just have to check a book out of the library at that time.**

**Maybe I'll see you there.**

**Maybe you will. Night, Alex.**

**Night, Nia.**

He put the phone away. He knew what his father had said. He knew his time as an Aegis was nearly up, and that he needed to focus on his life, his *destiny*. But with that destiny would come soul-crushing loneliness. In a few months, he would be trapped forever, and the shackles around his wrists were slowly tightening.

But when Alex thought about Nia, for the first time in his life, he felt free.

# 20

For the last few years, Nia lost herself in the world of Arumaya, the demigoddess who had sprung from her mind and allowed her to escape the real world. But when she was with Alex, she didn't want an escape. For the first time in a long, long time, the world in front of her felt just as exciting as the one she'd created.

They memorized each other's schedules and planned their mini-dates. Quick kisses on the stairwell. The brush of a hand as they passed in the hallway. When their free periods overlapped, they would always meet at their spot in the library. If Nia got there first, she would open her sketchbook, and continue creating new adventures for Arumaya. But when she saw Alex pop into the aisle, she closed the book on the worlds she'd created. For the first time in a long time, she was happy with the real one in front of her eyes. Every moment brought electricity and happiness, an escape from her fears and responsibilities and her mind. When they were together, Nia felt like she was flying.

He told her about his life and travels and what he'd seen. Foreign cities and fascinating cultures, as well as caverns full of fire and bone. Things that she would have never believed were possible. And she listened, rapt, terrified and exhilarated. But she taught him the joy of small intimacies. Holding hands and quick kisses. Texts that went all night long. Alex may have opened her mind up to worlds she never knew existed, but Nia loved showing him how to experience happiness in theirs.

Yet as much as she enjoyed the clandestine kisses and mid-day confessionals, she couldn't wait for their first official date. When they would have time to talk and enjoy an interesting reading and maybe even more.

When the day of the reading came, Nia waited at the end of her driveway for Alex. For some reason, she thought about Cinderella. A few years ago, Nia had watched the *Cinderella* remake with her mom. She'd never really cared for fairy tales, had never been one of those girls who dreamed of being swept off her feet by a dashing prince with cheekbones that could pierce leather. So when Prince Charming, who had yawned through suitor after suitor, asked Cinderella to dance after she arrived at the ball in her sparkly blue gown and decked-out pumpkin carriage, Nia rolled her eyes and made a sarcastic *Pfft.*

"That's extra even for a fairy tale. What kind of lame fairy godmother thinks the inside of a giant pumpkin smells romantic? Couldn't she conjure up a Rolls Royce?"

Nia had been sitting cross-legged on the floor, her mother seated behind her knitting a pair of socks for her first day of school. Her father was on the couch, his nightly glass of Cognac giving off a sweet, pungent smell.

"Can't you just enjoy it?" her mother said, mock-scolding her. "Sometimes you just need to step back from real life and let the fantasy in."

"That pumpkin probably gets better mileage than our SUV," her father said, sipping his drink slowly, savoring the taste. "What year is this supposed to take place anyway?"

Even now, Nia remembered the way he smacked his lips when he drank or ate something tasty. The sound used to annoy her. Now her guilt over those petty grievances practically gave her an ulcer. It had been so long since her father had been able to savor much of anything other than time. If only she'd known those moments with her parents, when they were still fully themselves, would end well before any of them were ready. She would have embraced them more than she had. And that guilt would never, ever leave her.

"I think it takes place in the olden days," Rivka said.

"When exactly *were* the olden days?" Stephen said.

"Please, I'm trying to watch the movie," Nia said.

"You criticize the movie but want us to stop talking so you can watch it?" Rivka said.

"I'm full of contradictions. Now can you *please* shut up?"

"Language," Stephen said.

"Okay, Mom, would you *please* refrain from using your vocal cords while I'm watching the movie that fetishizes the otherworldly powers of both impractical footwear and produce?"

"Much better," her father said.

A few weeks later, Nia began to notice that her father was losing weight. And soon after that, her mother began to forget things. It started off small, like where she put the measuring cups, where she left her car keys, realizing that she'd applied mascara to one set of eyelashes but not the other.

So maybe, she thought, *Cinderella* came to mind because that night with her parents was one of the last good times they'd shared. Or maybe it was because when she saw Alex walking toward her house, wearing jeans and a dark blue button-down over a clean white t-shirt, hands stuffed shyly in his pockets, Nia thought of what a grand romantic gesture that pumpkin carriage was supposed to be. Yet this cute boy walking toward her, without any pomp or circumstance, felt infinitely more romantic than any movie she had ever seen.

She felt a flutter in her chest as Alex got closer. Her palms began to sweat and she surreptitiously wiped them on the back of her pants. She was wearing flared jeans and a mint-colored top adorned with blue delphiniums that brought out her eyes. It was her favorite shirt, but she hadn't worn it in over a year. This top needed a reason to be worn, and riding in James's Mercedes or serving ice cream cones didn't quite fit the bill.

Tonight, she deserved to wear it. And this was the boy she deserved to wear it for.

"Hey," Alex said when he got to her driveway.

She waved back. "Hey yourself. You act like you're surprised to see me."

"Maybe I am? A little?"

"Did you think I'd stand you up?"

"Probably not, but moving here hasn't really gone at all like I expected."

"When I stand guys up, I like to make sure they don't live on my street. Otherwise, you know, awkward."

As Alex walked up the driveway, Nia's heart thumped with every step he took. She could smell his cologne. The scent was sweet, and though he'd definitely used one or two sprays too many, she didn't mind. As Alex neared, he raised his hand. She took it and he closed his fingers around hers. She could hear him breathing. She wanted to press her head against his chest and listen to his heart.

"So…what now?" Alex said.

"Now, we start the night off right," Nia said, leaning in.

Nia closed her eyes and pressed her lips against his and felt his hand gently brush against her side. She shivered.

"Are you cold?" he said.

"Kind of the opposite."

His smile widened.

"Come on," she said, taking his hand and leading him away. "The reading starts in half an hour."

"Go, Tree guy!" Alex turned to see Iggy sitting on his front porch. He was holding a bottle out like he was toasting them.

Nia laughed. "Thanks, Ig," she said.

Iggy whistled and took a swig from his drink. "Just have her home by eight or I'll get my chainsaw."

"It's already seven," Alex said in mock protest.

"So make the most of your hour," Iggy said.

"He'll have me home when I say he's going to have me home," Nia yelled at Iggy.

"Fair enough," Iggy said. "Have fun, you crazy kids." He took another swig.

As they walked on, Alex asked, "Does Iggy normally do that? Drink by himself?"

"Sometimes," Nia replied. "But only when things at home get really bad."

"What's going on at home?"

Nia sighed. "His parents are…difficult. That's putting it mildly. Not my place to go into more detail. But you do what you need to do to get by."

The streets of Whisper Valley were quiet. Nia and Alex held hands as they walked. She wondered if there had ever been anyone special during Alex's travels. Someone who made him shiver like he made her. She wished she could reach into his head and pull out the answers to every question she had without having to ask.

"Remind me who we're seeing tonight," Alex said as they turned onto Roanoke Way. "I've never been to one of these things."

"The author's name is Willoughby Williams," Nia said. "He's on tour for his new book, *Memories that Never Happened*. He's reading from it tonight at The Deckled Edge bookshop."

"There's no way that's his real name."

"Good call, Sherlock. His real name is Percy Sneed. I'm guessing he felt Willoughby Williams sounded more…literary?"

"I don't know. Willoughby Williams sounds kind of like an eighteenth-century haberdasher. You said Percy, er, *Willoughby*, is local?"

Nia said, "He grew up, like, five minutes from us on Billings Way. He's probably the only celebrity, and I use that term *very* loosely, Whisper Valley has ever had. You know, Death and his son notwithstanding."

"Are his books any good?"

"Meh. He tends to write about guys who refuse to grow up. You know, they're thirty-eight and own one towel and wash their sheets once a month and take six days to text a girl back because 'work got cray.' Meanwhile, my cousin Melissa texted me while she was literally in labor. I just hope the lame guys Willoughby writes about are confined to fiction."

"I refuse to comment on the grounds that it may incriminate me."

"Probably smart."

He removed his hand from hers. At first, she wondered if she'd offended him, but then Alex took something from his back pocket and held it out to her.

"I brought this for you," he said. "All the stuff about my dad and the Blaze and my future, that's *what* I am. This is *who* I am."

In Alex's hand was his copy of *A Cold Winter's Night.*

"This is what you were reading that day in the library," she said. "You said this book is the most special thing you own."

"It is," Alex said. "This book has traveled the world with me. So if you want to read it—"

"I wanted to read it the second I saw you holding it. I even looked into getting my own, but used copies were, like, four hundred bucks on eBay."

The illustration on the cover was the silhouette of a young boy walking alone into a bleak, snow-covered forest, the brilliant white undisturbed except for his footprints. Bare trees formed a canopy above him, their gnarled branches seeming to reach for him like claws. The moon hung in the night sky just beyond the forest like a watchful, malevolent eye.

Nia ran her hands over the cover. Traced her thumb along the pages. The book must have been read dozens, hundreds of times.

"Your tattoo," she said. "Let me see it again."

Alex rolled up his sleeve and held his forearm up. Alex's skin bore the silhouette of the boy from the book's cover, sharp branches reaching for him as he walked into the unknown.

"How did you even find out about this book?" she asked.

"Five years ago, we were living in Gothenburg, Sweden," Alex said. "I spent a lot of time alone. Shocking, right? One day, I was just walking along the bank of the Göta älv river and I found this little hole-in-the-wall shop that sold used books in English. I went in, figured I'd grab a few to pass the time until we left Gothenburg. For some reason, I couldn't take my eyes off the cover. I bought it for twenty Krona, which is about two bucks. It's the best money I ever spent."

"Tell me," she said, "why it's so special to you."

"The boy on the cover, his name is Sam. When the book starts, Sam is on a long car ride with his parents who are in the middle of a divorce. Sam feels alone, like he's been forgotten about. They're in the front seat screaming at each other like he's not even there. Then the car gets a flat tire, and when his dad pulls over to replace it, Sam runs off into the forest. But he gets lost. The whole book takes place over one night as Sam tries to find his way back to his parents. But something in the forest is hunting him. Can he find his way back before it gets to him? Does he even want to go back?"

"So what happens?"

"You'll have to see for yourself," Alex said. "The first time I read it I finished it in one day. I stayed up the whole night thinking about it. I was obsessed. Then I read it again, but took my time. A week later, I went to a tattoo parlor on Östra Skansgatan. I brought the book and showed the artist the cover. He didn't speak much English, so I basically pointed at the illustration and said, 'I want this.' Thankfully, he understood. It's a reminder that even when I feel alone, or scared, to keep going. Like Sam did."

"How did your dad react to the tattoo?"

"I hid it from him for about a month. He wondered why I was the only guy wearing sweaters and long-sleeve shirts in July. But he found out eventually. Nothing like getting a lecture on responsibility from Death."

"Couldn't he, you know, remove it?"

"My dad can do a lot of things. Spontaneous laser tattoo removal isn't one of them."

Nia laughed and caressed the book. It was just pages and binding and glue, but something about it felt *alive*. Like it was a conduit between them.

"This book means as much to me as anything in the world," Alex said. "And I want you to have it."

"Wait, you want me to *have* it?"

"Yup."

"Alex, I…"

"Just say yes."

"Okay. Yes. Thank you."

"There is one condition."

"You can't spring a condition on me after I've already said yes."

"You have to promise me you're going to read it."

"Are you kidding?" Nia said. "I kind of want to ditch you right now so I can go home and start."

Alex laughed. "Given where we're going for our first official date, it felt appropriate."

His hand found hers and she squeezed tight.

"Does it still hurt when you touch me?" she said.

He shook his head. "It feels like when you get into a hot shower. It might feel scalding for a split second, but you get used to it. And then it starts to feel really good."

"When you practically ran away from me on the bus, I thought I must have smelled or something. You should have told me the truth. I was about to buy a stronger deodorant."

"At first, I was scared by how it felt. I hoped it would go away."

She pressed her palm against Alex's face and kissed him.

"Are you glad it didn't go away?" she said.

"More and more every day."

"I bet you give copies of this book to all the girls."

"First off, I think there are a total of three copies of this book in existence. And other than the tattoo artist in Sweden whose beard was the length of my femur, I'm the only one who's touched this book since I bought it."

Nia opened the cover. She wondered how many miles the book had traveled. How many nights Alex had lain awake in bed, his mind lost in the woods within the pages. There was something about the cover that pulled at Nia's heart. Amidst the terror of the twisted branches and bleakness of the white snow, there was a sense of beauty. The small boy, wandering into the wilderness, ready to do battle with demons both real and imagined.

Nia held up the book. "Is it weird to say this might be my favorite gift ever?"

"Don't say that until you've read it."

"Okay," she said. "And I promise to give it back when I'm done."

"Nope. It's yours. But you need to give me something in return. Something meaningful."

Nia's lips curled into a smile. This would require some serious thought. She liked the challenge.

"You're on," she said.

They walked on hand-in-hand, taking their time in the crisp fall evening, unaware of the man in the black suit watching them from a distance.

# 21

The Deckled Edge was nestled between a wine bar and a hair salon on Primrose Boulevard, Whisper Valley's main shopping strip. One side of the storefront was floor-to-ceiling glass, in which dozens of books were displayed in careful arrangements. The adjacent wall was made up of a kaleidoscope of colored bricks. Reds and yellows and blues and greens and purples, like a wall of dreams. Nia had probably spent more money in The Deckled Edge than anywhere else in Whisper Valley. When Alex agreed to come, she felt for the first time in her life that she was with someone who wasn't merely interested in her to make himself happy, but because he found joy in her happiness too. And when he gave her his treasured book, she knew it was because he believed, like she did, that shared stories could create the deepest connection of all.

About thirty people were milling about in the bookstore waiting for the event to begin. Rows of chairs had been set up in front of a microphone stand. Stacks of Willoughby Williams's books were everywhere. Alex scanned the shelves with a deliriously cute smile on his face. It made Nia's heart sing to see him lost among the shelves. She prayed the noise in her head would stay away for the night and allow her to lose herself, if only for a few hours.

"Whenever my dad and I moved," Alex said, "I always found the nearest bookstore. When you don't have any real friends, made-up ones have to do."

"Made-up worlds can be better than the real one," Nia said.

"The real one has been growing on me lately," Alex said. He put his hand on the small of her back. She liked it there. It felt steady and sturdy.

"Me too."

Nia picked up a book called *The Blank Canvas* and showed it to Alex.

"This was one of the first books I bought when I first started to fall in love with illustrating. I probably read my copy as many times as you've read *A Cold Winter's Night*."

"At least your book taught you how to draw," Alex said. "I'd give my chances at surviving a night in a frozen forest fifty-fifty at best."

A woman walked to the podium and tapped a microphone. The crowd quieted.

"If you can please find a seat, we'll get this party started," she said. Once the crowd was settled in, she continued. "My name is Patty McKinlay and I'm the events manager at The Deckled Edge. Tonight, I'm honored to welcome back one of our favorite writers, Mr. Willoughby Williams. Mr. Williams is a Whisper Valley original, a Dubya V graduate, and we're always thrilled when he finds time to swing by The Deckled Edge. Now for an introduction, as though he needs it. Willoughby Williams is the bestselling, award-winning author of eight novels and two collections of short stories. His book *Freedom in a Jar* was made into a feature film starring Jake Gyllenhaal, and his story collection *Peas, Carrots, and Marmalade* won the Golden Wren award."

"That's a really big deal," Nia whispered to Alex.

"Ladies and gentlemen, please give a warm Whisper Valley welcome to Mr. Willoughby Williams!"

The crowd applauded. From behind a red curtain emerged a trim man in his early fifties, his beard brown on the sides and graying at the chin. He wore a pair of rimless glasses, a navy blazer, slim black jeans and pristine white sneakers. He looked like a high schooler who'd fallen asleep for thirty years. He smiled as he took the microphone.

"Friends," Willoughby said, spreading his arms out wide as though waiting for a group hug, "it feels good to be back in the Dubya V!"

The audience cheered. Nia clapped and Alex whistled. Behind her, someone shushed loudly and aggressively. Nia turned around to apologize, but when she saw who was sitting in the row behind them, her stomach twisted into a knot.

"James," she said. "What the hell are you doing here?"

"Um, same thing as you," James Mungro said. "Just keep it down. I want to be able to hear Willoughby Williams. Listen, I'm not here to start anything. I swear."

"How did you even know…?" Nia stuttered.

"You mentioned this reading to me a few weeks ago. You said you wouldn't miss it. I just assumed I was still invited."

*Please, don't ruin this*, she wanted to say. *Let me have some joy.*

Alex said, "If this is about you and me—"

"Don't be so conceited," Jame said. "I'm not here to get into anything. Actually, I came in part to apologize to Nia for what happened in the library. I let my emotions get the best of me."

Nia felt Alex take her hand and squeeze. A small gesture, but it said *I got you.*

"I don't buy your apology," Nia said. "You could have apologized a hundred time in school. I've never seen you within a mile of a bookstore."

"Is there a time limit on apologizing?" James said. "I came here for the reading. That's all. I promise."

Alex began to speak, but Nia put her hand on his knee as if to say, *Now* I *got you.*

"Talk is cheap," she said. "If you're being sincere, shut up and listen and leave us alone."

"Shutting up right now." James sat back and folded his arms across his chest.

Nia leaned close to Alex and said, "I'm sorry. I didn't know he'd be here."

"Doesn't change anything." He leaned over and kissed her as if to let her know it would be okay.

Willoughby Williams began his reading. Nia tried to lose herself in the words and the boy by her side, but the hummingbird in her chest was flapping its wings faster and faster and faster. Suddenly, she felt like her lungs were contracting, making it harder to breathe. She closed her eyes and evened her breathing, but the heat rose in her chest and climbed into her throat and filled her eyes. A single tear slid down her cheek and she brushed it away, praying she caught it before Alex noticed. But she could tell by the concerned way he was looking at her that he had, and suddenly she felt like the night's magic had been lost. She should have known this would happen. She should have known she wasn't meant to be happy.

"Are you okay?" Alex whispered.

Nia nodded, but she felt *far* from okay.

"It's okay if you're not okay," he said.

*It's okay if you're not okay.* For some reason, those words cooled the burning in her chest. *It's okay if you're not okay.*

"Sometimes I'm not okay," she said.

"Do you want to leave?"

"Absolutely not. I'm better when I'm with you. So if you try to leave early, I will chain you to Willoughby Williams."

"Good. Because I want to stay here with you. And Percy."

She smiled. Alex squeezed her hand again and she gripped it hard enough that he would have had difficulty letting go even if he wanted to, but she had the feeling he didn't.

When the reading was over, Willoughby closed his book with a flourish. The audience clapped, Willoughby took questions, and everyone headed up to get their books signed. James remained seated. He was on his phone and didn't seem to be very interested in getting a book signed. James had another motive for coming to the reading, Nia was sure of it. But she didn't know what it was. She knew she should've cut James off completely a long time ago, but every time she came close, she was reminded of what he'd done for her.

*He was there for you that night. If he hadn't been, you might not be here.*

They inched forward in line.

"So, what's the protocol?" Alex asked. "Since we're here together, do we need to buy two books?"

"I think we can get away with one," Nia said. She liked hearing him say *together*.

The man in front of them approached Willoughby Williams. Something about him struck Nia as odd. The rest of the crowd was slightly younger, more bohemian. The man wore an expensive black suit and shiny black loafers that reflected the recessed lighting. She could see deep purple shadows under his eyes, and his hair was so severely parted she could see his scalp. He looked like a mortician.

*Someone is overdressed*, Nia thought.

"A wonderful, passionate reading," the man said to Willoughby. His voice was smooth, refined. "This will be the first book of yours I've read, but if the rest of the story is of the same quality as the selection you read from tonight, I'm sure it won't be the last."

"Well now, sir, I appreciate that," Willoughby said. He opened the book to the title page and brandished a fountain pen. "Who can I make this out to?"

"Samael," the man said.

"Sam…"

"Ael. S-a-m-a-e-l."

"I've signed a lot of books over the years, but I don't think I've ever signed one for a Samael before," Willougby said as he scrawled his signature in the man's book. "What's the story there?"

"My father was a savvy businessman and a generous philanthropist," the man said. "He always said that this meant working with both the best and worst people humanity had to offer. He was very spiritual, a great believer in the duality, the complicated nature of man. In Talmudic lore, Samael is both a fallen angel and one of the lord's servants. My father saw a certain poetry in giving his son a name that represented that duality."

Willoughby whistled. "That is a hell of a story. Well, Samael, thank you for coming. My Twitter and Instagram handles are on my website. If you like the book, do me a solid and write a review and post about it on your feeds."

"You can be sure I will."

The man exited the line, and Nia and Alex approached Willoughby. The writer smiled.

"Who can I make this out to?" he asked.

"Alex and Nia," Nia said.

"You got it." As Willoughby signed the book, Nia noticed something that struck her as odd. Willoughby handed the book to Nia and they moved to the side.

"That guy ahead of us on line," Nia said, "the one with the funky name who looked like a lost member of the Addams family. I might be crazy, but I could have sworn he was taking pictures while we were getting our book signed."

"Seriously? He was taking pictures of you?"

"No," Nia said, "I think he was taking pictures of *you*."

"Me?" Alex said. "Why would he…?"

Alex scanned the store. He heard a jingle as the front door closed. The man in the black suit rounded the corner and disappeared out of sight. Alex began to walk toward the door, but Nia held his arm.

"I'm sure it's nothing," she said. "Everyone here is on their phone. He was probably just posting pics to Insta or something. Here, look what Willoughby wrote to us."

Nia opened the book and read Alex the inscription.

*To Alex and Nia –*

*A broken heart can never be full, and a full heart can never be broken. May your hearts remain full for a lifetime.*

*Willoughby Williams*

"Did he come up with that on the spot?" Alex asked. "Or do you think he writes that in every book he signs?"

"I'd like to think he made it up on the spot," Nia said. She handed Alex the book. "I want you to have it."

"No way. Tonight was your idea."

"I got a book tonight, now it's your turn."

"I can't argue with that," Alex said. "Thank you."

"Just so you know," Nia said, "this doesn't count toward our agreement. I have an idea for something special I want to give you. But it's going to take time. So be patient."

"Is it banana bread?" Alex said. "Because I love banana bread."

"I only make banana bread for people I *really* like," she said playfully. "I'm still on the fence with you."

As Nia paid, Alex picked a book off the Local Author shelf and thumbed through it. A wicked smile spread across his face.

"What?" Nia said as she signed the receipt.

"I have to get this," he said. He paid for the book and handed it to Nia. "This one's on me."

"*Haunted Houses of Whisper Valley*?" she said. "You must be kidding."

"All the haunted houses in this book are bogus," Alex said, "except one. There's one Perdita in Whisper Valley. One soul who untethered from her body before its Exortus could be completed. And we're going to meet her."

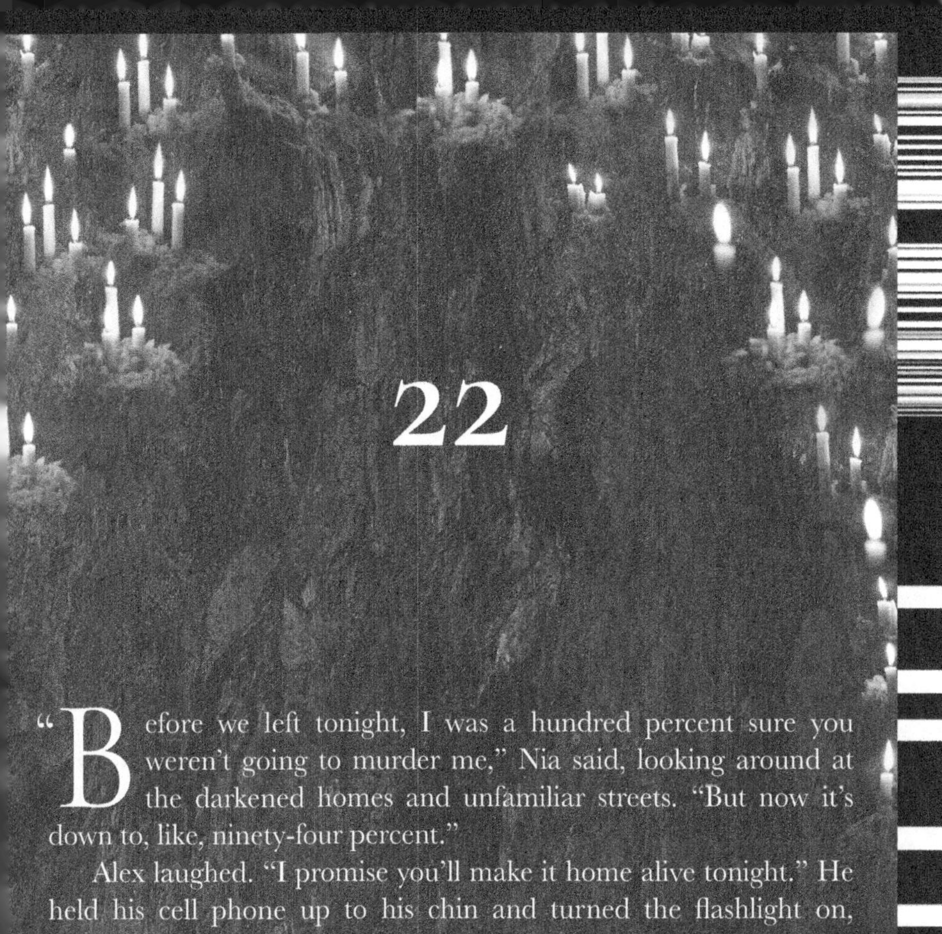

# 22

"Before we left tonight, I was a hundred percent sure you weren't going to murder me," Nia said, looking around at the darkened homes and unfamiliar streets. "But now it's down to, like, ninety-four percent."

Alex laughed. "I promise you'll make it home alive tonight." He held his cell phone up to his chin and turned the flashlight on, bathing his face in an eerie glow. "Or will you?"

"Now I'm only forty-eight percent sure I'm not going to murder *you*."

Alex flicked the light off. "I can live with those odds. Come on."

"Where are we going? And yes, I'm aware of the irony in asking that question given that I've lived in this town my whole life and you moved here, like, this morning."

"You know more about the Whisper Valley you see every day," Alex said, "but I know more about the Whisper Valley you don't see every day. Or more specifically *can't*."

"Now you're really freaking me out."

"Do you trust me?"

Nia looked at him and said, without hesitating, "Yes."

"Then come on."

He led her to 23 Vine, a dilapidated Victorian home with faded blue paint and cracked white trim. It had a wide, wraparound porch with stone railings, three dormers, and a cylindrical turret with oval windows. A faded For Sale sign was planted in the patchy, overgrown lawn.

Nia said, "Okay, what is this place, and how many murders were committed here?"

"No murders." He opened the haunted houses book and flipped to page thirty-two. He handed it to Nia and turned on his phone light so she could read. "But two deaths. And one of the dead is still here."

Nia read the page out loud. "Harold and Millicent Adams bought the home at 23 Vine Street in Whisper Valley in 1963. Harold died peacefully in his sleep from a heart attack. Millicent passed two years later in the same bed at the age of eighty-seven from complications due to diabetes. But whereas Harold passed on peacefully, Millicent did not. Ever since her death, visitors claim they can still hear Millicent roaming the house, searching for her beloved husband. When it's quiet, people have said they can hear a faint creaking sound and feel a chill in certain rooms. People who knew Millicent believe the sound is the rocking chair she used to sit in to watch her favorite soap operas and knit for her husband and their children. And if the light is just right, some have even said they can see the silhouette of her spirit, as dust particles settle in the exact spot that she died, like snowflakes on a coat."

Nia looked at him. "Is all this true?"

"I mean, it's probably a little over-dramatized, but when Millicent Adams died, her Ankou failed to complete her Exortus. Her soul became lost. A Perdita. So, yeah. The book is right."

"You're saying the ghost of a yarn-loving old lady still lives in that spooky-ass house." Nia closed the book.

"We don't use the term *ghosts*. It's derogatory."

"I'm sorry for offending any and all dead people," she said. "Now let's get the hell out of here."

"Don't you want to go in?" Alex said.

"I'd rather fill my shoes with razor blades and walk to Canada."

"Perditas aren't dangerous," Alex said. "That's another fairytale. They're just lost spirits. They're not malevolent—just lonely. Imagine existing in a permanent state of confusion, wondering where all your loved ones went."

"I'd rather not imagine that," Nia said.

"Most of what people assume about death and dying is wrong, based on centuries of myths and folklore. Untethered souls are more sad than scary, and Death isn't some guy in a robe who carries around farming equipment."

Nia took a breath. "Okay. Fine. Let's see your Perdita. But if I hear anything that sounds like 'Zuul,' I'm gone."

Alex took Nia's hand and led her toward the house. Unsurprisingly, the front door was locked. They went around the side. Alex tried the windows until he found one that was unlatched. He slid it open. Every breath sounded like a cannon shot. If a neighbor saw them sneaking around, Perditas would be the least of their problems. Alex ducked his head into the open window, the top half of his body disappearing into the dark. Nia waited. And waited.

"Alex? Everything okay?"

Suddenly, Alex yelped and his body jerked upward, slamming against the window pane. Nia's hand flew to her mouth.

"Oh my god, are you dead?"

Alex turned back, a goofy smile on his face that said *sorry not sorry*.

"You asshole. Now there's an eighty-seven percent chance I'm going to murder you."

"So I have a thirteen percent chance of making it out of here alive."

"And dwindling."

Alex swung his feet through the window, then held his hand out for her. Nia took it, glared at him, and climbed into the house.

It was in better shape on the inside than the outside. Nia expected to have to dodge cobwebbed chandeliers, spiders the size of Buicks, and furniture so filthy she could write her name in the dust. But the interior was fairly well-maintained. Somebody was trying to keep up appearances in the hope a buyer might overlook the home's sordid past.

Nia followed Alex to the foyer. A flight of carpeted stairs led to the second floor.

"Is it colder in here than it is outside, or is it just me?" Nia said.

"It's always colder when a Perdita is near."

"Why?"

"A body gives off heat. A soul without a body does the opposite."

"Shh," Nia said. "Do you hear that?"

They stopped moving. Nia held her breath.

"Is that…creaking?"

"Millicent's rocking chair," Alex said. "She's upstairs. Come on."

"I just wanted to go to a bookstore for a nice, pleasant reading," Nia said, "how did we end up in the *Grudge* house?"

"You were lucky enough to fall for me."

"I'm beginning to question my judgment."

"Do you want to go home?"

"Absolutely not."

"Good. Me either."

Nia followed Alex upstairs. Their footsteps were muffled by the thick carpet. She could feel her heart thrumming in her chest. When they reached the top of the stairs, Alex pointed to a closed door at the end of the dark hallway.

"She's in there," Alex said. "Do you feel the chill?"

"I do." Nia heard it again. A high-pitched creaking, like old wood straining under too much weight. They walked to the door and Alex gripped the doorknob.

"Feel that," he said.

Nia placed her hand on the bronze. It was ice cold.

"Perdita?" Nia said. Alex nodded. "I want to see her."

"You won't be able to see her. Only people with the Blaze can see souls. But you'll be able to feel her."

Alex opened the door. A gust of cold air washed over them,

making Nia shiver. The windows were closed. The room was empty. There was no furniture. No carpeting. Just a scuffed wooden floor in need of a good polish and windowsills in need of dusting. Moonlight shone through the curtainless windows, illuminating the floor and walls. Alex stepped inside and Nia followed.

"There she is," Alex whispered. He pointed to an empty space by the easternmost window. "Look at the air. The dust particles. The moonlight. Doesn't it look just a little *distorted*? Almost like a shimmering in the air."

Alex put a hand on Nia's shoulder. Warmth spread across her back and down her spine. She could make out a hazy outline, barely visible in the moonlight. "I think I see it," she said.

"Now close your eyes. *Listen.*"

Nia closed her eyes. She focused all her energy on the spot in front of her. She could hear it. The faint sound of squeaking. It reminded Nia of how her father, back when he was healthy and vibrant, would sit on her bed and read her stories, bedsprings groaning under his weight. The memory was so vivid she nearly gasped.

Then she heard something else. A *click click* like metal tapping against metal.

"What is that?" she whispered.

"You hear it too," he said.

"I do."

"Knitting needles," he said.

"Can she see us?" Nia said.

Alex shook his head. "She exists on her own plane, between the living and the dead. All she has are her memories."

Nia had visions of her own mother knitting, hands moving quickly but delicately, then slower and more cumbersome as the disease ate away at her mind. She could feel Alex's hand on her shoulder, warming her, steadying her. They stood there, silent, listening to the soft sounds in the moonlit room.

Nia should have been scared. Terrified. But she wasn't. She was overcome with curiosity and memory...and something else she couldn't quite place. She thought about the moment Alex told her who he was, how she should have turned and run. It would have been the smart thing to do. The rational thing to do. But for some reason, some elemental reason, she knew that doing the very irrational thing and letting herself fall for him felt very, very right.

"There's no way to help her?" Nia said.

Alex shook his head. "A Perdita can't be Exorted. And the only way to bring her back would be through Transference. Trading a soul for a soul."

"So she'll be alone forever," Nia said. "That's so sad."

"I told you Perditas were more sad than scary. Come on. Let's leave Millicent alone."

Alex took Nia's hand and led her back into the hallway. Alex headed toward the stairs, but Nia stopped.

"Everything okay?"

"In here," she said. She led him into an open room at the end of the hall. Nia drew the curtains back, revealing large bay windows, bathing the room in a soft moonlit glow. She closed the door behind them.

"Millicent didn't need to see this," she said. Nia turned toward Alex. She moved closer to him and looked into his green eyes. She felt his hands slide from her shoulders down to her waist. She closed her eyes and put her lips against his, and as she did, she gently unbuttoned his sleeve. She traced her finger along his forearm. She felt Alex shiver from her touch.

They parted briefly. She could still taste his lips on hers, feel the heat in his fingertips. Then Alex whispered, "I need to be honest with you."

"Don't tell me there's a Perdita in here too," she said. "I want you alone right now."

He laughed. "We're alone. But I've never done anything like this before. I don't really know what I'm doing."

Nia placed her hand against his cheek.

"Whatever you're doing, don't stop."

Alex nodded and laced his fingers through hers. "All these years I've felt like I've been missing out on something. I just never knew what it was."

"So what was it?" she said.

Alex merely leaned in and kissed her, warm and deep and full. Their bodies pressed against each other. She could feel his heart thumping, just as hers was, and the cold slipped away like it was never even there.

# 23

Byron Sonnum walked briskly through the Cavern of Orcus. Even though he had walked these halls many times over the last century, he was still astonished by the magnificence and grandeur of the underworld. The Cavern had been around since the beginning of time, and over a thousand Dominii had walked its halls before Byron Sonnum. It was living history.

As Byron walked the candle-lit corridors, several Mors turned to face him—at least as much as a creature without a face could actually *face* anyone. The Mors had once been human. Byron had sentenced many of these creatures himself, their sentient minds harboring hatred for him that would last for eternity. And though the Mors could not harm him, he still felt the lidless eyes following him, knowing they would do anything for the chance to tear him apart.

Eventually, the light began to dim. Fewer and fewer candles lined the walls. Soon, Byron found himself shrouded in total darkness. He could not even see his hands. It was then that he knew he had reached his destination.

"Dominus Sonnum," a voice boomed. "Please step into the light."

The voice was loud and deep. It came from everywhere and

nowhere. Above him. Below him. Rattling his bones, reverberating throughout the cavern, piercing him like a broadsword.

A circle of light appeared in front of Byron. The rest of the Cavern was pitch black, the kind of darkness that seemed to not only hide what lay within, but swallowed the light like an unseen, gaping maw.

Byron Sonnum stepped into the light. He met with the Conclave many times during his tenure, but this was only the third time he had been summoned. The first was when his father bequeathed the mantle to him. The second meeting brought him unfathomable pain and remorse. He thought about that meeting every day of his life. This was the third. Byron hoped he would never be summoned again until it was time to turn over the mantle to Alex. That he had been called here, now, was not a good omen.

"Dominus Sonnum," a female said, her voice like a thin dagger slipped between the ribs. "The Conclave appreciates you joining us on such short notice."

"Welcome, Dominus," came another voice.

"Dominus Sonnum, Lord of the Underworld, Keeper of the Ankou. Welcome."

Seven translucent figures then appeared from the darkness. They formed a semicircle around Byron. Seven souls. Seven former Dominii. The Conclave.

"Why have you called me here?" Byron said.

"Your Aegis, Dominus Sonnum," said one.

"He gives us pause," said another.

"Sincere pause."

"Grave concern."

"Perhaps you have a weakness for human folly that has blinded you to what is going on right under your nose."

"Speak to me plainly, and with respect," Byron said. "Tell me *exactly* why I'm here."

"Your *Aegis*," thundered one so loudly it seemed to cause the darkness itself to quake. "We have sincere doubts as to whether he has the temperament to uphold the Tenets. Your time as Dominus is nearing an end, Dominus. And your Aegis is…distracted."

"Alex is not just my Aegis. He is my son. And he will be a better Dominus than I have ever been," Byron said. "Better than any of *you* ever were."

"Your son, Dominus, seems to have far more interest in the living than the dead."

Byron's voice trembled with anger. "Which is why not a soul on Earth is better prepared to take my mantle. He was seventeen years old before he discovered the Dim, and when he did, he found the strength to keep it in check. I know not all of you can say that. Maybe what this Conclave needs is a little more humanity."

"Need we remind you, Dominus Sonnum," one disembodied voice said, "that for centuries, the ritual of Corpus Sanguis has combined the blood of a Dominus with the soul of a child to produce an Aegis. For thousands of years, the Aegis has come from the blood of the Dominus. Until Alex. We allowed you to forsake the ritual for this boy."

"You all know it was not that simple," Byron said. "We came to the conclusion that we could not risk performing the ritual after what happened. I couldn't—*we* couldn't—take a chance that it would happen again."

"That is why we allowed you take in this boy," a voice said, "to sever a possibly tainted bloodline. We hoped your Aegis—"

"My *son*."

"—would give our hallowed order a new start. Remember what is at stake, Dominus."

"You don't need to remind me of anything," Byron said. "I lost more than you could possibly know."

"Your emotions have clouded your judgment, Dominus. And you would do well to lessen your misplaced self-righteousness. There seems to be a trend of your Aegii defying the Tenets."

"Alex discovered the Dim on his own. And he pulled himself back," Byron said. "That alone should prove I was right to adopt him."

"He did show strength in that regard, Dominus. But your judgment has been off before."

"We are not monsters. We know the grief you carry. But we

have given your Aegis tremendous latitude. If Alex shakes our confidence again, we will have no choice but to reprimand him again. And go further if necessary."

"*No*," Byron shouted. "I will not permit you to threaten my son."

"Careful, Dominus. We don't have to remind you what happens to Dominii who defy us. The Cavern of Orcus could always use more help."

"I have served you dutifully for many years."

"Good. Then I hope you do not end up having to choose between your Aegis—"

"My *son*."

"Your *Aegis* and your duty."

"It won't come to that. Alex is just different."

"Your previous Aegis was *different* too. Perhaps it isn't the bloodline we should be concerned about. Perhaps *you* are the common thread."

"Just make sure your *son* is prepared to take your mantle soon, Dominus. We will not permit him to interfere with the balance of life and death."

"The Convergence is upon us, Dominus. The Quieting is coming. You and your Aegis must be ready at all times."

"How many will die in this Quieting?" Byron replied.

"Many. The spiritual turbulence will be mighty. You and your son will need all of your skills to ensure these souls are Exorted properly."

Byron took a deep breath. In his nearly ten decades as Dominus, Byron had served through dozens of Quietings. Each one full of loss and tragedy and pain. Whatever fate was in store for the people of Whisper Valley, it would be catastrophic.

"The next time we see you, Dominus," one of the seven said, "I hope it is as one of us."

Byron said, "When that day comes, my son will have already begun to carve out his legacy."

"Then go do your duty," one last voice said as the ghostly forms of the Conclave apparated back into the darkness, "my son."

---

When Byron returned to Marigold Lane, he knocked on Alex's door.

"Come in," Alex said. Byron entered. Alex was lying on his back, on his bed, his cell phone held above him as he tapped out a message. Comic books and graphic novels were strewn about the room haphazardly. "Hey, Dad. What's up?"

"Who are you texting with?"

Alex looked at him. "Do you want me to answer that?"

Byron walked over to the bed and sat down.

Alex sat up, surprised. "I don't remember you ever sitting on my bed. This must be bad. Did I forget to put away the milk this morning?"

"Enough jokes. Are you ready?" Byron said. "To take my place?"

"Why are you asking me this now?" Alex said.

"Because I just met with the Conclave. They're concerned."

"You met with them? And they told you that?"

"They did," Byron replied. "They don't care about explanations or rationale. They only care about the balance between life and death. They believe you're distracted. And that if you interfere in another Exortus, they have no qualms about making you suffer."

"Let me meet with them," Alex said. "Let me convince them I'm ready."

"An Aegis doesn't meet with the Conclave until they take the mantle except under extraordinary circumstances. Not even I met with them before I took over from my father."

"These aren't extraordinary circumstances?" Alex said.

"No," Byron said. "Not yet. Please keep it that way."

"I want to keep seeing her, Dad," Alex said. "As long as I do my job, it shouldn't matter."

"No, it shouldn't matter, but it does," Byron said, getting up from the bed. "I won't stop you from seeing her. But I will be watching to make sure the Conclave's concerns are unfounded."

"They are unfounded. I'm ready."

"Then you'll also need to be ready to say goodbye to her when the time comes."

"I can do both, Dad," Alex said. "I can be with her and do my duty."

"No. You cannot."

"And how would you know?"

But Byron had already closed the door behind him.

# 24

The upside to Nia living just down the street was that Alex didn't have a long walk home after kissing her good night. The downside was also that he didn't have a long walk home after kissing her good night.

They saw each other throughout the fall, meeting at their spot in the library during the day and gazing out atop Larrimore Hill in the evening. Nia had read *A Cold Winter's Night* in two days, apologizing for taking so long, blaming work and "family stuff."

She told him she'd fallen in love with the simple yet resonant story of the young boy Sam, forced to wander the white wilderness, the unseen monster a hair away from feasting on his flesh, and the parents who didn't realize they were pushing their son away until he was gone. She offered to return the book, but Alex refused. The story was hers now, he said, as much as it was his. In kind, he checked out reams of graphic novels and comic books from the library, stories of superheroes and adventure and distant planets, as well as smaller, quieter stories of love, loneliness, friendship, identity, and discovery. Then he would exuberantly text Nia nonstop about his discoveries like he was a kid who'd just learned about the existence of dinosaurs.

He would often see Iggy alone on the Molina front porch with red-rimmed eyes, beer in hand. They would wave, say they'd see each other at the bus stop, but otherwise pretend nothing was amiss. Iggy seemed to prefer the solitude. Alex wondered what was happening behind closed doors.

Most nights were spent alongside his father Exorting souls. He could feel his bonds with the Ankou intensifying. His powers were growing stronger. Despite his success, Alex's relationship with Byron was deteriorating. They barely spoke, and when they did, it was only about their work.

Every time he hung out with Nia, or saw Iggy, he tried not to think about the fact that his time in Whisper Valley would eventually come to an end. Because of that, he spent every moment he could with Nia. He'd wasted so much time over the years. He wanted to make up for it, to hold on to the kisses and laughter and small intimacies for as long as possible. He only had so many days to enjoy his life before his life became death.

One evening, walking home after a wonderful, drawn-out kiss in Nia's driveway, the taste of her ChapStick still on his lips, he saw Iggy sitting alone on his porch again, a drink in his hand. As Alex got closer, he could see that Iggy's cheeks were wet.

Alex stopped in front of the Molina driveway and said, "You okay, Ig?"

"Real answer or fake answer?"

"Real."

"Then no. Definitely not okay," Iggy said.

"Want to talk?"

Iggy seemed surprised by the offer. He smiled and said, "Sure. Pop a squat."

Iggy chugged the rest of his beer and tossed the bottle into a nearly full trash can. Alex took a seat. Iggy popped the top on a beer and handed it over. Alex took a swig and grimaced. It tasted like fermented Sour Patch Kids.

"Grapefruit shandy," Iggy said apologetically. "My dad finished all the good beer."

Alex shuddered as he drank. "At least I'm getting my daily dose of vitamin C."

"I admire your positivity," Iggy said. "You know, it's weird when you think about it."

"What's weird?"

"I mean, you live, like, twenty feet away from me and we see each other every day. But I really don't know anything about you. Or vice versa. I know you and your dad are basically nomads and you have a weird thing about foliage. And I know that Nia really likes you, which means you must be not be a total jerk because she's amazing. And I know that you seem to really like her back. But that's about it. We don't ever go deeper. For example, you can obviously see that I'm sitting here looking like I just poured a gallon of liquified onion onto my eyeballs. But you don't know why."

"So talk to me," Alex said. "Friends should be able to talk to each other about stuff. Big and small."

Iggy smiled. "I've never heard you say the word friend before."

"It has a lot of weight," Alex said. "I think that's why I've never said it. I've never been good with friends. Having them or keeping them. It's not that I didn't want to, but they were never a part of my life. Getting to know someone is permanent. And, well, our lives don't really have much room for permanency."

"Sounds like you've been dragged around your whole life without having much say in where you go," Iggy said. "Or who you spend time with."

"That's the understatement of the century," Alex said. He watched as Iggy drained his bottle, took out another, and popped the top. "Your folks don't care that you're drinking out in the open?"

Iggy made a *pssh* noise. "Doro uncorks her second bottle of Chardonnay by dinner. If I told her I was drinking a bottle of bleach, she'd just tell me not to use the good crystal."

"And your dad?" Alex said.

Iggy looked down. "Unless his girlfriend mentioned it to him, I doubt he'd even notice."

"His…girlfriend?" Alex said. "Oh man. Iggy. I'm sorry. I didn't know."

"It's actually better this way," Iggy said. "When my parents are under the same roof, it feels like there are two sticks of dynamite lit twenty-four seven and it's only a matter of time before they both go off. That's one of the benefits to training like a madman for track season. It gets me the hell out of the house."

"How long has it been going on?"

"A year? Two? Her name is Lisa. I think they met when she was his waitress at The Burger Barn, which is so cliché I want to vomit. He stays with her most nights, only comes home to get new clothes, check the mail, criticize me."

"Why don't your folks just get divorced?"

"Money. We don't have any, and if they split, they'd have to divide zero by two, which is mathematically impossible. Besides, I'm out of the house in a year and a half. It's harder on my sister since she's stuck with them another three years. We're both going to end up with so much in student loans we'll probably still be paying them from the grave."

"That really sucks. I'm sorry, Ig."

"Not to mention that when my dad *is* here, he rips my head off if I get any grades that begin with B-. Like he has any right to criticize me while he's off screwing a teenager. So to answer your original question: no. Doro doesn't give a rat's ass if I drink a few beers. Or eight beers. Anything to keep me out of her hair while she's on the phone complaining to her sister."

"To better days ahead," Alex said, holding out his beer.

Iggy smiled. "To better days." They clinked. "Your dad ever been married?"

Alex shook his head.

"I want to get married," Iggy said. "But not to anyone from Whisper Valley."

"What about Trevor?"

"Don't get me wrong, he's super hot and I do have a thing for swimmers. They have those crazy lat muscles that look like fins sticking out from their backs. But once I graduate, I want to wash my hands of this place. I'm sick of it. Know what I mean?"

"Not really. I've never stayed in one spot long enough to get sick of it."

Alex gestured at Iggy's eyes, which were still red and moist.

"Is this about your parents, or did something else happen tonight?"

"Something else," Iggy said. "This guy a few towns over. His name is Ellis. We hung out a bunch this summer and just kind of lost touch. It wasn't anything serious, but I just had one of those lonely nights where you text someone you probably shouldn't. Ellis texted me back to say that he was seeing someone and it was kind of serious and that I shouldn't text him anymore. I didn't think I'd care much, it's not like I was picturing our wedding, but for some reason it got to me. Hence the beers."

"I'm the last person in the world who should ever give out relationship advice," Alex said, "but I know enough to say that if Ellis doesn't want you, then he doesn't deserve you."

Iggy smiled at Alex, as though impressed. "Says the guy who's not good at giving relationship advice."

"If anything I say is worthwhile, it's a hundred percent sheer, dumb luck."

"On the bright side, if I'm single when I get to college, I'll be totally unencumbered to make some really terrible decisions."

"See? There's a silver lining in everything."

"Here's to making terrible decisions," Iggy said.

"To terrible decisions." They clinked again.

"So, what about you?" Iggy said.

"What about me what?"

"You and Nia. Seems like things are going pretty well."

Alex could feel his face reddening. "We're just hanging out."

"Hanging out," Iggy said, making air quotes with his fingers.

The flush had crept up Alex's cheeks and was probably now visible via satellite.

"I like her," Alex said. "A lot."

"That's obvious to anyone with eyes. Or ears. Or even a nose, since I could smell your cologne from inside a panic room on nights you two are *hanging out*," Iggy said. "Just tell me one thing. Are your intentions honorable?"

"Are they what?"

"Kidding. I always wanted to sound like a basic movie dad,"

Iggy said. Then he got serious, leaned forward and put his hand on Alex's shoulder. "You know by now that Nia is one of my absolute favorite people in the whole world."

"I know she is. Mine too."

"She likes you. A lot. She deserves to be happy. And I'm not just saying that as a platitude. *She deserves to be happy*."

"I hope I make her happy."

"You do. Just remember what I told you. Don't lead her on."

Alex paused. "Lead her on? That's the last thing I'd ever do."

"Maybe not intentionally. That girl has been through a *lot*. She's strong as a bull in a bulletproof vest, but being strong can also be absolutely exhausting."

"You're talking about her parents," Alex said.

"Have you met them?" Iggy said.

"No."

"Well, if you ever do, her dad will love you because you make his daughter happy and dads are pretty simple that way. Her mom will probably hate you."

"What? Why?"

"Because you're not sticking around," Iggy said. "And if Rivka Solomon knew her daughter loved a guy who wasn't going to be there for her long-term, she'd bury you in a shallow grave before letting her daughter get her heart broken. Have you and Nia talked about what's going to happen to you once you and your dad leave Whisper Valley?"

"How do you know we're not staying?"

"You said it yourself the first day we met. How many cities have you lived in? How many schools have you gone to? Let's be honest, you're not finishing high school at the Dubya V. Can you even say for sure you're going to finish the semester?"

"I can't," Alex said. "It's not up to me."

"Nia's dad will probably be gone within the year, if not sooner. Her mother's mind is long gone. Nia is the most loyal, loving person you'll ever meet. Anyone who hurts her deserves eternal damnation."

"I would never hurt her," Alex said.

"If you let her love you, and then leave, what would you call that?"

"I don't know. What if she came with me?"

"This isn't a fairy tale, Tree guy. Girls don't drop out of high school and abandon their sick parents to run away with some guy they met two months ago. Real life doesn't work like that. Nia is smart as hell. Hopefully, she'll get that mentorship and it'll open up some doors because the girl can draw better than I can breathe. But she shouldn't have to choose between having a life and having your life."

"I don't want to make her choose anything," Alex said. "I'm not that important."

"You're important to her," Iggy said. "Don't insult her by pretending you're not."

Alex nodded. "You're right."

Iggy took another sip. He was beginning to slur his words. "I'll bet she's already thought about what's going to happen when it's time for you to hit the road. Even if *you* haven't. Thankfully, she has people here who care about her."

"You're talking about you and James," Alex said. "Is that why he hates me? Was there something between him and Nia? Because it would explain why he's been a complete dick to me ever since I moved here."

"Nope. I know everybody likes a good love triangle, but it's not what you think. I mean, James is an asshole, and lord knows I've wished for terrible things to befall him. But he doesn't bat for the same team you do."

"Oh," Alex said. "I didn't know."

Iggy's eyes went wide. "Crap. Nobody's supposed to know. I swear, Alex, if you tell anyone—"

"Friends can trust each other, right?" Alex said. "I won't tell a soul. But how do *you* know?"

"How do you think, world's worst detective? James and I had a thing. Maybe we even *were* a thing."

"I didn't know that either."

"My friend, the things you don't know could fill a football

stadium. James and I made out after the homecoming party freshman year. I figured it would end there, but it didn't. It just kept going. God help me, I actually *fell* for the asshole."

Suddenly, James's demand to know what he and Iggy were talking about that first day made a whole lot more sense.

"You saw something in him other people didn't."

"I did," Iggy replied. "But it wasn't easy. He always insisted on meeting in super weird places, like abandoned factories, or by the railroad tracks, or, this one time, the middle of the woods. I didn't mind, though. The secrecy actually made it more fun. But one Saturday he invited me over to his house when his dad and teenaged stepmom were supposed to be gone for the weekend. And then they got back early and walked in to find us…"

Iggy trailed off. He took another sip.

"That Monday," Iggy continued, "James came in to school with a black eye. And suddenly this rumor starts going around that I got caught making out with Mr. Wyatt the music teacher, and Billy Wootens is running around calling me a skin flute player. Of course it was all a total lie. Billy got suspended, but it didn't matter. Mr. Wyatt left Dubya V. And there are still kids who mimic playing the flute if they pass me in the hall and no teachers are around."

"And you think James started that?"

"I *know* he did. That's what his father taught him to do. You embarrass the Mungros, they'll make you wish you'd never been born."

"You said Billy got suspended. What about James?"

"Nothing. Billy has always been too stupid to be clever. But James has a brain. Anyway, how do you prove how a rumor started? Dean planted this toxic seed in James that's just grown bigger and nastier over time. He's wanted James to be a cop ever since he was born. Carry on the family tradition. So when Dean saw the future chief of police on the couch with me, he wasn't going to stand for that." Iggy's voice grew angry. "James was the first guy I ever kissed. It meant something to me. I think it did to him, too, until…"

"You don't have to tell me all this," Alex said.

"I know," Iggy said. "But sometimes you have to tell *someone*, otherwise it just gets bottled up and turns into acid and eats you from the inside out. You know?"

"Not really," Alex said. "I'm sort of a pro at bottling things up."

Iggy laughed. "That's really not good for you."

"It took a while, but I'm starting to realize that. You know, it's funny. I came to Whisper Valley fully planning on minding my own business until it was time for us to leave. I was going to be totally incognito."

Iggy released a hearty laugh, followed by an even heartier burp. "And how's that going for you?"

"Pretty much a giant disaster," Alex said. He looked down at his beer. "I'm not so sure I want to leave this place."

"Well, whatever happens, wherever you end up, you'd better not repeat anything I've said to you tonight. Because I know where you live and I'm like a ninja, only faster and deadlier."

"I've always wanted to be friends with a ninja," Alex said. "So, I know I'm a little late, but are you still looking for a running partner?"

Iggy smiled. "Maybe."

"Because we've been eating way too much takeout from Leo's and I think my blood type is extra mozzarella."

"Then Alex my friend, you are a prime candidate for the Ignacio Molina fat-burning, ass-kicking, lose your dad bod fitness regimen," Iggy said.

"But I'm not a dad."

"Then no reason you should look like one," Iggy said. "Ooh, this is gonna be fun."

"As long as you promise not to leave me wheezing in a ditch somewhere."

"I make no promises. Meet me in front of my house tomorrow morning at five thirty. That's *a.m.* Running shoes, athletic socks, water bottle if you need one. Oh, and once we get you in shape for longer runs, Vaseline."

"Vaseline?"

"For your nipples. They're going to chafe against the inside of your shirt like crazy and the next time you take a hot shower it'll feel like someone hooked your nips up to a car battery."

"I literally have no words."

"Just be out here by five thirty. At five thirty-one, I'm gone."

"I'll be there."

Alex stood up to leave. Iggy got out of his chair and opened his arms wide.

"Come here," Iggy said. Alex took a step forward and found himself in an Iggy bear hug. "Friends gotta hug."

For some reason, the embrace broke something loose in Alex, and he wrapped his arms around his friend and held tight. When they disentangled, Iggy said, "Dude, are you…crying?"

"It's the pollen. Always gets to me this time of year."

Iggy smiled. "Sure it does. See you in the morning. Come ready to get your ass kicked."

"Can't wait. Thanks, Iggy. If you ever want to talk, you know where I live."

"Same here. See you tomorrow."

Alex walked home and watched Iggy go back inside. He liked this town. He liked caring for people who cared for him back. Whisper Valley had opened up a part of Alex, forcing him to use long-forgotten muscles, and it felt good. As he approached the front door, Alex looked up and saw his father standing at his bedroom window. Byron caught his son's gaze, held it, and then turned away.

# 25

Samael brought the glass to his nose and sniffed it. The glowing amber liquid smelled faintly like smoke and wood chips. He inhaled the aroma, deep and satisfying, then set the glass down on the table without taking a sip. He would taste the bourbon, in due time. Samael had drunk less than ten times in his life, so on the rare instances he did imbibe, he preferred to take his time, to savor the flavors. And tonight, Samael had much to savor.

The motel room Samael was staying in cost seventy-nine dollars a day. There were fancier, more luxurious options, but the more you paid for a room, the more the hotel's staff would dote on you. Remember you. Luxury hotels kept better security records. Samael preferred a hotel where the pimply staff kept their noses buried in their cell phones.

He sat at a cheap plywood desk upon which he had laid out dozens of photographs, schematics, emails, texts, and even flight records. He smiled. The Children of Azrael had outdone themselves.

As Samael put the glass to his lips, finally ready to savor his drink, there was a knock at the door. He put the glass down and opened the door.

"Morton," Samael said, "it's good to see you."

Samael shook his friend's hand. Morton Yen's grip was firmer than usual, and he did not return the smile.

"I wish I could say the same, Samael." Morton took a seat on the sofa and crossed his legs. He looked around the room, fixating on a strange brown stain by the boxy television. "You certainly didn't spring for opulence."

"Certain situations require a sacrifice in luxury," Samael said. "Though I do miss my fifteen hundred thread count Egyptian cotton sheets. I wasn't expecting you until tomorrow, Morton. Is everything alright?"

"You tell me, Samael." Morton stood up and went over to the desk. He spread the papers around, perusing each one. "Our people have done their work well for you."

"They have. And I'm grateful, as always." Samael eyed Morton. He had known the man for years. It was not like him to show up unannounced, and he could tell there was something off about his demeanor. "Why did you come here tonight, Morton?"

"Tell me everything you've found," Morton said. "I only saw bits and pieces of what my people collected. But it appears you've fit those pieces together."

"I believe I have," Samael said. He picked up a piece of paper and held it out to Morton. "I tasked our people with finding the birth certificate of a man named Byron Sonnum. Did you know what they found?"

"I do not."

"Nothing, Morton. They found *nothing*. At least nothing real."

Morton sat back. "Go on."

"Byron Sonnum has had many birth certificates over the years, but our people are well-versed at spotting forgeries. There is no official birth record at all for Byron Sonnum."

"There can be explanations for that," Morton said.

"Perhaps," Samael replied. He handed Morton a photo printout. "This is an undated photo of Byron Sonnum which our people found in a historical archive using facial recognition software. Based on the architecture and burned-out buildings, the photo appears to have been taken in the Netherlands shortly after the Rotterdam Blitz. Look at the eyes. The face. Now look at this."

Samael opened the Photos app on his phone and scrolled to a candid picture of a man entering an unremarkable home with the number 72 above the doorway.

"This is a photograph of Byron Sonnum. Taken *two days ago* outside the house he and his son are currently renting on Marigold Lane *right here* in Whisper Valley. These photos are of the same man. I moisturize every day, but even I would not look this good at his age. I believe that Byron Sonnum is Death."

Morton looked at Samael, then examined both the Rotterdam photo and the one on Samael's phone.

"It appears to be the same man." Morton's voice was impressed, but also reserved. Samael knew he and Morton had been down this path before, only to have their quarry vanish. "How did you come upon this man, Byron Sonnum?"

"Through his son," Samael said.

"His son?" Morton said, confused.

Samael pulled up another picture on his phone. It showed a teenage boy standing with a young woman in a bookshop. "That boy's name is Alex Sonnum. He is Byron Sonnum's son. Our people compiled flight manifests and property records dating back nearly thirty years. I can match Byron Sonnum's travels to dozens of catastrophes all over the globe. Do you know where Byron Sonnum was living twenty years ago, when my family's plane went down?"

"Where?" Morton said.

"In a town fifteen minutes away from the beach where I washed up. He was *there*, Morton. He *knew* that plane was going down because he was the one who caused it."

"Why would Death need to live anywhere?" Morton said.

"The best disguise is hiding in plain sight," Samael said. "By coming off as a normal man. A normal father. People don't ask questions if they assume you're one of them."

Morton thought for a moment. "Who is the girl in the bookshop with Alex Sonnum?" Morton said. "Death's daughter?"

Samael shook his head. "Her name is Nia Solomon. I believe she is Alex's girlfriend. She is inconsequential for our matters."

Samael told Morton about his conversations with James Mungro. About the car crash. He showed him the video of the fight in the library. Samael grew excited as he spoke, and watched Morton's reaction intensely. Morton Yen was not a man who displayed his emotions haphazardly, but even Samael could see a smile tightening at the corners of the man's lips.

Morton looked up at Samael and said, "You really think this is it? That this man Byron Sonnum is…him?"

"I think so, my friend. I believe Byron Sonnum does not have a birth certificate because he was never actually born."

"Then why does Death need a son?" Morton said.

"Several years ago, I spoke to a woman who had survived a train wreck outside of Istanbul. She said she had seen a strange man, accompanied by a young boy. I believe that man was Byron Sonnum, and that boy was Alex. I believe Alex Sonnum is Death's heir. Look at this."

He showed Morton more photos. The pictures showed Alex Sonnum and Nia Solomon entering a darkened home through a window.

"That house is located at 23 Vine Street in Whisper Valley. According to local urban legend, the house is haunted by a woman named Millicent Adams. In general, I don't believe in haunted houses any more than I believe in aliens or breakfast buffets, but Alex Sonnum went there for a reason. Some urban legends, as we know, are based on a kernel of truth. I believe Alex Sonnum went to that house because he knew this legend is true. Because he has a connection to the dead. Just like his father."

"These photos at the house and the bookstore—you took them yourself?"

"I did."

"It seems beneath you to be following teenagers around, Samael."

"You're going to lecture me on ethics while your people dug up enough information to put Dean Mungro in jail for a decade?"

Samael said. "Besides, when it comes to finding Death, getting your hands dirty is a necessity."

"Your hands seem to be dirtier now than they have in the past, Samael," Morton said.

"That's only because you haven't been paying attention, Morton," Samael replied.

Morton sat down on the couch. He took off his glasses and rubbed the bridge of his nose. "Even if all of this is true, Samael, and after all these years we have finally found Death himself, here's one thing I don't understand."

"What's that my friend?"

"You seem obsessed with not just Byron Sonnum, but his son. Why?"

Samael smiled. "I do suppose Death's family is somewhat relevant to my mission."

"You mean *our* mission, Samael," Morton said.

"Yes. Our mission. Of course."

"The Children of Azrael have spent years, untold hours, and a great deal of money to aid your efforts to find Death," Morton said. "We have hacked into untold databases to provide you with confidential information. We have spent the GDP of a small nation to uncover the secrets of Death because we, like you, are fascinated by the truths we might uncover. What it could mean for the future of science and theology. Our goals have always been to *learn* about Death, Samael. This talk about getting your hands dirty. The surreptitious photographs of those children. Your plans no longer seem to be about merely uncovering Death's secrets."

"You're right," Samael said. "I'm less interested in discovery and more interested in retribution."

Morton's eyes widened. "Retribution? What are you talking about?"

Samael stood up. He went to the window and looked outside. Rain had begun to spatter against the glass. Lightning shot down from the sky many miles away, and soon after that, a crack of thunder loud enough to make Morton jump ever so slightly. Samael did not flinch.

"You have been a good friend for a long time, Morton. And I appreciate everything you and the Children of Azrael have done. I never would have gotten this far without you. But there's one thing about which you are mistaken."

"Which is?" Morton said.

"Our goals were never the same," Samael said. "You and the COA wanted to find Death to study him. Learn from him. My goal, my *only* goal, Morton, has been to make Death suffer for what he did to me."

"Those are not the words of the man I've known for years," Morton said.

"You are correct. They are the words of the man you *thought* you knew for years," Samael said. "Death is not the only one who keeps secrets, yujin."

Morton went back to the desk. He picked up a sheaf of papers.

"This is madness," Morton said. He looked at a receipt. "What are these blueprints? And what in God's name are you planning to do with liquid hydrogen?"

"Even the scales, my friend."

"My people did not obtain any of this for you," Morton said. "Where did you get it?"

"To obtain certain items over the years, I have needed the assistance of the Children of Azrael," Samael replied. "Others, I'm quite capable of getting myself."

"So your plan is what, exactly? To *kill* Death? Samael, you've lost your damn mind."

"You have me all wrong, Morton. To make a man suffer, *truly* suffer, you don't kill him." Samael held up a photo of Alex Sonnum from the bookstore. "You tear out his heart."

"You're insane," Morton said. "It is clear you mean to harm people."

"I'm doing what I should have done from the very beginning. I should never have tried to chase down Death. I should have made Death come to *me*."

"You should be locked up, Samael. I have no choice but to contact the authorities."

Samael knelt down and placed his hand on Morton's arm, looked him in the eye, and said, "I'm asking you, as a friend, Morton, a friend of many years, not to do that."

Morton pulled away. "You give me no choice. From this point on, consider yourself cut off. You've gone too far."

Morton took one of the pages from the desk and went to the door.

"No, my friend," Samael said, "I haven't gone nearly far enough."

When Morton reached for the doorknob, Samael slid the blade into the back of his neck so fast the man felt nothing more than a slight pinch before he died.

The piece of paper Morton held fluttered to the floor, landing in the pool of spreading blood beneath him. In large, bubble lettering, it read WHISPER VALLEY SCHOOL CALENDAR.

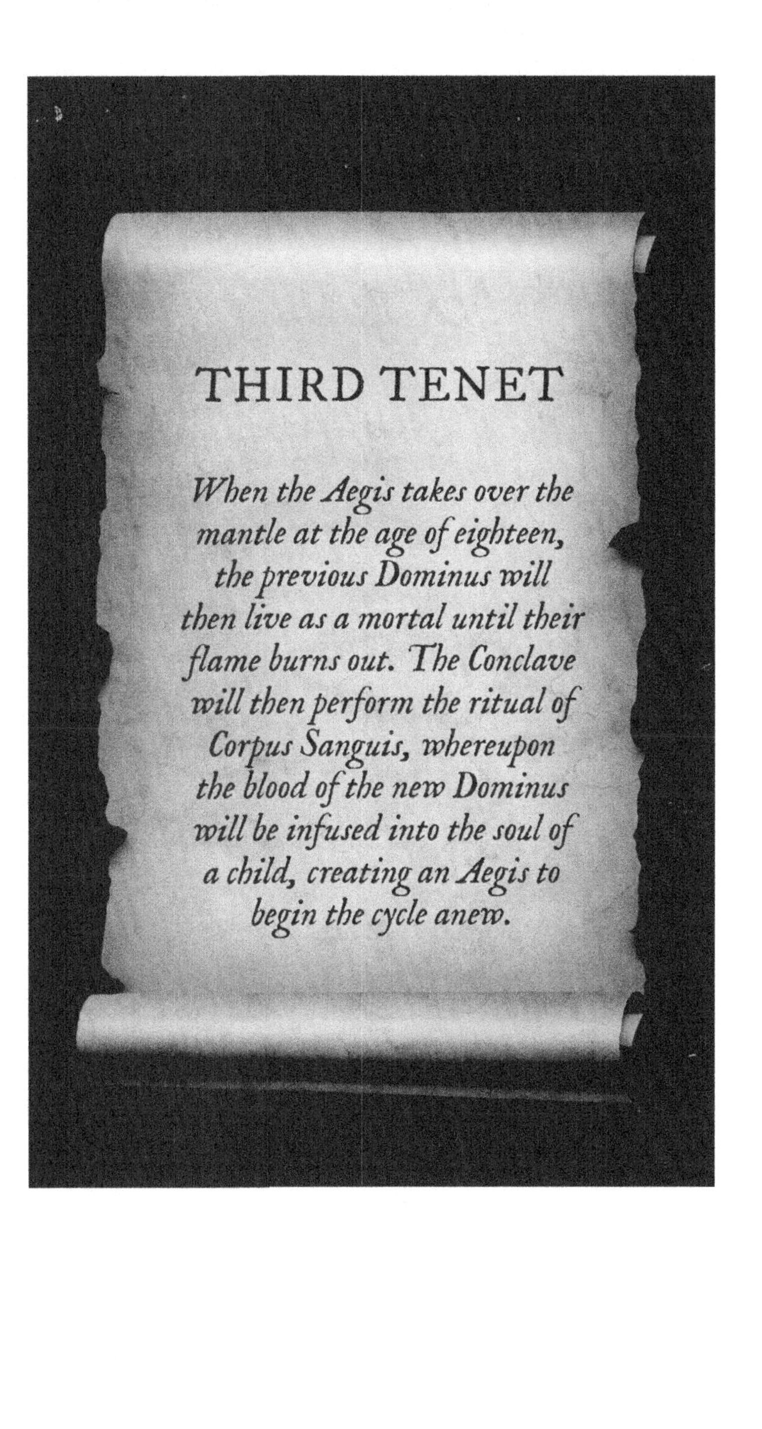
THIRD TENET
When the Aegis takes over the
mantle at the age of eighteen,
the previous Dominus will
then live as a mortal until their
flame burns out. The Conclave
will then perform the ritual of
Corpus Sanguis, whereupon
the blood of the new Dominus
will be infused into the soul of
a child, creating an Aegis to
begin the cycle anew.

# 26

When James heard the knock at the door, his breath caught in his throat.

"Who is—?"

Dean came in without waiting for James to finish the question. James bookmarked his Spanish textbook and turned around slowly. His father *never* came into his room at night. Not unless there was something wrong.

His father had softened over the years, but still had an iron grip that left marks on skin. Nine times out of ten, his rage was unavoidable. Occasionally, James was able to talk his way out of whatever punishment—warranted or unwarranted—awaited. He couldn't think of anything he'd done that day, but James also knew it didn't really matter. If his father was in the wrong mood, James would need three Advil, a shot of vodka, and an ice pack before bed.

But when Dean came into the room, James saw something he didn't recognize. His father's shoulders were hunched over and there was a look in his eyes that, in any other person, James would have recognized as…sadness? Seeing his father displaying even a hint of melancholy was unnerving. Because if there was one thing Dean was good at, it was reversing his feelings, turning sadness into anger, and projecting it outward. When bad things happened to Dean, it meant worse things for James.

Dean took a seat on James's bed. His father's eyes were red. He knew better than to ask his father if he was upset about something. He might as well sign his own death warrant.

"How you doin', kiddo?" Dean said. *Kiddo*. James hadn't been called that in a long, long time. It was an artificial term of endearment. James wondered what shoe was about to drop.

"I'm okay. Just working."

"What are you working on?"

"Spanish," James said. He showed him the textbook, in case his father had any doubts.

"Spanish," Dean said dismissively. "How exactly does learning Spanish serve you in the real world?"

"Maybe I'll study abroad in Barcelona. Or do business with a company in Guadalajara or Mexico City. Maybe once I'm on the force it'll help me communicate better with other officers or even witnesses and suspects. There are a million practical applications."

"We have people on the force who speak it so you don't have to," Dean said, "so that you don't end up wasting time on something totally useless. Meanwhile, I doubt you've even cracked the *Police Officer's Handbook*, which I gave you how many years ago? But you know what? That's a conversation for another time. That's not why I wanted to talk to you."

"Why did you want to talk to me?"

Dean stood up. He paced around the room slowly, like a lion surveying a herd of antelope. He perused the photos and plaques adorning his son's walls. He picked up a frame from James's desk and ran his fingers over the glass.

"I remember taking that picture of you and your mother," Dean said, surprised. The frame had sat on James's desk for the last several years, but this was apparently the first time Dean noticed it. "Do you ever talk to her?"

"Sometimes," James said. The truth was they emailed nearly every day. But he didn't want his father to know that.

Dean nodded. "Guess I can't really tell you to get rid of it, now can I?"

"Please don't," James said.

Dean smiled and put the frame back. "Suppose I can let it slide. Listen. I don't know how else to say this, so I'll just say it. Lillian is leaving."

"Leaving? Like, she's going out?"

"No. She's leaving me."

"Leaving you…holy crap, Dad, you lost another one?"

"Don't be a such a smartass," Dean said with enough anger in his voice to make James slide his chair backward. "Anyway, yes. She's going."

"Should I say goodbye?"

"She's already checked into a hotel. I suppose you can text her if you want. But she'll probably want some time to herself."

James nodded. "Can I ask why?"

"Some people just can't take criticism," Dean said. "The things I say to her, they're for her own good. If she's too dense to understand that, it's her problem. So it's just gonna be me and you, kiddo."

*Until you find some new twenty-three-year-old willing to sign the world's most ironclad prenup*, he thought.

Dean got up to leave. "Just figured you should know. So when you come down for breakfast tomorrow and she's not there you'll know why."

"Thanks for telling me."

Dean gripped the doorknob, but then he turned back to face James. "I meant to ask you. That guy that came to our house. The freak who wanted to talk to you alone. Have you heard from him since?"

James felt his blood turn to ice. "No," James said. "Like I told you, he was some private investigator digging up dirt on that kid Alex Sonnum and his dad. Alex is the one who assaulted me in the caf that day. His dad apparently owes some people money and that's why they move around so much. He knows cops and PIs don't always get along, which is why he was such a hardass to you."

"I ran a background check on the Sonnums after the crash," Dean replied, mulling over the words like a piece of food he couldn't decide was rancid or not. "It was strange. I couldn't find anything."

"Hence the PI," James said. "This guy probably goes outside the law to dig up dirt."

"Pretty far outside the law, considering the stuff he told me," Dean said. He took a step toward his son. "That man knew things about me, about us, that could be very damaging. You answer me, right now. Have you seen him since then? And god help you if you lie to me."

"I haven't seen him. I swear on Mom."

Dean seemed to soften. They both knew James did not bring up his mother lightly.

"I need to ask. Not as a cop, but as your father. Are you and that man…?"

"No, Dad. I'd never seen the guy in my life before that night."

Dean scratched the back of his head, as though trying to solve a particularly difficult puzzle. "He just wanted to know about the Sonnum kid. You're *positive*?"

"I would never lie to you," James said solemnly.

"Because I'll never be able to get rid of that image of you and that…*boy*. In my home. You know the one. Antonio or something."

"Ignacio," James said.

"Whatever. I'm not a praying man, and I despise laying my hands on my own son, but I prayed that night that you learned a lesson. You'll see this when you get older and marry a good woman and have your own family, but the most important lessons are the ones that are the hardest to teach. You think I'm hard on you, kiddo, well, you have no idea what life has in store."

James sensed that same anger he'd felt toward his father so many times over the years rising once again. He'd tossed James's mother out of the house with nothing, leaving James a raw, unsheathed nerve ending, ready to flare up whenever it was touched.

"I learned my lesson," James said. Just like he always said he did.

He could practically see Dean's blood pressure lower as the red drained from his face.

Dean breathed out. He nodded slowly. "Alright," he said. "You might not know it, but I'm *helping* you. You can't go through life soft, because people will hit you hard. If you're going to make anything of yourself, people need to fear what you're capable of."

"That's one lesson you taught me well."

Dean smiled. "I'm glad. Now if that man comes back, you tell me. *Immediately*."

"I will. And, Dad?"

"Yes, James?"

"I'm sorry about Lillian. I liked her."

Dean snorted a laugh. "You know, I'm not all that sorry. I think I wanted to like her more than I actually liked her. I didn't think she'd be so…difficult. So I'm glad it's over. Next time, I'll be more careful. Just remember that while you're slipping a ring on a woman's left hand, she might be trying to open up your wallet with her right."

"I'll remember."

"Good. See you in the morning." Dean closed the door.

James sat there for several minutes, waiting to see if his father would come back. Then his cell phone chimed with an incoming text. The ID on the screen read Billy Wootens. Dean knew Billy. He liked Billy. Maybe more than he did James. If a text came in from him while Dean was present, his father wouldn't think twice. Which is why he'd assigned Samael Zagan's number to Billy Wootens.

**You've outdone yourself, James. The County Clerk didn't give you any trouble when you asked for the files?**

**Nope. Told her I needed the blueprints because I was making a diorama. People love stupid dioramas.**

**That is quick thinking. You have a sharp mind. People underestimate you.**

James smiled. He'd always thought that. It felt good to hear someone actually say it.

**Thank you.**

**You have the mind. Now just have the patience. We're**

**almost there. And I promise you, our mutual friend will think twice before ever bothering you again. Fear is a powerful weapon.**

**I know it. If there's one thing I've learned, it's that if people cross you, you need to make them fear you.**

**They will, James. I promise you that they will.**

# 27

Nia saw Iggy delicately balancing a grilled cheese, corn on the cob, and bottle of water on his tray as he exited the cafeteria line. She was eating alone, a forkful of salad in one hand and a worn paperback book in the other. She waved him over and slid a folded piece of loose-leaf paper into the book to hold her place.

Iggy took a seat across from Nia and tore off a bite of his grilled cheese. "Weird not seeing you with a sketchbook open in front of you."

"It's in my bag taking a bit of a break while I read. How's the grilled cheese?"

"You know, it's actually not terrible. They may have even used real cheese today," Iggy said.

"Will wonders never cease. So, has Alex been surviving your morning runs?"

"For the most part. The first day, he made it almost a whole mile before he hacked up a lung. But he's working hard and making progress."

"Well, please don't kill Alex," Nia said. "I kind of like him."

"He did swallow a bug the other day."

"That's disgusting. Did you get it out?"

"Get it out? He *swallowed* it. There's no getting it out. I just told him it's good luck and to let people know if he feels anything crawling around his intestines."

"Thank you for ruining my lunch."

"I wouldn't worry about him. I get the feeling Alex is tougher than he lets on. One of those guys you'd want in your camp during the zombie apocalypse," Iggy said. "We did two and a half miles this morning, and at a not-super embarrassing pace. He can almost hold a conversation now while we run. Another year working with me and he'd have a shot at track. He's pretty tall, and our best hundred meter guy is graduating this year."

Nia ignored the comment.

"So, whatcha reading?" he asked. Nia held up the book and showed Iggy the cover. "*A Cold Winter's Night.* Sounds like the kind of book that would be perfect with a cup of hot chocolate and a roaring fireplace."

"It's not so bad with a glass of iced tea and a bowl of soggy salad," she said.

"How many times have you read it? It looks like the pages are about to fall out."

"My second time," Nia said. "Alex gave it to me. He's read it a thousand times. Hence the binding that looks like wet cardboard."

Iggy nodded. "From Alex, huh? *Timeo Danaos et dona ferentes*."

"Tell me, Cicero, what does that mean?"

"Virgil, actually. Roughly translated, 'Beware the Greeks, even when they bring gifts.'"

Nia put the book down. "Okay, now what the hell is *that* supposed to mean?"

"Come on, Nia," he said.

"Come on what? I'm not in the mood for games."

Iggy sighed and sipped his drink. "Okay. First off, let me say that I like Alex. A lot. And I don't say that lightly because I've let you know when your judgement has been, well, faulty."

"I feel like there's a *but* coming up."

"Okay. Storytime. Just bear with me. Two years ago, I met this guy. Simon. He was a freshman in college and home for the summer. We met at a bonfire, made out a little, and actually hit it off. We spent practically every day together that summer. As soon as I got off work at the movie theater, I'd go right to his place. I went *fishing* with him. And I *hate* fishing."

"I don't even think I've ever seen you eat fish, let alone fish fish."

"See? So, August comes and Simon is getting ready to head back to college. But somehow we're still going. I figure we'll eventually have the talk. You know, about how we're going to do the long-distance thing, pick weekends where I'd come visit and vice versa. The kind of talk you hate and look forward to. 'Cause on one hand it means you're not going to see each other very often, but the fact that you're even having it means you want to make it work. So a week before Simon goes back to school, we go bowling. He rolls a one seventy-something and I don't even think I break a hundred. I mean, he's even good at *bowling*, but that's beside the point. We went back to his place, and after we made out a bit, I put on this green sweatshirt he had lying around. It was a ratty old thing, but it smelled like him so I didn't care."

"Gross, but okay," Nia said.

"When I go to leave, I start to take the sweatshirt off, but Simon says no, I should keep it. It's his favorite sweatshirt but he wants me to have it. My heart nearly burst. I went home that night thinking I'm going take the sweatshirt with me when I go to college, wear it twenty-four seven, tell all my friends it's my boyfriend's, all that mushy shit. And then the next day, Simon texts me that it's over."

"No, he didn't."

"Oh, yes. Turned out Simon wasn't a big fan of the long-distance thing. I guess the sweatshirt was my consolation prize."

"What'd you do with it?"

"I kept it for a week, hoping Simon would change his mind. Then I texted him asking if he wanted it back and it took him three days to respond. He said, *Sorry, busy. ttys.* So that afternoon I drove to the dump and tossed it into a bin full of smelly crap where it belonged."

"I'm so sorry, Ig. That really sucks. Did you ever hear from him again?"

"Nope. I occasionally stalk him on Facebook and Insta. I think he's dating some Norwegian douchebag who looks like a six-foot-five mashed potato."

"So what you're actually saying, only it took you much, much longer to say it, is that because Alex gave me this book, he's planning to end it. Am I right?"

"I'm just saying that sometimes we give things meaning that they haven't earned. That the intentions of whoever gave it might be very different from what we think they are."

"I know Alex giving me this book meant something."

"I wanted so badly to believe that sweatshirt meant something too," Iggy said. "But maybe you're right. Alex does seem like one of the few non-terrible dudes at this school—present company excluded. But you know his deal. He's been enrolled in, what, ninety-eight schools? Do you think Whisper Valley is his last stop? Have you had the talk with him about what happens when he leaves?"

"No," she said.

"Alex and his dad don't stick around. They keep moving. And I still think they might be in witness protection."

"They're not in witness protection," Nia said.

"How do you know?"

"Just, trust me, Ig. They're not."

"Fine. Obviously, you know more about Alex than I do."

"Matter of fact, I do," she said.

Iggy pointed at the book. "At least your book doesn't smell like sweaty teenage boy."

Nia laughed. "Given how much time this book has spent with Alex, it just might."

"As long as your teenage boy smells better than mine did," Iggy said. "Look, I'm only saying this because I'm worried."

"About what?"

"You, stupid."

"Don't be," Nia said. "I know Alex better than anyone. I know his heart. And aren't you Alex's friend? Or have you just been pretending?"

"He *is* my friend," Iggy said, "but you've been my friend longer. Sure, perfect world we all go off to college and text all the time and hang out during Christmas break and bitch about our professors and the hunky RA on my hall I'll undoubtedly crush on. But there's something up with Alex. I know it, and you know it. Even if you don't want to talk about it."

"If I'm not talking about it," Nia said, "maybe there's a reason for it."

"Listen," Iggy said, "you have enough to deal with these days. I'm just looking out for you."

"And I'm dealing with all of it," Nia said. "At least the best I can."

"I can't say I've ever gone through what you're going through, but it's gotta be absolutely brutal to deal with given everything on your plate at home."

"It is," Nia said, "and Alex has helped take my mind off of it all. Not in a way that distracts me. In a way that lets me know that, I don't know, there's still happiness out there to be found, I guess."

"That does count for something," Iggy said. "Speaking of things on your plate, when do you hear about the mentorship in Austin?"

Nia sighed. "Soon? I hope? My luck, I'll get turned down the day of the Fall Ball and have to pretend to want to dance."

"I bet you get in," he said. "I know how talented you are."

"You should be my therapist," Nia said. "Whatever this is with Alex, I'm happier now than I was before I met him. He's not going to fix me. And that's not his responsibility. But spending time with him takes my mind off of things, even if it's just for a little while. And right now, that's more than enough."

"Do you love him?" he asked.

"I don't know. Maybe. Maybe I'm afraid to say yes."

"Look, I don't know what you and Alex talk about behind closed doors," Iggy said. "And for all I know, it's real. I *hope* it's real, because, hell, we could all use some good things happening to us. Plus, I'm pretty sure my romantic judgment radar was broken at birth. But I love you, Nia, and don't want to see you get hurt by giving your heart to someone who leaves you with nothing but a…"

"Sweatshirt."

Iggy nodded.

"Thank for looking out for me, Ig. In the meantime, please don't break Alex."

Iggy laughed. "I don't think he breaks all that easily."

"Neither do I."

# 28

That stupid sweatshirt. Nia couldn't get it out of her head. She never realized she could despise a piece of outerwear so much. She decided to walk home after school. Clear her mind. Think about what Iggy had said.

Nia had been in two and a half relationships, and at the risk of sounding clichéd, everything about Alex felt different—his freaky powers notwithstanding. She'd had two and a half boyfriends before Alex: Albert Hawkins in seventh grade (to the extent that you could really have a boyfriend in seventh grade), Justin Perlmutter freshman year…and Dimitri Florakis.

She met Dimitri the summer before sophomore year. He went to Caldecott High, he was cute and smart and a good kisser, and he never hesitated to hold her hand when they were together. And during the really bad times, when her parents were getting worse, even though she didn't think she loved Dimitri, that simple, human connection was often the only thing that kept her from falling apart.

That fall, her father's cancer spread. The doctors didn't think he'd make it another year. At the same time, her mother was diagnosed with stage two Alzheimer's. Nia had to stay strong for them. Every ounce of her energy was focused on people besides herself. Every day Nia woke up feeling like she was drowning, waiting, hoping, *praying* someone would help her too. Some days, she wondered whether it would be easier if she just let herself sink

So when Dimitri broke it off ("You just seem down all the time and that's not really fun"), Nia crumbled. It wasn't that she loved him. But Dimitri was a life preserver suddenly taken away and she was tired of treading water. Tired of being angry at the world for dealing her such an awful hand. Maybe it would be easier to sink rather than swim.

So, one night, she drove her parents' car to Larrimore Hill, parked, then leaned up against the wobbly fence, almost hoping it would buckle and save her from having to make the decision. She could hear the metal creaking and then, just before her world ended at the bottom of a ravine, she thought, *I don't want this.* There was only person who could understand. Who had been through this and chosen to live. Who could help pull her back from the edge.

Nia texted James Mungro.

*At LH. Help.*

She had been there for him. She prayed he would drop whatever he was doing to be there for her.

And he did.

James arrived at Larrimore Hill ten minutes later. His Mercedes had barely come to a stop before he ran up to her, took her hand, and pulled her back. She fell into him and they cried together, sobs coming in huge, crashing waves. James stood there, holding her. He ran his hand through her hair, and said, "You pull me back, I pull you back."

Like Nia, James also knew that depression was not a battle. It wasn't as if you vanquished your enemy and found peace. There was no permanent victory. A win one day only meant its armies would return, stronger than before, ready to fight you all over again.

She appreciated that James did not spew sugary platitudes like *everything is going to be okay*. Because neither of them knew for sure. And it was because of that moment atop the hill that there was a bond between them, no matter how thin it had been stretched, that would never break. They'd seen each other at their lowest. And so for all the things James had done, Nia always thought back to what he did for her that night. That if not for him, her father may have spent his final months alone.

But James was not Alex. He could never be Alex—for a lot of reasons. On one hand, Alex seemed like a normal guy. A *nice* guy. The kind of guy who would make her feel less alone because he, too, was alone and they could fill that aching need for each other. But there was the other side of him. The side she wouldn't have believed if she hadn't seen it with her own eyes. The side that had seen things, done things, that were beyond comprehension. How could death coexist with life?

Nia didn't know the answers to any of it. All she knew was that when she was with Alex, when she was held by him, felt his lips on hers, his skin on hers, all the obstacles and responsibilities and bad thoughts fell away and she felt…

In love.

There it was. The bell that could never be un-rung. The words that, even if she hadn't said them to Alex—yet—were in her heart.

Nia could think of a thousand things that had been holding her back, but none that had been pushing her. Between caring for her parents and the depression that felt like a truck on her chest pushing the breath from her lungs, Nia had never really stopped to think about what her future might look like. *Could* be like. Her life was a constant *now*, with no *then.*

For the first time, Nia's dreams felt like more than just illustrations on a page. There *was* a world out there. But her obligations and responsibilities still felt like weights tied to her ankles. Right now, not drowning was the best she could do. She cared about Alex. Deeply. But she needed to help herself first. Alex could not be her life preserver.

She was enjoying the exercise and solitude. She got too little of either one. The sun had begun to dip below the horizon, rich, golden rays stretching for miles. The day nurse would be there to take care of her parents for another two hours. It was a perfect night to keep to herself.

She passed by a bus stop and saw her reflection in the glass. Her skin was slightly flushed, her curly hair damp and clinging to her neck and shoulders. She smiled.

*I look cute.*

She laughed out loud. It was such a corny thing to think. But before she could overthink it, she took out her cell phone, snapped a selfie, and texted it to Alex.

*You make me smile.*

Alex wasn't there to be her life preserver. But he could be there to make her smile, feel good about herself when she needed it, feel the warmth in his arms when she desired it. She kept walking, eyes glued to the screen.

She didn't have to wait long.

Less than a minute later, she received a text back. There were no words. Just a picture of Alex, taken in what appeared to be his bedroom, with his phone held at a strange, unflattering angle with bad lighting. He had a crooked smile and bleary, tired eyes. Her heart sang.

She wrote back.

**You haven't taken many selfies, have you?**

**Was it that bad?**

**I plead the fifth. I like that you don't know what you're doing but you do it anyway.**

**I definitely don't know what I'm doing.**

**That's okay. It's still a cute pic. BTW Iggy told me you're ready for the Olympics.**

**Oh totally. If there's an Olympics for the cardiovascularly challenged I'd be internationally ranked. I hurt in places I didn't even know I had places.**

**Pain is temporary. Pride is permanent.**

**You stole that from a deodorant commercial, didn't you?**

**I might have.**

**Well, it feels good to use my body for something other than saving guys who try to run me off the road.**

**That's not entirely true. You do use your body for other things.** 😉

Nia watched as the dreaded three dots blinked for what seemed like an eternity. Then a new text popped up.

**I'm pretty sure there's an emoji for blushing but I'm not sure where it is.**

**Don't worry. I'd rather picture you blushing.**

**Just pretend I sent you a kissy face. Actually don't. Pretend I sent you some combination that's both witty and profound. Like an alien, a syringe, and the Norwegian flag.**

**A ghost or fire seems more appropriate. Almost home. See you soon, Alex.** 😘

**See you soon, Nia.** 🇳🇴

She laughed, put her phone away, put her earbuds in, and listened to the rest of an episode of *The Creative Brain* featuring a comics illustrator named Artis Moore whose work she admired. When she got home, she could hear the vacuum cleaner running upstairs and could smell fresh-roasted coffee and lemon Pledge. Nia wondered what it would be like to live in a house that didn't constantly smell like Arabica and sound like a Dyson showroom.

She went upstairs and changed into a pair of sweats and a t-shirt. She looked at the picture Alex had sent and smiled. She put her phone on silent, took a deep breath, and went into her parents' bedroom.

For all the complaints she might have about her house smelling like coffee and cleaning supplies, it was better than the bitter, acrid smell of antiseptic or the mildewed scent of illness. The television was playing on a low volume and her father was propped up in bed watching an episode of *Law & Order*. Two pillows supported his back, another one his head. She tried to remember him without all the tubes, with another fifty pounds on his bones, more hair on his head, and more color in his skin.

"They think this poor schmuck is the one who killed the girl," her father said, his words coming out in bursts between breaths, "but it's too early in the episode for them to have found the real killer. He's just a red herring."

"Isn't every episode basically the same?" Nia asked.

Her father shrugged, at least to the best of his ability. "I can leave it on and turn my brain off. There's something to be said for a story that wraps up all neat and tidy at the end. No loose threads. I can close my eyes and not wonder what happens next because it doesn't really matter."

Nia went to the side of his bed and knelt down. She put her hand into his, still not used to the tissue paper feeling of his skin, the rail-thin arms she used to believe could bend steel and carry her not just to bed at night, but to the ends of the earth. Her father closed his hand around hers and squeezed gently. She wanted him to squeeze *hard*, to grip her so tight she could feel her bones grinding together.

"So how was your day?" her father said, craning his neck to see her.

She sighed.

"That good, huh? Anything I can do to help? Someone you want me to beat up?"

Nia laughed and gazed adoringly at her dad. "I can't believe you're asking *me* how *you* can help. I always feel like I'm failing *you*."

"There are a lot of things failing me right now," her father said. "Unfortunately, they're all inside me. You haven't let me down since the day you were born."

"That's not true," Nia said. "You just don't know everything."

"Then tell me," he said.

Nia shook her head. "I can't put more on you."

"You're a woman, Nia, so I can talk to you—father to daughter. We both know I'm not going to be here much longer. I want every remaining breathe I have to count. And I don't want to go with any regrets. Or any secrets between us. I think I deserve that."

"You do," she said.

"Glad we're in agreement. So talk to me. What's on your mind?"

She took a deep breath and said, "I met someone."

A grin blossomed on her father's face, and the sight of it filled Nia's heart to bursting.

"I had a feeling," he said. "You've been smiling a lot more lately. Go on. Tell me about this someone."

"Do you really want to hear this?"

"If you don't start talking right now, I will leap out of this bed and lock you inside this room until you tell me."

"And I know you would," she said. "He's new."

"To what. The earth?"

She laughed. "No, to school. He and his dad just moved here at the beginning of the semester."

"And what has this boy done to deserve the affection of the amazing Nia Solomon?"

"He's just different," she replied.

"In what way?"

*So many you'd think your daughter was a raving lunatic.*

"He's sweet. He's thoughtful. He's a good—"

"If you say 'kisser,' I'm going to need to use one of those memory eraser things from *Men in Black*."

"I was going to say good listener. Most guys just want to talk about themselves."

"Was that a dig at me?"

"No, Dad, don't worry. I guess the difference is that Alex *shows* me he cares. It's a silly thing, but he knows how much I love illustration and graphic novels. So he checked, like, fifty of them out of the library so he could read them and talk about them with me."

Stephen whistled. "Don't tell your mother he did that. She'll say he makes me look bad."

"Nobody could ever make you look bad. I just feel like I know more about him in this crazy short time than anyone I've ever supposedly cared about."

"Well, aside from the fact that I'm going to have to live with not being able to invite him over for dinner, answer the door holding a shotgun, look him in the eye and ask him what his intentions are… he sounds like he might—and I stress *might*—be worthy of my daughter. But I get the feeling there's a catch."

"There is," Nia said. "I don't know if it can last."

"What do you mean if it *can* last?"

"Alex's dad travels for work. Constantly. Alex has been enrolled in, like, a hundred different schools, and Whisper Valley is just his latest stop on the never-ending itinerary. He could be gone in a month."

"Okay, but what about college? At least then he'll be staying put."

Nia shook her head. "He's planning to take over his dad's business. I don't know if he'll ever stay put."

Stephen tapped his chapped lips with an ashen finger. "That's a pickle. But even if he moves around, can't you two do one of those long-distance relationship deals? You know, nightly chats over SnapFace?"

"I'm not even going to bother correcting you," Nia said. "And no. We haven't talked about it. And I'm also not sure Alex's career goals really align with being in a committed, long-term relationship."

"So you're saying he wants to work in finance."

Nia laughed.

"If he leaves," Stephen said, "and you can't stay together for… whatever reason. You are still the most amazing, brilliant, ambitious, wonderful, beautiful young woman in the world. You will have princes and sultans fighting over you."

"I think you've watched more movies than I have, Dad. And I don't want a prince or sultan. I just want someone I can be myself around."

"That sounds—"

Suddenly, Stephen Solomon's eyes shut and his face screwed into a horrifying mask of pain. He cried out and doubled over, his hands balled into fists as he clutched his stomach. His breathing grew rapid and beads of sweat formed at his brow.

"Dad? *Dad*, what's going on? Should I call the hospital?"

*This can't be happening. Not now. Not now. I need you. Please.*

Then, just as quickly, her father's eyes opened. His breathing steadied. He sat back. His hands unclenched.

"It's alright," he said, catching his breath. "The pain comes and goes a few times a day. Hate to say I'm used to it by now."

"Jesus, Dad. This seems worse than usual. Is it?"

"It's not getting better," he said. "But please. Let me focus on you. That helps more than the pills."

"Okay. But if the pain is getting worse, you have to let me call the doctor. We can change your meds. Or get new meds."

"I'm always in pain. This, right here, makes it better," he said, gesturing to her.

"Well, thankfully, you never need to call in a refill for me," she said.

"All I was saying, before I was so rudely interrupted by my own body, is that you're seventeen. Your whole life is in front of you. You will meet a lot of people. Most will be wrong for you. Some will feel right and still be wrong. And one day, you'll meet someone who both feels right and *is* right."

"What if I want it to be him?" she said. "What if I *feel* that it's him? You and Mom met when you were our age."

"We did," he said, his eyes drifting away, as though recalling a happy, nearly long-forgotten memory.

"And you've made it."

"We have," he said, "through good times and, well, you know the rest."

"So what do I do?" Nia said. "I don't want to lose him."

"Let's get one thing abundantly clear. You never *lose* anybody. They only lose *you*. Because if they're dumb enough to let you go, it's their loss."

"Are dads born knowing the right thing to say," Nia said, "or do they study it?"

"Definitely not born with it," Stephen replied. "Ask your mother. I've said some of the absolute dumbest things that thankfully you were too young to remember. But, hey, I got better."

"A lot better."

He winked at her.

"I think what you need to do is see whether this Alex fellow is willing to make a commitment. That even if he isn't here with you, that he's *here* with you."

He brought Nia's hand up and gently tapped his chest with his finger. A tear fell from her eye and her father wiped it away.

"And what if he can't promise that?" she said.

"Then you have a whole lot of time to learn who you are yourself, instead of who you are with someone else. Your person will come, whether it's now or later. But you need to take care of yourself before you even think about taking care of anyone else."

"Sometimes it feels like I don't know how to take care of myself," Nia said. "And sometimes I feel like I'm slipping. I've…I've come really, really close to falling, Dad."

"Oh, my sweet baby girl, I promise to never, ever let you fall."

But as Nia's father held her in his atrophied arms, she knew that if she ever did start to fall, he would not be strong enough to pull her back.

# 29

Alex felt it when he woke up. A tingling sensation that started on his forearms, then traveled up to his shoulders, across his back, then down his spine. He shivered with recognition. Ankou. A lot of them. Four words went through his mind.

*The Quieting is coming.*

When the Convergence began, it would inform the Conclave of the site of the next Quieting. They would then alert Byron, and he and Alex would travel to the site to prepare. They did not know exactly when or where the Quieting would occur, just that they had to be ready. The closer they got, the greater the Ankou presence. Now, the confluence of Ankou was so strong in Whisper Valley that Alex felt it in his bones. Their time here was coming to an end.

He went to the window and raised the shades. Gorgeous golden rays streaked through the morning sky. The leaves had begun to change color. Whisper Valley was striking. Even amidst the bright hues of morning, Alex could see them. Flashes among the clouds. Shimmering white orbs among the orange and gold.

Two. Then three. Four. Five. Ten. Twenty. More. His heart sank with every Ankou he saw, because every one meant another soul would be Exorted.

Alex went downstairs and found his father already at the kitchen table.

"Morning, son," Byron said as he sipped his peppermint tea.

Alex made a small pot of coffee, then filled a mug and added a splash of cream and one sweetener. He stirred it, sipped it, then stood there, as if waiting for the response to a question he had not asked.

Finally, Byron said, "You felt them too. The Ankou."

"I did," Alex replied. "It's coming. The Quieting."

"It is. The Ankou are gathering. The Conclave told me that the spiritual turbulence will be tremendous. We'll need to be ready. Are you?"

"I think so."

"You think so?" Byron said. "Alex, I'm counting on you. We've done this before. Many times. This is no different."

"This couldn't be more different, Dad. We *know* these people."

"Thousands of people die every day, Alex. Since we arrived, four souls have been Exorted in Whisper Valley alone. You need to be able to detach from your emotions. An Aegis can afford the naïveté of guilt and remorse. A Dominus can't. You need to let it go."

"And what if I can't?"

"Don't say that, Alex," Byron said, his voice full of concern. "Don't you *dare* say that. You are already on *very* thin ice with the Conclave. If they feel you aren't going to outgrow this... *phase*... they have made it clear nothing is off the table. Thankfully, we'll be leaving Whisper Valley once the Quieting is over. That will limit your distractions."

"Distractions? Is that what you're calling Nia?"

"You can't prioritize one life over many, Alex. Once the Quieting is over, the Conclave will direct us to our next destination. We arrive, we depart after the Quieting, and repeat. The clock is running on our time in Whisper Valley."

"I just... I don't think I'm ready for it to happen here."

"The Quieting happens when it is meant to happen."

"Thanks for the helpful explanation, low-budget Yoda." Alex paused. "I'm not ready to go."

"We need to be ready to leave at a moment's notice. Why do you think we pack so light? Do you think I like owning just four pairs of pants? Even if you're not ready, you need to be ready."

"Your inspirational speeches are kind of terrible. You would be the absolute *worst* high school football coach."

"Well, then it's a good thing I've never had to fire up my resume," Byron said. "What's wrong, Alex? I've never seen you this disturbed during a Convergence."

"I don't know why. It's just never felt so real."

"In what way?"

"These people. They're my friends."

"Your friends?" Byron said. "We don't have friends, Alex. These people will be a distant memory in a year. You will forget them, and they will forget you. We are smoke. We linger for a few moments and then we are gone."

"I don't know if I want to be smoke," Alex said.

Byron's eyes narrowed. "Don't say that. You don't know what's at stake."

"I know *exactly* what's at stake. The lives of the people who live here. People I care about."

"You're talking about that girl."

"Don't say *that girl* like she's just a word. You don't know what it feels like, Dad."

"You're wrong, Alex. I know *exactly* what it feels like. I have lost more than you can *possibly* imagine."

He said the last two words with such anger, such remorse, that it shocked Alex to his core. He couldn't remember ever seeing his father display this kind of raw emotion.

"You told me after we Exorted Cory and Suzanne Westin that you understood what I was going through," Alex said. "What did you mean by that?"

Byron heaved a heavy sigh and said, "You care about Nia. I cared about someone like you did once too."

Alex let the word sink in. "You never told me that."

Byron sat back and smiled, as if seeing a memory in his mind.

"Her name was Sofia. I met her when I was a young Dominus living in a town called Morelia in Michoacán, near Lake Pátzcuaro. One day, I went to watch the local fisherman catch whitefish with their butterfly nets. Later that day, one of the fishermen returned to shore and his daughter came to help him with his catch. I was awestruck. She was the most beautiful woman I'd ever seen. Somehow I caught her eye and she smiled at me, and I was done. Two days later, I saw her again in the market and asked her to have lunch with me. I don't know why. At one point during the meal, she touched my hand and I felt this… heat. It felt like our power, only this one burned right into my heart. It was the most powerful touch I'd ever felt. I fell in love with Sofia over a plate of morisqueta."

"I've felt that too, Dad. With Nia."

Byron nodded. "I had a feeling."

"Why does it happen?" Alex said. "That feeling?"

"I don't know. I asked my father. He'd never felt it before. The best I can say is that it's elemental. Like how when two flames intertwine, their fires burn higher than they ever could alone. Sofia was my first and only love."

"What happened to her?"

"I was in Morelia for four months waiting for the Quieting. I spent every waking minute with Sofia. And then it happened. A tsunami decimated the town. Sofia was helping her father Miguel haul in that day's catch." Byron looked down. "We Exorted ninety-six souls that day. I buried Sofia and her father myself."

"Sofia didn't have to die, Dad. I need to warn people," Alex said. "I won't be able to live with myself."

"You will *not*," Byron shouted. "The Conclave will *kill* you. And I will *not* lose another child."

Alex's jaw dropped. The words hung in the air.

"What do you mean *another* child?" Alex said. "Dad, what are you talking about?"

"You are my son, Alex. But you are not my first child."

Byron sat there, staring at the table, and when he looked up at Alex there were tears in his eyes. Alex had never seen his father cry.

"I had a daughter," he said. "Her name was Evelyn. And she was the most beautiful little girl this world had ever seen."

"Was," Alex said. "You said was."

Byron nodded.

Alex felt his head spinning. "I don't even know how to process this. Why didn't you tell me? Was Evelyn adopted, too? What happened to her?"

"She was not adopted. You are the first Aegis who has not come directly from the blood of a Dominus. In the past, when a Dominus's flame burns out, the Conclave performs the ritual of Corpus Sanguis. They take the blood of the new Dominus and imbue it into the Exorted soul of a child. An infant. Young enough that the world isn't imprinted on them."

"You mean young enough so they don't realize their freedom is being taken from them."

Byron said nothing.

"So Evelyn came from your blood," Alex said.

"She did."

"What happened to her?"

Byron sighed. "It has always been customary for the Dominus to teach their Aegis how to control the Blaze and the Dim. To balance life and death. I taught Evelyn, but once she gained control of her powers, things began to happen. A neighbor's pet would go missing. I would find a deer in the middle of our cul-de-sac dead with no external injuries."

"Evelyn was using the Dim," Alex said.

"She was. I didn't know at the time. Or maybe I knew but didn't want to believe it. For some reason, Evelyn was born with this *rage*. I don't know how else to put it. Then people began to die. The Dim revealed a side of Evelyn that I can only describe as—"

"Evil."

Byron nodded. "There was something broken inside her. Something that could not be fixed or reasoned with. She could not control herself. She left us with no choice. A Dominus needs an heir. But if that heir is unstable, they cannot be allowed to take the mantle."

"So you Siphoned her," Alex said, his voice rising in anger and disbelief. "You Siphoned your own *daughter*."

Tears began to stream from his father's eyes.

"I did," Byron said. "Evelyn was broken. Her power would have only grown. But she was still my daughter and I loved her. And not a day, not a *minute* goes by that I don't feel that pain. I have simply had to live with it."

The Sonnums sat in silence for several minutes. Byron's tears ceased as suddenly as they appeared. He took a sip of tea, his hand trembling ever so slightly. Alex's mug had grown cold in his hands. Alex knew his father was thinking about the moment he'd taken his own child's life. He couldn't fathom that kind of pain.

Then Byron looked at Alex and said, "I've kept too much from you for far too long. You deserve to know the whole truth."

"About Evelyn?"

"About yourself." Byron closed his eyes and said, "Evelyn used the Dim on your parents."

The coffee mug fell from Alex's hand and shattered on the floor.

"What did you say?"

"You were born seventeen years ago to Gregory and Barbara Howard. They were your parents. Evelyn killed them."

Alex's head throbbed. "You told me my parents *abandoned* me."

"That was a lie," Byron said, "to protect you from a truth even I couldn't face."

"My whole life I've felt unwanted," Alex said, seething. "*You* let me think that."

"You are not unwanted," Byron said. "You are *loved*."

"Evelyn. She..." Alex couldn't even say it. The words were bile rising in his throat, rancid and raw. "Your daughter killed my parents."

"Yes."

Alex felt the room begin to spin. His stomach was empty, but if it hadn't been, everything would have come right back up. Alex's whole world felt like it had tilted on its axis.

Alex slid down to the floor. Byron sat next to him and reached out his hand. Alex slapped it away.

"You've lied to me," Alex said, "so many times. I don't even know what's true anymore."

"I never lied about Evelyn," Byron said.

"You never *told* me about Evelyn. And you lied about my parents. You told me they left me. That they didn't want me. I've gone my whole life thinking I was just *abandoned*, when the truth was they were taken from me. By *your* blood."

"I never told you because I didn't want to hurt you. But I was only protecting myself from the pain of telling you the truth."

"So your daughter killed my parents, then you adopted their orphaned son? So, what, was I some replacement kid? Like your goldfish died so you got a new one?"

"Not at all. I couldn't love you any more, Alex, whether you're from my blood or not."

"I've never been your son," Alex spat. "I'm just a kid whose life you destroyed and took pity on. That's why you never told me about the Dim. You were worried that if I knew how to use it, I might be another Evelyn."

"I was," Byron said, "but it was a foolish concern. You are not like her."

"You adopted me because the Conclave didn't trust your bloodline. They were worried that performing Corpus Sanguis would lead to another...Evelyn. I bet you didn't even want me, but the Conclave forced you."

"That is not true," Byron said. "After what Evelyn did to your parents, I went to see you at social services. Nobody told me to go. You were this tiny child at the bottom of this enormous crib. I remember the linens were so filthy. And all these people walking around, ignoring you as you cried. It tore my heart in two. I knew I was responsible because I refused to see what Evelyn was. I thought about what might happen to you. If you were lucky, a loving family would take you in. But not every child is so lucky. I looked into your eyes, and when you saw me, you stopped crying. You *smiled* at me. And at that moment I knew I could not leave your fate up to chance. I would raise you as my own and love you for the rest of your life."

Alex felt his cheeks grow hot. Tears sprung to his eyes, but he willed them to go away. He refused to cry, not now, not for this. Not for him.

"If you love someone," Alex said, "you don't lie to them."

"You'll have a hard time finding a parent who hasn't failed their child in some way."

"Missing your kid's soccer game is *not* the same thing as hiding that your daughter killed their parents. This is why the Conclave has been on my back all this time, isn't it?"

"In part. What Evelyn did shook the Conclave. It's why they've kept such a close watch on you. It's why they're concerned about you and Nia."

"Nia is the best thing that's ever happened to me," Alex said. "I don't want my life to just be…death. I want to *live.* With her."

"Maybe she is the best thing that's happened to you. But will you be the best thing that's happened to her?" Byron said. "She's, what, seventeen? Does she want to give up her future for this life?"

"You're assuming I even still want this life."

"We have a greater calling. The mantle of Death keeps balance in the world. That job is entrusted to me, and soon it will be entrusted to you. We live with pain because we have to, for the greater good. If the Conclave feels you can't be trusted, you could be…" Byron trailed off.

"Siphoned," Alex said.

Byron nodded. "You don't have the evil inside you that Evelyn did. But if the Conclave believes an Aegis can't perform their duties, it doesn't matter what's in their heart."

Alex sat there. Silent. Byron slid closer to Alex and put his hand on his son's shoulder.

"I am sorry," Byron finally said. "For everything. I know how hard this is because I have loved too. I never wanted you to get your heart broken like mine was. When you're a child, you accept your fate. As you get older, free will rages against the constraints of destiny. My destiny led me to you."

"Was it worth it?" Alex said. "The path that led you to lose Sofia, to Siphon your own daughter?"

"Love is pain," Byron said. "A pain I wouldn't even wish on a Mors. It never leaves. It is a weight around my neck every day of my life. But any pain I may have endured is a drop in the ocean compared to the suffering so many would feel if we let the balance tip. By taking Evelyn away, I was saving others. That's how I was able to live with it."

"I thought you said you didn't care about each life," Alex said. "That we were part of something bigger."

"Every great thing is made up of many small things," Byron said.

Alex felt like a hand had reached inside him, grabbed his heart, and twisted it.

"I *need* you, Alex," Byron said. "I haven't been the perfect father. Love is not an excuse for my failings. I should have trusted you with the truth. The Tenets teach us about our duties to the dead. But they teach us nothing about our duties to the living."

Byron extended his hand.

"Everything I've done means nothing if you are not there to take my place. I've always believed you could be better than me, that you could learn from my failings. Will you help me? Son?"

Alex looked at his father's hand. He did not take it. Alex stood up and said, "I don't know anymore."

Then Alex walked out of the house.

# 30

Alex had never been inside Nia's house. She'd never invited him, and he never thought to ask. In fact, he was glad she hadn't. What the hell would she say if Alex met her parents?

*Hey, Mom and Dad, this is my boyfriend, Alex. He's really sweet and takes good care of me, and by the way he's next in line to rule the underworld. Can you pass the chicken piccata?*

The distance between their homes may as well have been an ocean. Today he was going to cross it. He needed to see her. He needed *her.*

It was a gorgeous late fall day. The kind of day that should have been spent under a tree somewhere, Nia curled up in his lap as they both read, stealing quick looks at each other's books and longer kisses. But that morning had upended his world. Right now, Nia felt like the only constant he had.

As soon as he knocked on the Solomons' door, he realized he should have texted her first. He didn't even know if she was home. Plus, her parents were ill—would he wake them? This was just a bad idea. Alex turned around to head somewhere, *anywhere*, but then the door opened.

"Alex?" Nia said. She looked surprised, but the good kind of surprised. "Is everything okay?"

"I missed you."

"I saw you yesterday."

"It's been a long day." Alex took her hand, gently caressing her palm with his thumb. He leaned in and said, "May I?"

Nia smiled and pulled Alex toward her. "You may."

They kissed, lips touching ever so slightly. She pressed her palm against his face and he put his hand on her hip, and Alex felt like he might just catch on fire on her doorstep.

When they parted, Alex said, "Can I come in?"

The smile on Nia's face slid away.

"I don't know if that's a good idea right now."

"Let me guess. You have a hidden room filled with the headless corpses of previous boyfriends."

"You nailed it. But I was planning to show you my decapitated head collection next week. I figure if I'm going to date anyone, they need to be comfortable with the fact that they might end up with their head mounted in our dining room."

"That's alright I've always admired taxidermy."

Nia smiled, but she still seemed hesitant.

"It's alright," Alex said. "I get it." He turned away.

Nia put her hand on his shoulder, stopping him. She stood in the doorway, silent. Finally, she said, "Okay. But please be quiet. My dad might be asleep."

"In another life, I was the world's greatest cat burglar."

"See, if you were a normal guy, I'd know you were joking. But given, you know, *you*, I'm only about eighty percent sure."

"I'll be quiet," he said.

"Then come in." Nia took his hand and brought him inside.

"Shoes," she said. He took off his sneakers and left them by the door.

They crept up the stairs in their socks. Hers were pink and fuzzy. His were white with holes in the toes.

"Is your mom here?" Alex said.

"She walks to Brady Green most mornings," Nia said. "She brings a thermos of hot lemon water and gets a poppyseed bagel with scallion cream cheese and just sits on a bench for a while. Sometimes she eats her food. Sometimes she doesn't. Sometimes she'll come home with an uneaten bagel and make herself another one. And I always make sure she has her phone's GPS turned on just in case."

"You keep an eye out for her," Alex said. "You keep an eye out for everyone you care about. I hope you feel enough people keep an eye out for you."

"Sometimes," Nia said. "Kind of sucks having to always be the responsible one."

She led Alex down the hall to a closed door. "This is my room," she said. She opened the door, took Alex's hand, and brought him inside. When he saw what was inside, his breath left him and a wondrous smile spread across his face.

"Holy crap," he said. "Did you do all this?"

Nia's face flushed. She smiled, shy and proud. "I did."

Nia's room was covered floor to ceiling in artwork, illustrations, sketches, and storyboards. Colors and creativity radiated out from every inch. Blues and reds and oranges and greens and yellows, pencils and inks, blacks and whites and shades of varying density. Alex looked up. Half the ceiling was plastered with incredible, detailed drawings of other worlds, creatures, heroes, villains, and planets, like a brilliant, cosmic Sistine Chapel.

He recognized Arumaya, the demi-goddess, with her white, feathered wings, curly, reddish-brown hair, lustrous skin, and golden armor. He saw gods and goddesses, heroes and villains, beauty and ugliness, ordinary people and extraordinary people. Nia's room looked like someone had reached into the most incredible, creative brain in the world and splashed its contents around like they'd been shot from a fountain of pure imagination.

He couldn't help but remember all the rooms he'd lived in over the years, with their bare, blank walls, devoid of pictures, photos, mementos, or anything at all. Nia's room looked like it belonged to someone. Alex's rooms all looked like they belonged to no one.

"I don't know what to say," Alex said, "other than I hope you have an agent or a manager or someone who can turn all of this into a movie. I mean, this is just crazy."

"Crazy in a good way or crazy in a 'I belong in a padded room' way?"

"Both? You would definitely have the coolest padded room in history. I'd come visit."

She laughed. "My dad likes to say that flattery will get you everywhere."

"Well, does it?"

She came to Alex, looped her arms around his neck, and kissed him deeply. He closed his eyes and lost himself in her. Nia's room made Alex feel like he'd entered the pages of an exciting book.

"What's that one?" Alex said, his mouth half covered by Nia's lips.

She turned around. He was pointing at a sketchbook on her desk, its illustration mostly covered by other books and colored pencils. Nia quickly disentangled herself from Alex, went over to the desk, and turned the sketchbook upside down.

"When you gave me your copy of *A Cold Winter's Night*, I promised I'd give you back something just as special," Nia said. "I haven't forgotten. I've actually been working my butt off on it. It's just not ready for public viewing."

"Seriously? You're making something and you're not going to let me see it?"

"Do chefs let people watch them while they cook?"

"You've obviously never been to Benihana."

"If you try to sneak a look before it's ready, I hope the Blaze can replace lost limbs, because no joke, I will chop off your hand."

"I think you have been to Benihana."

"I promise," Nia said, "you'll see it when it's ready."

Nia tucked the sketchbook onto a shelf. Alex noticed an open envelope on her desk. He saw that the return address was Austin, Texas. His eyes widened.

"Wait," he said. "Is that…?"

Nia nodded enthusiastically. "Yup."

He went to the desk and picked up the papers. "Can I look?"

She nodded, beaming. Alex began to read.

*Dear Ms. Solomon –*

*We are pleased to offer you a full scholarship for the forthcoming Austin Illustrators Collective – Winter Session. This scholarship includes tuition for the program, as well as travel, food, and accommodations. If you accept this invitation, please return the enclosed form by the deadline. Upon receipt of your acceptance, we will begin the process of scheduling your sessions and pitches. We look forward to welcoming you to the AIC, and can't wait to see what you create!*

"Holy shit!" Alex said. He ran to Nia, picked her up, and spun her around. She laughed giddily and wrapped her arms around his neck as he kissed her. "That's amazing. Nia, I'm so happy for you."

"I'm kind of happy for me too," she said.

She sat on her bed. She motioned for Alex to join her. He sat down next to her, his skin warming as they touched. He wanted to reach out, to hold her, pretend that they were the only two people on earth and that they had no other future, no other responsibilities, no other obligations than what they chose for themselves. Her acceptance to the program proved it. Their future was theirs to make.

"Is everything okay?" Nia said. "You've never wanted to come over before."

"You could have invited me over," he said.

Nia sighed. "It's hard for me here. When I'm with you, I like to get out. It helps me remember that there's more."

"I get it. And I'm sorry for showing up unannounced. I just needed someone to talk to."

"Someone meaning not your dad."

"You know more about me than my dad ever did."

"Well, I'm here. Talk to me."

Alex rubbed his head. His thoughts were going a million miles an hour and he couldn't grab onto any of them long enough for them to make sense. But he had to try.

"I've always felt like everything was laid out for me. Where my life was going. My dad told me what I was meant to do, where I would go, and I just followed him down that road. Now the road feels like it leads to a crater. Every time he says the word *destiny*, I want to hurl."

"Did something happen?" she said.

"Well, you, for starters," he said.

"Me? What do you mean?"

"I never saw you coming. Not in a 'I stepped out from the curb and didn't see that Mack truck coming' kind of way, but in a 'Dorothy realizing the world isn't only black and white' kind of way."

"Phew, because for a second I thought you might be calling me a Mack truck."

Alex pressed his hand to Nia's face and brought his head close to hers until their foreheads touched. He whispered, "I've been all over the world. And you are the most beautiful thing I've ever seen."

He heard Nia take a sharp breath. He could feel the warmth in her cheek where he held her.

She kissed him, then sat back. "Tell me what happened."

"My father. There's just so much he never told me. So much he lied to me about."

"About who you are?"

"Not just that. About who he is. He had a daughter before me."

"Oh my god, Alex. And you didn't know?"

"Nope. And his daughter. She died. And then Byron adopted me. It feels like he took me in just to fill that void, that he only chose me out of a sense of obligation and guilt. And it *sucks* to think that."

"Alex," she said, "look."

Alex looked at his hands. They were shaking. The tips of his fingers were glowing bright red, like burners on an electrical stove. Nia held her palm over his, then quickly pulled away. He clenched his fist together to put out the flame.

Just as he closed his hand, Nia's door opened and a woman of about fifty entered. She was plainly dressed, wearing a floral-patterned blouse and checkered pants that looked about twenty years out of date. Her eyes lit up when she saw Alex sitting on Nia's bed.

Instinctively, Alex stood up.

"I'm so sorry," he said. "I—"

"You should know better than to apologize, James," the woman said. "It's been so long since I've seen you in our house. Have you been hiding from us?"

Alex looked at Nia. She sighed.

"Alex," she said, "this is my mother, Rivka."

Alex held out his hand. "You have a lovely home, Mrs. Solomon."

"No need for such formalities, James," she said. Rivka stepped forward and pulled Alex into a full-bear, awkward, mother-smother hug. She held it for what felt like a month, then finally let him go. She looked Alex up and down with a smile. "Either you got shorter or I got taller."

Alex looked at Nia and raised his eyebrows as if to say, *What do I do?*

She mouthed, "Just go with it."

"Can I bring you anything?" Rivka asked. "Juice? Tea? Coffee? Do you drink coffee?"

"I do, but I'm okay right now. Thank you, Mrs. Solomon."

"How long have we known each other? Call me Rivka."

Alex looked at Nia. *Known each other?*

Nia did not respond.

"Well, if you change your mind, just say the word. I believe your father is out golfing with my husband. I'll make some sandwiches and lemonade. It was so good to see you, James. Nia, don't you dare let this one go."

Rivka winked at her daughter then kissed Alex on the cheek and left. Nia closed the door.

"Nia..."

"My mother has stage three Alzheimer's," Nia said. "She was diagnosed about five years ago. Right now she has moderate cognitive decline. She can still take care of herself and has her motor skills. But it's only going to get worse."

"Jesus. Oh, Nia. I'm so sorry."

"My dad isn't golfing. He's dying. I come home every day and do everything I can to try to make however much time they have left as painless as possible. You're a respite from all this. I never wanted you to come here because I wanted to keep the good and the bad separate." She paused. "But I don't know if that's possible."

"You have every right to do whatever you need to do," Alex said. "If I'm a respite, consider me the happiest respite ever. If you want to tell me more, the bad with the good, I'm here for you."

She took a breath, composed herself. "I bet you're asking why she thought you were James and why my dad was out with Dean Mungro."

"The question did pop into my head."

"My father worked as a real estate appraiser for twenty-five years," Nia said. "The Mungro family owns properties all over the county. He did a lot of work for Dean and Dean's friends. Sometimes he spent twelve hours a day in homes that were newly constructed or renovated. Homes that hadn't passed safety inspections, or where the property owners said they had but lied."

"So your dad and Dean were close."

"A big chunk of his living came from Mungro properties and referrals, so I think we just ignored…everything else. Whisper Valley isn't Silicon Valley. You don't give up a good job because you don't like your boss. And we didn't know those houses were unsafe until it was way too late."

"So you and James were friends?"

"We were," she said. "James used to be kind and fun, but his dad just wore him down. Dean is the kind of guy who would criticize a well-done steak for not being tough enough. He's a bastard and he made it impossible for James to live with himself or be true to himself. He never wanted a son with his own mind, he just wanted another one of himself. It's like telling a giraffe not to be a giraffe anymore, it should be a tiger. You never end up with a tiger, just a confused, fucked-up giraffe."

"James has done some pretty bad things," Alex said.

"You can blame someone for the bad things they've done while also having empathy for the pain that caused them to do it."

"His pain has caused a lot of other people pain."

"Empathy doesn't mean you ignore the bad things," Nia said, "it just helps you understand where they come from. The world would be a whole lot better if people had more of it."

"I grew up being told *not* to have empathy, that caring too much was a bad thing," Alex said. "I'm starting to realize how messed up that was."

"Maybe you and James aren't all that different," Nia said.

"Maybe not."

"I think James and I got along because we were always both a little bit broken," Nia said. "We were two puzzle pieces that didn't fit in anywhere. James is the angriest person I know, but he never had an outlet for that anger. And he was tired of depending on Dean to put out fires that he was responsible for setting because he pushed James to be something he wasn't. So, one night, James swallowed a bottle of his stepmom's Vicodin and washed it down with a quart of vodka. Then he texted me. I got there just in time to help him throw it all up."

Alex stayed silent.

"Then, last year, with everything going on, I just broke. My folks, a stupid breakup…I couldn't carry the weight of it anymore. So I went up to Larrimore Hill. Alone."

"Jesus, Nia…" Alex said

"I texted James because I really thought I might go through with it. I pulled him back when he hit bottom, and that night he came and pulled me back. I know he's done some pretty shitty things. But part of me is, I don't know, stuck with him, because we saved each other."

"Do your parents know about this?"

"No. Rivka still thinks Dean Mungro is basically SuperCop. She doesn't stop about *all the wonderful things he's done for your father*. Doesn't matter that half the homes the Mungros owned were built in the 1970s and coated in lead paint or dripping with asbestos. Or that they'd fumigated the place an hour before he got there and *forgot* to tell him. That Dean Mungro is the person most responsible for my dad's Mesothelioma. My mom still has these insane visions of her precious little girl wearing a beaded white gown and walking me down the aisle to become Mrs. Nia Mungro. Before she got sick, she had this roadmap for my life in her head. Now that map is gone, and I've had to care for everyone but myself. So for a moment, it felt easier to give up than to have to keep carrying it all. And it's also why I'm going to have to turn down the scholarship."

"What are you talking about?" Alex said. "Why would you do that?"

"After my dad's most recent set of PET scans, the doctors said he probably won't last more than three months. Right now, my mom can take care of herself, but it's anyone's guess how long that'll last. If I leave, I'm choosing to spend fourteen of my dad's final days away from him. And if he died while I was somewhere else drawing cartoons, I'd never forgive myself."

"You can get a nurse. Someone to help."

"We have someone come in part time," Nia said. "I chip in what I can. It's not much. Dean Mungro contributed for a little while, I think more for legal reasons than altruistic ones. Every dime we have goes to co-pays and hospital visits and medications."

"Can't you sue Dean?"

"We thought about it," Nia said. "Even talked to a lawyer. The bottom line is Dean and his family have money. We don't. It would take years and cost hundreds of thousands of dollars with no guarantee of anything. I'd have to drop out of school and get a full-time job to pay for it, and Dean could still win and bleed us dry. And no matter how it ended, it still wouldn't save my dad."

"Please don't turn the scholarship down," Alex said. "It could change your life."

Nia's voice broke as she choked back tears. "And not being there for my dad when he passed away could ruin it."

"Let me help you. Let me carry some of the weight."

"That's not your job, Alex. You can't help carry what's in my head," she said. "It's not just the scholarship. Or my parents. It's not something you can put your hands on and just *heal*. I need someone who knows it's not their job to fix me, but just to say that sometimes it's okay to not be okay."

Alex felt a surge of emotion in his chest, hot and fierce. He didn't know how to handle all of this information. The only other person he'd ever had any responsibility to was his father. But his father never needed a shoulder to lean on. He never needed someone to prevent him from bending or breaking. Alex's obligations were wholly to ensure his own future—nobody else's. Trying to understand everything Nia was going through was like trying to grip sand. Maybe he could catch a grain here or there, but most of it would slip through his fingers.

*I know more about how to deal with the dead than the living.*

"Are you going to be here in a year?" Nia said.

"Am I what?"

"Going to be here. In Whisper Valley. Next year."

"I… I don't know."

"Yes, you do," she said. Nia took his hands and placed them on her waist. He felt the familiar fire surge through him. "Will you be here in a year? In six months? In a *week*?"

"*I don't know*," Alex said. He felt a tear slide down his cheek. "Our time here is running out. I don't know when. But sooner than later. And when it's over…"

He trailed off.

"You're leaving."

He nodded. Then he looked into her eyes and said, "Come with me."

He had no idea why he said it, but it had come out and it felt right.

"What?" she said, startled.

"Come with me. Leave with me."

"You want me to leave with you and your dad?"

"No. Just me. The two of us. Let's just go. We can create new lives. I don't know what the hell we'll do, but we'll figure it out. You and me."

"What about your dad? Your job?"

"He can get a new Aegis."

"Do you even want that? You've spent your whole life preparing to take your father's place. Do you really want to abandon all of that?"

"I…I don't know."

Nia removed her hand from Alex's. "My family needs me, Alex. And I have dreams that aren't only about who I want to wind up with. I want to *be* someone. If I can't go to Austin now, I'll find another way another time. I'm not willing to forget about what I want just so you can escape. Running away won't help me figure out my future, it *robs* me of it. You don't get rid of your problems by pretending they're not there."

Alex knew he was being irrational, that she couldn't leave. He ached for simplicity, to remove all their obligations, all their obstacles. But that wasn't going to happen. Alex looked around the room. He marveled at the explosions of color and creativity. He thought about what his father had said that morning.

*The Tenets teach us about our duties to the dead. But they teach us nothing about our duties to the living.*

"*Please,*" Alex said.

She didn't answer. He'd never begged for anything in his life. He thought about his father. The pain and vulnerability he'd shown. How, despite the lies, despite the hurt, despite his future being laid out for him, before he even had a chance to know what the hell he was getting into, Alex had made a promise. Just like Nia had made a promise to fulfill her duties as a daughter, Alex had made his own to fulfill his duties as a son. Deep down, he still wanted to make his father proud. To prove he could handle the responsibility.

Deep down, Alex knew he was going to leave Whisper Valley.

"I made a promise to my father a long time ago. And I want to be the kind of person who keeps his promises."

"I told you that you were a respite," Nia said. "But I don't want it to be temporary. I don't want *you* to be temporary."

"I'm not," Alex said, but the words came out more as a plea than a statement.

"If you can't promise me that you're going to stay," Nia said, taking her time sounding out each word, knowing the weight behind them, "then I want you to go. Now. If you leave now, I'll bend. If you leave in a year, I might break."

Those last three words—*I might break*—cut into Alex's heart. Then he realized what he had to do.

"Then I should leave," he said. "But I refuse to let you carry that weight alone."

Alex opened Nia's door. He immediately caught the sour, despairing scent of sickness. Alex followed it.

"Alex?" Nia said. "Alex, what are you doing?"

There was a sliver of light under the door at the end of the hall, where the smell was strongest.

"Alex, stop," she said, but he had already entered the room.

Alex's breath caught in his throat. He saw a frail man lying in bed, hooked up to tubes and machines. He was sickly, gaunt, maybe a hundred and thirty emaciated pounds on a tall, withered frame. His skin was pale yellow, with deep purple bruises on his arms and neck. His lips were blue, his breathing ragged. His legs looked like broom handles beneath the blanket.

Nia's father didn't just look like he was at Death's door—he looked like he was stepping over the threshold.

Alex approached the bed.

"Alex…" Nia said apprehensively. "What are you—?"

Alex put his hands on Stephen Solomon's chest and closed his eyes.

Then he heard Rivka Solomon shriek, "*What are you doing to my husband?*"

He ignored her. The warmth began to swell in his chest, spreading out through his veins and arteries and into his limbs. He felt Rivka grab his shoulders from behind. She dug her nails into his skin and tried to pull him away.

*I'm sorry, Mrs. Solomon*, Alex thought as he held on, *but I promise you'll understand.*

Then the flames burst through his fingertips and the Blaze flowed forth from Alex into the body of the dying man. He saw Nia's father's eyes flitter open and then the world went white.

The next thing Alex knew, he was lying on a dark blue carpet, one arm out in front of him like he was hailing a taxi and the other tucked beneath him at a painful angle. He could hear sounds but could not make out what they were, as if he were listening to a conversation from underwater. Then his breathing steadied. He got to his knees and stayed there until the world came into focus.

"Stephen! Stephen, *talk to me*. Stephen, what happened?"

The voice belonged to Rivka Solomon.

"I have no idea. What the hell is going on? Nia? Rivka? Why do I feel…fine?"

The voice belonged to Stephen Solomon.

Alex staggered to his feet. Nia and Rivka were kneeling at either side of Stephen Solomon's bed, each holding one of his hands. They were crying.

His bruises were gone, blue veins no longer visible beneath nearly translucent skin. The legs underneath the blanket no longer looked like branches but like logs. His eyes were no longer glassy, but clear. Stephen Solomon looked *alive.*

Nia and Rivka were draped over Stephen, crying tears of joy. Stephen sat up and pulled his wife and daughter close to him as they embraced, weeping. Stephen's face was a mixture of utter joy and complete confusion, as if maybe he'd dreamt his sickness. He looked around. The bed. The medications. He winced as he found the needles still protruding from his veins. He seemed to realize this wasn't a dream—you didn't feel pain in a dream—but he couldn't explain how this was real.

Nia, her arms still wrapped around her father, turned to look at Alex. He could see joy and grief in her face. They both knew why he'd done it. Then before Nia could ask what would happen to him, Alex said, "I'll be okay."

They both knew he was lying. Then he felt it. He knew it was coming, but didn't think it would be so soon. The familiar purplish-black coloring started to creep into his skin. The pain was moderate now, but it would grow. He had to hurry.

There was only one way to fix this.

It was time to confront the Conclave.

# 31

Alex stumbled out of the house, but collapsed to a knee in the Solomons' front yard. He managed to get back up, but had to brace himself on a tree. His strength was gone. The grip of the Dim on his body was intensifying, the pain rising up from his feet to his ankles and knees. He gritted his teeth as he walked to mask the agony. He knew the Conclave wouldn't let this one slide. But he had a plan. Sort of. Maybe ten percent of a plan.

As he lurched across the street, Alex saw Iggy doing hamstring and quad stretches in his driveway. Iggy saw Alex and waved. Alex's legs gave out and he fell to his knees. Iggy ran over, put Alex's arm around his neck, and helped him to the curb.

"Holy shit, dude, are you okay?" Iggy said. "You look like absolute hell. Are you sick? Did you get food poisoning? Did you tie one on last night?"

"Just help me," Alex said, getting the words out between labored breaths.

"Are you coming from Nia's?" Iggy said. "Alex. Did you—?"

Alex nodded.

"Oh, Alex. Oh man, I'm so—" Iggy's words caught in his throat. "Alex, your arms…"

Alex looked at his arms. The Dim was rising, discoloring his skin visibly.

"Just help me," Alex said.

Iggy helped Alex back to his feet.

"Let me call 9-1-1," Iggy said. "You look like…you look like James did in that video."

"*No*," Alex shouted through gritted teeth, "I have to go. I have to go *now*."

Alex pulled free of Iggy. The pain was getting worse. He saw the hurt in Iggy's eyes, and even as the Dim poisoned him, his heart hurt for pushing Iggy away with no explanation. Then the front door of the Solomon home opened. Nia's father stepped out. He shielded his eyes as he looked around the neighborhood, as though he wasn't used to direct sunlight. He probably hadn't seen the street through clear eyes in years. Nia and Rivka were behind him, in the doorway, holding hands. Rivka's hand covered her mouth as though she couldn't believe what was happening.

Then Iggy said disbelievingly, "Is that Nia's dad?"

Alex said nothing.

"Holy hell, I haven't seen him in, like, a billion years. I thought he was at death's door," Iggy said. "Did you see him when you were over there? Alex, what the hell happened this morning?"

Alex did not reply. But Stephen raised his hand and nodded, a silent acknowledgment.

*Thank you.*

Then Alex turned and stumbled back home to 72 Marigold. He threw open the front door to find his father sitting at the counter, sipping a cup of tea. When he saw Alex, he put down the cup and stood up.

"Alex, what did you do?"

There was no more strength left in Alex's legs. He fell to his knees. His father grabbed him by the shoulder. With his remaining strength, Alex shouted, "Take me to see them. *Now*."

"The Conclave? Alex, that's forbidden, I—"

"TAKE ME OR I'M DEAD."

Byron nodded, placed his palm on his son's forehead, said *Evanescet*, and they were gone.

---

They appeared in the Cavern of Orcus. Alex looked down. The Dim had receded. His body was once again his own. He breathed a sigh of relief. *If I'd died*, he thought, *at least I wouldn't have had to go very far.*

Mors appeared on either side of them, collecting extinguished candles and casting malevolent glances at the Dominus and Aegis who had descended into their dark, unwelcoming home.

"Alex," Byron said, "you used the Blaze again, didn't you? What are you thinking? They're going to—"

"Kill me?" Alex said. "Maybe. But I have something to say to them and to you before they do. And I know they can hear me down here. I don't want any more lectures about my duties or my destiny or whatever. You were right. I couldn't go on pretending I was normal. So I'm done. I'm done *pretending* to be a student. A teenager. A kid. I'll take over as Dominus when I turn eighteen. You have my word. But I'm done playacting like I'm prepping for the SAT and college visits and thinking about what my major is going to be. I want us all to move on."

"Move on? You just used the Blaze, Alex."

"On Nia's father. Consider that the price of my recommitment. And given the lies you've told me, I think that's a pretty fair price."

Byron looked at him, as if weighing Alex's words. Finally, he said, "Let's go."

They walked through the cavern. One of the Mors seemed to hiss at Alex through his lipless skull. Alex flipped the Mors a double middle finger, small flames bursting forth from his fingertips. The Mors recoiled, nearly toppling over. Alex blew his fingers out and pretended to holster them.

"I think that might have been the most powerful middle finger in history," Alex said. He gave another Mors a middle finger and this time it did not move, just followed Alex, its eyes rotating in their fleshless sockets.

"Given the gravity of this situation, I don't see how you can joke," Byron said.

"Gallows humor," Alex said. "I can't think of anywhere more appropriate for it."

"I don't know how the Conclave will react to this meeting," Byron said. "But if you don't take it deadly serious, you're not leaving this cavern."

"I'm taking them as seriously as life and death," Alex said. "Because I know that's what's at stake. But come on. You can't tell me you never wanted to mess with the Mors."

"They're spending eternity as disintegrating carcasses doing my bidding," Byron said. "I think I've messed with them quite enough."

The light in the cavern grew dim as they walked further into the darkness. The candles receded into the gloom, the dancing flames fading into shadow. Then, when they were shrouded in darkness, a circle of light appeared directly in front of Alex's father. He stepped into it. Alex waited. And waited.

"I can't see anything. Can I get one of those too?"

A circle appeared in front of Alex and he stepped into it. His pulse began to quicken.

"Dominus Sonnum," came a thundering, baritone voice from the void. "We see you've brought a guest."

"A guest who desecrates the Tenets," came another voice, slightly higher-pitched, but laced with anger. "He has used the Blaze to prevent an Exortus for the second time. I say we Siphon this sad excuse for an Aegis and be done with it."

Alex began to wonder if this was a really, *really* bad mistake.

Then seven glowing forms appeared before them in a semicircle. They each floated a foot off the ground, their ghostly visages visible through a translucent sheen. Their faces appeared to be somewhere between life and death, skin and bone.

"Alex has something to say to you all," Byron said.

"We should not listen to a word this apostate says," said one member of the Conclave.

"Hush," said another. "We may not have a choice."

Alex smiled inwardly. That was what he was hoping to hear. He had a tiny bit of leverage over the Conclave, and they knew it.

"I doubt any of you had the courage to ask to speak to the Conclave in person when you were an Aegis," Byron said. "And with all due respect, every single one of you has broken or *bent* a Tenet. Even you, Father, so don't judge my son without being judged yourself."

Byron pointed at one spirit who did look strikingly like an older, bearded version of him.

"Your father?" Alex said. He pointed at the wraith. "You're my grandfather. Um, hi, Grandpa."

"You are not my blood," the former Dominus said.

"But I'm still your grandson," Alex said. "What should I call you? What was your name before you got, you know, *here?*"

"Before I became a member of the Conclave, I was known as Arthur Sonnum. You may call me Dominus. Aegis Sonnum—Alexander—desiring to speak with the Conclave is either incredibly brave or incredibly foolish."

"Why can't it be both?" Alex said.

He heard whispers in the dark. The seven members of the Conclave spoke among themselves. Without the heat from the thousands of candles, there was a chill in the air—if it even *was* air. Alex shivered.

"Aegis Sonnum." Yet another voice rang out in the darkness. "Once again you have used the Blaze to prevent an Exortus. This man, Stephen Solomon, would have been Exorted eight days from now. For this defiance, you should be Siphoned."

*Eight days*, Alex thought. *Nia's dad would have been dead in eight days.*

"You have been an exemplary Dominus, my son," said Arthur Sonnum. "The Ankou have maintained order and discipline I have not seen in many years. The number of Perditas has remained steady. You have set the bar high."

"Thank you, Father," Byron said. "I think my son would like to tell you what he told me."

"Young man," Arthur Sonnum said, "you being permitted here is a rare occurrence and a privilege. Make use of your time."

"I'm here because you all know what I've done," Alex said. "I used the Blaze on two people: James Mungro and Stephen Solomon. I'm here to recommit myself to my duties."

"That is a bold statement, Aegis," Arthur Sonnum said. "Why should we believe any promise when you have proven so consistently untrustworthy?"

"Because you don't have a choice," Alex said.

"Alex..." Byron said.

"Young man," Arthur said, "be careful with your choice of words. Our patience with you is not thin. It is nonexistent."

"I'll get right to it, then. I am adopted," Alex said. "I'm the first Aegis not born from Corpus Sanguis. Byron adopted me because his first Aegis, Evelyn, was born bad. She needed to be Siphoned. And the reason you didn't perform another ritual of Corpus Sanguis after Evelyn's Siphoning is because you were afraid my father's bloodline was tainted. Which means you were concerned that *your* bloodline was tainted. You were worried that another Aegis from the Sonnum bloodline might follow in Evelyn's footsteps and use her powers to kill. Am I wrong?"

The silence from both the Conclave and Byron answered Alex's question.

"And my guess is that Evelyn wasn't an isolated incident. She wasn't the first Aegis who went rogue. You were concerned about your bloodline even before Evelyn. She just confirmed your fears."

Silence.

"By adopting me you could start a new bloodline, separate from my father. Separate from you." Alex pointed at Arthur Sonnum. "If you kill me now, and have to perform another ritual using my father's blood, you're basically flipping a coin."

"We adopted once," Arthur Sonnum said. "We could do it again."

"And maybe you'll get the greatest Aegis of all time. The LeBron James of Aegii. Or maybe you'll get someone who wants no part of this. Or maybe you'll get another Evelyn. You have to make a choice: the devil you know, or the devil you don't. Well, I'm here. Right now."

Alex saw his father lower his head. He reached out his hand. Alex looked at it, confused by the gesture of paternal intimacy. Alex reached out his hand as well, and Byron clasped it. He squeezed Alex's hand once, tight, then let go.

"I will recommit to my duties as Aegis," Alex said, "But I'm done fitting in. Some of you might be able to turn what you feel on and off. I can't do that. So I'm going to stop pretending I'm something other than what I really am."

"And what would that be, Aegis?" Arthur Sonnum said.

"My father's son."

There were murmurs from the darkness as the Conclave discussed Alex's comments.

"What about the girl?" the female voice said. "Your father has voiced his concerns to us. And to you."

"What will you do about the girl, Aegis?" another Dominus shouted.

"Her name is Nia," Alex said.

"Your voice drips with insolence," Arthur Sonnum said. "No doubt your fondness for her drove you to use the Blaze on her father. Your heart has clouded your mind, Aegis."

"Dominus Sonnum," said another voice, "your son came here allegedly to assuage our concerns with his conduct. To prove he is capable of becoming the next Dominus. He has yet to convince us of that."

"Alex…" Byron said.

Alex took a deep breath and closed his eyes. He could feel an ache in his chest. He thought about Nia, about his lips on hers, her hand in his. He thought about her room. The illustrations. The worlds she'd created, the mind she possessed that he'd only just begun to understand. But she had a life. He had to let her live it.

"I'll never see her again," Alex said. "My emotions will no longer interfere with my duties."

"Good. But you must agree to one more commitment," Arthur Sonnum said. "Both of you."

"What is it?" Byron said.

"Alex will take over as Dominus on his eighteenth birthday. As you know, a Dominus is relieved of their immortality once turning over the mantle. And once their fire burns out, they become a member of the Conclave. However, you, Dominus, will agree to extend your flame's duration in order to mentor your son."

"For how long?" Byron said.

"Until he earns our faith. And in the event your son goes back on his word, you will retake the mantle until we find a suitable Aegis."

"You want me to mentor Alex," Byron said, "or monitor him?"

"What is it that the living say?" Arthur Sonnum replied. "Tomato, to-*mah*-to."

"You will Siphon Alex if he disobeys," another spirit said.

"Only a Dominus has the power to Siphon an Aegis," Arthur said. "If your son uses the Blaze again, you will need to take his life. You are our contingency plan."

"No, I'm your loaded weapon," Byron said.

"Call it whatever you desire. You will both agree to this arrangement, or Alex does not leave this cavern."

"Alex, I—" Byron began.

"I accept," Alex said. "I've spent seventeen years with you, Dad. I can handle a few more."

"We gave Evelyn Sonnum the same warning we are now giving you, Aegis. Consider her fate."

"I have," Alex said.

"Aegis Sonnum," Arthur said. "The Conclave accepts your recommitment to your duties. You may continue to follow the path of the Dominii. But if you interfere with another Exortus, the last face you see before your soul is ripped from your body will be that of your father."

The words cut through Alex like a dagger. He looked at his father. Byron's face was impassive. He wondered if Byron had the same confrontation with the Conclave before he siphoned Evelyn. If she'd been given the same warning Alex was being given right now.

"Dominus Sonnum, Aegis Sonnum," Arthur said, "do you accept this decision?"

"Yes," Byron said.

"Yes," Alex said.

"Good," Arthur said, "then be gone."

There was a flash of blackness, somehow even darker than the darkness of the Conclave's room itself, and then Alex and Byron were back in the foyer of 72 Marigold Lane.

"Dad…" Alex said. He did not finish the sentence. He didn't know what else to say. He could still hear the words of the Conclave as they promised to make his own father kill him. He closed his fist, as if hoping he could somehow feel Nia's hand in his, but he felt nothing.

Byron turned to Alex. He placed his hands on either side of his son's head. Then he leaned forward until their foreheads were touching. Alex felt grief for his father. For what he'd been forced to do all those years ago. What he was being forced to commit to now.

Alex was nearly as tall as Byron. He remembered being a little boy, how his father used to tower over him, a mountain of a man with the power of a god. Now, they were almost equals.

"I love you," Byron said. "We will live this life together."

"We will," Alex said, even if he knew, deep down, that what he really meant was that Alex was going to live this life alone.

# 32

Iggy was walking down the Dubya V hallway toward AP Calculus alongside Arvind, Francine, and Ayesha.

"He hasn't been in school in a week," Iggy said. "I mean, I live next door to Alex and it's like he just disappeared off the face of the earth.

"Tell me the truth," Ayesha said, "would it be creepy if one night I threw rocks at his window?"

"Creepy? Yes," Francine said. "Illegal? Also yes."

"I heard he got expelled for that fight in the library with James," Arvind said. "And then Dean Mungro threatened to have him charged with attempted murder, so Alex's dad pulled him out of school to go on the lam."

"Go on the lam?" scoffed Ayesha. "Are we in an old-school gangster movie?"

"Maybe," said Arvind.

"That's all bs," Francine said. "Alex's dad is in a secret branch of the military. James Bond kind of stuff. I heard he's getting deployed to North Korea to defuse all the nukes and install a new democratic government."

"You have no idea what you're talking about," Ayesha replied.

"I bet Alex is one of those child prodigies who solves time travel on chalkboards and can see complex equations dancing in thin air. He probably got hired by NASA to plan the next space shuttle launch using nothing but body odor as fuel, so he didn't need to spend any more time with us plebians in Whisper Valley."

"You're all wrong," Iggy jumped in. "Alex is actually an Avenger. He's currently in a HeliCarrier flying over the Bermuda Triangle getting ready to battle an army of mutant zombie parakeets with Captain America and Thor."

They sneered at Iggy.

"We're serious," Arvind said. "People just don't up and leave school mid-semester without saying a word unless something is up. Especially when they just got here. And given all the shadiness about the fight with James, a lot of people think Alex was hiding something. You live next door to him. You guys have your morning jaunts. I mean, Alex and his dad are still living next door, right? So what gives?"

Iggy stopped at his locker, opened it, and took out his calc textbook. He put it into his backpack, then locked it back up. Arvind, Ayesha, and Francine stood around him, waiting for a response.

"The truth is I have no idea," Iggy said. "I see the lights in their house go on and off, but the most I've seen of them is through the windows. I don't know. I wish I did."

"You guys are friends, right?" Francine said. "You really don't know what's going on?"

"I don't," Iggy said. "And frankly, it's none of my business. And it's none of yours either. He's a good dude. Let it go."

"We're just asking," Arvind said. "Alex will just end up becoming one of those Dubya V urban legends. Like whether or not the seniors really drove a tank into the gym for homecoming in 1996, or if Principal Oberman really got fired last year because he was having an affair with Jessica Singletary's mom."

"I heard they got married and moved to Switzerland," Francine said.

"Antigua," Ayesha said.

"Whatever," Iggy said. "They're all just rumors. You're all joking, but you don't realize how much rumors can hurt people."

"You're right," Arvind said. "I'm sorry, Ig."

"I don't think anyone except for Alex and his dad know the real answer," Iggy said, "and none of us are entitled to the truth."

"I bet *she* knows," Ayesha said, pointing toward the other end of the hallway, where Nia had just left homeroom. Her shoulders were hunched over even though her bag didn't look particularly heavy.

"Go wear your tinfoil hats somewhere else," Iggy said, sighing. "I'll catch you conspiracy theorists later. And leave Nia alone."

He walked away from his friends and went up to Nia. "Howdy, neighbor."

She smiled at him, but there was a sadness behind her eyes. "Hey, Ig," she said. "What's up?"

"Oh, you know, just enriching my nubile young mind," he said. "How are you?"

"I'm okay," she said. "Just getting ready for language arts."

"It's me, Nia," Iggy said. "How *are* you?"

"Guess I'm not really that okay."

"Listen, I'm not gonna ask what happened with Alex or why. I just want you to know if you ever need to talk, I love you, I live thirty seconds away, and my folks have a stupid good liquor cabinet."

Nia's weak smile solidified into a real one. "Thanks, Iggy."

"By the way, I saw your dad getting the paper this morning when I got back from my run. He looked good. Like, *really* good."

Nia sighed and nodded. "He's doing good. He's doing really, really good."

"'Cause I think last time we talked about family stuff you said he didn't think he was gonna be around much longer."

"He wasn't supposed to," Nia replied. "It's just…it's a miracle."

"A miracle," Iggy said. "You said he was stage four."

"He was."

"And then it just…cleared up? Like acne?"

"Like I said. It's a miracle. Please don't ask any more questions. My dad is healthy, he can help my mom, and that's all that matters."

"You're right," Iggy said. "I'm happy for you."

Iggy wrapped his arms around Nia and held her tight. She hugged him back. When they separated, Iggy said, "So, Ms. Solomon. You're single. I'm single. The Fall Ball is coming up. You see where I'm going with this."

"You're single? You mean Trevor hasn't succumbed to your wily charms yet?"

"I know, what the hell, right? What else does a guy have to do to get the captain of the swim team to fall into his waiting arms?"

"Give it time," Nia said. "He'll come around."

"Maybe. But until Trevor realizes the error of his ways, I'm going to the Fall Ball solo. So what do you say? Care to be my date?"

"That depends. Can you dance?"

"When I was little, my mom used to say that my dance moves looked like I was being electrocuted. But the flip side is that I'll make you look better. And hey, if I embarrass myself, at least it'll take your mind off of ghost boy."

"Ghost boy?" Nia said.

"You know, how Alex disappeared without any explanation. He ghosted everyone," Iggy said. "Why, what did you think I meant?"

"Nothing," Nia said. "So, Fall Ball. It's a date."

"We're on. I have a brand new suit, so you'd better have a cute dress."

"As a matter of fact, I do," she said, "and it'll be nice to have a reason to wear it. I have no doubt you'll look quite dashing."

"Would you expect anything less?" Iggy replied. "But just so we're clear, I'm totally going to use you to make Trevor jealous."

"I take great pride in being a pawn in your diabolical game."

"Fantastic. We're on," Iggy said. "Okay, gotta run to chem. Catch you later."

"Hey, Ig," Nia said.

"Yeah?"

"Thank you."

Iggy blew her a kiss, then jogged off to class.

Before Nia closed her locker, she moved her European History textbook and picked up the worn copy of *A Cold Winter's Night* underneath. She caressed the wrinkled cover, felt a tug at her heart, then quickly closed it and walked away.

# 33

Because Alex had gotten used to getting up early to run with Iggy, his internal alarm now woke him up at the buttcrack of dawn. Which meant he had a solid eighteen hours to kill before he went back to sleep—and there were only so many Exortus to perform. Every minute felt like a month. There was too much time to spend living inside his own head. Too much time thinking about what he'd given up.

Iggy had texted him on Monday asking if he still wanted to meet to grab the bus. Alex had texted back, **Go without me**. Tuesday, Iggy had texted, **U coming?** And Alex had written back, **No.** Wednesday, Iggy simply wrote, **?** And Alex sent back, **N.** Just **N**. Iggy stopped texting him after that, and Alex deleted the chain from his phone. One day, Iggy rang the doorbell after school. Alex refused to answer it, so he had Byron tell Iggy that he was okay, just "taking some time off." Naturally, that wouldn't answer Iggy's zillion questions, but hopefully he would take the hint and stop asking. He didn't care what excuse his father had given Dubya V for his absence. It didn't matter. A year from now, Alex would be a memory.

He had no plans other than to stare at the ceiling and wait for the next Exortus. Wait for the Quieting. The tremors from the Ankou were growing stronger.

He willed himself not to look at his phone. To see if she'd texted. To obsess over old messages and photos. He should have deleted her text chain as well, but he couldn't bring himself to do it. So he lay there, unmoving, trying to find ways to occupy his disquieted mind.

Meals with his father were largely silent. The meeting with the Conclave hung over them like a lead blanket. Byron sipped his peppermint tea and Alex would read the entire Internet, and then they went their separate ways. He had never felt so alone in his life.

To his surprise, as the weeks went by, he even began to miss school. He missed being challenged and stimulated. He used to complain to Nia and Iggy about boring teachers and too much homework, but the alternative, he'd discovered, was a black hole of boredom.

Everything on TV was terrible. It was bad enough at night, with infomercials and Z-grade action movies, but during the day it was all soap operas and game shows only truly bored people would ever watch. Which meant Alex watched every minute of them.

Twenty-two days after he left Nia's house, Alex woke up feeling like a pile of absolute dog crap. He stared at the ceiling for what felt like a hundred years, ignoring the hunger pains in his stomach and the crick in his neck. He looked at the blank white walls, the room he'd never bothered to decorate because, well, what was the point? He'd never decorated rooms in the other cities they'd lived in. Personalizing a space gave it a sense of permanence. Alex never expected his life to have any sort of permanence. He looked over at the small bookshelf. For some reason, it pissed him off. What a goddamn *idiot* he was lugging all those books around from continent to continent, city to city, like some baby refusing to get rid of his blankie. He would be a Dominus soon. It was time to grow up. It was time to leave the past where it belonged.

He took a box from the closet and tossed in his travel guides and photobooks and mementos. Then he lugged it downstairs and threw everything into the fireplace. He repeated this until his shelves were empty. Good riddance to a life he'd pretended to live.

Alex picked up the tourist's guide to Toowoomba, Australia. He had purchased it at a grocery store in Hooper Centre and carried it to three different continents. Now, he couldn't stand the sight of it.

Alex felt anger rise inside him. He didn't know who or what it was directed at, but suddenly he felt a heat flooding through him, his body a cauldron, his veins lava-filled tributaries.

He looked down and saw that the book was on fire. The pages were crackling, blackening, shriveling. Flames licked his palms, darting between his fingers like lizard tongues, yet his skin remained unblemished. He could feel the searing heat, but it did him no harm. He turned the book over and watched it burn. Then one of the flames licked at his sleeve and Alex dropped the book onto the floor. He stamped it out before the fire could feed on the carpeting.

He looked at the charred pages on the floor, the ashes scattered about. The room smelled like smoke. He went to the fireplace and removed a lavish hardback called *Seeing Japan* and opened the cover. Its pages were filled with hundreds of lush photos of Japan, its landscapes, its cities, its homes and countryside. He'd bought it at the Roppongi Tsutaya bookstore in Minato City, a gorgeous bookshop with gleaming hardwood floors, brick columns, and visible silver piping running along the ceiling. He remembered carrying the book back to their small apartment, sitting on his bed, and turning the pages slowly, savoring the images. He remembered feeling a tremendous sense of distance, of solitude, knowing those photos were the closest he would ever get to seeing the country's full splendor.

Alex removed another book from the fireplace. And another. And another. Until all the books had been rescued and piled up on the floor. Then he heard his father call from upstairs.

"Alex?" Byron called. "Is something on fire?"

"I burned my toast, no biggie."

Alex quickly piled the books back into the box and dragged them upstairs, then scrubbed the charred remains of the Toowoomba guide out of the carpet.

By the time he finished, he was out of breath. The fireplace was empty. The floor was (reasonably) clean. It made him think about Nia's room. Color and shade and shadow and *her* covering every inch. Alex wanted to lie down in her bed, to stare at her ceiling. He wanted to watch her draw Arumaya, to try to envision the telepathic connection between her brain and the page. How she chose which colors went where, what each planet would look like, her fingers dancing as she created an indelible image that, until that moment, did not exist anywhere but her mind.

He thought about why he'd made the decision to stay with Byron, to continue his path toward the mantle of Dominus. Did he actually believe in the mission? Or was it because it was all he'd ever known? For years, Alex had wanted to feel normal, to experience life and love and heartbreak and remorse and all the mistakes and messiness that sounded terrible but in actuality was the *good* stuff that made someone who they were. From childhood, he'd been taught that life was merely the time bookended by birth and death. Living in Whisper Valley was the first time he'd really given thought as to what came between.

Alex went back up to his room. His cell phone was on the nightstand. He watched it, hoping it might light up with a text. When nothing came, he swiped it on. He opened the Photos app and, knowing it would twist his heart, scrolled through.

Pictures of Nia. Pictures of him *and* Nia. A selfie Iggy had taken after their longest run together, three-point-one miles, a full 5K. Alex had been so out of breath he thought he would barf, legs aching like they'd been hit with hammers. But he'd also felt tremendous pride. Iggy had pushed him. And he'd responded.

He'd taken more pictures with Nia than anyone else in his life, combined. He could still feel her lips as she kissed his cheek, her springy hair tickling his neck when she lay her head on his shoulder. The way, when she kissed him, she would ever so gently trace his lower lip with her tongue. Living with the dead was Alex's destiny, but he had never felt more alive than when he was with Nia.

He wanted to make his father proud. Deep down, he believed he could be a Dominus. But he also wanted to feel human. To live and laugh and hurt. His father had said *love is pain*. But sometimes pain let you know you were alive.

He opened his text chain with Nia. Scrolled through their dozens and dozens of messages. Funny, random thoughts. Selfies they'd sent each other, his always a little off-center, out of focus, lighting that made him look like he'd been living inside a hermetically-sealed cave. But Nia always seemed to like the fact that Alex was unpolished. She saw things in him he didn't see in himself. And he was the moron who let it go.

He kept scrolling until he found the very last photo she'd sent him.

The accompanying text read:

**I bought a dress for the Fall Ball. Is it too forward to ask you to be my date?**

She'd even sent him a picture of the dress hanging in her closet. It was a lime green scoop neck dress with a fitted bodice adorned with sparkling beads in spiral patterns. He remembered picturing her wearing it, maybe dancing with her, his hands on her waist, her arms around his neck. Just close enough to feel each other, to look into each other's eyes and tune the rest of the world out.

Then he saw something else in the background of the photo. Something he hadn't noticed before. He zoomed in. There was a portfolio on her desk, next to an illustration that was, unfortunately, cropped out. But on the cover of the portfolio, in perfect cursive, was written:

*For Alex.*

He felt a lump rise in his throat. It was the gift she was working on for him. Again, he felt his anger rising.

He'd committed himself to follow his father's path. He wanted to prove he could handle the job, be a better man. A better Dominus. He'd promised his father. He'd promised the Conclave. *My emotions will never interfere in my duties again*, he'd said. He could stay true to that. His vocation was balancing the life and death of others. There had to be a way to balance his own.

Alex knew what he had to do. He checked the time. The Fall

Ball was starting in less than an hour. He just hoped he had clean clothes.

In his closet, Alex found a pair of good jeans, a dark blue dress shirt, and a brown sport coat, all thankfully ironed and wrinkle-free. But he still needed to get there without alerting his father. He'd cross that bridge when he came to it. He had no bike, it was too far to walk, and if his dad saw an Uber pull up outside, it was over. He looked out the window and saw Iggy get into his parent's car and drive over to the Solomon house. He smiled at the thought of Iggy and Nia going to the ball together. He missed them both so much it ached.

Alex locked his bedroom door. He needed time to get ready. Because he had an idea.

# 34

As promised, Iggy picked Nia up at six fifteen on the dot. She was waiting inside and smiled when she saw him pull up in his parents' hybrid. As Iggy walked up the driveway, Nia felt her father's strong hands on her shoulders.

He gave her a peck on the cheek and said, "Have a great time, hon."

"You're going to wait up for me, aren't you?" she said.

"It's been a long time since I've been able to wait up for anything. So yes. I'm going to wait up for you. Hope you're okay with that."

Nia hugged him and said, "I'm okay with that."

She still wasn't used to her dad being up and about, moving with both grace and confidence—plus a little bit of welcome clumsiness. He was still getting used to the changes. He had begged Nia to tell him what happened. He knew it had to do with the Sonnum boy. Nia told her father that she'd made a promise, and she intended to keep it. And after everything she'd been through, everything she'd done for him, she hoped he could respect that. She could tell it didn't sit well with her father, but he reluctantly agreed.

"If you ever want to talk," he said, "I'm listening. I haven't said this in a long time—but I can wait."

Rivka was knitting on the couch. Nia leaned down and kissed her mom on the cheek.

"Have fun, sweetie," her mother said. "Give James my love."

"I will, Mom." She turned to her dad. "You two will be okay?"

"We will," he said, taking his wife's hand. "I told her we could watch her favorite cooking show."

"You hate cooking shows, Dad."

"True, but it's time for you to let me take care of her for a bit. If it makes her happy, it makes me happy."

"And that makes me happy," Nia said.

No matter how suddenly and painfully her relationship with Alex had ended, he had given Nia her father back. The tradeoff was that every time she looked at her dad, she felt a twist in her heart, love tinged with pain.

The doorbell rang. Stephen opened the door with a scowl on his face that would make Michael Myers run away screaming.

"Now what in the hell do you want?" her dad barked.

Iggy's face drained of all color. "I..."

Stephen clapped Iggy on the shoulder and said, "I'm just messing with you, Iggy. It's good to see you, son."

"Oh. Thank god. Because I didn't bring a change of underwear."

Stephen laughed. Then his face turned deadly serious. "Now, I like you, Iggy. I might even trust you. But I'm not impressed by the fact that you needed a three-point turn to pull into our driveway."

"I have my license," Iggy stammered.

"I have a license too. The 007 kind. So I want Nia home by ten p.m. No exceptions. We have a family plot at Woodlawn Cemetery, but I doubt anyone would notice if the wrong body was buried there."

Stephen's face softened, his lips widening into a wicked smile. "I'm kidding again, Iggy."

"Now I think I might actually need that change of underwear."

"Hey, did Nia tell you she got a scholarship to that program in Austin?" Stephen said with immense pride.

"No, she did *not*," Iggy said, shooting Nia an "I can't believe you didn't tell me but it's okay because holy crap I'm happy for you" look.

"Tell him, hon," Stephen said, beaming.

"Two weeks in Austin over winter break," she said. "Full room and board."

"It's about time this young woman starts taking care of herself instead of everyone else," Stephen said.

"That. Is. Amazing," Iggy said. "When they make your comic books into a bazillion-dollar movie starring some hot A-lister in Spandex, I fully expect an invite to the premiere."

"Don't get ahead of yourself," Nia said. "It's just a start."

"That's seriously amazing," Iggy said. "Speaking of which, you *look* seriously amazing."

"You're not so bad yourself," she replied, noting his periwinkle blue suit and deep red tie. His hair was neatly parted down the side, and he was wearing cologne that smelled like a salty-sweet ocean breeze. "In fact, you look downright handsome. And you smell nice. If Trevor Michaelson doesn't fall head over heels for you, I'll have no choice but to add him to my ever-growing list of idiot guys."

"You two have fun," Stephen said. "But not too much. I own a shovel."

"Don't worry, Dad, I'm in very good hands." Nia looped her arm through Iggy's.

"So am I," Iggy said.

He led her to the car, opened the passenger door and helped Nia in.

"I know your goal is to make Trevor jealous," Nia said, "but you'd better not leave me alone on the dance floor without fair warning or this will be our last date."

"Hey, doesn't Trevor have a brother?"

"He's in sixth grade, Iggy."

"Waiting makes the heart grow fonder."

"First, that's not how the saying goes, and second, ew."

"Don't worry. If Trevor finally comes around and wants to hang out while you're off with Alice, I'm totally ditching you. But if it's you and me, it's you and me."

"Hang out?" Nia said.

"Hang out. Or something."

"Fingers crossed for you to 'or something' with Trevor tonight."

"See? You're the best date ever already." Iggy leaned over and kissed Nia on the cheek. "Now let's go hit the dance floor and make everyone jealous."

---

The Dubya V gymnasium was a square one-story building painted blue and orange, the colors of the Whisper Valley Tigers. When Iggy drove up, they could see a steady stream of their classmates entering through the metal double doors. Nia couldn't wait to get in and dance and let her mind empty.

Nia reached for the door handle, but Iggy said, "Don't you dare."

"Well, look at you, Prince Charming," Nia said. Iggy came around to her side and opened it for her. She got out and looped her arm back through his. "You're setting the chivalry bar way too high for any guys I date from this point on."

"Good, because I was thinking about starting a YouTube series called 'How to Treat a Lady.' Sort of *Queer Eye* for dating."

"If I had any money, I would invest in that," she said.

"I'll hold you to that after the *Arumaya* movie comes out."

They walked toward the gym. Inside, Ms. Hopper, the comp sci teacher, was checking off student attendance. She found Iggy and Nia on the list and said, "You're all set, Mr. Molina and Ms. Solomon. Now go have fun!"

Iggy bowed to her, and Ms. Hopper curtsied back. They had retracted the bleachers and raised the basketball nets in the gym to allow more space. Strobe lights had been hung across the ceiling, with colored cellophane draped over several spotlights turning the gym floor various shades of yellow, blue, orange, and green.

A DJ booth was set up at the far end with a laptop plugged into the sound system. Snack tables were set up with water, soda, chips, M&Ms, pretzels, and apples. *Who the hell eats apples at a school dance?*

Nia wondered. Then she saw Mikey Lederman grab one, clean it with a napkin, and take a bite, which answered her question.

"Blinding Lights" by The Weeknd was playing. The dance floor was already crowded. Others were mingling on the periphery, separated into cliques, or trying to gather the courage to ask a crush to dance. That was high school romance in a nutshell. Nobody willing to make the first move, so innumerable crushes went unrequited.

Nia was hungry, but the snack options weren't very appealing, and she didn't feel like brushing cheddar-flavored potato chip crumbs off her dress. Nia's friends peppered her with questions about her father. His sudden, miraculous recovery had been huge gossip at Dubya V, though it had thankfully been overshadowed by Billy Wootens being caught selling Adderall and getting suspended indefinitely.

They asked her about Alex, how she was holding up after the breakup. She smiled and said she was doing okay. The questions came with such pained, sympathetic looks that it made Nia want to puke. She hated feeling pitied, and hated knowing that her response and attitude would then be dissected like a frog in biology.

"People will forget he existed by Spring Break," Alice said, and Nia wasn't sure if that made her feel better or worse. Alex had left a hole in her heart, and every fake-sympathetic question felt like prying open a still-healing wound.

Iggy headed out to the dance floor and called for Nia. She was happy to join him. At first, she felt self-conscious, wondering if anyone was looking at her, watching her, studying her reactions. Was she too sad about the breakup and being dramatic? Was she not acting sad enough because she was an ice queen? Every emotion could be ripped apart. Why was she even here? She felt like a spotlight was on her, the darkness creeping in yet again. But just as it was about to overwhelm her, Iggy put his hands on her shoulders.

"Hey, screw everyone else," he said. "Just dance."

"Let's go," she said.

She took Iggy's hand. Nia closed her eyes and let the music take over. She danced with Iggy, other friends hopping in and out, and the darkness fled her mind. She was having a ball. The playlist was fire. And to her surprise, Iggy could *dance.*

After five songs they took a snack break. The front doors were open, a fall breeze cooling the hot gym.

"I haven't seen James tonight," Nia said, tossing back a few M&Ms. "Have you?"

Iggy shook his head. "He's probably off machine-gunning baby seals with Billy. I'd prefer not to think about him. James has pissed off enough people this semester he probably knows he's as welcome at school functions as scabies."

Nia nodded. Better that James wasn't here. They'd mostly avoided each other since the night at the bookstore, which was probably for the best.

Iggy downed a cup of water, then his eyes widened. He gestured excitedly toward the far end of the dance floor.

"Did you see that?" he said.

"See what?"

"Trevor Michaelson. He was just looking at me."

"I didn't see it. But that doesn't mean it didn't happen."

"Listen, Nia, I need you to be my eyes and ears. If Trevor *sees* me looking at him, then he'll *know* I was looking at him."

"And why would that be a bad thing?"

"It wouldn't be a bad thing. It would be the worst thing to happen in the history of humanity."

"Sure you're not being a little overdramatic?"

Iggy thought for a moment and said, "No."

"Haven't I heard you say that playing it cool is overrated?"

"I've also said, 'Do as I say, not as I do.'"

"Go talk to Trevor," Nia said.

They finished their drinks. "All of Me" by John Legend came over the sound system. Iggy held out his hand and said, "May I have this dance?"

She placed her hand in his and said, "You may."

He led her to the dance floor and gently placed his hands on her sides. She loosely draped her hands over his neck. They danced, slowly but awkwardly.

"I think Trevor just looked at you," Nia whispered.

"If you're messing with me, our friendship is over."

"Come on, I wouldn't do that to you. There, he did it again!"

"No way. Holy crap. Are you serious?"

"I said I wouldn't do that to you, Ig. You should ask him to dance."

"If you're wrong, and I embarrass myself and end up having to go live in a cave for the rest of my life out of shame, I'm going to be pissed."

"Just go to him. If you don't, you'll always wonder what might have happened if you did."

"But what about you?"

"Don't worry about me. You've already been the best date I could have ever hoped for."

"Okay, I'm gonna go talk to him." Then Iggy looked over Nia's shoulder. A smile spread across his face. "You know, I think I'd prefer to take runner-up in the best date category."

"What do you mean?" she said.

"Turn around," Iggy said.

Nia turned around. When she saw him, her breath caught in her throat.

Alex was walking toward her. He looked handsome, almost unbearably so. His brown hair was neatly combed. He wore nice jeans, an ironed blue shirt, and a sport jacket that made him look, dammit, *dashing*. She felt like her heart could burst.

"Just go to him," Iggy said. "If you don't, you'll always wonder what might have happened if you did."

Time slowed to a crawl. Every step he took seemed to take a year. Nia could feel her cheeks growing warm. When Alex reached her, he held out his hand. Nia took it.

"I know this is a total movie thing to say," Alex said to Iggy, "but may I cut in?"

"You'd better cut in *right this second*," Iggy said, stepping back. "Besides, I have the captain of the swim team waiting for me. Allegedly."

"It's good to see you, Iggy," Alex said.

"It's good to see you too. You know, I warned Nia there was a chance you were going to leave and never come back. I'm glad you proved me wrong."

"Thanks for looking out for her."

"I always will. Speaking of which, one of these days I expect an explanation for just what the hell happened the other week. But right now, I have a hot guy to potentially embarrass myself in front of."

Iggy extended his hand to Alex. Alex ignored it, and instead wrapped his arms around Iggy and pulled him in tight hug.

"Ugh, you're a good hugger," Iggy said. "Now if you'll excuse me, I'm going to try out for the captain of the swim team."

Iggy walked away, leaving Alex and Nia alone.

"May I?" he said.

"You may."

Alex placed his hands on her hips and gently pulled her toward him. Their bodies pressed against each other just enough that Nia felt that familiar crackle of electricity. She'd missed it more than she knew. She put her hands over his shoulders, fingers brushing against the hairs on the nape of his neck. She felt Alex shudder.

She looked him over. "You clean up pretty well."

"Honestly, it's a miracle I had clean clothes. This whole grand romantic entrance wouldn't have been so grand if I smelled like the inside of my closet."

"I never thought I'd see you again."

"I'm sorry," Alex said. "I need to get that out there. I'm not okay without you. I don't know if I've ever been fully okay to begin with. And I know you're not my life preserver either. But when I'm with you, I'm a lot closer to being okay than I am without you."

"I am too," she said, and then he kissed her and everything else stopped mattering.

"I told you I don't know what I'm doing," Alex said, "but that doesn't mean that if I do the wrong thing, I shouldn't try to fix it."

"What about your dad? Your future?" she said.

"I made a promise to my dad," Alex said. "I intend to keep it.

But I want my future to include you. I don't know how it's going to work. But I'll do whatever it takes to figure it out."

"I will too," she said.

"And I swear on my life that any time I'm not with you, you will always be with me." Alex put her hand on his heart. "Do you think we can try to make it work?"

"I'd rather try than lose you."

"It's ok to not be ok," Alex said. "But I'm much more ok with you than I am without you."

"I am too."

They danced. Silently, effortlessly, locked in each other's arms. She placed her head against his chest and closed her eyes. For all she knew the entire school was watching them, but she didn't care.

When she opened her eyes, Alex was looking at her.

He said, "I love you, Nia."

"I love you too."

The words came out before she even had a chance to realize what she was saying. But they were the four truest words she had ever said. They kissed, and she leaned into him.

*This is home*, she thought.

When they finally disentangled, Nia looked around. Most of the junior class, plus faculty, was staring at them. She had no way of knowing if it was because of their public make-out session, or the fact that Alex had reappeared out of nowhere with no explanation. But she didn't care. She loved him. She believed him.

"So, what now?" she asked.

"Um, I don't know. This was basically the extent of my plan. If you hadn't kissed me back, I probably would have just gone home and ordered a pizza and moped with the Ankou for the next hundred years. They're not very good conversationalists."

"That would have been a shame."

"Seriously. We'll make this work somehow. I promise."

"I know we will."

Alex leaned in to give Nia another kiss. She closed her eyes. But Alex's lips never met hers. She opened them to see what stopped him and immediately froze in fright.

Standing beside them was a man. He was tall and thin and wore a black suit with a black shirt and black tie. He was not a teacher and certainly wasn't dressed like a parent. And his creepy-close proximity to them felt like a purposeful invasion of space. For some reason the man looked familiar, but Nia couldn't place him. Either way, a very bad feeling chewed at her insides.

The man was staring at Alex, smiling broadly.

"Alexander Sonnum," the man said.

"Who are you?" Alex said.

"My name is Samael Zagan. Twenty years ago, your father killed hundreds of people and watched my family burn."

"What—?" Alex said.

Alex saw Ms. Hopper walking toward them, eyes locked on the stranger. "Sir, sir! You can't be here!" she said angrily. "Are you a parent? Did you sign up to be a chaperone?"

"Don't worry, I'm not staying," the man said. Then he turned around and walked toward the gym entrance.

"What the hell was that?" Nia said.

"I have no idea. But I don't like it."

"Me either. I have a bad feeling," Nia said. "Let's get out of here."

"Is it just me, or did he look kind of familiar?" Alex said.

Nia thought for a moment, then snapped her fingers and said, "The Willoughby Williams reading. *That* was the guy I could have sworn was taking pictures of you."

"Holy crap, that's the same guy?"

"Alex, what did he mean about your dad?"

"I have no idea, I swear, but I'm going to find out." Alex ran after the man. Nia and Ms. Hooper followed. "Hey, you. *Stop!*"

But when the man walked through the gym entrance, he turned around and slammed the double doors in Alex's face. His face was visible through the small windows in the doors. The man smiled, and then there was an audible *clink*. Alex tried to open the doors, but they wouldn't budge.

"Alex," Nia said, a chill running up her spine. "Alex, *look*."

Through the narrow gap between the doors, they could see a

thick chain held together with a massive padlock. The man had locked them inside.

He smiled at Alex and said, "Your father watched my family burn. I've waited a very long time to return the favor."

The man stepped back from the doors and took something from his pocket. When Nia saw what it was, a wave of pure terror washed over her.

"*No*," Alex said, shaking the doors. "Not now. Oh my god, *please no*."

A crowd had gathered by the entrance. Nia said, "Alex, what's going on?"

Then the man tossed the lit book of matches toward the door, and a wall of flame shot into the night sky.

He turned to her. His face was ashen. "This is the Quieting."

The flames raced around the gymnasium, licking the walls and wrapping it in a terrifying red and orange embrace. Samael watched the brick begin to blacken, eyes wide with delight. It was more beautiful than anything he could have ever imagined. This was his retribution. Twenty years in the making. A family for a family. And when it was over, he knew Death would come.

"What the hell did you do?" James Mungro ran up to Samael, sheer horror in his eyes.

"Isn't it wonderful?" Samael said, his eyes fixated on the glow.

"You told me you just wanted to scare them!" James shouted.

"Do you hear all those screams? I believe they're quite terrified," Samael replied.

"You didn't say you'd kill people!"

"Nor did you ask," Samael said. "You were quite content to keep your head in the sand. Thank you for your assistance, James. I can honestly say I could not have done this without you."

"You're a goddamn psychopath," James said. "I hope you burn in hell."

Samael looked at the young man. "To paraphrase what Winston

Churchill once said, 'I am prepared to meet my Maker. Whether he is prepared to meet me is another matter.'"

James stared in horror at Samael, delight etched on the madman's face. Then James ran off into the night.

---

The screams began all at once. One moment the gymnasium was filled with music and dancing, the next it was a furnace in hell. Alex felt the tremors instantly, like a tuning fork had gone off inside his bones.

*The Ankou. They're coming.*

The music had stopped. The lights had gone out. The power had either been cut, or the circuits had been shorted by the flames. In the darkness, Alex could see dozens of cell phones out as people frantically called 911. But given the speed at which the flames had wrapped around the building, help would not arrive nearly in time. And given the presence of the Ankou, Alex realized with terror that it was not meant to.

"Come on!" Nia shouted. She threw off her heels and sprinted to the back of the gym. Alex followed. She gripped the handle of the emergency exit door, but yelped and pulled her hand back.

"Don't open it!" Mr. Ryerson shouted from behind them. "There's a fire behind that door. If we open it, the backdraft could kill us all."

"Get the bleachers out!" Nia shouted. "We can reach the windows from them!"

Smoke had begun to fill the gym. The heat was rising every second. Students and faculty began to haul the bleachers out from the wall, creating a makeshift staircase.

"Pull the tarps out!" Mr. Ryerson shouted, pointing at the baseball field tarps that were rolled up against the wall. "Everyone underneath! Cover up!"

Students and faculty rolled the tarps out and began huddling underneath.

"Down on the floor!" Mr. Ryerson shouted. "Smoke rises! Get down!"

People dropped to the ground. Some were taking puffs on inhalers. Many were already coughing. Time was running out.

Once the bleachers were out, Nia ran up the steps to the row of windows. The heat had already caused the glass to spiderweb. Nia looked out.

"What do you see?" Alex said. Nia shook her head. Alex's heart sank.

"The fire is all the way around the building," she said. "Even if we could break the windows and get everyone through, there's no way we'd be able to make it past the flames. It's a dead end."

Nia came back down. Suddenly, there was an enormous crash from above. Alex looked up. The glass in the ceiling skylight had shattered.

"Look out!" Alex cried as the shards rained down. A guy screamed and grabbed his arm where glass sliced his skin.

Through the empty skylight, Alex saw them. The Ankou. Dozens and dozens of them were circling above the gymnasium, glowing vultures waiting to Exort the soon-to-perish people below.

Alex looked around. He saw Iggy holding hands with Trevor Michaelson. Arvind, Ayesha, and Francine were huddled under the tarps, hugging each other, knowing these were their last moments together.

He looked at Nia, standing next to him. All those moments they shared, whispers and kisses and touches and glances. How just moments ago they had told each other they loved each other, how they would make it work, and now they would be reduced to ash.

Alex's life to that moment flashed through his mind. His earliest memories with his father. When he first learned who he was; who Byron was. The day in the woods when he placed his hands on the dying man's heart and brought him back from the brink of death. All the travel. All the miles. All the days spent alone. How he had grown up desensitized to life, each soul no more than a flickering candle that had reached its end. Alex had sworn to uphold the Tenets. To follow in the footsteps of his father.

He knew what he had to do. It would hurt. He wouldn't survive. But these were his friends. He sure as shit wasn't going to let it end for them like this.

"Iggy! Trevor!" Alex shouted. "I need you both! Nia, you too!"

Iggy and Trevor Michaelson ran over, holding their jackets over their mouths.

"I have a plan," Alex said.

"Talk," Iggy said.

"I need you and Trevor to round up a bunch of people. *Big people.* Hell, the offensive line if you can. See that trophy case over there?" Alex pointed at a large, thick metal case housing Whisper Valley trophies and memorabilia. It was nearly ten feet high and six feet wide, and solid metal. It should work.

Trevor said, "What's the plan?"

"I need you to push the case over to the front doors."

"You mean the double doors that are locked with a raging fire outside?" Iggy said.

"That's the one. Nia, tell the teachers to herd everyone over by the front doors and to be ready. They're going to need to move fast, and we have to help people who can't run."

"Got it," Nia said.

Iggy looked at Alex like he'd sprouted a third head.

"When I give the signal," Alex said to Iggy and Trevor, "I need your team to push the trophy case over."

"Push it over?" Iggy said. "What the hell are you talking about?"

"Trust me," Alex said. "Now *go!*"

Alex's heart pounded. The smoke was burning his eyes. Alex went to the front door. He could see the chain. The paint on the metal doors had already begun to bubble. He thought about the Toowoomba guide, how he'd held the burning book in his hands. He felt the pain just like anyone—but pain was skin deep. He could take it. It was time to fight fire with fire.

Alex took several deep breaths, then gripped the metal handles on each door. Immediately he could feel a searing pain shoot through his fingers and palms, hotter than anything he'd ever felt before. He screamed.

"Alex!" Nia shouted. She ran to him.

"NO!" he yelled. "Stay back! I got this!"

The metal had to be over a thousand degrees, but even though Alex could *feel* the insane heat, his skin remained unbroken. Alex had paid attention in chem class. Metal only melted at temperatures topping 2,500 degrees Fahrenheit. He couldn't even be sure that the Blaze could rise above that kind of heat. But the Blaze wasn't the only weapon in his arsenal.

Alex pulled the doors toward him. They were locked tight on the outside. He peered through the small crack he'd created until he could see the thick metal chain looped through the door handles.

The crack was narrow. Maybe the width of an arm. But it was enough.

"Alex?" Nia shouted. Fire was poking through holes where bricks had fallen out of the walls. They had moments before everything collapsed. "Alex, *what are you doing*?"

"Just make sure everyone is ready!" he yelled. He rolled up his sleeve, then Alex stuck his hand through the crack, through the raging flames, and gripped the metal chain.

The pain was unreal, like he had stuck his hand into the mouth of hell itself.

Alex closed his eyes. The Blaze began to simmer inside him, spilling into his arms and fingers. Then, while the flames burst forth from his fingers, Alex began to channel his anger. His anger at the lies, at all the years he spent alone, all the days he felt like he was living someone else's life. He felt the Dim surge through him, roiling inside him, igniting the Blaze like nitroglycerin.

The pain in his arm was beyond comprehension. Then with one burst he released all the built-up energy into the hand that gripped the thick chain. Alex could see smoke begin to rise from the metal. Then, slowly but surely, he felt the metal begin to soften. The chain was melting in his hand. Alex could feel his body draining. He began to falter. His legs grew wobbly. And when he couldn't hold on any longer, he yanked as hard as he could. The chain broke apart and clattered to the ground.

Alex pulled the doors inward, then collapsed onto the gymnasium floor. He could see a wall of flame outside, at least six feet high. He felt like all the life had been sucked from his body. For one terrible moment he thought he might have been Siphoned. But only his father had the ability to do that. He was still alive, at least for now.

From the ground, with the last of his energy, Alex shouted at Iggy, "Now!"

"Come on!" Iggy yelled. Four burly guys had taken hold of one end of the trophy case to push, while another four had taken the other to pull. "One, two, three, go!"

They slid the enormous case along the ground, inch by inch, then set it in front of the open doors.

"Now *push*!" Iggy shouted.

All eight took positions along the back of the case, trophies facing the fire. On three, they all grunted and shoved the case toward the flames. Once it was directly in front of the fire, they all pushed and the monstrous cabinet toppled over. The glass shattered, trophies and plaques falling into the flames. The case itself had landed atop the fire, creating a makeshift bridge. But it wouldn't last long.

"Everyone, go!" Nia shouted. "One at a time, too much weight and it'll break!"

"Move fast," Iggy added, "metal conducts heat. This thing is going to turn into a frying pan!"

One by one, the students made their way over the trophy case. Two students picked up another who was wheelchair-bound and carried him across. As more and more went over, Alex could hear the case begin to buckle. There were a hundred and thirteen students in the school, plus faculty. There were at least a hundred and twenty people inside the gym. They were moving too slow. Not all of them would make it.

Alex tried to stand up, but he was too weak. He just kept waving the others through.

Nia tried to help him up. "*Come on!*" she yelled.

"I can't!" he said. "Just go!"

"I'm not leaving you!" Nia said, soot covering her face.

"Please," he said, "I can't watch you die."

"Then don't! Get up, Alex. *Get your ass up!*"

She managed to haul Alex to his feet. By that time there were about thirty students and a handful of faculty left inside the gym. Trevor Michaelson went to cross, but as soon as he stepped onto the case, it collapsed. The fire engulfed the metal. The entryway was again blocked by flames. Alex couldn't see another way out.

He managed to get to his feet. He was wobbly, but standing. Nia looked around. There were no other trophy cases. Nothing large enough to create another bridge. They were trapped.

"Are there any other exits?" Alex said.

"No," Mr. Ryerson said, coughing into his hand. "Just this and the emergency doors. And those are..."

He trailed off.

Alex kissed Nia and held her close.

"I'm sorry," Alex said. "For everything."

Then Alex saw a bright light outside the front doors. It seemed to be getting nearer, growing brighter and brighter. He held Nia. This was it. This was the end.

*The Ankou*, he thought. *They're coming for us.*

At least they would be together.

But then something occurred to him. Ankou came from *above.*

The beams of light weren't from an Ankou. They were from a car.

"Move!" Alex yelled.

The people in front of the door dove to the side as the vehicle crashed through the entrance to the gym with a crunch of metal and glass. It slammed into the broken trophy case and dislodged it from the entrance. The car came to a stop right above the flames, which immediately began to lick hungrily at the chassis. Then Alex saw who was behind the wheel. James Mungro.

"Go!" James shouted from inside the car. "Get out of there!"

"Come on, Alex!" Nia shouted. She wrapped Alex's arm around her shoulder and helped him over to the car. They hoisted themselves up onto the hood. Alex could feel the heat coming off the metal as they climbed onto the roof, then down onto the trunk, the fire bracketing them on both sides. Then they leapt off the back of the car onto the pavement. The rest of the students and faculty did the same.

James was still inside the car. The windows began to crack. The driver's side door would open right into the fire. He was trapped.

Once everyone was out of the gym, Alex turned back. Flames were licking the sides of the car. He could see James inside, looking for an exit.

"Go!" James shouted. "It's gonna blow!"

Alex looked around. He found a metal pipe, climbed back onto the trunk, and smashed it against the rear windshield. He brought the pipe down over and over until he'd created a small hole. Then he crouched down and yelled to James.

"Come on!"

James slithered into the backseat. Alex kept beating on the glass, the hole growing larger and larger. He could feel trickles of blood streaming down his arms.

"Kick!" Alex said. "We're almost there!"

James kicked repeatedly at the rear window. Finally, one of the sides dislodged. Alex jammed the pipe between the window to create a lever. James pushed with his feet and the windshield peeled off. Alex tossed it aside, then reached in and held out his hand, slick with blood. James grabbed it. Alex pulled him out and they both leapt from the trunk and ran.

They didn't make it more than twenty feet before the car erupted in a fireball that sent the chassis ten feet into the air, the impact knocking them to the ground. The metal came crashing down just feet from where they lay, its twisted husk continuing to burn.

Nia ran over and knelt down beside them. "Are you okay?"

James nodded. So did Alex.

"I'm pretty sure," Alex said to James, in between gulps of air, "that you should have your driver's license revoked."

"I'm sorry," James said. "For everything."

"We'll deal with you later," Nia said.

"Thanks for coming back for me," he said.

"Thanks for coming back for *us*."

"I owed you," he said to Alex. He looked at Nia. "I owed you both."

"Consider us even."

They all stood up. Dozens of classmates and faculty were gathered in the parking lot, watching the gymnasium burn. Alex could hear sirens getting closer. They would have been far, far too late to save anyone. From what he could tell, there didn't seem to be any major injuries, just some cuts and bruises and smoke inhalation. Alex looked up at the sky. The Ankou were gone. The Quieting had been prevented. He did not know what would happen next. The Conclave would not be so kind this time. In fact, they were probably preparing to use the Dim on him at that very mom—

"Alex Sonnum!"

Alex went cold. He knew that voice now. He turned to see Samael Zagan walking toward them. And he was aiming a gun at Alex's heart.

"I want your father to be here to see his family die," Zagan said, his voice crackling with unhinged, desperate insanity, "just like he did mine." Alex heard a *click* as the safety went off.

From the corner of his eye, he saw James running full speed at Zagan, driving his shoulder into the man's ribs. Zagan uttered an *oomph* as they both fell to the ground.

When Zagan's body hit the pavement, there was a crack of thunder. The gun had gone off. Then there was silence.

Alex stood there, waiting, *expecting* to die. But instead, he felt nothing. No pain. The shot had missed.

"Alex?" It was Nia. A bloom of red had begun to soak through her dress. Then she crumpled to the ground.

"No!" Alex screamed. He ran to her and cradled her in his arms. He tore off his jacket and wrapped her in it. Her eyes were wide with terror. Her mouth opened but no words came out.

"No!" he screamed. "Please, *please* no. Nia, stay with me! Somebody help us! *Please! Help us!*"

He placed his hands on her chest and drew every ounce of energy he had to bring forth the Blaze. *Come on*, he thought. *Faster.*

But his body was spent. He couldn't muster the energy for the fire.

"Please," he whispered, willing his body to listen. But it would not. The heat would not come. "*Please!*"

Nia put her hand on his face and said, "Alex, I..."

Nia did not finish her sentence. Her eyes were open, but she was not blinking.

*Oh god. Oh god, no. Please no.*

He held his mouth against hers, but felt no breath come from her lungs. He pressed his fingers against her neck, but felt no pulse.

She was gone.

Alex screamed into the night and clutched Nia's body against his, cradling her head against his chest as he howled. James and Iggy kneeled down next to Nia, tears streaming down their face.

"Nia," Alex said, sobbing. "Nia, please come back."

He felt a gentle tremor and looked up. A single, solitary Ankou was descending from the heavens.

"Get out of here!" Alex shouted. "Stay away from her!"

The Ankou continued its descent.

Then Alex saw Samael stand up. He still held the gun. He watched the scene with a strange, almost puzzled look on his face. Then he began to walk toward Alex, limping slightly.

"You monster," Alex seethed, tears running down his face. "You could have just come for *me*."

"Many innocents died along with my family," Zagan said. "Any collateral death is all on your father."

"My—" Alex began to say, but then he stopped. His eyes widened. Words failed him. Zagan turned around to see what Alex was looking at.

Byron Sonnum was standing at the edge of the parking lot. He wore a black suit with a white shirt and black tie. His polished black shoes reflected the orange glow of the flames. His hair was combed back. He was staring at Alex.

The words of the Conclave echoed in his mind. *The last face you see before your soul is ripped from your body will be that of your father.*

"I'm so sorry," he whispered to Nia. "I love you." Then Alex looked at his father, tears staining his cheeks. But Byron did not approach Alex. Instead, he began to walk toward Samael Zagan.

Zagan cocked his head. Recognition flashed across his face.

"I know you," Zagan said. "I've been looking for you my whole life."

Then Zagan raised the gun and fired five shots into Byron Sonnum.

The bullets disappeared into Byron, absorbed into his chest like drops of water. Byron kept walking. Zagan pulled the trigger again but it clicked empty. He reached into his pocket and took out a handful of bullets, half of them falling to the ground with a *plink.*

Alex watched as Byron's shadow began to grow. But not just his shadow: *him.*

Byron's body stretched out into the sky, impossibly large, his face receding into darkness, his suit unfolding into a flowing black robe. He grew and grew until Byron loomed over Samael like a dark mountain. A hood covered his face. Then, Byron raised his head. And Samael began to scream.

Byron's face had become a great, bone-white skull. Human eyes glowed in its dark, fleshless sockets. The face had no lips. No cheeks. No tongue. No flesh except for two large, lidless eyes.

From the robe's sleeves extended two pairs of skeletal hands, each inhumanly long and ending in long, slender fingertips. The skeletal right hand reached behind its back and retrieved an enormous scythe, its handle long as a person, moonlight glinting off the blade which looked sharp enough to slice through steel.

Death walked toward Samael. It held the scythe with both hands, flames and shadows dancing in its eyes. Alex was too terrified to move.

Samael stumbled and fell, crawling backward on his hands as Death came closer.

"Get away from me," Samael said, swinging the gun at Death. "*Get away!*"

He swung the gun again, but this time Death caught Samael's wrist and lifted him into the air. Then Death held up his scythe, the shimmering blade reflected in Samael's eyes.

With a swooping motion, Death swung the scythe and impaled Samael with the enormous blade. Death then lifted the blade into the air, but rather than cleaving Samael in half, the scythe ripped a glowing form from his body.

Death had Siphoned Samael Zagan's soul.

Samael's lifeless body fell to the earth. Yet his soul hung from the end of the blade, quivering in the darkness. It glowed in the night. Samael's soul looked around, confused, as if trying to understand what was happening.

Then Death looked up. So did Alex. Dozens of Ankou flew down from the sky and latched onto Samael's soul, which uttered an inhuman scream. The Ankou ripped his soul from Death's scythe and began to drag it downward. The soul howled and clawed at the air as it slipped beneath the earth, leaving nothing but Samael Zagan's empty body crumpled on the pavement.

Alex watched all of this unable to speak, unable to breathe. Then, when Samael and the Ankou were gone, Death began to walk toward him.

Alex had prevented a Quieting. He'd defied the Conclave. He had been warned. There was no coming back. He knew the punishment. He was ready.

"Take me," Alex said. "I don't want to be here without her."

Alex closed his eyes and waited to be Siphoned. To feel the blade of Death tear his soul from his body. But there was nothing. He opened his eyes. Standing before him was not the true face of Death, but his father.

"I'm sorry, Dad," Alex said, his words choked out between sobs. He looked down in agony at Nia's lifeless body. "I just loved her so much."

Byron knelt down and put his hand on Alex's cheek. He smiled, then leaned forward and kissed his son on the forehead.

"It's not your time," Byron said. "Live your life. And never forget that you are my son."

Byron looked up at the sky. A lone Ankou descended from the heavens. It was coming for Nia's soul. Byron raised his hand and closed his fist. The Ankou stopped in its place, hovering just feet from Nia's body.

Then Byron placed his hands on Nia's heart and began to breathe deeply. Heavily. Byron gritted his teeth. He was in tremendous pain.

"Dad?" Alex said. He felt a tremor beneath him, surrounding him. "*Dad?*"

There was a flash of light, blinding Alex. Alex blinked. The street eventually faded back into focus. And then he saw his father's lifeless form on the ground.

"*Dad!*"

The Ankou that had come down for Nia instead floated to the body of Byron Sonnum. It changed shape, elongating into the guise of a human. A hand reached down. A slender hand. A woman's hand. Alex watched as his father's soul reached up and took it. The Ankou had taken on the guise of a young woman Alex had never seen before, but she looked at Byron like she'd loved him for a lifetime.

*Sofia.*

Then the Ankou lifted Byron's soul from his body and they both disappeared into the heavens.

Alex felt something stirring in his arms. He looked down and saw Nia. She was *looking* at him.

"Alex?" Nia said. She looked down and saw that she was wrapped in Alex's coat. "Alex, what happened?"

Words failed him. He simply brought her to him and kissed her and cried.

With the girl he loved in his arms and the body of his father on the ground beside him, Alex didn't know how his heart could simultaneously be filled with both endless love and bottomless grief.

# 36

TWO MONTHS LATER

"Nia, Alex, the car is here!"

"Almost ready, Dad! Alex, can you help me close this?" Nia said.

Alex looked at Nia's overstuffed suitcase and frowned. "If you try to fit so much as one more toothpick in there, I think it's going to explode."

"Snarky comments later. Help now."

"Okay, sit on it."

Nia sighed and sat on her suitcase. Alex zipped it up, then stood back proudly.

"Trust me," he said, "when it comes to packing, you want the guy who moved a hundred times before he was old enough to drive."

Nia put her hands on her hips and looked around her bedroom almost wistfully. "Guess we're ready to go. You know, once we get to Austin, I'm going to realize I forgot something important. Like pants."

"Pants are overrated," he said. "So, are you excited?"

"Excited. Nervous. Anxious. Terrified. Ecstatic. Basically, I'm feeling totally throw-up-able."

"Is that a word?"

"I'm officially making it a word." She checked her watch. "We land at one thirty, Texas time. The program will have a shuttle waiting for us outside baggage claim."

"And you're *sure* you're okay with me coming?"

"Am I sure?" Nia said. "If you said no, I'd knock you unconscious and stuff you into the overhead bin."

"As long as they still serve mini pretzels or those weird blue potato chips in the overhead bin, I'll agree to those conditions."

"I want you there," Nia said. "I know when this is over, you're going to be away a lot, and I want to make the most of every second we have until then."

Alex smiled. She kissed him, but there was a sadness beneath it that Nia picked up on. She took his hand.

"If you're not ready…" she said

"I'm ready," he said, squeezing her hand. "I need to go with you. Just…sometimes it hits me all over again. This is the first time I've ever traveled without him. My dad was the only family I had."

"Well, now you have me," Nia said. "I can't replace him, and I won't try. But as long as you have me, you'll always have family."

"Then I'll keep you as long as you'll let me. You okay with that?"

"Am I okay with that? I get to tell people I'm Death's girlfriend."

"Please don't," Alex said. "The Conclave had to grit their teeth and hold their nose when they gave me the mantle of Dominus. Thankfully, they didn't have a choice. Without a Dominus or Aegis, the world would become a giant Perdita-fest overnight. You know what they say: the devil you know is better than no devil at all."

"I don't think anyone has ever said that. And Perdita-fest sounds like the worst music festival of all time. Are you getting used to being Dominus?"

"Like breaking in a new pair of shoes. Only, you know, with slightly bigger consequences. I've already had to banish two Ankou, and after I stopped the Quieting at the gym, there's been more turbulence than normal. I'll come back here after Austin, but I don't know how long I'll have before I have to leave again. I have a lot of work ahead of me."

"I'm going to miss you."

"Me too. Just know that when I'm not here with you, I'm here with you." Alex placed his hand on Nia's heart and kissed her softly.

"Long as you promise not to fall for any hot French Perditas," she said.

"You'd just better hope that Marie Antoinette was properly Exorted."

Nia laughed. Then she turned serious. "I want you to know I will always be grateful for what your dad did for me. I wish I'd gotten to know him better. But I promise I'll take care of his son for the rest of my life."

"He would have liked you. A lot."

"Speaking of your dad, I distinctly remember you telling me that all that stuff about the Grim Reaper was just folklore and fairytales."

"My dad used to talk about becoming the true face of Death when I became Dominus. I always thought he meant it figuratively."

"Meanwhile, I'm glad we're getting out of here now," Nia replied. "The whole town feels like it's become Area 51 with all the news crews and tabloid journalists trying to figure out just what the hell happened at the gym."

"My dad always told me denial is the best course of action. And the only people who were capable of seeing what really happened are me and Samael Zagan. And I'm the only one who's still above ground. What about your dad?"

"At some point, I'll tell him the truth. He deserves that. But he said he'd wait until I was ready to tell him."

"When we get back, I think you should tell him," Alex said. "There have been too many lies. Besides, I'm in love with his daughter. And Iggy told me he owns a shovel."

"That sounds like a great plan," Nia said. "The 'telling my dad' part, not the 'my dad burying my boyfriend in the woods' part."

"Let's get out of here, then. I wouldn't mind getting away from the reporters constantly stopping by to ask if I knew Samael Zagan."

"Hey, speaking of that hellbound psychopath, did you see this article today?"

"No. Every time I hear that name it's like nails on a chalkboard. Let me see it."

Nia took out her phone, opened a website, and handed it to Alex. The headline read:

MOTIVE STILL UNCLEAR IN ZAGAN ATTEMPTED MURDERS

After a thorough police and FBI investigation into the fire set by Samael Zagan that nearly killed dozens at the Whisper Valley High gymnasium, motives for his terrorist acts remain unclear. Witnesses say Zagan did not make any statements before locking the gym doors and setting fire to the building. Students and faculty were able to pry open the padlocked front doors and, along with the quick thinking of WV student James Mungro, managed to save dozens, if not hundreds of lives. Except for a few minor injuries from debris and several treated for smoke inhalation, there was remarkably no loss of life from those inside. Many are referring to the incident as The Miracle at Dubya V.

There were, however, two fatalities after the nearly-catastrophic events: Zagan himself, and Byron Sonnum, father of Whisper Valley student Alex Sonnum, who had come to find his son. Autopsies concluded that, despite the odd circumstances, both Sonnum and Zagan appeared to have died from natural causes. Conspiracy theories have been prevalent since the incident, with several witnesses claiming that Zagan shot Nia Solomon, a junior at Whisper Valley High, before perishing. Yet no gunshot wounds were reported, and all students and faculty were fully accounted for. Some have even made outlandish claims regarding supernatural occurrences, which police have chalked up to the effects of smoke inhalation.

Authorities are still looking into Samael Zagan's professional dealings and murky finances. Zagan himself was the lone survivor of the infamous Plata Air crash twenty years ago which killed 147 people, including Zagan's father, mother, and sister. In the ensuing years, those who knew Zagan said he had developed an unhealthy obsession with finding those "responsible" for the crash—though the disaster was said to have been caused by faulty equipment rather than any sort of malicious activity. Zagan opened up a store, Zagan's End, which specialized in occult-related items. Tax returns showed millions of dollars in annual income, but many of Zagan's colleagues claim he had a great deal of unreported income, and correspondence has shown ties to a large global "death-obsessed" community called the Children of Azrael which one former member caustically described as "Dungeons and Dragons for rich, bored people." Police found years of correspondence between Zagan and Morton Yen, 52, a fellow member of the Children of Azrael, whose body was discovered just days before Zagan's attack at the gymnasium. Zagan is the prime suspect in Yen's murder.

Items from Zagan's End are scheduled to be auctioned off, with the proceeds and Zagan's estate earmarked for the family of Morton Yen, to help rebuild the Whisper Valley High gymnasium, and to various other charities.

"I'm just glad his money will go to help people," Nia said. "I don't know if I'll ever be able to take a PE class in that gym again."

Suddenly, Alex felt an ache in his chest, the way it did after a hard run with Iggy. Sometimes the grief came in droplets. Sometimes in waves. Sometimes it overwhelmed him. For the first time in his life, Alex needed to swim on his own.

"Hey," Nia said, putting her hand on his cheek, "are you okay?"

"I think so. I just miss him so much. I knew he wouldn't be around forever. But I thought we'd have more time. There's so much I wish I'd said. And not said."

"I have a feeling he knows what you wish you'd said," Nia said. "Remember what you told me. It's okay to not be okay."

He smiled and she kissed him.

Their embrace was interrupted by Stephen Solomon's booming voice.

"I'm not paying for waiting time!"

"Let's go before your dad throws me out the window," Alex said.

"One quick thing," Nia said. She knelt down by her bed and took out a leather portfolio. It read *For Alex* on the front in gold lettering. "I thought about throwing it out or setting it on fire that day you left. I'm glad I didn't."

She handed it to Alex. He took it from her, unzipped the portfolio, and carefully opened the cover. When he saw what she revealed, Alex's jaw dropped.

He was looking at the most gorgeous illustration he'd ever seen. The picture was of two people, arms entwined in an intimate embrace. He recognized the young woman in the picture as Arumaya, Nia's superhero, with her curly reddish-brown hair and white, feathery wings. Sand swirled around her as a blood red sun beat down from above.

In Arumaya's arms was a young man. His hair was white and he wore a dark robe that draped down from his wrists like a wizard's. His frost-colored hands held Arumaya's waist. Behind him was a snow-dappled forest, with gnarled tree branches creating a canopy over them. Snow encircled him in a sort of polar vortex, mixing with the sand Arumaya had conjured up from the earth. It was as though their very embrace merged the sand and the snow into a powerful cyclone. Above them, the sky was an otherworldly amalgam of blues and reds, fire and snow.

"This is Kalter," Nia said, pointing to the young man. "He was born to Kaldus, emperor of the ice world of Frigga, and his mistress Galdene. When Kaldus's wife, Enestra, found out about Kalter, in a rage she sent her forces to execute him. Kalter was forced to flee into the icy forests. During his flight, Kalter was lost in a snowstorm and fell unconscious on a steep mountainside. But instead of killing him, the mountain granted Kalter powers to help him survive the cold—and fight his enemies. He has the ability to manipulate any substance that's below a freezing temperature. He can create snowstorms, use snow boulders as weapons, or create ice bridges for travel."

"He kind of looks like—"

"You?" Nia said. "I suppose there's a resemblance. Arumaya and Kalter joined forces to combat their respective enemies, realizing they were far more powerful together than alone. Through their bond they can merge their individual powers to create something even greater: an ice sandstorm. You know, to battle evil and save the world and all that good stuff."

"Where in the world did you get the idea for this?"

"I've always loved Norse mythology. Like the story of the giant Ymir, who was created when the fires of Muspelheim melted the ice from Niflheim. When Ymir was killed, the world was created from his body. These two elements, fire and ice, combined to make something far greater than themselves. But even though they both have really cool superpowers, when it comes down to it, Arumaya and Kalter are really just two lonely people who found each other."

"Who can also create badass ice sandstorms."

"I mean, of course."

"Does it have a name?" Alex said. "The illustration."

"I was going to call it *A Song of Ice and Fire* but, unfortunately, that was taken."

Alex shook his head. "I'm literally speechless."

"You're not literally speechless, or you wouldn't have been able to say that you were literally speechless."

"You know what I mean. I love it more than anything in the world. Present company excluded." Alex kissed her. "If you show that at the mentorship program, they'll go insane."

"Nope, this one stays here. It's just for us. I have other things to show in Austin. Besides, I want Arumaya and Kalter to watch over my folks while we're gone."

"Heaven help any supervillains who try to mess with your parents while we're in Austin."

They brought their suitcases downstairs. Stephen and Rivka Solomon were waiting for them by the front door. They hugged and kissed Nia.

"Do you have everything you need?" Mr. Solomon asked Nia. "Do you have your medication?"

"I do. And I'm speaking with my therapist over Zoom next week."

"Good. Time for you to put yourself first."

Rivka embraced Alex, and Stephen gave him a firm handshake.

"Nia won't tell me what happened to me. She said she made a promise to someone. I have a feeling that someone is you. I'm not going to break my daughter's trust by asking you if I'm right. All I'll say is this: thank you for giving me back to my family."

Alex just nodded and said, "I'm glad you're back too, sir."

"Just don't do anything to hurt my daughter, or I will bury you underneath the school. Now get out of here, you two. Go have the time of your lives."

"We will," Nia said. "Love you both."

"We love you too," Rivka and Stephen said together.

They went outside. Snow had begun to blanket Whisper Valley. Alex saw Iggy standing at the end of his driveway, wearing a sweatshirt, a green headband, and warmup pants with the Dubya V logo. He waved. Alex and Nia waved back.

"You'd better not get lazy in Austin, Tree guy," Iggy shouted. "Because when you get back, I don't care if it's negative a million, we're not done training."

"I look forward to freezing my ass off with you, Ig," Alex said. "See you soon. You and Trevor had better still be together when we get back."

"Your lips to the ears of the relationship gods up on high," Iggy said. "Have fun. I expect constant texts and pics. And, Alex: don't do anything crazy like defy all laws of physics and nature and the space-time continuum or something like that."

He winked at Alex, then blew Nia a kiss.

Alex and Nia loaded their bags into the trunk and climbed into the backseat. They waved at Nia's parents as the car pulled away. For the first time in his seventeen years, Alex's future felt uncertain. Unclear. And he was okay with that. He had made two promises: to his father, to continue his legacy, and to Nia, to always have her in his heart, no matter the distance between them. He planned to keep both promises.

"I love you," he said to Nia.

"I love you too."

"We'll make this work. I have no idea how. But we will."

"I know."

Nia leaned over, put her hand on Alex's sleeve, and kissed him softly. He felt the familiar heat in his arm. He hoped to feel it for the rest of his life. She was going to turn Austin on its head, and he couldn't wait to watch.

Nia looked out the window as the neighborhood sped past them. Alex could still feel the heat from her hand on his arm. He looked down, but to his shock he saw that she'd removed her hand from his sleeve. And there, where her fingers had rested, were several small, circular scorch marks on the fabric.

Alex looked at Nia's palm. A faint orange-red glow emanated from her fingertips. After a moment, it was gone. She hadn't noticed it, or the marks she'd left on his sleeve.

"Nia, your hand, it—"

"This is the farthest I've been from home in a long time," she said, interrupting him. "I'm really glad you're coming with me. I know we'll figure things out."

"I am too. And I know we will."

There would be a time to talk. To figure out the future. As they sped toward the unknown, Alex thought about his father's last words.

*Live your life. And never forget that you are my son.*

Alex promised to remember them.

The End

# ACKNOWLEDGMENTS

People like to say that writing is easy. You just open up a vein, and let it bleed onto the page. Well, *The Reaper's Son* wasn't me opening up a vein. It was opening up my head, and my whole heat. And I wouldn't have had the courage or need to publish this book without the readers and the dreamers, the people who love nothing more than to translate words on the page into images in their mind and feelings in their soul. *The Reaper's Son* is a book about two lost souls. But this book is for all the lost souls out there, myself included, who see ourselves in Alex and Nia, and know that sometimes what we want to say takes time, and love, to get out.

Thank you to Amy Tannenbaum and Jessica Errera at the Jane Rotrosen Agency, for working through many (many, *many*) drafts of this book. Their contributions were innumerable and invaluable.

Thank you to the brilliant cover designers who helped me boil the essence of this story into images: Mimi Bark who designed the paperback, and Sandra Maldonado who designed the hardcover and interior. And to Painted Wings design who did the splendid (and super cool) edges.

To the readers who have read my previous books as Jason Pinter, and who have embraced this alter ego. Glad you came along for the ride. And for the readers who have just recently discovered me, whereby through *Dating & Dismemberment* or my TikTok feed, welcome to the madhouse. Glad you could make it. We're all a little bit crazy here, in the best possible way. Enjoy your stay, and don't forget to tip the bellhop…

Words evoke images. Images evoke feelings. Feelings can change our lives.

Thank you all for changing mine.

# ABOUT THE AUTHOR

A.L. Brody is the fantastical alter ego of Jason Pinter, and the author of *Dating & Dismemberment* and *Weddings & Witchcraft* in his Mating & Monsters series. As Jason Pinter, he is the internationally bestselling author of numerous acclaimed, bestselling thrillers, including *Hide Away, A Stranger at the Door, Past Crimes,* and more, which have nearly two million copies in print worldwide. He lives with his family in a cave in the pit of despair (aka New Jersey). Visit him on X and Instagram at @JasonPinter or on TikTok at @Jersey-BookGuy.

Made in the USA
Las Vegas, NV
30 October 2024